If Two Are Dead

By the same author:

The Thomas Dordrecht Historical Mystery Series

Die Fasting [1758]
Great Mischief [1759]

If Two Are Dead

THOMAS DORDRECHT IN 1762

JONATHAN CARRIEL

iUniverse, Inc.
Bloomington

If Two Are Dead

iUniverse books may be ordered through booksellers or by contacting:

iUniverse
1663 Liberty Drive
Bloomington, IN 47403
www.iuniverse.com
1-800-Authors (1-800-288-4677)

ISBN: 978-1-4697-9124-1 (sc)
ISBN: 978-1-4697-9125-8 (e)

Printed in the United States of America

iUniverse rev. date: 4/16/2012

Cover art and design by David T. Jones

Three may keep a secret, if two of them are dead.
—Benjamin Franklin, *Poor Richard's Almanac*

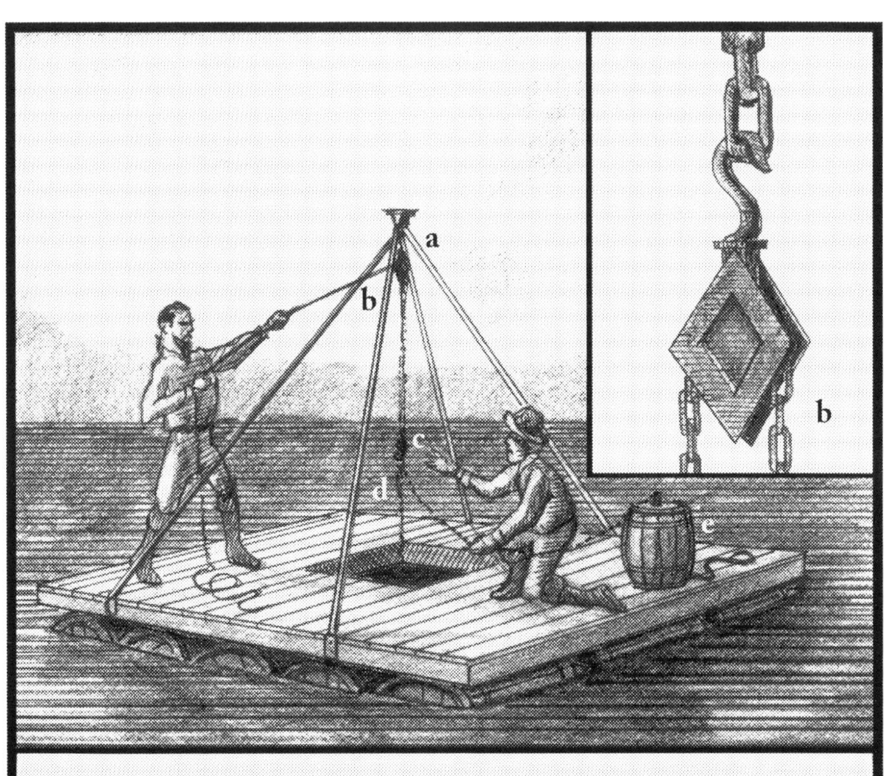

a *Hoist*

b *Pulley*

c *Hook*

d *Mooring chain*

e *Mooring float*

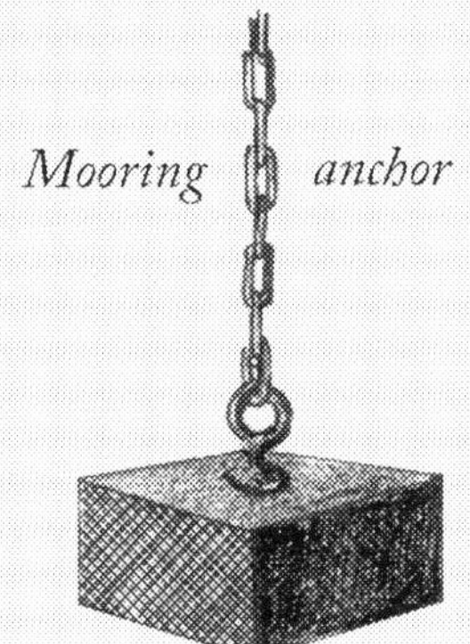

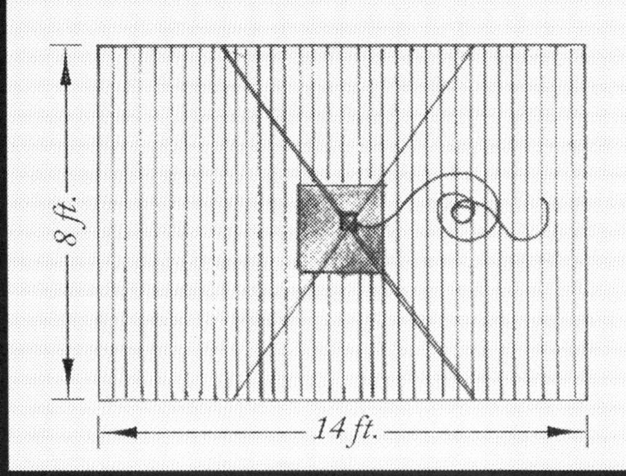

The Cow

and its attributes

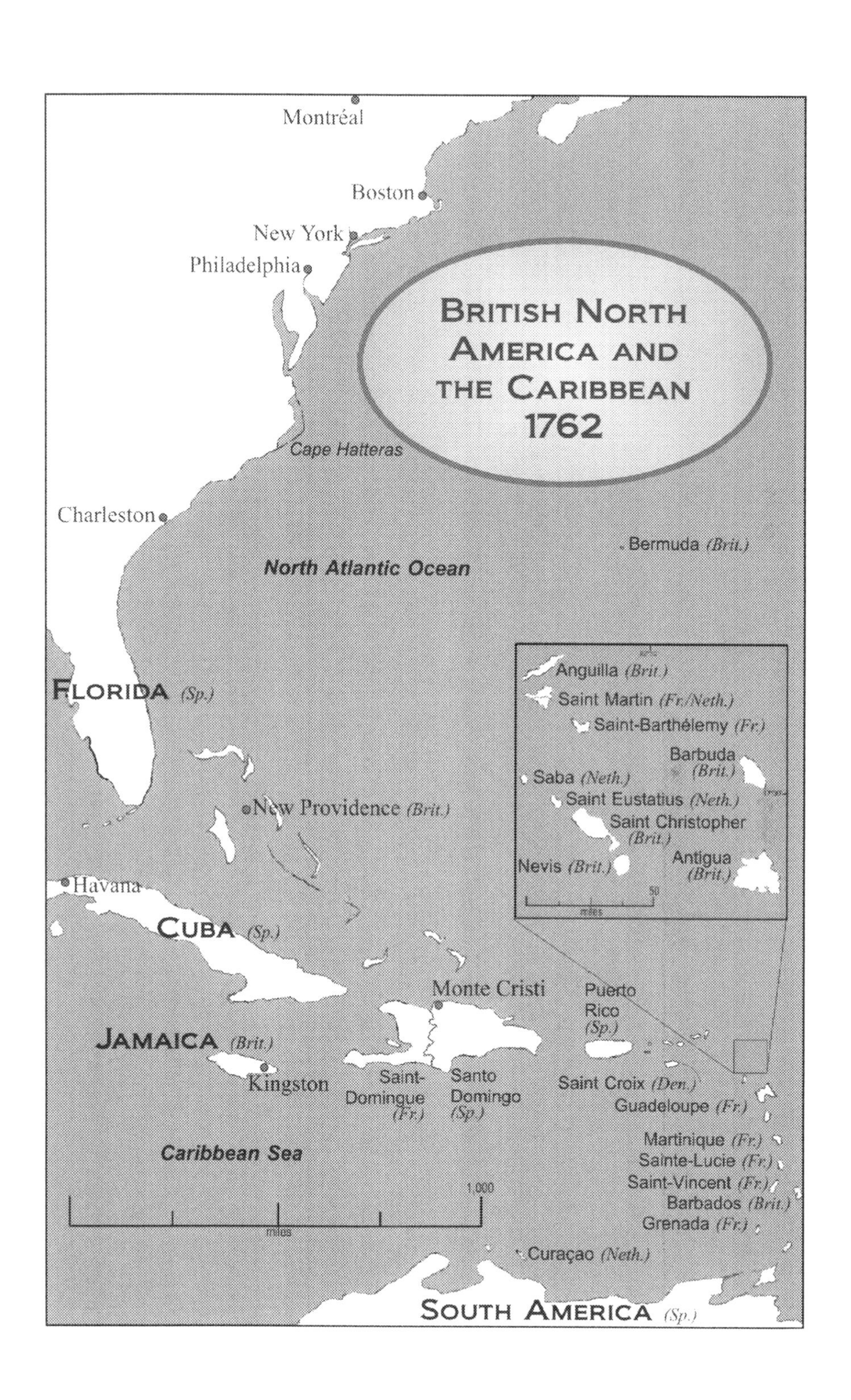
BRITISH NORTH AMERICA AND THE CARIBBEAN 1762
Montréal
Boston
New York
Philadelphia
Cape Hatteras
Charleston
Bermuda (Brit.)
North Atlantic Ocean
FLORIDA (Sp.)
New Providence (Brit.)
Havana
CUBA (Sp.)
Monte Cristi
Puerto Rico (Sp.)
JAMAICA (Brit.)
Kingston
Saint-Domingue (Fr.)
Santo Domingo (Sp.)
Saint Croix (Den.)
Guadeloupe (Fr.)
Martinique (Fr.)
Sainte-Lucie (Fr.)
Saint-Vincent (Fr.)
Barbados (Brit.)
Grenada (Fr.)
Caribbean Sea
1,000
miles
Curaçao (Neth.)
SOUTH AMERICA (Sp.)
Anguilla (Brit.)
Saint Martin (Fr./Neth.)
Saint-Barthélemy (Fr.)
Barbuda (Brit.)
Saba (Neth.)
Saint Eustatius (Neth.)
Saint Christopher (Brit.)
Nevis (Brit.)
Antigua (Brit.)
50
miles

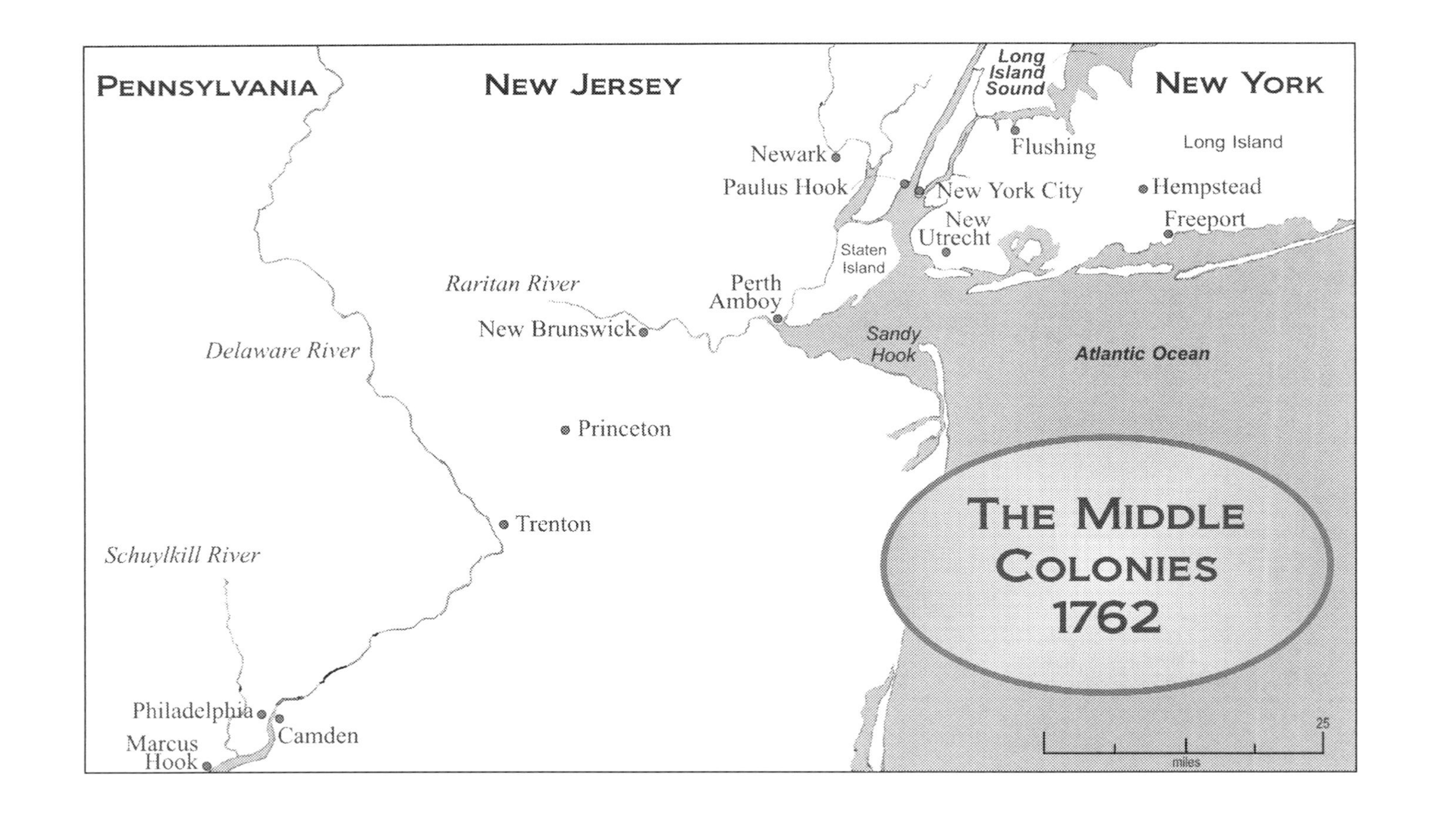

The Middle Colonies
1762
Pennsylvania
New Jersey
New York
Long Island Sound
Flushing
Long Island
Newark
Paulus Hook
New York City
Hempstead
New Utrecht
Freeport
Staten Island
Raritan River
Perth Amboy
New Brunswick
Sandy Hook
Atlantic Ocean
Delaware River
Princeton
Trenton
Schuylkill River
Philadelphia
Camden
Marcus Hook
25
miles

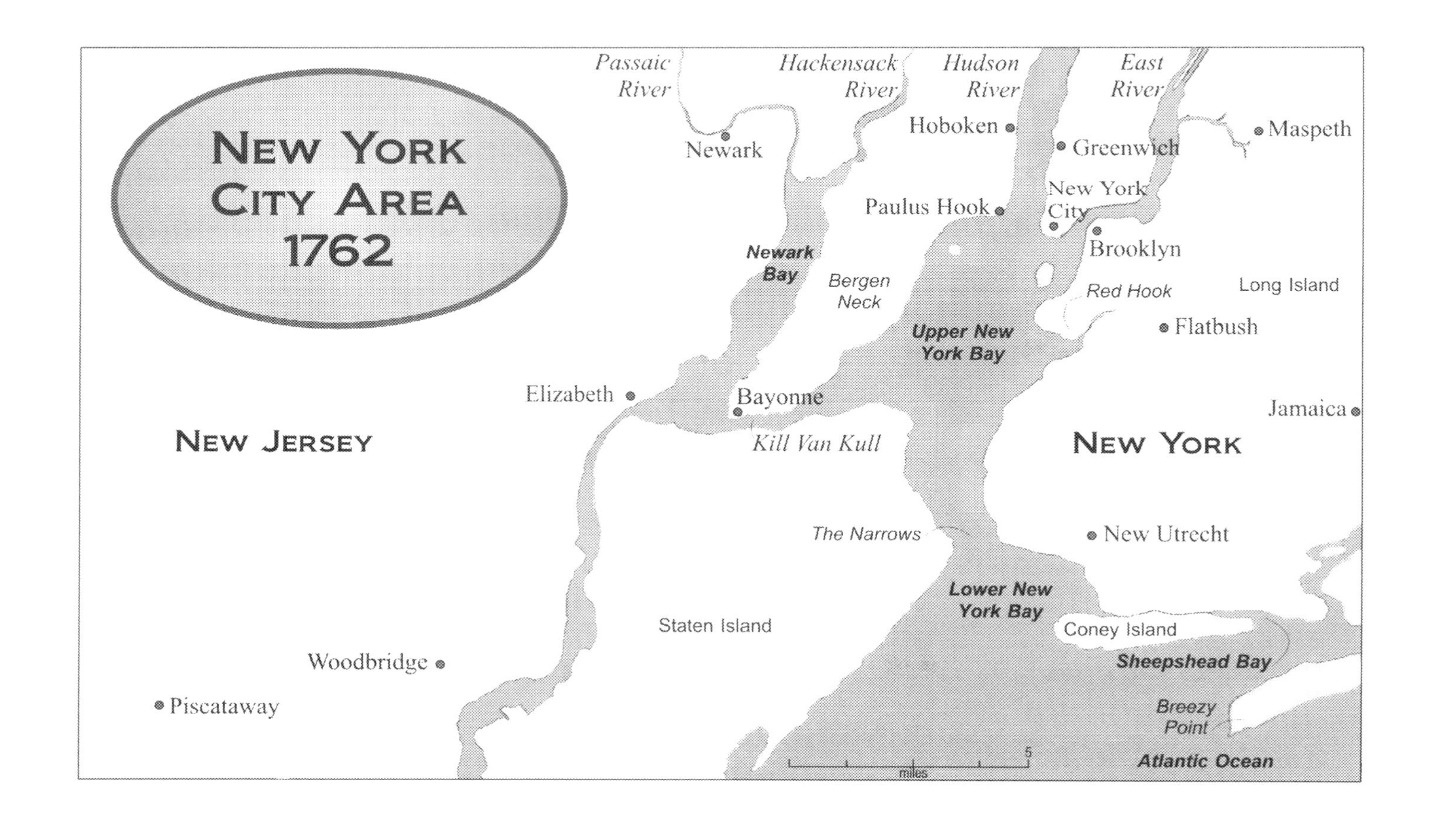
New York City Area 1762
Passaic River
Hackensack River
Hudson River
East River
Newark
Hoboken
Greenwich
Maspeth
Paulus Hook
New York City
Brooklyn
Newark Bay
Bergen Neck
Red Hook
Long Island
Flatbush
Upper New York Bay
Elizabeth
Bayonne
Jamaica
New Jersey
Kill Van Kull
New York
The Narrows
New Utrecht
Lower New York Bay
Staten Island
Coney Island
Woodbridge
Sheepshead Bay
Piscataway
Breezy Point
Atlantic Ocean
5
miles

List of Potential Witnesses
Prepared by Thomas Dordrecht for John Tabor Kempe, Esq.
September 15, 1762

NEW YORK CITY	
Benjamin Leavering	Merchant
Thomas Dordrecht	Merchant's clerk, Castell, Leavering & Sproul
Liam McCraney	Coroner's assistant
Abel Jennet	Constable
Aston	Driver (slave to N.Y. constabulary)
Mrs. Roberson	Hostelry proprietor
Captain Enos Trent	Master of merchant snow *Dorothy C.* (currently lying N.Y. harbor)
BROOKLYN & KINGS COUNTY	
Billy	Tavern owner, *The Jug*
Lenoor Steenburgh	Tavern owner
Flora Norts	Patron, *The Jug*
Titus	Patron, *The Jug*
Rykert Dordrecht	Farmer, New Utrecht, N.Y.
PAULUS HOOK, N.J.	
John Meed	Tavern proprietor
"Miss" Paulette	Tavern patron
Saartje Van Narden	Inn proprietor
Johan Van Narden	Inn proprietor
Wendell Brush	Fisherman/oysterman
NEW BRUNSWICK, N.J.	
Mr. Lewes	Stable owner
PHILADELPHIA, Pa.	
Sam Drucker	Coachman, Convenient Coach Co.
Reuben Castell	Merchant
Evelyn Sproul	Widow (née Leavering) of Daniel Sproul

Miss Rhoda Leavering	Elder sister of Benjamin Leavering
Francis Goode	Retainer (free black) of Castell, Leavering & Sproul
Christopher Enniston	Merchant's clerk, Castell, Leavering & Sproul
Captain Peter Wardener	Master of merchant brig *Four Daughters* (currently at sea)
Samuel Low Aldridge	Merchant, Aldridge Brothers
Ichabod Dabney	Solicitor, Aldridge Brothers

Author's notes: The above is a *fictional* document, prepared by Thomas Dordrecht for the express purpose indicated. It is not a comprehensive list of all characters in *If Two Are Dead*. New Utrecht is today a neighborhood in the southern half of Kings County, New York—commonly known as Brooklyn. Similarly, Paulus Hook is a small section of the modern metropolis of Jersey City, New Jersey. Saint Eustatius is a tiny island in the West Indies; relatively insignificant today, it was notorious in 1762. Interested readers are invited to view further historical information that may be found on the author's website, www.JonathanCarriel.com.

Chapter 1

Tuesday, March 23, 1762

"Dead, you say?" my employer spluttered.

All the hubbub in our busy office halted. It was exactly what the man had said.

"But that's impossible!"

"I'm afraid it must be so, Mr. Leavering," the man persisted, the curiosity of his Scottish accent dissipated by the substance of his message. For a second, he and Leavering stared at each other in grim silence.

"What on earth brings you to believe this could be Mr. Sproul?"

"It's—"

"Sproul is the very portrait of health—a man of enormous vigor!"

"Mr. Leavering, I know nothing of him, but this pamphlet was found on the man's person." He held out a slim, bound, new-looking tract. Leavering grunted uneasily on seeing the spine, and he appeared unwilling to take hold of it. The visitor turned the cover. "It was this—"

Leavering gasped on beholding the bookplate and reared backward as if struck.

Glasby practically threw Mapes out of his chair in order to get it behind Leavering. "Do sit down, sir!" he begged. Leavering collapsed so heavily, I feared the chair would splinter to the floor. "Thomas, brandy!" Glasby whispered urgently. "And, uh …" He nodded at the dumbfounded group of clerks, agents, and carters in a frantic hint that I should try to manage some privacy. While pouring from the decanter, I reciprocally whispered to Mapes to clear everyone from the room.

Leavering took a swallow and coughed but stared silently ahead, breathing huskily. "Do loosen your neckcloth, sir, I pray you!" Glasby fussed. Red-faced, Leavering slowly obliged, taking measured sips. Given his advancing years, his substantial girth, and the unprecedented disruption, the uncharacteristic torpor that suddenly overtook him was not unnatural. Glasby faced the tall, somber bringer-of-news. "I didn't catch your name, sir? I'm John Glasby, Mr. Leavering's second at this office."

"Liam McCraney, assistant to the public coroner. I'm very sorry to …" He gestured awkwardly about the room.

"What exactly … ?"

"At six fifteen this morning, sir, the constable reported a dead man—a gentleman by appearance—found in an alleyway near the New Jersey ferry. It seems he must have been taken ill and gone there to lie down—"

"Into an *alleyway*?" I broke in incredulously.

"So it seems, *um* …"

"This is Thomas Dordrecht, my assistant," Glasby muttered.

"Your servant, sir," I affirmed mechanically, chagrinned by my impertinent outburst.

"To lie down?" Glasby resumed. He gulped. "There is no suggestion, then, of …"

"Of foul play? No, no, none at all. Rest assured, there!"

"But that makes it all the more incomprehensible! I know Sproul well, myself, and a sturdier man of forty-eight or so you'll—"

McCraney looked suddenly hopeful, as if he truly wished to oblige in the matter. "Well, perhaps then … I came because we must, of course, obtain positive identification, gentlemen. None of us knows the man. Mr. Sproul was—*er*, is not from New York, I take it?"

"Castell, Leavering & Sproul is originally a Philadelphia firm, sir. Mr. Leavering moved here three years ago to expand its business. Castell and Sproul are his partners."

"Mr. Sproul often visits here, then?"

"No, actually. This was … this is his first appearance here. We …" Glasby suddenly looked lost.

"We are anticipating his arrival at any moment today," I furnished for him. "He wrote that he expected to reach Paulus Hook, or at least Newark, last night, so—"

"There must be some error!" Leavering exclaimed, suddenly revivified. He slammed his fist down on the arm of the chair. "Must be! This cannot be Daniel Sproul!"

"All we had to go on was this book, sir. A gentleman down at the Royal Exchange recognized the surname and directed me here."

The connection of the book with a corpse made Mr. Leavering blanch again, but he stood up, resolved. "We must attend to this at once!"

"I shall go with you, of course, Mr. Leavering," Glasby announced.

A practical decision seemed abruptly to bring our employer back to his usual self. "*Um,* no. Thank you, John, but someone must be here if he … when he … and besides, Mr. Helden is due presently to talk about the flour consignment. I'll take Thomas with me."

"You're sure?"

"Of course. This is all a mistake! We'll be back in thirty minutes. Let's be off, lad."

Mr. Leavering grasped his walking stick, opened the door for Mr. McCraney, and followed him out and down the stairs. I grabbed my coat, exchanged a worried nod with Glasby, ignored the stares of Mapes and the others, and rushed after them.

On reaching the bright sunshine of the street, Mr. Leavering briefly looked about Peck Slip as if he had no idea where he was. "What we must see is adjacent to the poorhouse, Mr. Leavering," McCraney tactfully asserted.

"Yes!" Immediately, he turned and strode off toward the Common, having instantly calculated that walking would be more expeditious than any form of transportation. Mr. Leavering is a tall and portly man of sixty-four years, whose frankly ungainly appearance causes people unfamiliar with his gentle nature to scatter from his approach, particularly when he is urgently purposive, as now.

McCraney and I, however, dodged the crowds as we struggled to keep up with him. When McCraney stepped in a horse's leavings crossing William Street, we fell further behind while he balanced on my shoulder to clear his boot against a step. "I feared for your employer's heart at first, Dordrecht," McCraney panted as we resumed our pursuit, "but I perceive he remains capable of strenuous exertion." Probably not a decade older than me, he seemed impressed with Leavering's stamina.

"He is a man of many surprises, you'll find, but I admit I, too, was concerned."

McCraney cast me a glance of curiosity as we both automatically jumped to avoid a cart that was being backed into a loading dock. "Mr. Sproul is more than a partner to Mr. Leavering. Important as that relation is, he is also his son-in-law."

"Oh my!"

"Father to his only grandchildren."

"Ah. How awful, then, if ... You still fear for Mr. Leavering, then, when it comes time to look?"

"I ..." I wanted this to be a mistake every bit as much as my superior did. "I'm glad he shall not be alone," I mustered.

McCraney cast me an appraising glance, which I interpreted as disparagement of my apparent youthful bravado. "It is not necessary that you also view the body, Dordrecht. If you'd rather—"

"I was in Abercromby's army at Ticonderoga four years ago, Mr. McCraney," I said plainly. "I can stomach a corpse."

But his intuition was correct that I was not looking forward to it.

The morgue was located in a small outbuilding on the north edge of the Common, between the poorhouse and the new barracks, which were now sitting desolately half-empty. The main floor of the structure was apparently the headquarters of such constables and night watchmen as the town could afford. We proceeded down to the cellar, which, to my relief, had a full standing room and windows at the level of the ground outside that permitted light and air and kept it from smelling as foul as I'd anticipated. At the foot of the stairs was a desk with a few chairs next to a door made of heavy timbers. McCraney dropped his hat and the book on the desk, which

I took to be his own. "Are you quite ready, gentlemen?" he inquired considerately. "This can be—"

"Please do get along with it," Mr. Leavering said hoarsely.

"Of course, sir." McCraney had to lift the door in order to push it open. Inside was a room the size of a drawing room, walled only by the rough stone foundation. In the middle was a table covered by a coarse, woolen blanket with an all-too-familiar shape beneath it. Mr. Leavering moaned briefly, as the shape clearly matched the slight and diminutive figure of his partner. Mr. McCraney moved to the far side of the table, took hold of a corner of the blanket, and again looked to Mr. Leavering for an indication. I noticed my employer was trembling—something I'd never seen in nearly three years of his employ—and I confess my own stomach was churning. McCraney pulled the blanket down and uncovered the bust.

"*Ah!*" Mr. Leavering virtually shrieked, both hands flying to his mouth. "No! *No!*" He abruptly turned, fled out the door, and collapsed at McCraney's desk, weeping profusely into his handkerchief.

McCraney hurriedly replaced the blanket and we followed. He observed Mr. Leavering closely for a minute; then, evidently convinced he was not endangered, produced a glass of water from a sideboard and handed it to me to give to him. "All I have here, Dordrecht," he whispered apologetically.

I placed the glass on the desk in front of Leavering, who was facing the wall, wracked with more emotion than I'd dreamed him capable of. "I'm ... so terribly ..." Not looking backward, he emphatically waved me away.

McCraney caught my eye, nodded me back into the larger room, and shut the door. He put a glass of water into my own hands, and I was surprised how much it relieved me. "I'm very sorry, Mr. Dordrecht," he stated. I merely nodded, trying to get a grip on my own emotion. "I take it we do have a positive identification?"

"I ..."

"Were *you* personally acquainted with Mr. Sproul?" he asked.

I drew myself upright and faced him. "I ... only met the gentleman once, for a mere half-hour. It was near a year ago, when I was on my one business trip to Philadelphia."

"I see. But you, too, have no doubt that this is, in fact, Mr. Sproul?" I must have looked baffled. "I have no wish to distress your employer further … and it is often more certain if persons *not* as intimately connected can make the identification."

"Oh."

"Ah, and I have not yet shown you this." He lifted the blanket slightly from the middle edge of the table, took hold of the corpse's right forearm, and, with difficulty, twisted it outward so I could see the top of the hand … which instantly banished my last doubts. "Very noticeable," McCraney remarked of the old-but-terrifying scars on the thumb and top of the hand.

I sighed and nodded. "Mr. Glasby once related to me that Mr. Sproul was raised on a farm twenty miles out of Philadelphia that was attacked by … Delawares, I think … His father was killed, and a savage was about to brain the boy as well when his mother, having managed to reload the musket, shot him dead. But the tomahawk dropped on his hand, and his dexterity was impaired all his life."

"You do make positive identification, then? We could spare Mr. Leavering, you see. Your signature will be as adequate as his, if you would."

"Of course." He produced a printed form from inside the sideboard and filled it out. After inspecting it, I signed. Then there was another paper, which he completed and gave me, explaining that it should be given to the undertaker, so the body and clothes could be reclaimed. I placed it inside my jacket. These formalities completed, we both seemed at a loss for words.

Mr. Leavering was still sobbing inconsolably, and I was reluctant to disturb what little privacy he had.

"Mr. McCraney, have you not got any notion what on earth brought Mr. Sproul to this pass?"

McCraney looked relieved at the prospect of more dispassionate discussion. "Frankly, Mr. Dordrecht, it is as baffling a matter as any I've ever seen. You say the man was in good health?"

"Mr. Leavering and Mr. Glasby say so, and certainly that was my impression a year ago." I recollected my brief conversation with the deceased, which had not touched on our mutual business at all.

"In fact, he and I shared the recreation of canoe-paddling—which can be rather demanding exercise."

"Particularly for a man of his years. Near fifty, I believe Mr. Glasby said?"

"My understanding, yes."

"Looks considerably younger. Hair's barely touched with gray. And his face is … remarkably composed for an individual suddenly overtaken."

"How so, sir?"

"A man suddenly stricken with a fatal apoplexy or asphyxiation or befouled food usually expires with an expression of great pain or alarm on his face. Not to mention vomit on his person. I hope I'm not distressing you?"

Had I been as close to Sproul as Mr. Leavering, I daresay he would have been, but my curiosity was now regaining the fore. "No, sir."

"Whereas Mr. Sproul appears perfectly calm, indeed asleep, and his corpus was found to be clean." A thought struck him. "The book suggests he was of the Quaker persuasion. Is that so?"

"Oh, very definitely. But not at all a zealot. His father-in-law would not have loved him if he were a zealot."

"I ask only because there was no hat found. His garments are what you'd expect of a Quaker—well-made, but plain cloth without embellishment—but don't they always wear those odd, flat hats?"

I tried to think of the men I'd seen leaving the Friends' Meeting House on Crown Street. "I'm not sure it's required of them, Mr. McCraney, but come to think of it, Mr. Sproul was wearing just such a hat during the one interview I had with him."

"Strange. You'd think a man traveling, particularly, would want his hat?"

"Aye … Surely there must be *something* to explain this calamity?"

"Well, can you bear looking again? I was planning to wait until you were gone, but …"

We moved back to the table. "Can you at least estimate *when* Mr. Sproul was deceased?" I asked, blurting a new thought. "He was found at six fifteen? That's nearly four hours ago now."

McCraney pulled the blanket down to the waist, and I forced myself to look as if through his eyes—the eyes of one who had no personal relation to the corpse. It was hard not to think ill of oneself for so purposely invading another's privacy. Yet Mr. Sproul's fine features were as serene as if an undertaker had already prettified him. I jumped, however, when McCraney pulled an eyelid open to examine the eyeball. "Sorry!" Finding nothing to remark, McCraney attempted to open the jaw—Mr. Sproul's lips were parted, but the mouth was nearly closed—but soon gave up. "*Rigor mortis* is in full force, here. I think he must have yielded up the ghost earlier in the night, but I've really no idea when exactly."

"Uh huh."

"Can you help me turn him up on his side?" He pushed as I pulled. I had to banish grim memories of handling the dead and wounded during my stint in a provincial regiment. McCraney examined the back and legs. His nether underlinen had been left on him; all I noted was that it was unsoiled. "Nothing. Absolutely nothing." We settled it—*him*—back down, and shook our heads. "I wondered if perhaps he was struck by lightning … but my understanding is that the victims always have burn marks on their skin somewhere."

"And there was no storm last night."

"Grasping at straws!"

"Ah! Actually, Mr. McCraney, correct me if I'm wrong, but I did handle corpses up north, and … Does this body not strike you as unusually cold to the touch?"

McCraney looked a trifle surprised, but immediately pressed his palm onto the corpse's midriff. "It's not a warm day, Mr. Dordrecht," he said cautiously.

"Aye, but for the first week of spring, it's blessedly pleasant."

"That's so." He pressed his palm back onto his own forehead, perplexed. "I know: we'll compare him with the other one!" As he moved toward the far wall, I realized with a start that the dark heap of rags I'd barely noticed on the floor against the wall … was another corpse. "This one came in just an hour after Mr. Sproul," McCraney said almost cheerfully. "I was just about to walk out in pursuit of kinfolk of Mr. Sproul when Jennet brought this *bravo* in."

He squatted down, grasped the blanket, then checked himself. "Oh. This fellow's not as composed a sight, Mr. Dordrecht!"

I gulped. "Very well."

He casually pulled the blanket back, revealing the snarling and bloodied face of a thickset man not much older than me, with wild hair, a fortnight's stubble, a deep, old scar across the forehead ... and numerous holes in his filthy shirt surrounded by dried blood. "No question what did in this lout!" McCraney said, opening the shirt to put his palm directly on the chest. *"Hmph!"* he grunted. He stood up, walked back to the table, felt Sproul's chest again, and repeated the action on the stabbing victim. "I can't imagine why, but it *does* seem to me that this one is not as cold as Mr. Sproul."

"Where and when was this one found?"

"What did Jennet say? He was spotted on the Hudson riverbank just north of town, shortly after dawn, by a workman on the Greenwich road. But no one called the constable until somewhat later."

"A knife fight, do you suppose?"

"Could be. But they know who this one is, at least. He's spent many a night as a guest of the city fathers—the jail, not the poorhouse." He attempted to manipulate the corpse's arm, but found it resistant. "Probably been dead since well before dawn too. But I ... I can't explain why there should appear to be a difference in body warmth, Mr. Dordrecht."

Just then, there was a commotion outside that brought a fresh spate of weeping from Mr. Leavering. Another voice was heard.

"A woman?" McCraney asked. He automatically straightened his neckcloth, and then thought to cover the two corpses again.

I recognized the voice with warm relief. "Mr. Glasby's wife," I explained, "a great friend of the Leaverings." There was no reason to add that Adelie Chapman Glasby was also a great friend to me. We were about to open the door when I realized that she, too, was in tears. I turned back to the assistant coroner and cleared my throat. "This constable, Jennet? I might want to talk to him. It's all just ... so peculiar."

"I don't know what help Jennet could be to you, Mr. Dordrecht. I'm afraid his mental acumen is naught to speak of, although he's at least one of the honest ones. But his shift is from midnight to noon, so you'll find him just upstairs daily at midday, when he reports in."

"I see. Thank you. And … you've been very helpful."

"Not an easy matter for anyone," McCraney said modestly. "Good heavens!" he exclaimed, striking his palm against his forehead. "His purse, his effects!" He rushed to unlock a cabinet opposite the door, from which he extracted a leather coin purse, the contents of which he spilled out onto the sideboard. At his request, I counted up the score of coins, which totaled two pounds, eight shillings, sixpence—substantial proof that Mr. Sproul had not been molested either before or after his demise. "Could you bring the clothes over, please?" he requested, nodding at a table in the corner and pulling out an inventory sheet.

I moved to collect the garments, wondering how severely affected my own reason must be, given that I'd not previously noticed them and, worse, not thought to inquire about them. But I'd not taken two steps back when I was stopped cold. "Mr. McCraney! These garments are reeking of liquor! Of rum!"

McCraney turned to me, quill in hand, looking perfectly stunned. "But that's …" He met me in the center of the room, lifted the bundle to his nose … and gagged. He absently set them back in my arms. "I … I don't see … There's no trace of alcohol on his person, Mr. Dordrecht."

"You're certain? But how could—"

"Perfectly certain. I always check for that."

"Surely you must have noticed when you removed the clothes for the examination?"

McCraney looked ill with embarrassment. "The slave does that," he said. "Given the absence of wounds on the body, I barely even looked at his clothes."

"How could there be this much of spirits on the clothes, and yet no trace on the man? None on his undergarments!"

"Well, I can hardly say, but I dare not be squeamish about offenses to my olfactory sense, Mr. Dordrecht, I make a point … If you can stomach it, I suggest you compare the *bravo* to Mr. Sproul, in that regard."

Though greatly tempted to take him at his word, I was now just dubious enough of McCraney's abilities to feel compelled to make my own inspection. Stifling my repugnance, I knelt beside the wild fellow's corpse, pulled back the blanket, and inhaled next to his mouth. It was quite foul, but there was one predominant odor. "Rum!"

"Aye," McCraney said. "The bane of this city, Mr. Dordrecht!"

I summoned more courage and repeated the effort on Mr. Sproul's corpse … and detected nothing.

"I doubt Mr. Sproul ever even indulged in tobacco," McCraney observed.

I tried again, and again noticed nothing. "I recollect Mr. Glasby remarking as much once," I said, glad to replace the cover. "And it was common knowledge that he never drank. But how … ?"

"I can only suppose the liquor was spilled on him in some accident."

"Which … may have occurred after his decease, as well as before?"

McCraney shrugged. "That's as plausible as anything."

I sighed heavily, rather exhausted by the accumulation of imponderables. McCraney completed the inventory, and I signed it.

The voices outside were calmer.

I opened the door and heard Mr. Leavering moaning, "How am I ever going to tell her?" He was still facing the wall, shaking his head.

Adelie Glasby, one hand on his shoulder, turned toward me, her handsome face stricken. "Is there any—" she mouthed.

Doubt, I knew she meant. I shook my head and gestured to indicate the scars on the corpse's hand.

"Oh dear heaven!" she breathed. She looked back at Leavering. "Does he need to stay here?" she said softly, asking both McCraney and myself.

"No ma'am," McCraney answered. "Mr. Dordrecht's handled all the immediate matters. Does he live far away?"

"Hanover Square," I asserted.

"We have a wagon outside. I'll have the slave drive you home."

"That would be most kind, sir," Mrs. Glasby said warmly.

McCraney ran up the steps to make arrangements, and Mrs. Glasby and I began cajoling Mr. Leavering into walking out to the street. It took upward of ten minutes to get him into the wagon with her beside him. Even in the wagon, Mr. Leavering kept his face buried in his hands. It was horrible to see a man of such fortitude and enterprise—I rather hero-worshipped him—brought so fearfully low. I gave the slave a tuppence, and gave the purse to Mrs. Glasby. "What *happened*?" she whispered.

"They don't really know, Adelie," I said, having long before been excused the presumption of informal address. "I'm at a loss too. I … If you need me, I should go back to the office."

Leavering moaned, and she turned to comfort him. I nodded to the slave, and finally they were off.

I was fifty paces on my return, when I heard McCraney calling my name. He ran toward me, waving the very book that had first led him to our office. "It fell onto the floor," he explained breathlessly.

"Ah! Thank you yet again," I said, taking it and waving farewell.

He touched my elbow. "Have I seen that extraordinary woman somewhere before?" he asked.

I smiled. Mrs. Glasby certainly does make a strong, positive impression. "You may have, Mr. McCraney. She is possessed of a fine singing voice and has several times appeared in concert at Trinity Church, among other places." Absently, I gestured southward with the book, as if every New Yorker did not know perfectly well where Trinity was.

Something flew out of the pages, startling both of us. I bent over and picked up—four playing cards … of an unusual design that struck me as possibly foreign. Mystified, I turned them over several times before stuffing them back into the book.

"I thought Quakers disdained playing with cards?" McCraney said.

I could only shrug and shake his hand as we parted again.

My supervisor and patron, John Glasby, was horrified when I confirmed what he'd surmised from our extended absence—that McCraney's corpse was in fact Mr. Sproul—but he dutifully managed to preserve his outward manly composure. "Adelie's gone back to the house with Benjamin?"

"Aye. Thank you for sending her. Her arrival was a great solace to us both. They should be home by now, and I expect they've broken the news to Mrs. Leavering."

"Sproul dead!" Glasby exclaimed breathlessly, his face slack. "I simply can't … can't …"

I shrugged helplessly.

"And this man, the coroner, has *no idea* what caused it?"

"He said it would probably be ruled a misadventure. All that can be observed for certain is that his heart ceased beating." Glasby sat heavily on his desk. "And if that's not implausible enough, his coat was saturated with rum."

"*Rum!* Impossible! Sproul was adamant in—"

"I know, John, I know. But there it is." We sat speechless for a minute, no consoling phrase coming to mind.

Finally, Glasby shook his head, sighed, and stood. "Well! We've got to decide what to do here. I'd like to set you and Mapes in charge for the rest of the day, Thomas. I think I should go to the Leaverings' directly, in case I can be of any assistance. Helden's straightened out, so you needn't worry about that."

I handed him the form for the undertaker. "Benjamin Leavering is *not* his usual self," I asserted.

"No doubt. I can't imagine what this will do to him. We should be closed, tomorrow, Thomas, for at least one day—a show of respect. The man was a partner of the firm."

"Yes, sir."

"Can you handle all the staff, then? Oh, and get some crepe for the door? And post a notice?"

"Of course. Would it be appropriate for me to come over after work?"

"I'm sure. If they're indisposed, they'll be frank enough to tell you."

As Glasby collected his effects, summoned, and spoke to Mapes, I resolved to raise a matter of purely personal concern. I caught him at the door. "I'm sorry to be so forward, Mr. Glasby, but … do you imagine this event will change the plan to have me voyage with the *Dorothy C.?*" I was already entered as the supercargo on her next voyage to Santo Domingo in the Caribbean. It would be my first international business trip—my first ocean trip—and I'd been anticipating it for over a year.

Glasby looked blank for just a second. "Ah, I don't know, Thomas. Shouldn't think so, although … with one partner dead and another incapacitated by grief … Who knows how long it'll last? He and Mrs. Leavering will travel back to Philadelphia, I feel sure of that, but … I know how much you want to go, but … it's too soon to decide that." He knew as well as I the ship would be laden and ready within a week. "If Mr. Leavering can spare a moment to think about the business, I promise I'll ask him. Certainly, Helden's flour will have to go, one way or another." He straightened his hat and departed.

I gritted my teeth, almost ashamed to contemplate the pettiness of my hopes when compared to the turmoil facing the Leavering and Sproul families, but it would be a bitter disappointment if this tragedy were to prevent me from sailing.

There was no point in fretting it. I threw myself into the tasks at hand. When the church bells struck twelve, I recalled that I'd contemplated stepping out to see if the constable McCraney had named might alleviate some of my perplexity. Not possible. Perhaps the morrow would offer a better opportunity.

An extraordinary, but very pleasant friendship had developed since the fall of 1759, when I had been taken on as a *de facto*, though not a legally-bound apprentice by Castell, Leavering & Sproul, between Mr. and Mrs. Benjamin Leavering, Mr. and Mrs. John Glasby, my eccentric cousin Charles Cooper, and myself. Neither the Leaverings nor the Glasbys had any family in the city, and Charles and I were as yet unmarried and unencumbered. Though separated by decades in age, we six found ourselves largely harmonious in sensibility, interests, and opinion. I, the youngest of them, felt enormously privileged to be included in their supper parties, discussions, and excursions—blessings over and above my opportunity to learn the lucrative and challenging business of importing and exporting goods by ship.

I therefore had little hesitation in presenting myself early that evening at their handsome home on fashionable Hanover Square, in the East Ward, to offer my condolences. Mr. Glasby met me at the door. "Ah, Thomas!" he said softly. "You just missed your cousin. All settled at the office?" I nodded affirmatively. "Very good. Mr. Leavering took to his bed immediately on his arrival here, but Mrs. Leavering's bearing up, despite the awful shock of it. Adelie and I have done what we could, but it's a sad, sad household."

"Ah. I should like to pay my respects."

"Yes, yes, come in, of course."

Hermione Leavering was, like her husband, a large, rotund, and plain person of some three score years. If anything, however, she was usually even more gentle, bright, candid, and jolly of disposition. Since moving to New York, she had thrown herself into some of the charitable endeavors that have supporting women's auxiliaries, making many friends—several of whom, having seen the tokens of mourning I had posted on our office door, had apparently already visited to extend their sympathies. Mrs. Glasby, sitting next to her in the drawing room, rose upon seeing me and encouraged me to take the seat while she fetched me a glass of cider.

"Thomas, my good lad. Thank you for coming!"

Though she was able to get the words out, I could sense that she was still reeling from the blow. "Please accept my profoundest sympathy, Mrs. Leavering."

"Thank you, Thomas, I …" She clutched my forearm. "Thomas, I understand it was you who … at the coroner … Benjamin was so overwrought! Is there any, the slightest, doubt that …"

I had to look away before facing her. "Dear madam, I grieve to tell you, there may be others whose comely face and figure might be confused with his, but … the scars on the hand were not mistakable."

"The *right* hand?" she demanded.

"Aye, ma'am, the right."

She clutched a handkerchief to her mouth with both hands for half a minute, struggling to restrain an outburst of tears. I fear I had just extinguished a last ray of hope. "Oh, I wasn't really dreaming that … We have already posted a letter to my daughter. The hardest thing I have ever written! Adelie had to transcribe it for me, I couldn't hold the pen! It's all so unfair, so unjust! If it wasn't blasphemy, one would … We—none of us—even have the slightest inkling what Daniel was doing, coming to New York. He'd written us to expect him, but … Evelyn will presently turn forty, but he need hardly have traveled here to arrange a celebration. In *March*, for heaven's sake! No one travels in March when it's not necessary!" She was not normally a babbler, and she shortly caught herself. Mrs. Glasby handed her a small glass of brandy while her husband added a log to the fire.

It seemed a not inappropriate moment to change the subject. "I have to return this object to you, ma'am," I said, producing the book, "which was inadvertently separated from his purse and effects at the coroner's."

"Very odd of Daniel to travel with *only* two pounds!" she exclaimed. "Nothing makes any sense!" This thought took me aback. Were I to carry two pounds eight and six in my purse, I'd think myself quite flush; but on second consideration, Mr. Sproul was a well-to-do businessman in the middle of a trip that would have to last at least a week … "I'm sorry, my dear. The book?" I put it in her hands. She winced on beholding the *ex libris*. "Ah! We had Mr. Franklin—*Doctor* Franklin—print these up as a Christmas present, oh, fifteen years ago." She turned to the title page. Despite my customary infatuation with books, I'd not ventured so far, being greatly busied at the office. It was a volume by the Quaker minister John Woolman—widely regarded in New York City as an obstreperous madman—entitled *Some Considerations on Keeping Negroes, Part Second*. "Oh, of course," Mrs. Leavering said mildly. "Daniel thought the world of this gentleman, and this is just published. It was Daniel, you know, who persuaded Benjamin to manumit his three slaves before we moved here. That's not even legal in this province. Daniel could be *very* convincing!" Glasby nodded sadly. Mrs. Leavering absently began to read the book.

I cleared my throat, a recalled curiosity getting the better of me. "If I may, ma'am," I said, taking the book again and riffling its pages, "I wonder if you've any idea how these came to be stuffed inside?"

The sight of the playing cards did not seem to disturb her at all—though both Mr. and Mrs. Glasby's eyes widened with surprise. "*Hmpf*," she grunted, amused. "Well, we all have feet of clay, you know! If my dear son-in-law had a *peccadillo*, it was cards. He just loved to play card games. The other Quakers were most disapproving. Even my daughter was most disapproving! But he was very sociable, and he found it agreeable and relaxing, so I thought, wherever was the harm, *eh?*"

"That ... couldn't have anything to do with there being only two pounds in his purse?" Glasby asked tentatively.

"Oh no! Daniel was emphatic that he never ventured more than a penny a card, though it sometimes irked his playing partners. He said he was flayed for risking too much on the one hand, and not enough on the other!"

"He certainly knew his own mind!" Mrs. Glasby said admiringly.

"Oh yes! Well, thank you, Thomas. These must belong to a deck they have at home. I'll give them to Evelyn."

I knew a little about cards. "They seem to be from a continental set," I ventured. "These are the four *Varlets*, not Jacks. Probably pulled out for a game of Whist."

"Really? Curious! Are you a regular player, then?"

"Oh no, ma'am, but you may recall, my family owns a tavern over in Kings County. And tavern-keepers always maintain a deck or two for the amusement of their clientele."

Mrs. Leavering's eyes were glazing over. "I think it's time we should leave our hostess alone, gentlemen," Mrs. Glasby said.

The lady whimpered slightly, but did not protest the idea. "All the arrangements are made, ma'am," Mr. Glasby said gently. "Adelie and I will be back at eight in the morning to do what we can. The weather looks to hold, so I thought it would be easier to sail to Perth Amboy and go overland from there. Happily one of our own coastal boats—the *Janie*, Captain Ford—can oblige us. Even has a reasonably comfortable cabin. Barring the unforeseen, you should be in New Brunswick tomorrow night, and Philadelphia by Friday Noon at the latest."

"Oh, that's good. And the, *uh*—"

"The undertaker will bring the casket directly to Peck Slip by eight thirty. High water will be at nine thirty."

"Ah. Thank you all so much for everything."

Under a lighted tavern sign at the corner of Nassau Street, I bade goodnight to Adelie and John Glasby. "I don't know whether the inexplicability of his death makes it harder or easier to bear," Adelie sighed. "On the one hand, you have no one and nothing to blame, so you can concentrate on simple grief, but—"

"But on the other hand," John continued for her, "it's just maddening that you can't explain it. Can't *begin* to explain it!"

"It nags so at you!" she concluded with a shrug.

Chapter 2

It had never before happened on a weekday in the thirty months I'd been working for the firm, that I had awakened in my room in the boarding house and not had to get directly to work. Given the distressing circumstance, the unexpected holiday brought only the briefest—guilty—pleasure; but at first I was at a loss as to how to employ myself.

As none of the New York staff would be expected to venture to Philadelphia for the funeral, I daresay the traditional rationale of closing the firm was that all of them should immure themselves in their various houses of worship to repent of their sins, contemplate God's mercies, and pray for the soul of the deceased. But after two years in Manhattan, I had still not affiliated myself with any of the Reformed congregations—yet another failing that deeply irks my family and their neighbors in my hometown. Perhaps I will stop in at Middle Collegiate … if the spirit moves me.

Though sunny, it was still just cold and blustery enough to discourage any notion of retrieving my canoe from its winter storage.

By the time I'd sat down to breakfast in the common room, however, I'd resolved to spend the morning at the New York Society Library, where I am now proud to be a full member in my own right. The clerk there looked askance when I requested the volume that Mr. Sproul had been carrying, but dutifully reported that, while they'd not yet acquired a copy, he could fetch me its predecessor, written a decade ago. It was just a brief tract, ostensibly directed solely at fellow Quakers, and yet its implications were staggering. Apparently this fellow John Woolman thinks everyone everywhere should immediately set all of his slaves at liberty! His scriptural argument is certainly close-reasoned, and he calls also on the most enlightened morals of our time, yet … can one not see the chaos that would ensue? What on earth would happen *next?* Imagine that Mr. Sproul thought highly of this lunatic!

I borrowed several other books and stayed in the reading room until three-quarters past eleven was chimed, but I found myself constantly remonstrating, in fantasy, with the mad Quaker. I was glad to have a project that would shake my mind of him!

By noon, I had enjoyed a bracing walk back up to the Common. I did not stop to talk with Mr. McCraney but went up the stairs of the little building to search out Officer Jennet. He arrived a few minutes later—a large, lethargic man in his thirties who seemed reluctant even to talk with me, much less to show me where he'd found Mr. Sproul … until I offered a shilling to make it worth his while. Then he brightened up and even sought permission from his superior to borrow the wagon and the slave. The latter, Aston by name, also brightened on seeing me; I guess tuppence had been overly generous for his exertions yesterday! We set off directly, with the tolerant superior urging the slave to be quick about the business.

Aston whistled gaily as he drove us westward to the river—a small, lively contrast to the big constable. I couldn't decide whether he was atypically cheerful for a slave … or simply unhinged. Jennet ignored both of us until I began querying him. "Have you ever before found a gentleman lying dead in an alleyway?"

He appeared to suspect I was jesting. "No." I waited. "Last fall, there was two duels fought by the redcoats, but the seconds took the corpses to the undertakers, so we didn't have to bother with them."

"Is it unusual to find two dead men in one day?"

"This time of year. August, however …"

"Four stiff ones we found, one Sunday last summer!" Aston sang out. "And *hoo,* did that morgue stink when—"

Jennet elbowed him. "This is it," he announced as Aston reined the horse.

"Already?" I said. "Mr. McCraney said he was found near the ferry. That's another three blocks."

Jennet shrugged. "Right over there's where he was." We were on the river road just north of Vesey Street. On the east side of the road were two incongruous structures looking directly onto the muddy shore: a large warehouse and a three-story building that appeared to be a fairly respectable inn. There was an open area between them about ten feet wide; both structures had windowless walls facing it. There was a six-foot-high wooden fence across most of the frontage, with an open entry on the warehouse side.

"Show me, please."

Jennet sighed heavily, but the three of us clambered off the wagon and walked across the road into the alleyway. It was filled with neat stacks of barrels, crates, a two-horse wagon harness, and, of course firewood. There was one uncluttered corner that even had some grass left on it. "There," Jennet said, pointing at the wood pile.

"*There?* Not over on the grass?" No reaction. "How?" Jennet impatiently nodded at the slave, who gamely sat on the ground and leaned backward against the corner of the wood pile. He splayed his legs and arms out and bent his head all the way back.

"Didn't have his mouth open, Aston," Jennet ventured. Aston closed his mouth and eyes, but kept his head arched backward. "Aye. That way."

It took me seconds to voice my unease. "It's the most uncomfortable position he could ever have chosen!" Jennet and the slave cast questioning looks at each other. "You're sure he was lying there, against the corner of the pile, not just over here, where the logs at least wouldn't dig into his back?" Aston nodded. "And his head was all the way back, not slumped down on his chest?"

"Aye."

Aston saw me looking at the relatively comfortable-looking plot of greenery. "It be dark here at night."

That was, of course, true, particularly as the moon was in the last quarter. Could Sproul possibly have been here before sunset?

I shook my head, the whole scene being unfathomable. "You noticed the rum on him?"

"*Hoo,* couldn't miss!"

"Man must've been dead drunk to spill so much on his clothes," Jennet said.

"Waste of good liquor!"

"But he *wasn't* drunk," I protested. "McCraney says there was no liquor in him, only on the clothes."

The two looked at each other unbelievingly. "*Somebody* were drunk," Aston said.

"Did you look about for any other property he may have had? I'm thinking particularly of a hat—a flat, Quaker hat."

Both shook their heads. "We searched all 'round," Jennet said.

The total improbability of it all then nearly overwhelmed me. "What about *luggage?*" I asked, realizing no one had even mentioned it yesterday. "Surely a man on a week's journey must carry some luggage!"

"Maybe it got stole?" Aston said.

"Stole the luggage but not his purse?" Jennet chided him.

"If he was truly ill," I mused, "I suppose he might have dropped his luggage, and then someone claimed it as found goods." But the really baffling question was, why had Mr. Sproul not headed directly to his in-laws after he disembarked on Manhattan? Or, if he was taken ill and wandering distractedly in the wrong direction, why did he walk into an alleyway when a decent looking hostelry was to hand? "Is this a respectable establishment, Mr. Jennet?"

"Roberson's? Ain't no ill-fame attached to it."

"Uh huh. Was it they who found him?"

"Aye. She sent a boy to fetch me."

"At six fifteen?"

"Aye. I took his pulse, I seen nothing could be done for him. I went back to hall, called for Aston and the wagon. We got back here, loaded him in, Aston took him to McCraney, and I went on about my rounds."

"He must not have been stiff at that time, then? He flattened out?"

"Beginning to be stiff. It took us a while."

"He was cold!" Aston asserted. "Like that beggar woman we found in the snowdrift."

"Not *that* cold, Aston," Jennet countered. "She was hard as a rock."

"Colder than the other one we found yesterday!"

I was startled to hear this comparison voiced independently. "Did you happen to remark that to Mr. McCraney?"

"McCraney?" Jennet exclaimed. "He don't much talk to us!"

"This is the burly fellow with big teeth and an old scar on the forehead? Killed in a knife fight?"

Both of them snorted derisively. "Oh no," Jennet said, "Meshach Hager weren't killed in no honest fight."

"How so?"

"Must've been taken by two or more. Someone held him back while another one did for him."

"Why do you assume that?"

"No cuts on his arms or hands," Aston asserted, "just stabs in the chest. Never had a chance."

"Good lord."

"Don't waste no sighs on that one," Jennet said. "A bad 'un. He'd have done the same if he could."

"You have any hope of finding who killed him?"

Jennet sighed and shrugged. "We'll keep ears open, in case any fool brags of it, but—"

"Not a prayer, and who gives a damn!" Aston said gleefully.

"You mind your place!" Jennet snarled at him; but I could tell it was toothless, and the slave had merely stated the obvious.

"Was he lying in the sun? Could that have kept his body warmer?"

"Too early for that. You know the foundry, two-thirds the way to Greenwich? There's a big oak on the river side of the road. That's where he was. Had to go back to the hall and fetch Aston all over again."

Morbid curiosity was distracting me. "What happened to the body? Did anyone come to claim it?"

"Him? Nah. Jones makes a sketch just in case family comes for them, but we had that one put under before the morning was out."

"Efficient!" I said sardonically.

That seemed to amuse the slave, but not the constable. "Aston has to be getting back, Mr. Dordrecht," Jennet said sourly.

"Of course. Thank you both." I gave Aston his obviously anticipated tuppence, and he bowed with an overstated flourish that could easily have been interpreted as insolence … if one had a mind to interpret it that way. Jennet got on the cart, and Aston drove it away. Neither offered more than a nod in farewell, and neither, I noted, had indicated the slightest curiosity about my reasons for this inquiry. As they turned the corner into Vesey Street, I began to wonder myself.

But the sudden, inexplicable demise of a perfectly healthy man is surely a natural curiosity, I reflected. Had Mr. Sproul unaccountably expired in the peaceful bosom of his parlor, it would still have been an anomaly of general interest. Learning further details of this tragic event was possibly one service I could offer to assuage the anguish of my employers and their families. I climbed the steps and let myself into the empty foyer of Roberson's hostelry.

"Just a minute, I'll be right with you!" a woman's voice called. I had only enough time to note the wall's four hand-colored prints of scenes from the gospels when a stout, harried, plain woman of middle years came in from the back, wiping her hands on her apron. "Good day to you, sir," she said, smiling at me. I was chuffed that she seemed happy at my appearance even though I was not even wearing my business suit. "I'm Mrs. Roberson. Would you be interested in a room?"

"I'm afraid not, ma'am," I said, knowing—from personal experience—that it would disappoint her. "Just some information, if you can spare me a minute."

"Oh?" She squirmed, too polite to refuse me outright.

"I shan't detain you long, Mrs. Roberson. This concerns the … corpse discovered outside here, yesterday morning."

"Ah!" she gasped, her sympathies evidently aroused. "What a terrible thing! Jennet told me this morning they now know at least who the poor gentleman was."

"Uh yes. My name is Thomas Dordrecht, ma'am. I'm an employee of the shipping firm of which the deceased, Mr. Daniel Sproul, was a partner."

"Ah, such a fine-*looking* man! His wife must be greatly distraught."

"I daresay, ma'am, if her parents are any indication." I had to explain the family's situation in detail—but I noticed she no longer seemed in haste to resume her chores. "Can you perhaps tell me who discovered him, ma'am?"

"Oh, it was me, sir. First thing, every morning, we have to replenish the firewood. But my husband was cleaning the grates, and I'd sent the boy off to market, so I went out to fetch the wood myself, and … I hate to tell you, but my first thought was, it was a drunk. In nice weather, they sometimes wander into the alley after being thrown out of *The Clam Digger* just down the road, though usually they pass out on the ground. I was much put out until I saw that his clothes showed him a gent, no matter the smell on them. I still shoved him pretty roughly, I'm afraid, because … Even though his head was tilted back, it took me half a minute to realize he was dead, not just sleeping."

"The coroner believes he was not in fact drunk, but the liquor was on his clothes, not in his belly."

"Oh my! I *knew* he wasn't the sort!"

"This was at six fifteen, then, ma'am?"

"Oh no, somewhat earlier. That was when Mr. Jennet got here, after the boy had located him down by the ferry dock." A black lad of twelve or so years passed silently by us carrying an armload of kindling—"the boy" in question, I surmised. "Do they still have no idea what killed the poor man?" she asked. "All Jennet could tell me was *heart failure*. I could've told them the man's heart had stopped!"

And that, I confirmed, was in fact apparently still the full sum of medical opinion. "Did you see anything else that might have belonged to him, ma'am? A hat? Luggage? Or anything otherwise out of the ordinary?" She shook her head. "Any evidence that the man had been ill on the ground, perhaps outside the premises?"

"No. Trust me that I know what to look for!"

"No doubt, ma'am. My parents run a hostelry and tavern, too, over in New Utrecht."

"Ha!" We shared a rueful smile. "His waistcoat was buttoned wrong," she remarked all of a sudden. "One button off, all along."

Odd … but I'd frequently enough walked out the door before realizing I was incorrectly buttoned. "Perhaps, if he were feeling indisposed and tired—"

"I suppose."

A more important question occurred to me. "Mrs. Roberson, do you recall the night before? When was the last time anyone here went out to the alley?"

"Oh … oh yes, of course, we had a party in the private room that carried on interminably, and Willard had to go bring in more wood for their fire."

"That would have been … around ten o'clock?"

She looked at me disbelievingly, and I realized I was thinking in Kings County terms. "On after midnight, Mr. Dordrecht!"

Midnight! "And. of course, Mr. Sproul was not there, at that time?"

"Oh no. We'd have evicted him! Were he drunk, that is, begging your pardon. If Willard had found him ill, we'd have summoned assistance."

"Of course, of course." Baffled again, I was momentarily at a loss. "I suppose he might have arrived on a night ferry, he was coming from New—"

"Last run's at dusk," she asserted flatly, shaking her head.

And of course she was right again. Even the Brooklyn ferry only runs into the night at harvest time. Could Sproul have wandered for hours or passed out somewhere else before collapsing at Roberson's? Again I was at a loss. I pulled out my change purse. "I thank you for your time, Mrs. Roberson. May I … offer you a *pour-boire,* perhaps?" This *was* getting a tad expensive, I thought to myself.

"Oh no no no, Mr. … uh, sir. It's all so distressing. Please do give his widow my sympathies."

"Of course, ma'am. Thank you and a good day to you!"

Notwithstanding the respectability of Roberson's, *The Clam Digger*, located a mere block and a half further south, was as gamy an establishment as any I'd seen—and my employment on the East River waterfront had taken me past plenty of them. Any public house that catered to mariners or blacks, or worse—as here—both, was held in the lowest esteem by the gentry of our town. Yet at midday, I felt no special qualm in ordering a much-desired ale. I held up the sixpence I'd intended for Mrs. Roberson, and the brutish-looking publican forthrightly assured me that no gent remotely resembling Mr. Sproul—hat or no hat, luggage or no luggage, rum-soaked coat or no coat—had darkened his doors in years, much less the past two days. Neither, I surmised from the scowls of his patrons, had any gent resembling *me*. I drank up and moved on.

I was in greater luck at the ferry dock, as the ferry was in and waiting for the wind to increase or the current to abate. "Can't manage with both no wind and heavy flow of the water," the garrulous, bewhiskered captain told me. "One or the other betimes, but not both!" I sacrificed yet another sixpence and learned that he alone manned the ferry—except in midsummer, when his otherwise useless nephew made the dawn run. I described Mr. Sproul in detail and asked when he had been brought over. "But I don't recall any such gentleman, young fellow," he assured me. "Certainly not since the ice broke up three weeks ago."

That couldn't be right. I described Mr. Sproul a second time, and he assured me a second time that he had plenty of opportunity to take note of all his passengers, and that no such gentleman had taken his ferry this calendar year.

Feeling nearly panicked by my vertiginous bewilderment, I demanded to know whether anyone else might have transported our firm's principal into New York. "Well, I'm the only ferry here. Down at the Narrows, you have Denyse's ferry, and twenty miles up, there's Dobbs ferry … There's other boats that cross the river, of course, but not such as take the general public with them for hire."

I was preparing to examine him a third time when the breeze picked up. He held out his palm expectantly, and I was so thrown, it took me seconds to hand the sixpence over.

Dumbly, I watched as the ferryman hoisted his sail and, pressing his customers into casting him off, took the wind for Paulus Hook, directly across the Hudson. I staggered off the wharf to Cortlandt Street where, for a full minute, I stood irresolutely still on the edge of the road.

Mr. Sproul's death had come up so suddenly and unexpectedly and overwhelmingly that it was just now becoming clear to me that it wasn't merely *how* Mr. Sproul had died that made no sense. *When* he died and *where* he died also made absolutely no sense. He had written that he *hoped* to reach Paulus Hook by Monday evening—and certainly one could hardly expect to do better when traveling from Philadelphia at this time of year. And yet, without having crossed over by the public ferry, he somehow wandered into the alleyway next to Roberson's inn between midnight and dawn … and expired. One incongruity was piled atop another!

Presently, not having any clear object in mind, I retraced my steps north, stopping in front of *The Clam Digger*, Roberson's, and the alleyway, each time looking in vain for anything new. Hoping to clear my head, I then kept walking, out of town and past the orchards, hoping the fresh air might revive my wits.

After a mile or so, I came upon the foundry, a much larger and more prosperous-looking enterprise than my Uncle Frederik's brickworks, which is located in the middle of the island well east of this spot. Carts were moving loads of ore, sand, hay, and firewood to and fro, horses were neighing with the effort, a laden barge was being towed off the little private dock, men were shouting greetings or orders, and soot was spewing from the chimneys. The wind had risen to a fitful breeze, and I feared it might veer in direction and send the soot down upon me. I looked again toward the river and noticed the great oak. I walked toward it, thinking to separate myself from the befouling consequence of a minor wind shift. This was the spot where Jennet had located Mr. McCraney's *bravo*—a fellow whose fate he, the constable, and the slave had all been certain merited no concern or even second thought.

And in truth it was Mr. Sproul's fate that occupied me—or perhaps it was my own. The realization that one could work hard all one's life, earn the esteem of colleagues, the respect of neighbors, and the love of family … and still be arbitrarily struck down without warning by some incomprehensible thunderbolt of Zeus … was a thought to incapacitate the strongest. Leaning against the tree trunk, I was about to sink to the ground when I perceived a dark red spot on the grass; rain had not yet erased the pool of blood that had recently been spilled there. Habitually, I looked about, but found nothing more to relieve the mystery of that incomprehensible death than I had of Mr. Sproul's.

I made my way eastward through the fields to the old Indian trail that runs the spine of Manhattan, and thence back to town. I was, in fact, moved to spend some moments in Middle Collegiate Church, where I sat alone on a pew in contemplation, if not quite in prayer. I realized with some shame that I was allowing myself to become prey to despondency, and that that was not acceptable. Mr. Sproul's own example, I thought, must preclude that! He, after all, had seen his father brutally taken from him as a mere boy, and yet he overcame whatever crisis of faith and motivation he must have felt to build a business, his city, and his family. Could I do less?

Enough! I found myself a hearty meal, drank a quantity of good ale, and took myself home. There I pulled out my guitar. It had been some time since I'd practiced, and the effort was restorative. I went early to bed.

The office of Castell, Leavering & Sproul, which, I am happy to say, is normally busy, was unusually so after being closed over an entire workday. Mr. Glasby, taking full charge for the first time, looked somewhat beleaguered by the necessity of fulfilling Mr. Leavering's functions in addition to his own, and he assigned me half a dozen projects before I'd removed my jacket. It was late in the day before I even thought to voice the conundrum that had so preoccupied me the afternoon before, but Glasby was still too agitated even to grasp my intent. "Yes, yes, Thomas," he said impatiently. "Have no fear, I wrote to Mr. Castell for his thoughts about your trip. We should be hearing back by Saturday. Now, have you examined the *Edward Blandings's* manifest?"

Oh yes, my trip, that too! It had barely crossed my mind yesterday. But my report on the manifest took the better part of an hour. Just as

I was again about to change the subject, Mapes claimed his attention for a complicated scheduling matter at our warehouse.

When this chaotic situation had persisted into Friday, I began to wonder whether I should trouble Glasby with my perplexities about Mr. Sproul at all. What purpose would it serve? However successful we were, affording time to indulge mere curiosity was an option only for the wealthiest, and my excursion and conversations had uncovered no more than curiosities. Perhaps we should simply have to live with our confusion regarding the sad death of Daniel Sproul, as we had to live with confusion regarding so many other tragedies. Every shipping company, of course, had its own grim private tale of a ship that had cleared one port for another and then disappeared without a single trace of its crew, rigging, or cargo. Every family, my own—*alas!*—not excepted, had its memory of a cheerful and frolicsome infant who simply didn't wake up one morning.

On Saturday, Mr. Castell's reply was received, leaving the decision about my trip in Mr. Glasby's hands. And when, after hours of debating himself, Mr. Glasby acceded to it … the enigma of Mr. Sproul's demise slipped completely into the background.

Chapter 3

Mr. Glasby had postponed his decision until near the last practical minute. I had considerable preparation to get under way, given that I might be abroad for as long as six months. Things had been well in hand until all plans had been disrupted four days ago. Now needing to catch up—and in truth, relieved and wildly excited—I begged his permission to depart at our usual Saturday closing hour of two thirty, despite the firm's backlog of business. Much to Cyrus Mapes's annoyance, he gave it to me.

Chief among my priorities was a visit to my family in Kings County, which was imperative for business, as well as personal reasons.

Mr. Leavering's intention was that I should travel with the *Dorothy C.* as a supercargo—that is, an individual who would have naught to do with the working of the ship, but was nonetheless more than a passenger, because of his responsibility for the security, marketing, and trading of some or all of the cargo inside it. As the captains of merchant ships generally perform these functions in addition to commanding their vessels, it is a matter of some delicacy to add a supercargo into a ship's company—particularly when, as in my own case, they are very young fellows of no more than apprentice rank. When I'd first been introduced to Captain Enos Trent last October, he had seemed amenable to the idea; however, his enthusiasm for my presence was markedly diminished ten days ago, when the ship returned from Monte Cristi harbor, our destination on the eastern—Spanish—half of the north coast of Santo Domingo island. When Glasby explained that I should be responsible only for the sale and exchange of the flour and foodstuffs, while Captain Trent would retain control of the sale and exchange of maritime supplies, he appeared only slightly mollified. In fact, the principals of the firm were perfectly satisfied with Trent's handling of the ship and the crew, but less so with his commercial transactions, and were seeking a way to break apart those traditionally joined functions, in the hope of improved results all around.

As a supercargo, one is entitled to the status and perquisites of a mate, but can only be commanded to assist the ship in emergency. Another perquisite—a consideration tendered in view of the hazard of travel—is the right to have carried aboard a substantial quantity of goods that the supercargo intends to sell on his own account, strictly separated from the firm's merchandise and, for that matter, the captain's equivalent private account. On first learning of the possibility of this trip, I had solicited my family and neighbors in New Utrecht for goods that might fetch higher prices in the Caribbean than locally, and my immediate need was to arrange their final delivery to Peck Slip on Monday.

And, of course, I felt duty bound to bid my family good-bye in advance of a long and arduous voyage—one that they, landsmen to a soul, were certain would be my last. Therefore, I rushed back to my rooming house, gathered a few necessities, and was lucky to catch the afternoon ferry to Brooklyn town, from which it is a mere five-mile walk south to New Utrecht.

Although no daffodil had yet been so forward as to show its face, the day was mild, and spring's promise could be detected in the damp air. My mood lightened the further I got from the city. Aiming to complete a parcel of my personal cargo, I did not go directly to my family's abode in New Utrecht, but stopped first at the town's smithy—an enterprise that I had reorganized some while back so that it was owned by wealthy Meneer Teunis Loytinck, manned by our family's slave Vrijdag, and, thanks to the latter's diligent efforts, profitable to all concerned through a complex sharing arrangement. The burghers of the locality, otherwise lacking a blacksmith and having previously known Vrijdag as his late predecessor's assistant, generally overcame their prejudices and availed themselves of the services of an independently operating black slave.

"Good afternoon!" I called to him—in Dutch, of course, Dutch being the primary tongue in New Utrecht, even though most of its residents, even the bondsmen, are bilingual.

"Good afternoon!" he repeated, smiling awkwardly. Though Vrijdag and I had had innumerable dealings with each other and had known each other since we both were children, neither of us was able to articulate an easy form of address. He is too proud to call me "Meneer Dordrecht," and I am too proud to demand it from one not reciprocally permitted the dignity of a surname. My brother, for whom he is compelled to work as a field hand for one hundred ninety days a year, insists on "Meneer Harmanus," and Vrijdag complies—for the sake of peace, I imagine. But we two affect to deal with each other as if neither had names.

"How is business?" I asked him.

"It pick up. Spring. But I think last year, more."

"Ah. That could be true. Half the soldiers have left New York City now, you know. Seven thousand up and gone from a city of twenty thousand! My employers say that will have to affect all our markets."

Vrijdag grunted unhappily, but shrugged it away. "Have four crates full!" he announced.

"You do? Show me!"

This was the crux of the transaction that brought me here: from wrought-iron rod that I'd purchased for his stock, he'd laboriously manufactured thousands of three-inch nails. Whenever his demand for horseshoes, hinges, and door latches had slackened, he'd turned to the nails, knowing I could sell any excess in the city for far less than those imported from Britain. I inspected a couple at random from each of the heavy boxes—evenly tapered to a fair point, with a well centered flat head. "Excellent! Did you count them?"

"Six gross, exact, each case."

"You're sure?" I teased—instantly regretting the habit.

"Plus one, each case!" he retorted, to my pleased chagrin.

"Ha! You know I plan to take these to Monte Cristi? I'm told I can get much better money for them there than in the city."

"On boat? What if—" He caught himself, but he was still apprehensive.

"If the boat goes down? You're out of luck … but not as out of luck as I am!" We both snorted our nervous manly contempt of danger. "But my company's ships do come back, as a rule, and richer!" For a second, he still looked undecided. "The ferry to *Manhattan* could go down, Vrijdag!" I grew impatient with him—and myself, thinking of how bizarre my business acquaintances would regard even the thought of discussing such a decision with a slave—but I did reckon that I had, after all, ventured the capital for the iron stock, and was therefore by rights entitled to the disposition.

"You sell Vrijdag nails far away?" he asked, cocking his head.

"Aye!"

He liked that. "Ha!"

Noticing that daylight was fading, we turned to the arrangements for sealing and marking the crates, and for their inclusion on the cartload I was planning for Monday morning.

As we had no means of greeting, so we had no ordinary form for parting. I simply touched his elbow and said farewell. He merely nodded, and did not—as he once had—jump.

At my family's home—a public hostelry known as *The Arms of Orange*, the largest structure in our tiny hamlet—the first individual I came across was my disgraced father, the now universally disdained town drunk. I had availed myself of our famous brick privy in the yard, and was entering from the back intending to surprise my mother in the kitchen, when he came shambling out. He looked even worse than the last time I'd seen him at Sinterklaas—unshaven, his hair a tangle, his clothes filthy. He was stuffing a morsel of cheese into his mouth. "Hello, Pa," I said.

"*Eh?* What are you doing here?"

"Come to say farewell, Pa, before my trip to the Caribbean."

"What! Caribbean! Only a damn fool gets in a boat if he doesn't have to, boy!"

"My employers desire me to serve as the supercargo, Pa."

"Oh, so you have to?"

He was a trial to anyone's patience, but I remembered the man who had been my honored progenitor before his morals collapsed some years back. "I'm very eager and excited to go, Pa."

"Mad!" he grunted, shaking his head and starting away to the stable.

"I was hoping for your blessing, Pa!"

The look he gave me wrenched my heart—surprise, a flash of pride, and hope—quickly extinguished. "*My* blessing?"

"Aye." Now he looked suspicious. "I'm seeking all the blessings I can get, Pa."

He grunted and continued on his way. "Try not to get yourself drowned, boy!"

"Thank you, Pa," I managed.

My sister-in-law, Anneke, was looking on through the top of our Dutch door, drying her hands on her apron. "Welcome home, Thomas," she sighed, opening the lower door. "I'm afraid he's worse than ever. Harmanus now refuses to talk with him."

That took me aback. My eldest brother was such a model of pious rectitude, he put most clergymen to shame. For him to so ignore the commandment to honor the father meant that Pa's lapses had touched new depths. "Where does he eat? Where does he sleep?"

She looked furtively back toward the kitchen. "We have to keep him away from the children and the customers, Thomas. I feed him before everyone else, then he goes away, sometimes for a couple days. He has a crony up in Brooklyn. On cold nights he goes back to your mother's room, but we've fixed a pallet for him on the floor."

We stared at each other for a second. "He's brought it on himself," I ventured lamely. Anneke nodded and shrugged and turned back to the kitchen, and I quickly requested and got the more cheerful news about everyone else. She herself, I learned, was expecting her eighth child early in the autumn. "Congratulations!" I exclaimed, wondering what she really thought.

"God's will and God be praised, Thomas!" she said simply. "I'll tell your mother you've arrived."

"Don't wake her!"

"She asked me to!" Picking up a cleaned chamber pot from the bureau, Anneke climbed to the second story, and I walked on into the main room, where the eldest pair of her six surviving offspring disrupted the peace of the two guests by noisily embracing me.

However gratifying that was, I had to shush them for the customers' sake. "Do you suppose Grootmoeder will recognize me?" I asked Berendina, the eldest—and my favorite.

She shook her head. "Only Papa and Cousin Bertie, Uncle Thomas. Oh, and Auntie Geertruid."

"Well, we have to try, don't we?" We walked over to the fireplace, where my grandmother was asleep in her rocker, her knitting spilling onto the floor. I bent down and gathered it back into her lap, and then kissed her cheek. "Hello, Grootmoeder!"

"Oh!" she said, coming awake with a start. "Hello … sir." But she smiled in response to my smile.

"You dropped your knitting." There was no comprehension. I put the yarn and needles directly into her hands, and she smiled again and began working. But even I could tell that she was no longer connecting to her previous efforts. I kissed her again and went back over to the table where the children had been engrossed in their studies—in addition to tending to the customers.

"Are you really going all the way around the world, Uncle Thomas?" Hendrik asked eagerly.

"Well, not quite, lad," I said. "I'm going a long way, but even that's not a tenth of the way around the world."

"Aren't you afraid that whales will eat your boat?"

"Well … no."

"Are there cannibals where you're going, Uncle Thomas?" Berendina asked in all seriousness.

"No, sweetheart, I'm heading to a quite reasonably civilized place, the island of Santo Domingo, which Columbus discovered over two hundred fifty years ago."

"But aren't they all papists there? Won't they force you to kiss a crucifix?"

I had to laugh. I might have asked the same questions when I was their age. Fortunately, Mother came in just then, and *she* cross-examined me regarding every article of clothing I was planning to take. She being the business manager of all family enterprise, we discussed how the inn was faring, and I then explained the details of my arrangement with Vrijdag. Anneke asked me to fetch a keg of cider from the cellar that she deemed too heavy for the children. Hendrik held a candlestick while I searched it out. "Do you miss your Auntie Elisabeth, lad?" I asked. He nodded glumly as I shouldered the keg. "Ah, so do I!" It had been a year since my beloved younger sister had married and moved in with her husband's family in the next county, but even though I'd been delighted with the marriage—to Roderick, the youngest brother of my particular friend, Marinus Willett—I still found her absence palpable. One knows that change is a constant in life, but still …

"Oh Herr Thomas, Herr Thomas!" greeted me as we emerged from the cellar. It was Joachim, my brother's German indentured servant—who seems to have decided, ever since I arranged our purchase of his indenture, that I walk on water. He knuckled his forehead and pulled the keg over onto his enormous shoulder, saying "I take, I take!" and hurried to deliver it to Anneke.

Harmanus and I greeted each other with a civil handshake. There was peace between us at long last, but I still feel the weight of his bewildered disapproval of all my choices in life. Harmanus seems at heart to believe that every man should be a farmer just like himself—with a few exceptions such as the clergy and the military and the royalty, I suppose—and that anyone who is *not* is likely some sort of heretic. But he was in a fair mood this evening. "I do have to thank you for Joachim, Thomas," he allowed sincerely. "He may be a simpleton, but he does work. I hope I can persuade him to stay on when his contract runs out." We discussed the neutral subject of the progress of his farms until supper was at length on the table.

Harmanus now sat at the head of the table, I observed. For years, he had left that chair empty and sat on its right, in deference to our negligently absent father; now the break was so bitter and final that all pretense was gone. It was good of him to include a prayer for my safe return as he said grace.

We were seated at the two tables of our main room. The children were at one table with Grootmoeder and Joachim, both of whom were oblivious that they weren't seated with adults. Harmanus and Mother headed the other, with the two guests of the inn joining Anneke and me in the center. One was a quiet farmer from Hempstead *en route* to a funeral in New Jersey. The other was a garrulous man of affairs from Perth Amboy, selling the intricate reins and harnesses for pairs of horses, oxen, and goats, many parts of which were manufactures imported from Britain. He was particularly interested in my forthcoming voyage, and I was so full of excitement that we were well into dinner before Mother inquired whether the firm would miss having my services on the spot … whereupon I was moved to relate the tragedy that had occurred during the past week.

They were all completely stunned. "The man *just* died?" Mr. Fuller, the commercial traveler, said incredulously.

"It is my cousin whose funeral I am attending," said the other morosely, "but he was kicked in the neck by a cow."

"It does sometimes happen that apparently healthy adults expire of a sudden," my mother said thoughtfully, "but *some* reason—apoplexy, food poisoning, heat stroke, asphyxiation—is always visible, as far as I've ever heard."

"Was it fun to identify the body, Uncle—?" Hendrik began enthusiastically … before his parents' furious scowls silenced him. I concurred that it was hardly appropriate to discuss such matters at the dinner table.

"This is not Mr. Leavering you're speaking of?" Anneke demanded. She, my brother, and Mother had had occasion to meet Mr. Leavering and the Glasbys since I became employed there. "I could understand, given his age and great weight—"

"No, no, this was Mr. Sproul, his partner and son-in-law, from Philadelphia, who was very trim and at least fifteen years younger."

My brother seemed the most disconcerted of all. "This was a man of great piety, I believe you told us last year?"

"Aye. A Quaker, of course, you understand."

Harmanus still looked thoughtful. "I bought the ox from a Quaker up in Flushing. Of course his theology is repellent, but I had to admit the … earnestness with which he held it, he—"

Mr. Fuller coughed delicately, and Harmanus reddened with the realization he'd overstepped the bounds appropriate to polite discussion—particularly for those who hope to retain paying customers.

For my own part, I was astounded at my brother's unprecedented effusion of liberality! Would he say a kind word for Anglicans next? "I believe Mr. Sproul was even some sort of lay preacher, Harmanus."

Mother sighed. "It is extremely mysterious."

"Let us know if you learn anything more, Thomas," my brother said. "I'd be very curious!"

Even more startling! I couldn't recall Harmanus Dordrecht expressing *curiosity* about anything in his life. Perhaps his dense theology was rocked by the extreme capriciousness of this "Act of God?"

After supper, Hendrik evaded his parents and caught me having a pipe out in the street. "What's it like, identifying a body, Uncle Thomas?" he demanded eagerly.

I decided to humor his ghoulishness, though I couldn't match his enthusiasm. "It's a necessary duty, Hendrik, not a pleasant one."

That didn't discourage the lad in the slightest. "What made you sure it was Mr., uh, the man from Pennsylvania?"

"Well, there was no difficulty with the identification, Hendrik, he hadn't been disfigured. But mainly, Mr. Sproul had a distinctive scar on his hand from a wound he got when he was your age."

"Oh! And he still had it?"

"That's the rule with scars."

"Oh. Why doesn't anybody know how come he died?"

"There's nothing to indicate the reason, Hendrik."

"Hekserij?"

Oh dear. "I don't believe in *hekserij*, Hendrik. Only folks who are going daft, like Grootmoeder, believe in witchcraft anymore."

Hendrik looked dubious at this optimistic overstatement. "Then what—"

"We have to learn to live with things we can't explain, lad, rather than making up a reason, like *hekserij*. We hope that science will bring us to enlightenment someday, but we mustn't pretend we have an explanation when we don't."

"But—"

"Aha!" Mother was standing in the doorframe. "You!" she commanded, pointing to my nephew. "Prayers and bed! Directly!"

"Yes, ma'am."

"You're sleeping with your brothers tonight, so Uncle Thomas can have his room back!"

"Yes, ma'am." He trudged off, but dutifully kissed her cheek when reminded by a tap on the shoulder.

"I forgot to mention, Thomas—you and I and Katryne and Lodewyk have been invited by the Van Voorts to join them for dinner tomorrow, after church. I understand you have business to conduct with Vrouw Van Voort ..."

"Yes. Officially it's with her grandfather, of course." Teunis Loytinck still kept up the pretense that he ran his own farms.

"Oh yes. But it's thoughtful of Marijke to make it into a social occasion."

And good business, I thought—actually rather flattered that *my* business with her apparently merited a special effort. But, of course, she and Mother and Katryne Nijenhuis have also become close friends in the last years.

Dominie Van Voort, the pastor of our town's church, though more succinct than his predecessor, whose sermons are recalled with shudders a full decade after his demise, can nevertheless hold forth considerably longer than I truly care to endure. And I wasn't the only Dordrecht who was elbowed more than once! This time the subject was grace. Is one born with it? If not, can one acquire it? Through good works? Through prayer? Through faith? Through grace? *Gracious!* my lamentably parodistical mind tacitly interjected. *Can I acquire grace through grace? Through saying grace? Or is it something my dancing instructor can teach me?* The temptation to burlesque is one I stifle with difficulty. For good reason, I avoid subjecting myself to Sunday services!

At length it was over, and I had a chance to socialize with the townsfolk before dinner. "Oh, sweet heaven, I thought he'd never give out!" a low voice whispered in my ear—my cousin Bertie Hampers. Bertie was still a free spirit, despite living with his in-laws—who were fulsomely congratulating the dominie, and despite being father to three—soon four—children. He was the only adult in the town who expressed the emotion I would feel if someone else told me of a planned excursion to the Caribbean—envy. I regretted not having more time for him as the social hour concluded, and Mother and I joined Vrouw and Meneer Nijenhuis in walking out to the Loytinck house, where the Van Voort family lived with her now somewhat mellowed grandfather.

"Does old Loytinck ever manage to attend kerk?" I asked Lodewyk Nijenhuis.

"Every now and then," he said, amused. "*She* is now as regular as anyone."

"Naturally!"

"Naturally. Being the dominie's wife entails certain responsibilities, as I'm sure your mother and my wife explained to her when they counseled her to marry him!" he added slyly.

"But that's worked out, I take it?"

"Amazingly well, Thomas. Whoever thought they'd manage two children at her age? But they're thrilled, old Loytinck is pleased, the dominie minds the kerk, his vrouw minds the farms, slaves handle the children, and all's well in New Utrecht!"

I shook my head with wonder at the unexpectedly happy fate of a couple so mismatched to all appearances. "Tell me, does the old boy ever carouse with my father as he used to?"

"No. Thomas, I'm sorry, but nobody here *talks* to your father any more, much less carouses with him in public."

I groaned. "You?"

"We used to be friends, lad, but I can't penetrate the fog of spirits any longer. I grieve for him, I really do."

We arrived on the porch of the house—rather excessively called a mansion by the townsfolk—and were welcomed inside by the adults of the family. Again, I was amused to see how Marijke Van Voort towered over her husband, and how she carefully deferred to him—at least on all issues that did not truly concern her. Mother and Katryne, I mused, had contrived a great change in the once very remote and awkward Marijke Katelaar. The dominie was effusively responding to a polite query from Lodewyk, which was actually only a request for clarification of a point in the sermon. I cautiously paid my respects to the patriarch, whose shoulders were finally just a trifle stooped. "Good day to you, Meneer Loytinck."

"Well, young Dordrecht! Word has it you're to be embarked to the islands?"

"Aye, sir, on Tuesday, if all goes well."

He snorted. "Better not wait, lad, there's more bad weather afoot!"

It was a gray day, but I hadn't sensed anything ominous. "You think so?"

"My knees never lie, boy."

Being so addressed was a provocation, but I bit down on my annoyance. I suppose being nearly four times my age entitles one to address men of twenty-two as *boy*. "Are you satisfied with our arrangement regarding the smithy, Meneer Loytinck?"

That forced him to think. "I consider it acceptable, Dordrecht," he allowed. "We're breaking even, and the town needs a smith." I knew better than to expect thanks for the idea and the negotiations. "I'm rather amazed that you get such good work out of that black! He never did more than the minimum when I owned him."

Now I regretted raising the issue altogether. Eight years ago, Loytinck had ordered Vrijdag beaten half to death when he'd run off. I had nothing to reply. Certainly I didn't want to mention that Mother was holding the slave's savings in the hope that he'd someday buy his own freedom.

Vrouw Van Voort came to my rescue by voicing a demand that I tell the company all about my voyage. The subject being very much in the forefront of my mind, I was able to expatiate on it until well after the first remove. "Do they allow you to take aught for yourself, Thomas?" Katryne asked.

"Oh yes, that's customary. I'm taking some of Aunt Betje's meat pies and some of my brother-in-law's good beer, but they're actually for my own sustenance on the trip, as I understand neither will survive the whole passage. Then Mother has spared me six kegs of her hard cider, which my employer suggested I can use as compliments."

"But you're permitted to market goods on your own behalf, are you not?" Lodewyk interjected.

"Yes. I'm taking four crates of Vrijdag's nails. They sell well enough in the City—forty percent less than British nails—but I understand the premium is far higher in the sugar islands."

"The slave is *making* nails?" Meneer Loytinck demanded rather incredulously. "I hadn't realized that!"

"Oh yes. His local business is both seasonal and erratic, so I bought him some rod iron stock from a finery forge in Pennsylvania with which my firm has relations, and he's been hammering them out whenever his work slackens."

"Oh, excellent, Thomas," Lodewyk began, "that's—"

"But Thomas," Dominie Van Voort interrupted, looking vaguely puzzled, "isn't that … *illegal?*"

Everyone looked slightly disconcerted—briefly. "I suppose it is, sir, but—"

"But what?"

"But aside from the fact that everyone in America does it, we—"

"Hardly a justification, Thomas!"

"I admit that, of course, sir, but the point is that it's … *unjust* to make it illegal for us in the colonies to manufacture our own nails!"

"Unjust?"

"Forgive me," Vrouw Nijenhuis said, "but how does it come to be that it's illegal to make *nails*, for heaven's sake?"

"The Parliament of Great Britain has so decreed, my dear," her husband responded.

"For nails and a great deal more!" I declared.

"When was this?"

"Well before the war," Loytinck asserted.

"It's not nails, specifically, as I understand it, ma'am," I said, recollecting a discussion in our office some time back. "It's the refined, milled iron from which the nails are made. Nothing fabricated from our refined iron—nails, chains, tools, hardware—is in accordance with the law, when made here."

"Here? In New Utrecht?"

"Anywhere in North America, ma'am. The idea, I believe, is to support the manufacturers of Britain—"

"By ruining the colonists who must buy British products when their neighbors could make them so much cheaper!" Nijenhuis asserted, thumping the table. Everyone was startled to hear him—normally the mildest of farmers—declaim with enthusiasm.

"That's the opinion of my employers as well, sir," I affirmed. "We in America are supposed to content ourselves with shipping raw materials to Britain, where they have claimed an exclusive right to convert them into finished goods, which they then ship back to us and the rest of the world. We're supposed to be mollified by the fact that we have guaranteed purchasers in Britain and a free trade within the empire."

"Works out well enough on the whole, wouldn't you say"—I shot a glare in Loytinck's direction lest he again call me *boy*—"*um*, Dordrecht?"

Mother smiled ever so briefly as I continued: "It works in some respects, sir. It does encourage the mining of raw materials here and the manufacture of finished goods in Britain and the ability of English and Scottish merchants to export them, but there are many effects of these mercantilist laws that are terribly harmful, not only to us in New York but, as Dr. Franklin contends, to the empire as a whole."

"Oh, *Doctor* Franklin!" Loytinck exclaimed.

"But the injustice of the matter lies in the distinction made between Britons in Britain and Britons in the colonies. Why should we be prohibited from making and selling nails when they are not?"

"Hear, hear!" Nijenhuis exclaimed—in English, slyly pointing up the irony of the fact that all of us Dutch-speakers consider ourselves Britons every bit as much as the Virginians do. Everyone smiled.

Except the dominie, tenting his hands over his plate. "But Thomas, if it's *illegal* ..."

I fear I simply gaped at him. Could the man truly be so otherworldly, so naïve? Half of the business of Castell, Leavering & Sproul—of New York City! Of all America!—was not in full conformity with British mercantile law. What did he think our province's prosperity depended upon? I caught Vrouw Van Voort's nervous eye. In what did he think my commerce *with his wife* consisted?

He did not comprehend it. "We must render unto Caesar that which is Caesar's, Thomas," he asserted mournfully.

"But if Caesar is contending that things are his to which he has no right ... ?" Nijenhuis challenged.

"I do rather wish the Son of God could be prevailed upon for an analysis of our specific circumstances, Dominie!" I wheezed.

"Thomas, *please!*" Mother said, suppressing her smile with difficulty.

"I'm sorry, I'm sorry!"

Then the whole table fell to laughing, and Vrouw Nijenhuis happily recalled that she was dying to tell the other ladies of a new bonnet shop she'd discovered on her last excursion into town.

An hour later, Vrouw Van Voort and I—and her grandfather—excused ourselves from the party to visit their barn, which was but a few yards from the house. A gust of cold wind buffeted us during the few seconds we were out of doors. "You see!" Loytinck gloated.

"It is indeed getting brisk, sir," I conceded, eager to avoid any contention with his knees.

"Stanley, our foreman, went to his Anabaptist meeting this morning," Vrouw Van Voort remarked, "and told me just before you arrived that the ships in Sheepshead Bay were tugging at their anchors!"

Though eager to get on to the matter of our commerce, this was too great an anomaly for me to ignore. "*Ships?* In that little bay?"

"Well, yes, that's what he said."

"Eben Stanley knows naught of *ships*, granddaughter," Loytinck observed.

"He said there was one with three masts, Grootvader!" Loytinck shook his head. "The sands outside that bay open and close, depending on the last big storm, I'm told," Vrouw Van Voort continued. "And Reuben—the kerk's servant—said other large boats have been putting in there recently."

"Can we get on with this? I'm wanting my nap!" Loytinck nagged.

"Of course, Grootvader," she replied. We followed her to a corner of the barn. "These are the ten barrels we're consigning, Mr. Dordrecht."

"Aha!" I spent a few minutes examining the barrels for tightness, turning one or two around and on their sides with some difficulty.

"I presume you'd care to choose one for inspection?"

"Please." I pointed to the one that had staves that seemed imperfectly fitted. Meneer Loytinck clumsily began to attack the head of it to force it open, but he had trouble simply holding the hammer. I held my peace rather than set him off by volunteering to assist. Finally we had it off, and I dug as deeply as I could with a scoop to bring up a quantity of grain. Though not a farmer myself, I am the grandson, son, and brother of one, and I was fully able to judge that the barley remained salable, unmarked by rot or pests. "Excellent!"

"The cooper is coming first thing in the morning, Mr. Dordrecht, to reseal the barrel just before we put it on the cart for Brooklyn. Stanley and three of our men should be at Peck Slip before noon."

"Very good."

Loytinck excused himself, to my profuse thanks for his assistance and private relief for his absence.

"We had hoped to sell all the barley to the troops here," his granddaughter said, "but they've left us!"

"I understand there should be no trouble disposing of grain in Santo Domingo, Mevrouw," I said, "though I can't guarantee what we'll be able to get for it."

"I'm hoping you can find us a favorable price, Mr. Dordrecht!"

"I shall certainly do my best, ma'am!" Particularly as we'd agreed on an eighteen percent commission!

After giving her further instructions for marking the barrels, we walked back to the house. She stopped on the porch, however, even though it was rather chilly outside. "I hope you were not offended by my husband's qualms, Mr. Dordrecht? I honestly don't know where—"

"Ma'am, I hope you and he were not offended by my forwardness!"

"Actually, although I am in agreement that there is nothing reprehensible about evasion of the mercantile strictures, even though it's called, *um*—"

"They presume to call it *smuggling*, ma'am," I said rather too brutally.

"Yes …"

"Many take them to task for rendering it necessary, however."

"Yes. But what does worry me is the thought that any of these products might end up in the hands of our country's enemies, the French."

I swallowed. Leavering and Glasby had catechized me on exactly how to behave if challenged with this practice by officialdom—to feign horror while emphatically and unconditionally denying any knowledge of such commerce—but how could I possibly prevaricate with this good woman of my hometown?

"Nothing we are taking can be construed as contraband, ma'am," I first hastened to assert. "At least, not under normal circumstances."

"Normal? How is that, Mr. Dordrecht?"

"My employers maintain that contraband consists only in warlike stores—weaponry, ammunition. They contend all other goods have no taint, and that they are following traditional precepts of freedom of the seas first asserted by our Dutch forebears over a century ago."

"But?" she demanded, after a pause.

"But Parliament and the military commanders here among us now insist that nothing, nothing at all, may ever be traded with merchants of the enemy country. Goods that people require in peace as well as wartime are forbidden. Clothes, shoes, nails, shingles, and foodstuffs are all deemed illicit."

"But they do succor the enemy's soldiery, do they not?"

"Oh perhaps, ma'am, but more to the point, they enable everyone else simply to survive. The islands of the Carib Sea produce naught but sugar. There are thousands of civilians there—women, children, men, and slaves by the ten thousands—who are completely dependent for their food on their trade with us in North America. If we obey these cruel dictates and fail them, there will be mass starvation there. I am told we can depend on it!"

I was surprised at my own vehemence. I had often observed Mr. Leavering, Mr. Glasby, cousin Charles, and my firebrand friend Willett declaiming against imperial interference in our trade, but I'd generally listened without participating. It was pleasing that I'd not gotten my tongue knotted as I restated these ideas! But she still seemed hesitant. "I just hate the thought that any of this grain might nourish a man who would raise his saber against any lad from this town!"

For a second, I was at a loss for a rejoinder—but only for a second. "If we had to judge the character of everyone we exchange goods with, Mevrouw," I argued, "why, all commerce would immediately grind to a halt! Do you have any guarantee that the grain you sell over in New York City will never sustain a thief? That the barley you sell to my brother-in-law's brewery in Flatbush will never contribute to the inebriation of a rapist?"

She examined me dubiously. "You yourself, I well recall, Mr. Dordrecht, once faced the fury of Montcalm. Can you truly be so indifferent to the thought that we might in any way support those who would attack others from this county who joined the king's forces?"

Whew! She was an even tougher customer than her husband! "I ... Ma'am, we all have to take risks, and ..." Glasby had told me that our firm had in fact smuggled foodstuffs to Québec while I'd been in the army; also that that action had helped stave off a famine among the populace following a disastrous harvest. "I hope I'd consider, ma'am, that the replenished soldier looms larger in the imagination than do the many more helpless and innocent civilians caught in the crossfire!"

"Hmm!" she murmured noncommittally. "Very well. We do wish you safe passages, Mr. Dordrecht!" At last she opened the door.

Small talk had been exhausted long before. Lodewyk Nijenhuis, his wife, and Mother were all struggling to keep their eyes open as the dominie rehearsed the themes of his next sermon. "Thomas!" Mother said, jumping up. "We must get back directly! I trust my son has not driven too hard a bargain, Vrouw Van Voort?"

"Oh no, Vrouw Dordrecht, and our terms were decided some time ago. This being the Lord's day, we were of course merely discussing last-minute details." Dominie Van Voort nodded emphatic approval, and the party presently dispersed.

And very shortly thereafter, I begged that my love be conveyed to my absent siblings and hugged everyone good-bye. Excitedly foreseeing the wonders I'd report when next I would see New Utrecht, I commenced my march back toward the town of Brooklyn.

Captain Trent threw the entire office into disarray on Monday morning by announcing that, given the deteriorating weather, he intended to leave on the morrow's morning tide, rather than the planned afternoon tide. He saw no problem with this revision, as virtually the only items not yet stowed on the *Dorothy C.* were my private account goods. Suffice it that I had a most full and busy last day running back and forth from the office to the wharf and into the hold of the ship.

At eight p.m., I trudged through a heavy drizzle to *The Brimming Bumper*, where, by prior arrangement, I was to dine with my cousin Charles Cooper, who wanted to treat me to "the last good meal you're likely to get for half a year." Where Charles got the cash for this extravagance—and where he gets the wherewithal for his daily bread—I don't know, and never expect to learn. Charles is past thirty and yet he still lives in a small room of his parents' house and has never enjoyed regular employment. When my curiosity had once gotten the better of me, Aunt Janna had rather huffily insisted that he does pay them rent. At that point, I decided never to inquire again. We have slowly become friends. Although he never mortifies me by shrieking "Tommy!" when encountering me on a public street, as once he did, he can still be embarrassingly effusive. However, he remains close to all the rest of my circle, and is unfailingly curious about *everything* and informative about *everything*, so … he always interests me.

I had already downed half a flagon of ale by the moment he joined me. His absurd wig, drenched from the rain, looked even worse than usual, but I'd long ago given up hope that it would bite the dustbin. "What ho, cousin mariner!" he bellowed, causing others to stare, uncomprehending, at my person.

"And 'Ahoy there!' to you too!"

"My, my! Off to the Caribbee this time tomorrow!"

"Tomorrow *morning*, it's been changed. Six thirty! I'm afraid I can't dawdle over supper if I hope to get any rest."

"You're going to have weeks to do nothing *but* rest, silly boy!"

"Charles, *please!*" I protested.

"Well, it's true," he blared on, ignoring my objection. "That is, presuming you can get any sleep while being tossed like a feather in a—" The serving girl—actually she must have been near to forty—appeared, and he broke off to ogle her bosom. "Martha, my adored one!"

"Mind where your hands wander, Mr. Cooper!" she said with more toleration than one might've expected. She pulled away and one of Charles's hands was indeed exposed, fondling the back of her thigh. I wanted to crawl under the table, but both instantly regained their poise—How often had this scene been rehearsed?—and she inquired what we *gentlemen* would have tonight.

I quickly placed an order for stew and another ale, but Charles took two full minutes to decide, teasing the hapless servant all the while.

"Finally!" I exclaimed when she was released. "Charles, you really—"

"You're off to the Mount? To Monte Cristi? To trade with the dons, of course, who have only the entire southern continent to grow their staples!"

Sarcasm, as usual. The settled fiction of trading at Monte Cristi was that we British colonials were dealing solely with the Spanish and other neutrals. It was sheer happenstance that a virtually unpopulated bay on the north-central coast of Santo Domingo island was deemed convenient for this. We were completely oblivious to the thought that our produce might be traded again scant hours later to the hostile French, whose coastal barges had but fifty miles to run to a harbor on their half of the island. The French possessions are completely employed in the fabulously lucrative business of sugar, rendering them dependent on our trade for all else, and quite ready to pay dearly for it. "Mr. Glasby says the New Englanders have become quite brazen of late, sometimes trading with a Spaniard while a Frenchman hovers behind a curtain, not merely listening but prompting the Spaniard how much to bid!"

"Better than the prisoner-exchange ruse, Thomas! Are you taking a prisoner with you?"

The ruse in question involves traveling directly to a French port under a white flag of truce, carrying one or more French prisoners of war to be exchanged for English. The private ship performing this notable public service is entitled, as compensation for its trouble, to exemption from the hated prohibition on trading. Competitive bidding for the requisite French prisoners had at one point gotten quite heated along our seaboard! "No, we're instructed to stay with Monte Cristi. Mr. Leavering wishes to avoid trouble now, as he believes the war must be over at any moment."

"Very sensible of him. Except that it should have been over a year ago. It's eighteen months since we've completed our glorious conquest of the giant icehouse!"

I sighed, hoping to avoid another of his political rants. Charles is possessed of ardently unconventional objections to our war that just happen to be shared by the Philadelphian principals of my firm—a position that binds him into our social circle. But by way of changing the subject, I wondered aloud if Charles might be informed on one worrisome rumor. "I did want to ask you, is there any truth to … I heard that Pitt—"

"That bloody jackass!"

"—was plumping to involve the empire in a new conflict—"

"With Spain, the damned fool! Well, you needn't worry there, Thomas. The lunatic former prime minister is mercifully out on his backside at last, and the entire idea is too preposterous for anyone with an iota of sense to contemplate!" That was all I needed to hear, and I hoped Martha's arrival with our plates would put an end to it. It didn't. Charles resumed his ogling and his oration in the same breath. "Is it not the epitome of madness to start a new war when one is already bankrupted by the first one, *eh?* The opposition contends that, having succeeded in divesting the French of continental possessions, Mr. William Pitt now wants—"

"The 'Earl of Chatham,' they've ennobled him!"

"Yes, and I'm sure there's a most foul tale to be told someday … Mr. William Pitt actually wanted to repeat the feat with the Spanish! Notwithstanding an exhausted army and navy! Notwithstanding that his European allies are stalemated in Germany! Notwithstanding—"

"My stew is excellent! Are you pleased with the ham?"

Charles had the grace to realize I'd heard all this before. He broke off, took a mouthful of his meat, and pronounced it quite acceptable. For a few minutes we spoke of Mrs. Glasby's forthcoming theatrical project, a stage production of *The Recruiting Officer,* which was the sole event that might have tempted me to pass on my voyage. Presently, I was finished with both my glass and my plate; Charles was barely halfway through. "Martha!" he roared. "Another beer for the sailor lad!"

"Charles, thank you, but I really—"

"I insist, Thomas, I insist!" His countenance became suffused with the surprisingly predatory look it gets when he's finally ready to discuss something in earnest—when he thinks you have *information* he wants. One of Charles's "hobbies," it is my dubious privilege to know and to have to keep secret, is writing slanderous and disquieting letters to the editors of our newspapers, for which he uses the grim pseudonym *Sejanus* …

Feebly, I protested once more before giving up. A new glass arrived, and I swallowed a draught. "Captain Trent thinks we're in for some—"

"What happened to Mr. Sproul, Thomas?"

Exasperating! I am desperately trying to check every last item off my list and get *some* rest, and he opens a question as amenable to definitive solution as who killed the little princes in the Tower! "You know as much as I—"

"I do not, Thomas, or I wouldn't be asking."

"We had a letter today. He was buried on Saturday afternoon. There were near four hundred mourners. Mrs. Sproul has required sedation …"

"Thomas! What *happened* to the man? I've never even heard the report of your session with the coroner."

"Truly there's naught to tell, Charles."

"A man known to be healthy on Sunday is found stone cold on Tuesday morning, and his corpus reveals *nothing?*"

The purgatorial terror I'd felt last week in Middle Collegiate in the face of total incomprehension swept back over me of a sudden, like a spell of dizziness and nausea. For seconds I couldn't speak as Charles scowled angrily at me. The wry thought, *Trust Charles to demand the impossible!* brought me back. "Grootmoeder has got young Hendrick thinking it must be *hekserij*, Charles, and in all honesty, I can't do much better."

"No. No! We must do better! There was *nothing* on the body?"

"Not a thing that would suggest a natural, unnatural, or *supernatural* cause of death!"

He scowled again. "Adelie said the clothes had been befouled?"

"Aye," I affirmed, now regretting my flippancy. "Smell of rum all over them. But the coroner, McCraney, swore there was no rum in him or on his person."

A sneer. "Did he put his nose to the test, I wonder?"

"I put *my* nose to the test, Charles!"

Charles abruptly sat back. "I beg your pardon, cousin," he said.

"And he had over two pounds in his purse, so clearly no one had interfered with the body."

"Unless …"

"Unless what, Charles? There's not the slightest suggestion of foul play here. There's not the—"

"I heard you went back to the coroner's the day your office was closed?"

How'd he know that? I hadn't even told Glasby. No matter. "Aye. I did."

"Well?"

He wanted every detail of my exchanges with the constable, the slave, the landlady, the barman, and the ferryman. With his observant questions, it took an hour to accomplish. Nine forty-five was tolled by the church on the corner. I reiterated my helpless belief that, not only was the cause of death inexplicable, but the time and the locale were as well.

"I want to know more about *why* he was traveling to New York in the first place!" Charles asserted, flabbergasting me. "Mrs. Leavering was adamant that she had no idea what was on his mind, and that such a visit was unprecedented."

"She … mentioned that to me too," I said, realizing that the observation did deserve more weight.

"Was anything happening at the firm? Anything unusual about your voyage?"

"Oh no. The firm has ships coming and going all the time. And I'm sure Leavering and Glasby would have said so, if Sproul had hinted any concerns about the business."

Martha was hovering about impatiently.

"It's all very unsatisfactory, Thomas!"

Unsatisfactory! As so often with Charles Cooper, one is simultaneously tempted to throttle him and to laugh in his face. With some difficulty, I refrained from either. Charles was prevailed upon to pay the long-suffering waiting girl, I thanked him, he wished me luck, and we parted fondly, as cousins should.

As I wearily climbed up to my room, shaking my sodden greatcoat, I reluctantly had to concede him one truth: what was known about the death of Daniel Sproul *was* unsatisfactory.

And there … I would have to leave it.

Within minutes of reaching my room, I was blessedly horizontal, ready for sleep, wanting sleep, needing sleep, and believing it critical that I get sleep. Yet sleep did not come. Over and over I rehearsed my list, sure though I was that all had been readied. Yes, I had packed the ledger books. The dictionaries were already aboard. The barley casks had been marked as I'd instructed. Vrijdag's crates were firmly braced in the center of the hold. All four of my shirts were in my portmanteau. Both the landlord and his slavewoman had been twice reminded to wake me without fail at four thirty …

Two o'clock struck. It had been useless of me to annoy the landlord with reminders if I were never going to fall …

Amsterdam of old. Which looked something like … Albany! My wrists were bound in front as a spear-point at my back forced me across a rainy stone plaza full of horrified but disapproving people, then down two hundred steps of a circular stairway. "Why I am here?" I cried—to no avail. "Of what am I accused?" No answer. "You've no right!" I screamed as I was shoved inside a room and the door slammed behind me. But it was no ordinary closet. It was the infamous drowning cell! Close-fitted white tiles lined the floor, the four walls, and the back of the door to the height of eight feet. The steel-helmeted spear-carrier scowled down from the open ceiling … as did my late Grootvader and … Colonel John Bradstreet. I hammered the door with my bound hands. "Let me out!" Water suddenly began pouring into the cell from an orifice out of reach at the top of the wall. Within seconds, my feet were soaked. A few seconds more, and it had covered my ankles. Suddenly I noticed the wood and leather apparatus taking up the bulk of the room: a pump! I grasped its handle and pulled up and pressed down, causing a sucking gurgle. The water was nearing my knees. I stroked again, feeling a pressure against the effort. And did it again, when I sensed that the water level had not risen. Frantically, I pumped … and the level slowly dropped. I pumped until I could see the wet floor, and then halted, panting. But the water kept pouring in, the rate never changing. The men above looked on silently, indifferently. Again my ankles were covered, again I pumped it out, again I halted to catch my breath. And again and again the cycle repeated. Each time my exhaustion increased, and my ability to keep pace lessened. The water reached my waist, my chest, my neck, my mouth …

"Masta Dodrick, Masta Dodrick!" I was being shaken. Pushed under! Suddenly it was totally dark, save for a blinding candle on a shelf. "Masta Dodrick, you has the evil spirits!"

"Ah ah!" I bellowed, lashing out, striking the spirit—her—in the chest, and sending her backward. "What? What! Oh my God!"

"It's Bessie, Masta Dodrick. The spirits got you?"

"What? Bessie?" Slowly I began to see familiar objects … of my room. And the landlord's servant. "Oh! I'm sorry! Did I hurt you?"

"No. It's half-four, Masta Dodrick. Four thirty!"

It took extraordinary effort to pull myself together. But I somehow did, and I lugged my heavy portmanteau through hateful weather—rain so cold you wished it were snow—to the ship, which was rocking more than one would like in the fresh breeze. It took strength and courage to climb the gangplank in dim light, where I was greeted by the frowning captain. "What the devil took you so long, boy?"

"Sir? It's just quarter-past, sir!"

"Well, the flow has changed nonetheless, hasn't it?"

"I have to make one more run over to the office, sir."

"What! I'm ready to cast off!"

The office door was barely thirty paces from the gangplank. "It will take but a minute, Captain Trent."

Trent growled with dissatisfaction. "See that it does, Dordrecht!"

As I rushed down the gangplank my feet slipped from under me, and I landed hard on my rump on the dock. Though it hurt like the devil, I realized nothing was broken, stood up shakily, and limped on toward the building. I used all fours to climb the steps and found my colleague Cyrus Mapes at the landing, gaping. Four years older than me in age but not as high in rank in the firm, Mapes smirked as he opened the door to the office. Though we manage to get along, I always feel he'd not be sorry to see me dismissed. "Your backside is quite a sight, Dordrecht!"

"I just took a tumble, Mapes." I retrieved the object for which I'd come.

"A *guitar?*"

"Trent estimates the trip will take over three weeks."

Mapes grunted, and then recalled a duty. "Oh! This arrived just minutes ago, in the post."

He handed me an envelope. From Mrs. Leavering, of all people! I hastily set the guitar down and tore it open. It was the four playing cards, with a note explaining that she'd asked her daughter about them and been assured they did not belong to Mr. Sproul. As they looked valuable, she hoped that I might be able to find the true owner and return them. I blankly stared at the lot. The bell of the *Dorothy C.* rang furiously. "Mapes! Do me a favor and stuff this in my desk, will you? Thanks!"

"Fair winds and following seas, Dordrecht!"

"'Bye!"

"Well!" Trent exclaimed sarcastically after I'd again negotiated the gangplank, which was hauled in immediately after I achieved the deck. "Our young supercargo has joined us at last! *Finally* we can go, lads!" He waved me to one side and blew a whistle as I attempted to ask a question. I saw the hawsers being hauled aboard. Within a minute the ship was moving out into the East River.

Still panting, I watched the shore retreating through the dismal rain. Ten days ago, I'd imagined this moment—brilliant sunshine, scudding clouds, the Leaverings joining Mr. Glasby and his beautiful wife to wave me good-bye …

The one stevedore who'd released our lines from the bollards was out of sight indoors before we'd gotten out of the slip.

Chapter 4

For a full minute I stood witlessly to the side of the main deck in the rain, ignored by all as the complicated procedure of being towed backward into the main channel, dropping the tow, and raising sail was effected. Finally I noticed that my portmanteau, as well as my guitar case, was getting soaked, and realized it was nobody's job but mine to get them below. Of course I had been down in the cabin several times before and knew where I was to stow my personal dunnage, but it had never looked so gloomy and close on those occasions as it did now. The guitar fit into the niche Captain Trent had shown me, but it was all I could do to stuff the portmanteau into its tiny cubbyhole. A wave of exhaustion came over me, but the cramped bunk that I'd earlier imagined would be all right now looked profoundly uninviting.

The black crewman came down, hunting for an article the captain had asked him to fetch. Feeling the necessity, I asked how calls of nature were answered. For a second, he looked as if he'd been queried by a horse. Finally, he simply pointed to a door I'd never noticed and returned to his duties. I opened it with some trepidation. To say the sight was not pleasing is an understatement, but I remonstrated with myself to the effect that it, the cubbyhole, and the bunk would serve … because they *had* to serve.

Presently relieved, I patched my dignity back together and decided I really should not sleep through my first great departure. I climbed back up to the deck. We were now in the middle of the upper bay, and the city was fast receding into the sodden gray morning. The crew was still preoccupied with trimming the sails, so I returned to my out-of-the-way spot to watch. There was a sailor nearby, looking upward in great concentration, evidently directing the activities of others in the tops. He was most curious in his person, given that, while his face and form were not unpleasing, he was apparently not exactly a mulatto, but a mix of all the races of mankind, with Mohawk and Lascar blood blended in atop that of Europeans and Africans. I stared with some amazement at the jewelry bedecking his ears, neck, and fingers until distracted by the captain's call of "Two points to windward!" and the helmsman's "Aye, aye!"

I turned back toward the bow as the crew strained to haul the sails further in, and … "My *hat!*" I screamed. The sudden increase in wind had torn it off my head. For two seconds, it seemed it might drop harmlessly to the deck, but a gust took it outward and it landed upright on the surface of the water. I groaned mightily with dismay. The exotic fellow came toward me, his head cocked. "Can't we go back and get it?" I wailed.

He stopped dead and, to my intense annoyance, burst out laughing. "Go *back?* For a *hat?*" he guffawed.

"I *need* that hat!" I roared, incensed. "I just bought it! It cost a lot of—"

"That'll be all, Parigo," said a deep voice I recognized as that of the mate, Mr. Fox. "What seems to be the problem, Mr. Dordrecht?"

"My hat! Can't we …" It was still visible a hundred yards behind us. "Would it really be so much trouble to go back for it? Surely—"

Fox shook his large, homely head. "Not possible, sir, simply not possible," he pronounced … and walked away, leaving me speechless with frustration.

"Wouldn't go back if it was *you* overboard, cully!" Parigo rejoined—grinning as if that were somehow an amusing statement. Seeing what I trust read as outraged indignation on my face, he added, "Oh maybe—seeing as you're the boss's grandson and all—maybe we'd make a try at it."

The thought that the *Dorothy C.* might so casually leave me to drown in sight of my home county—and would have second thoughts only on the basis of misinformed ancestry—infuriated me to distraction. "A *try!*"

"You'd be shaking hands with Davy Jones long afore we ever got sails down, and anchored, and lowered the jolly boat, and got back to haul you out of the bay!"

"Nonsense, I can swim!"

"Oh you can, can ye?" he said, surprised but still shaking his head. "All very well, but the waters'd claim you nonetheless. Down by Santo, you'd have a prayer if the sharks ain't too hungry, but here, now … That's water's *cold,* matey! Nobody last in cold water."

"But it's inhuman to—"

"Parigo, that topsail is *luffing!*" Fox hollered—and the sailor instantly turned his back on me.

Furious, I turned away from *him* and saw that my hat had disappeared, New York Island had disappeared, and even the Kings County shore had disappeared into the fog, though we were approaching the Narrows on the Staten Island side. Perhaps some notion of the glorious adventure of ocean travel was disappearing also. I thought of making one more appeal to Fox, but the concentration on his face resolutely suggested, *Not now!* Sick with dismay, I overset my previous resolve and decided to bury myself in my bunk.

But confronting the bunk with the intention actually to get *into* it brought on a new level of misery. While the common seamen slept in hammocks that swung freely, the six officers' bunks were built permanently into the sides of the ship, three on top of each other. The lowest one on the starboard side had been assigned to me. Mr. Fox and the captain were to be directly above. All resembled nothing so much as coffins, barely long and wide enough to accommodate a average-sized man lying on his back, with a five-inch board retaining him on the open side. Being just shy of six feet in height, every time I moved I would bump my head or my feet or my hands. With great difficulty, I maneuvered myself inside it—my home for the next many months—and fretted that I'd suffer a recurrence of the nightmare that had so terrified me—*When?*—just four hours before.

But after a long interval of bemoaning the hat and the bunk and the weather and the nightmare ... I fell sound asleep.

"Mr. Dordrecht!"

I was poked on the shoulder. "Mr. Dordrecht, do you care for any of the burgoo?"

Mr. Fox favored me with a rare smile, and I saw Captain Trent and others nod behind him. Disoriented, I rose—and knocked my forehead hard on the bunk above.

Grunts were the closest I got to any expression of sympathy. "Won't be hot forever, young fellow!" Fox said, turning back to the others, who were seated at the mess table in the center of the cabin. It took me two full minutes to extract myself and sit down with them. As I'd never undressed, I felt only mild embarrassment at being disheveled, but was too cross to stop and repair myself. There were three men about the table to whom I'd never been introduced; no one volunteered, and my mood was so distant, I rudely failed to request it. Fox placed a bowl in front of me and—still slightly dizzy from the blow to my head—I quietly began eating it.

"Enjoy it now, lad," said one. "It never gets any better!"

They laughed. I might have too, normally, but today I stared morosely at the stew. They gabbled on while I summoned the resolve to put the first spoonful in my mouth. It was not the most repulsive comestible I'd ever tasted, but ...

"Are we not less heavily stowed than on our last cruise?" one of them asked Captain Trent.

"Oh aye, to be sure," he replied. "We're at least four inches higher in the water. Mr. Leavering is concerned to grasp the advantage while it lasts."

"Because he, too, thinks the war is over?" Fox suggested.

"So he said."

"Surely that can't be to our *dis*advantage!" the first exclaimed.

"I don't know. Leavering asserts that trade invariably slackens after a war." Trent sucked on his pipe. "I had one dinner with him and Glasby, before, *um* ..."

"Yes, yes," Fox murmured. They all knew about Mr. Sproul, of course, I surmised.

"He remains optimistic about the business—over the long haul—"

"Ah," sighed the first man.

"But he believes commerce may be tight over the next many months, and—"

The companionway door was opened, letting in a blast of cold air. "Mr. Fox?" a voice called from the deck.

Fox mopped his lips and rose to answer the summons. Conversation ceased. "A man of war is being piloted into the harbor," he announced.

Trent scowled and drummed his fingers on the table as two of the officers hurriedly finished their bowls, struggled into their coats, and pulled themselves up to the deck. I noticed snowflakes swirling down as they did. "I'd best keep an eye on her, Mr. Fox," Trent said uneasily. He rose and followed the others.

Fox sat back down and glumly finished his bowl. The other man—a red-haired Irishman with oddly jumpy eyes, nearer to my own age—looked as if he wanted to start a conversation, but thought better of it.

I finished my bowl and suddenly realized what was so peculiar. "Harbor?" Both men looked at me quizzically. "We're not moving!"

The Irishman laughed aloud, but Fox quickly scowled him into silence. "We're at anchor, Mr. Dordrecht. We put down here in Sandy Hook Bay two hours ago, to wait the storm out overnight. The shoals are difficult enough when visibility is perfect, and the wind is not on one's nose."

Waiting? All these men idled? Were they not trained to deal with bad weather? It seemed to me I should investigate and perhaps enter a protest on behalf of our employers. I rose and started up the stairs.

"Watch your—"

"Ow!" I clobbered my skull again, so hard that I fell back against the steps and lay there, blinking.

The Irishman approached, his eyes dancing. He roughly took hold of my head and parted the hair—causing more pain. "Bugger's not bleeding," he told Fox dismissively.

"He's 'Mr. Dordrecht' to you, O'Malley," Fox snapped.

"Oh, aye."

I essayed standing upright, holding onto the bulkhead.

"Mr. Dordrecht, may I suggest also, that you should put a coat on before taking the deck? It's turned very cold, sir."

My dizziness passed. "Thank you, Mr. Fox," I wheezed. That meant dealing with the portmanteau. With many tugs back and forth, I wrenched it out of its cubbyhole. It then took two minutes to extract the coat from the bottom of the portmanteau and to replace it in its hold. Both men recoiled as I put the coat on—repulsed, I suppose, by its odd beads and tassels. "It's my old Indian coat," I felt impelled to explain. "I won it when I was in the army up north. I never wear it in the city anymore."

"Indeed," Fox said with great distaste. O'Malley crossed himself, his eyes bulging.

"Perfectly good coat!" I insisted. "Very warm!" Obviously they remained unconvinced. I moved toward the steps.

"Watch your—" they both warned … just in time.

"Thank you, gentlemen."

I carefully hauled myself up the steep entry and gained the snow-covered deck. The fresh air was shockingly pleasing—no matter that I gulped snowflakes in with it. Captain Trent and several men were looking off the stern. I turned and faced forward … and at first could make out nothing but a world of grayish white. I walked toward the port rail, actually sliding once, and hung onto the shrouds as I got my bearings. A bell on another ship was rung three times, from which I inferred it must be half-past one in the afternoon. To my left, I could see no border between sea and sky, but looking downward, the slate water reassured me that there must be one. Finally, dead ahead a hundred yards, I discerned the low spit of the Sandy Hook peninsula. We were facing northeast, I reasoned, the direction from which all our storms come. Though we still felt the wind smartly whistling through our rigging, the sands had broken the power of the ocean's waves—which I am told can be fearsome, but which I have yet to experience. Contemplating the scene directly, I dismissed all thought of protesting our delayed departure!

Picking my way across to the starboard rail, I realized there were over a dozen other merchant ships anchored in the bay—probably waiting out the storm, just as we were. Turning aft, I saw the huge man-of-war towering above the rest, two hundred yards off our quarter. I moved back to the stern and addressed myself to the captain. "Do we know which one that is, Captain Trent? I don't recall having seen her in New York's harbor before."

Trent reared back, apparently annoyed—whether because he disliked the coat or because I perhaps wasn't supposed to speak to him without invitation, I couldn't tell. He grimaced and sighed. "She's the *HMS Enterprise*, Mr. Dordrecht. Fifty guns. We've seen her occasionally in the Caribbean."

"More than we'd like!" O'Malley larked—and Fox shot him another warning look.

"She doesn't seem a particularly modern ship," I observed hesitantly.

"No," Trent agreed. "Built way back in King William's time, I'd venture. Now serves mostly as a courier or a convoy ship. Since we didn't see her on our last cruise, we're speculating she's come with dispatches all the way from England."

"And I think she's had a hard time of it," Fox said. "Look at the ratlines on the starboard mizzen," he added, handing Trent the spyglass.

"Hmpf!" Trent grunted. "Patches all over. Not proper shipshape!" He and Fox shared a sardonic smirk. "If you don't mind, Fox, I'll retire for a while. Keep an eye on the weather!"

"Aye sir!" The captain, a spry man despite his weather-beaten fifty or so years, walked easily to the companionway. "You'll keep this snow swept off, Fox?" he called as he stepped down.

"Aye aye!" A gesture to the youngest of the sailors presently resulted in a cleaned deck.

I spoke to the chief mate. "Am I not seeing something, Mr. Fox? What is so very not-shipshape about the *Enterprise?*"

Fox reddened. "I'm, *uh*, afraid we were being facetious, Mr. Dordrecht."

"How's that?"

"Well ... you note that there are many more patches on *our* ratlines than on *Enterprise*'s? We in the merchant service tend to be somewhat jealous of the resources commanded by His Majesty's

Navy, you see. And … perhaps rather sensitive to the condescension we perceive from them toward our calling."

I had heard similar expressions in our office. "Aha, you consider that you achieve a good deal more with far fewer assets and men?"

Fox shifted uneasily. "That's the gist of it, sir. I … don't mean to speak ill of the navy, of course."

"Of course." I took another turn around the deck and reluctantly decided there was naught for me to do but go below and try again to rest. There I was pleased to find that Trent had lit an oil lamp and was at the table, reading. "May I share your lamp, Captain Trent?"

"Surely, young sir, that's what it's here for."

With relief that I'd not be forced into inactivity, I rummaged my current reading out of the portmanteau and sat down. "Up to *Second Chronicles*, I observe," I said, making some effort at conversation. "Quite an accomplishment!"

"It's my fourteenth reading, Mr. Dordrecht," he announced simply.

My jaw went slack. Fourteen times through the *Bible!* "My goodness!" I finally pushed out.

"And you?"

Oh dear. I had a dozen books aboard for serious study, but at present … "A, *uh,* popular novel, sir." I flashed it in front of him, not really wanting him to see that it was Mr. Smollett's notorious *Roderick Random*.

"A … novel," he said, incomprehension plain on his face. "I see."

He returned to his reading, and … so did I.

Shortly after seven bells were rung, I heard Fox's voice from above, loud with agitation. "He must be out of his senses! Call the captain!"

O'Malley's head burst through the companionway. "Captain Kelsey's under way, sir!" he shouted. "He's waving as if he wants to speak to you!"

"What the devil?" Trent muttered, quickly saving his place and rushing out. Curious, I did the same—remembering to duck in the nick of time.

"—a sudden his men are in the tops and he's hauling in his anchor," Fox was saying, gesturing at the approaching merchant sloop.

"Enos!" a stout figure on its windward bow yelled in our direction. "*Get the hell out of here!*"

"Francis, are you mad?" Captain Trent yelled back. "In this weather?"

"*Enterprise* has her boats out!" Kelsey shouted, moving aft as his ship passed our stern. "They pressed six men off the *Chadwick*, of Edgartown!"

"Oh dear God," Trent muttered as O'Malley pointed at a two-master at the south end of the bay. I noticed a rush of activity on a nearby merchant vessel.

"But the shoals …" Fox moaned.

"I can't risk losing any more hands," Kelsey yelled from his quarter, "I'm two men shy as it is!" Duty done, he turned to face ahead, but immediately turned back to us. "Oh! And don't go to the Mount!"

"*What!*" Trent shrieked, moving toward the bow to keep pace. "Why ever not?"

Kelsey cupped his hands around his mouth as his craft moved swiftly away. "*Because we're at war with Spain!*"

I looked aft and saw that virtually the whole crew had joined me as I followed the captain to the bow. After a couple stunned seconds, they turned their eyes on Captain Trent, who shook himself and turned purposively in a circle, scanning the anchorage over our shoulders, coming to rest facing northeast. "All hands on deck!" he said at last. Fox pulled out his whistle, but Trent caught him. "Softly, softly!"

"Parigo, get everyone out of the forecastle," Fox said urgently.

Trent and Fox were presently issuing orders as fast as they could talk. Four men were climbing the ratlines, while others were arming the capstan. Trent himself took the wheel. I moved to the side, impressed by the spectacle.

"Dordrecht, grab that broom and clear the snow again!" Fox yelled.

For a second I stood immobile, absurdly resenting an order to do menial work. "I thought … Is this truly such an emergency, Mr. Fox?"

Fox wheeled toward me, red-faced. "They could take it into their heads to press *you* into their navy, man!" he said furiously. "Get cracking!"

I swallowed my petulance and got cracking directly. Ignored by all, I repeatedly pushed the accumulating snow into the scuppers and overboard. The fall was actually less heavy than it had been when I'd come up earlier. Two of the sailors, I noticed with horror, were barefoot.

The next three hours kept the entire crew in a state of intense concentration. Once we rounded the hook, the ocean swells I'd so eagerly anticipated began elevating and lowering our entire world in a slow, disorienting, wholesale fashion I'd never known in the bay or on the river. Parigo spent the entire time at the rail, throwing the lead-line and calling out the depth of the water beneath us as we reached the troughs. As I recalled that the *Dorothy C.* has a draft of eleven feet, hearing him call *fifteen* six times in a row was breath-stopping. When that was once followed by, "By the mark, thirteen!" I nearly fainted. The precise draft was eleven foot, *three inches!* I corrected myself. But then, yes, we were four inches higher in the water than usual! "By the mark, fourteen!"

Captain Trent had soon entrusted the wheel to a helmsman. He spent the entire horrible afternoon with his spyglass practically glued to one eye, as his other monitored the compass. After we lost track of Kelsey's ship, the barely visible sand spit was our only landmark for over an hour. Finally, I saw Trent focusing on a faint line of highlands; when their summit bore due west, he told the helmsman to head up two points—at which point Parigo's calls rose and Fox looked ready to weep of relief.

The snow had ceased not long after our departure, but I'd not dared to utter a word. I was surely cold and miserable—but what of the wretches lacking shoes? Fox seemed to notice my presence of a sudden. "You may retire below if you wish, Mr. Dordrecht," he said hoarsely.

"Are we out of danger, then, Mr. Fox?"

He seemed barely able to locate me in the murky dusk. "No. We are out of the *worst* danger." I might have pressed him for more detail, but he moved away to relieve several others.

I did not linger to while away an interlude in chat. I was in my bunk three minutes later.

The storm continued over the next two days, moderating slowly as we progressed southward. There were frequent, cold rain showers, but no more snow. The principal officers' mood appeared greatly relieved, but they remained distantly polite to myself. For exercise, I walked about the *Dorothy C.*, at last truly making her acquaintance. She is what is known, for some bizarre reason, as a *snow*—a two-masted vessel, simple in design and, for a merchantman, swift, with both square sails and fore-and-aft sails. She is ninety-eight feet in length and thirty in beam, and carries some hundred fifty-four tons in her holds—which, thank heaven, do not quite descend to thirteen feet below the water line! Somehow, all of it is worked by a complement of only nineteen men. Rather against my rational will, I found myself becoming *fond* of "her," conceiving that "she" had gallantly preserved me from the horror of the naval press. Would an ocean voyage turn me into a lunatic, the kind one sees betimes in the city, carrying on extended conversations with their horses?

The attitude of the regular seamen was also remote, which was perplexing. Though easy with each other, they continued aloof from me, close to the point of rudeness. At first I thought they were wary of my status, but presently I realized, with impatience and some contempt, that it was prejudicial aversion to my Indian coat. Even Parigo kept his distance.

As I rolled myself out of my bunk on the third morning, I sensed a change in weather even down in the cabin, the air being a little warmer and much drier. However, the motion of the boat was strangely unpredictable, with odd hesitations and lurches, in addition to the steady rising and falling. I took the deck wearing only my waistcoat, and nearly stumbled when the boat yawed just before I grasped the ratlines. Holding on, I looked about in bright sunshine and was able to see the horizon—and nothing else—at every point in the circuit. An observation struck me just as the chief mate approached. "Mr. Dordrecht? Good morning. Are you well?"

"Mr. Fox, the ocean is *blue!*" Marveling, I pointed down at the spectacular sapphire color of the water.

"But of course it is, Mr. Dordrecht."

"I mean, it *is* blue. I thought that was ... a figure of speech, a conceit, you see."

A smile of tolerant amusement finally creased his face. "Indeed it is blue, Mr. Dordrecht. I wished—"

"I thought it was gray."

"I am relieved that you are in good health. We are crossing the great current today, which accounts for the odd motion of the vessel, and ... If your constitution should ever be overtaken, sir, I hope you will remember that the starboard rail is currently the leeward one?"

It took some seconds before I grasped what he was talking about. "I'll do my best, Mr. Fox! How long will it take us to traverse the current, do you think?" I at least knew that it was common practice to cross the wide, northbound stream as quickly as possible.

"Most likely by this time tomorrow, sir."

"Aha. Would it be all right if I were to read up here on the deck?"

"As you will. We have no chair for the purpose, I fear. And pray take care not to trip any of the lads. Perhaps there, by the bulkhead?"

He pointed to a wall of the forecastle. As I'd have to sit on the deck itself, comfort was out of the question, but it would be preferable for an interval to the murk of the cabin. "Thank you kindly."

After breakfasting—my appetite had only grown since we left—I availed myself of the spot Fox had suggested and happily immersed myself in my story. When six bells chimed, I looked up and was startled to behold a cat. It was standing in the forecastle companionway door, examining me rather suspiciously. "Puss-puss?" I whispered, tapping my fingers on the deck to entice the beast over. It yawned. "Puss-puss-puss?" Diverted, I rubbed my hip to indicate that a good scratch might be its reward for neighborliness. The cat stretched, took a few sure-footed steps in my direction, and sat down. Evidently regarding my efforts with disdain and indifference, it began to clean itself. It was an ordinary amber tabby, except that it was missing tufts of hair in several places. I set my book down and patted my lap. Puss now looked as if it were giving this weighty matter serious consideration and took more steps in my direction.

I put my hand out, palm open and up, and scratched it behind its ear—a ministration it deigned to accept on some provisional basis. Finally, it crawled into my lap, curled up, and commenced purring and flicking its tail as if satisfied to have received its expected royal obeisance. I retrieved my book and noticed O'Malley at the port rail, watching all this with an expression of great anxiety on his face. He turned away the instant our eyes met. Bemused, I scanned about and saw Parigo at the starboard rail with virtually the same expression. He made a better show of shamming preoccupation with the belaying pins, but I was in turn inspired to keep a surreptitious watch on him as I resumed reading. Twice—before my curiosity gave out—I felt certain that Parigo was deliberately calling the attention of his mates to my familiarity with the *cat*, and that something more was at stake than domestic sentimentality.

It was two days later—the weather as perfect as the Almighty can make it—that the mystery was revealed. I was again reading on deck. Having finished the disturbing and thought-provoking Smollett novel, I was now studying a more respectable text in commercial relations. Mr. Parigo—the boatswain, I'd learned—settled himself opposite me against the weather rail and commenced splicing lines together, a curious and intricate task. Though I was ready for conversation, I felt a social awkwardness that precluded it … until the cat reappeared from below. "Does the tabby have a name, Mr. Parigo?"

He grinned, displaying quite a brilliant flash of teeth, including one of gold. "Aye, sir, she is Dorothy. Named for her mother!"

"Her dam is also aboard the ship?"

"Her mamma *is* the ship! You may thank her them rats have less chance of attacking your grain barrels!"

"Aha." I patted my lap and, after half a minute of imperious disdain, Dorothy the cat padded over and availed herself of it. "Well, I do thank her indeed!"

Parigo grinned inordinately. "She's what convinced us you was safe, Mr. Dordrecht. We had thought maybe you was a Jonah until she accept you!" His smile abruptly disappeared as he realized he'd blurted out too much; he attempted to cover his confusion by vigorously addressing his task.

I know what a *Jonah* is, however, and was disconcerted to think my presence aboard might be regarded as fatal bad luck. "The cat …"

"She know these things, Mr. Dordrecht." Perhaps he noticed the very perturbed look I'm sure was on my face. The lives of *Jonahs* were not insurable by Lloyd's of London. "Oh of course *I* never think that! Fact, I won a handful change off you. Lads had betting pool, how long you'd hold your supper once we was in the stream. I put tuppence down to say you'd hold it in, and you does!"

"Indeed," I groused, aware that he had neatly changed the subject. "Well, congratulations!"

"Won off O'Malley too. Said he never last three bells, and he don't!"

"Ha."

"I'll make you new hat, since I owes you!"

"A hat? My word! Not necessary, Mr.—" But he had cut off a strand of the manila line and was bringing it over to me. As I had gotten sunburned, my scruples were overwhelmed by the thought of how very convenient a hat would be.

Parigo pulled my head forward from the bulkhead, placed the line about my skull at the temples, and tied an overhand knot to mark the circumference. "Old sailcloth I makes. Not fancy like that you lost, but keep the sun off."

"Well thanks, Mr. Parigo," I said as he sat back down.

"We have gam tonight! All crew. Saturday, eight bells. You have music? You bring?"

Even puss seemed suddenly alert at the prospect of a party. "Well! Of course!" And he, I, and Dorothy the cat resumed our several occupations.

Curiously enough, I had once before enjoyed a shipboard party, but that had been on a military transport calmly anchored in the Hudson River south of Albany. This evening we were under way in the black Atlantic night, our deck heaving in the swells, all our sails set and pulling us strongly toward our destination. Nonetheless, the sailors had no difficulty singing, drumming, and even dancing. And of course they had no difficulty enjoying the extra tot of grog that Captain Trent allowed them. They were effusive in welcoming the guitar, as the only instrument they had otherwise was a fife, which was played quite well by the black sailor—whose name, inexplicably, was Sergei. He and I had some trouble tuning to each other. Once coordinated, however, we managed to play—or at least accompany—every popular tune or chantey that came to mind. Many had uncountable verses that only one man knew. Parigo, who is possessed of a pleasant tenor, rendered two songs so bawdy I blushed with the thought that my *brothers* might ever hear them! Men would dance as we played, usually one at a time in a sort of self-absorbed trance, hopping wildly about despite the shifting floor. Even O'Malley was so inspired for a moment. Trent watched it all from the weather rail, benignly smoking his pipe; Fox was stalwartly holding the wheel. The "gam" went on throughout the evening and might have continued longer had not the eighth bell signaled a change of watch and, more critically, the arrival of *Sunday.*

The lantern was extinguished and the party quickly broke up. Several of the sailors shyly thanked me for playing as they moved to their hammocks or their watch stations. Sergei and Parigo—all I could make out was grinning teeth—patted my shoulder as they left. Captain Trent said goodnight, which he'd never done before, and Fox allowed "Well done, sir!" Still excited, I stayed on deck for several moments, leaning back against the ratlines, looking upward in awe at the heavens—more spectacularly displayed than I'd ever, ever seen them. When my neck could take no more, I fell to contemplation of the men aboard the vessel, on whom my continued ability to enjoy any stars at all was now completely dependent. The action of *Roderick Random* dooms the hero to be pressed into the Royal Navy; had I come earlier to that episode, I'd have shoveled the snow overboard with my bare hands! But it also unflatteringly describes the discipline and social relations on a British Navy vessel. Perhaps the natives of Britain are more informed of navy practices—and I had myself been shocked at the casual way Redcoat officers denigrated, flogged, and *hanged* their hapless common soldiers on the New York frontier—but the contrast to our ship's crew was still stark. The *Dorothy C.*'s discipline did not strike my admittedly untutored eye as lax, and yet ... there was no shrieking of orders, no taking of names, nobody carrying a knotted rope to "start" a momentary laggard—and no weekly floggings. When the prospect of the trip had first been bruited, I questioned Mr. Leavering on the subject, and he told me that Captain Trent does indeed possess the legal right to flog or, in extreme cases, to hang his sailors. He also assured me that, while any captain who did so would avoid prosecution, he would also be unlikely to garner repeat commissions. So far from being royalty, our captain didn't even have private quarters in which to sleep.

Captain Trent was nonetheless *God's* representative on our high seas, as I observed when attending his "service" the following morning. Though it was a quite informal affair, the men regarded it with the utmost seriousness. A hymn was sung *a capella*, Fox and O'Malley each gave a sober reading, and Trent mumbled an incomprehensible sermon … that I'd happily trade for any of Van Voort's polished orations, as it consumed but a tenth of the time. Late that afternoon, Parigo presented me with a serviceable canvas hat. He seemed shyly embarrassed by my extravagant gratitude.

Given that certain death awaited anyone who'd be so bold as to venture beyond the ship's perimeter—that is, overboard—it was surprising how little sense of confinement I felt. On Tuesday morning, I realized we'd been out a week, and I'd not even begun to make good on Mr. Leavering's injunction to learn all I could of seamanship and navigation. I presently taxed Captain Trent and Mr. Fox with my desire to do so. Mr. Leavering, I told them, had desired me to achieve at least the equivalent knowledge of an ordinary seaman before we reached Monte Cristi.

Their faces, which had seemed both glad and supportive of my ambition, suddenly darkened. "I thought you told him, Fox," Trent said.

"Beg pardon! I thought you had."

Trent shrugged and faced me. "Mr. Dordrecht, we are, *uh,* not going to Monte Cristi!"

I was speechless … but I sensed I should not have been so surprised.

"You do remember Captain Kelsey's warning to us, sir?" Fox said. "If the government, in their wisdom, have brought us into war with Spain, we can no longer legally enter a Spanish port any more than we can enter a French one."

My expectations were quickly reoriented, as that much was not contestable. "How is it that Captain Kelsey should have come to know this?"

Trent sighed. "My guess is, the men of *Enterprise* let it slip to the New Jersey pilot, and he made it his business to tell all he could in the harbor."

"I see. But then, where *are* we heading? To Jamaica, as our clearance papers suggest?"

Fox laughed aloud. "Oh heavens, no. Never make any money there!"

Trent drew on his pipe. "I suppose I ought to have consulted you, as the firm's representative, Mr. Dordrecht, but there really is only one practical alternative. Our course is set to return to Statia—that's Saint Eustatius island."

"Dutch," Fox asserted. "Neutral as a matter of high principle!"

And an untaxed, tariff-free port. Everyone in commerce along the Atlantic seaboard was vividly aware of minuscule Saint Eustatius, the notorious "Golden Rock" of the Lesser Antilles, as loathed by belligerent militaries as it was loved by all their long-suffering victims. "But … isn't that a great deal farther, Captain Trent?"

He shrugged. "Five hundred miles. Five days."

"We do have provisions to last?"

Both men laughed. "I should certainly hope so, Mr. Dordrecht," Fox said. "Ships are not infrequently becalmed for a month *en route* to the islands!"

Despite the warmth of the cabin, I shuddered. "You've been there before, Captain Trent?"

"It's been a couple years but, yes, many times. Mr. Leavering will be glad for you to make its acquaintance!"

And as my mind raced through the alternatives they pointed out on the large-scale chart—Jamaica, New Providence in the Bahamas, Danish Saint Croix, and Curaçao, far to the south—I quickly came to affirm his judgment. We presently returned to the subject of my education, and Trent decreed that, for as much as I could tolerate it daily, Parigo, O'Malley, Fox, and he himself would teach me operations, steering, sail-handling, and navigation, respectively. Fox proposed to begin immediately.

My relaxed sojourn was thus abruptly terminated. But as Mr. Leavering had propounded, a *shipper* should be fully conversant with all aspects of ships and shipping, not just with cargo.

Even though my lessons progressed pleasantly enough, the officers still seemed distant to me: Trent evidently regarding me as a burden imposed by his employers; Fox as a delicate, out-of-his-element lordling; and O'Malley as if I were trying to claim his position by proving him unfit for it. I tried to view these reactions with equanimity, given that my purpose—like theirs—aboard the *Dorothy C.* was hardly to form friendships, but to perform my duty toward our mutual employers. Nonetheless I found myself positively enjoying my time with Uzal Parigo, the only man aboard with whom, to my surprise, I felt truly at my ease. It was a surprise in that I had never felt anything approaching friendship back home with a dark-skinned man—a rough collegiality, perhaps even respect, yes, with Vrijdag and some others, but never *ease*. Parigo had a cheerful, breezy confidence that made all land-based prejudices evaporate—at least for me. If Trent noticed the regard the boatswain and I developed for each other, he ignored it; Fox undoubtedly thought it another peculiarity of landsmen; and O'Malley viewed it with contempt.

During the next fortnight—with winds that were never unfavorable and varied from light to strong without again reaching gale force—I particularly appreciated my navigation lessons with the captain. He taught me to take sights of the sun, moon, and stars, and walked me through the simple mathematical reductions needed to determine our latitude, and the laborious ones necessary to estimate our longitude. It was critical to reach sixty-two degrees thirty minutes west, which he deemed a safe line between Saint Maarten and Antigua and, more importantly, their respective shoal islands of Anguilla and Barbuda. Once we'd reached it, the course was set due south, but we continued to take sights carefully every dawn and dusk, to ensure we'd not drifted east or west.

"Haven't I read that there are ship's clocks, nowadays, sir," I asked him one morning after a particularly tedious and fraught computation, "that can more easily and accurately enable the determination of longitude?"

Trent laughed gently. "Oh there are indeed, Mr. Dordrecht! Wonders of modernity! But have you any notion what they might cost?" I hadn't. "One of them would cost near as much as the *Dorothy C.* herself!"

"Ship on the port beam!"

I hastened to the deck. Despite the brilliant sunshine, I could see nothing but whitecaps on a sapphire sea. "They can see farther from the masthead, of course," O'Malley said condescendingly from behind the wheel.

"Yes, Captain Trent has explained to me that at the mainmast's height of eighty-five feet, one can see seven miles beyond what we can see on the deck," I shot back, restraining my irritation.

"What's her heading?" Fox bellowed upward, ignoring both of us.

"She's seen us!" was the answer. "Southwest."

"Masts?"

"Three. A warship!"

Fox told a seaman to wake the captain.

"Friend or foe?" I couldn't help demanding.

"Not much difference!" Fox muttered, grimacing. He paced back and forth nervously. "Oh I shouldn't say that, of course," he amended. "We've never seen the French Navy, nor the Spanish, but everybody's privateers are very dangerous to us, and—"

"*British* privateers?" I asked, shocked.

"The worst. It's probably the Royal Navy, however, and they'll just delay us three hours while they check over all our stores in the hope of contraband." Trent appeared, and Fox joined him in conference.

"Why does he say 'hope' of contraband?" I asked O'Malley.

"If they find any, they can condemn the whole ship as a prize, can't they? And the Admiralty Court awards *them* half the value!"

I had known that … but it was very different—horrifying—to be subjected to the reality of it—to be seen as prey by one's own countrymen. Trent shrugged stoically and went back below. I looked at Fox quizzically, anticipating frantic calls for action that did not come. "We're still too far from port to dream of escaping, Mr. Dordrecht," he said. "We must hope for an honest and preoccupied British lieutenant." He lit his pipe. "And a tolerant one."

"There's *nothing* we can do?"

"If we were closer, we might jettison our fresh water to lighten our burden and increase speed. But we have no chance today of outrunning any but a crippled navy man or privateer. We shall have to see what comes. We *have* endured this before." He sat on the rail and morosely contemplated the sail that had just appeared as a speck on the eastern horizon.

He might have endured it before, but I hadn't, and I found it agonizing to contemplate the various possibilities. Would our dubious but painstakingly crafted papers be dismissed as lacking *bona fides*? Could it be that an agent of our king would confiscate Vrijdag's nails or Marijke Van Voort's barley? Might my own private stores be construed more illegitimate than anything else aboard and somehow made the occasion for the condemnation of my employer's entire venture? Losing the *Dorothy C.* would not ruin the firm, but it would surely set us back.

"British!" the masthead man yelled. "Navy!"

Some relief showed in O'Malley's eyes. "You can add a prayer that they have a full complement too, Mr. Dordrecht!" He was sincere—his usual off-hand asperity was absent.

"They could press our men *here*, on the high sea?"

"Indeed they could. They might do just that!"

"Where do they draw the— They wouldn't cripple us, here in the middle of the ocean?"

"I've never heard of them taking more than half."

"Half!"

"Very unlikely. They pressed two off us once, three years ago."

No wonder all the men looked as anxious as I felt. "Do they ever take … officers?"

"Seldom. The petty officers, if they've lost their own." Alarmed, I scanned about for Parigo, who was calmly painting the dinghy in the waist. "Oh, don't worry about your colored friend. They looked him over once, and he was savvy enough to forget all his English and babble like an idiot in Portugee."

I was containing my vexation with him when the lookout called down, "It's the *Artemis*, Mr. Fox, I'm sure now!"

Fox exhaled sharply, and sent a man down to inform the captain. "She's caught us twice before, over at the Mount," he said, in response to my undoubtedly worried face. "Pretty straightforward. Knows there are bigger fish to fry."

"And both times on our way in," O'Malley added. "Better than homebound, loaded with sugar!"

Fox scowled at him and he held his tongue. "Ah, she's hull-up now. Be with us in an hour. You may as well explain to Mr. Dordrecht how we heave to, O'Malley. I shall make a last check of the hold."

And though I could barely concentrate, O'Malley coolly passed the time elucidating the procedure for bringing the boat safely to a dead halt in mid-ocean. When the *Artemis* was a half-mile away, Fox sent for the captain, who appeared on deck wearing the heavy blue coat he'd worn when I first met him in our Peck Slip office. The two off-watch officers who'd been sleeping followed him, yawning. "Let's heave to now, Fox," he said, "to show how eager we are to be cooperative with His Majesty's Navy."

"Aye aye, sir." On Fox's call, the square sails were furled, O'Malley headed directly into the wind, and the fore-and-aft sails were backed on opposite sides. The ship's noise and motion dramatically ceased.

"If you'll let me handle this, Mr. Dordrecht?" Trent murmured. "Please simply affirm all that I say—and don't volunteer *anything*."

These were precisely Glasby's instructions, so I nodded. Presently the *Artemis* loomed alongside us and hove to even more smartly than our crew had done. A gig was lowered off her starboard side, and a crew of nine sailors clambered down into it, followed by an elegant young officer wearing a sword. They cast off and were bumping our port side three minutes later. The officer—exuding imperial authority although I think he was actually younger than me—introduced himself as Lieutenant Griggs of *HMS Artemis*. Trent gravely welcomed him aboard and invited him, Fox, and me below.

Griggs sat down at the head of the table, declined refreshment, and commenced his business as automatically as if he'd been at it all his life. Most likely, he had! He first examined our clearance papers and demanded to know why we were not heading for Jamaica. Trent said we had learned from a chance encounter off Carolina that war had broken out with Spain, and he had decided to stay away from the hostile Greater Antilles. Fox nodded. I nodded. He demanded our manifest and was presented with the one drawn up for this eventuality—as opposed to the true manifest buried underneath Trent's bunk. "You, of course, have no thought of selling this flour or this barley to any but British or neutral traders?"

"Certainly not, Lieutenant."

Griggs then itemized a tattered printed list of proscribed goods, upon which numerous handwritten emendations had added or deleted specifics. Trent solemnly avowed that none were aboard. Fox and I followed suit, though all of us knew we'd be in considerable difficulty if our perjury were disclosed, and all of us knew that sail cloth, turpentine, pemmican, and nails were in fact aboard. "I require you to show me your hold now, Captain."

"This way, Lieutenant."

The inspection—I think Trent and Fox somehow anticipated it—was perfunctory, a very brief look. Fox loosened the bung of one barrel of flour and presented a spoonful to the lieutenant's satisfaction. Had Griggs exerted himself to look behind and underneath, he would have easily found the turpentine and the nails. I had to wonder why he did *not* exert himself, as he seemed otherwise quite punctilious and exacting. I was also surreptitiously watching to see if Trent crossed his palm with any coins, but felt certain he did not. Griggs shortly proclaimed the inspection at an end, and Fox and I straightened the hold while Trent followed Griggs back to the cabin.

"He didn't even *try* to inspect everything!" I whispered to Fox.

"No, thank heaven."

"But … why has he stopped us at all, then?"

"He has to put in his reports."

"But … he wasn't bribed, surely?"

"No, thank heaven. Some of them … Not this fellow."

"What's the point, then?"

Fox shrugged. "The government thinks it wants to control all the commerce, but the lads doing the inspecting know that's impossible.

So what you've just seen is what happens in practice—when we're lucky."

"Then all the worry we had—"

"Trouble is, you never know. All you really know is what happened the last time you were inspected."

"But—"

"Is that latch caught firm? Let's get back."

In the cabin, Griggs was signing a receipt that would certify us in the event of another detainment—which in fact would save us some hours when we were accosted by another navy man on the morrow. But he never condescended to relieve our minds on the remaining misgiving occasioned by his visit. It wasn't until he reached the rail, said, "Good day to you, Captain, you're free to go," and disappeared, that we understood with great relief that none of the crew was to be taken from us.

"Three cheers for King George?" Fox asked quietly as the gig pulled away. I gathered this was something of a tradition.

"Oh the devil with it!" Trent snapped—though his face remained impassive.

As the sailors got us moving forward once again, I watched the retreating warship with increasing annoyance. By what possible right, I wondered, could that uniformed young popinjay ever have asserted that we were *not* free to go? Perhaps I was spending too much time with my vehement cousin Charles, but the whole episode, war or no war, suddenly struck me as an outrageous imposition.

My state of mind was such that a resumption of my lesson with O'Malley was out of the question, so I went down to the cabin to fetch my reading—and was embarrassed to find Captain Trent on his knees facing his bunk, in an attitude of fervent prayer. "I beg your pardon, sir, I didn't mean to—"

"No, no, lad, I'm just done," he said, rising. Stupefied, I stared at him. "I was praying for forgiveness, of course! I do beg you to believe, Mr. Dordrecht, that I am not in the habit of bearing false witness."

"Indeed, never, Captain Trent!"

He shook his head vigorously and sighed. "Sometimes the honest ones"—he nodded at the spot where Griggs had seated himself—"are the hardest to bear. The honest ones sincerely believe they're serving king and country and God, even as they make it impossible for humble men to earn a living!"

I grunted affirmatively.

"A queer world betimes, Mr. Dordrecht!"

Our due-south course put us on perhaps the easiest point of sailing, a beam reach, given the Caribbean's prevailing, easterly trade winds. This made life aboard considerably more relaxed, quieter, and literally less tumultuous. Everyone found it easier to sleep.

Just before dawn, two days later, I was dozing in my bunk, the steady snoring of those above me the only audible sound.

A faint call from the masthead far above broke the silence: "*Land ho!*"

I jumped so unthinkingly that I knocked my head silly on Mr. Fox's bunk, the first time in three weeks that I'd forgotten. The fact that it made me dizzy didn't stop me clambering out and noisily forcing on my boots. "Please be quieter, Mr. Dordrecht!" Fox moaned.

"Mr. Fox, they've sighted *land!*" I exclaimed, barely suppressing a shout.

"*Um,* yes, I should hope so," Fox mumbled, turning his head away.

"Should I … Should I wake the captain?"

Fox turned back to me and sighed. "Only if it's five hundred yards dead ahead, Mr. Dordrecht!"

I was so excited, I didn't even recognize that he was jesting. With the thought of urgently verifying whether it *was* five hundred yards dead ahead, I grabbed my hat, stuffed it on … and crowned myself on the companionway lintel. Fox and I both groaned as I grabbed the rail-rope to keep from falling. A few seconds of blackness later, I slightly more cautiously resumed my climb.

When on the deck, I asked O'Malley eagerly, "There's land?"

"So he tells me," he replied, pointing aloft.

I turned all about—causing more dizziness. "*Where?*" I nearly shouted.

"Right where it's supposed to be, Mr. Dordrecht."

I wanted to throttle him! "Where?"

"Where God put it thousands of years ago!"

I couldn't see a thing. "*Wh—* Parigo! Whereabouts is the landfall?"

Parigo had been watching the exchange with more amusement than I found in it. He motioned me forward to the starboard rail. "You see dark, purple clouds on horizon?" he said, pointing just off the starboard bow. "When sun rise, they turn into peaks of hills. Couple hours after that, you see whole island."

"But which island? Statia?"

"No, no, no!" O'Malley sniggered, shaking his head—and I was embarrassed to recall having been told that Saint Eustatius was too small to be the first seen, particularly because the others were closer, in front of it. "It's either Saint Maarten or Antigua. We hope the former."

I knew I should remember why, but I was too excited not to ask. "Why is that?"

"Because if it's Antigua, we've gone fifty miles too far, of course," O'Malley said condescendingly. "Not to mention there's a whacking great reef dead in front of it!"

"Ah. When will we know?"

"All in good time!"

I looked to Parigo in exasperation. "In few minutes, when sun come up," he said.

"Uh huh!" *How would I bear the wait?*

Saint Maarten it proved to be, identified twenty minutes later by the configuration of its hills. I tore myself from the rail to look at the paper drawing that outlined the contour of the island as seen from the northeast, our vantage. But I immediately rushed back, thrilled by the metamorphosis from cloud to faint mountaintop, to multiple green hillsides that presently merged into one landmass. Eventually, sandy and dark rocky shores appeared, flocks of birds flew overhead, a rainstorm came and went—producing a magnificent rainbow, and tiny human beings could be seen *walking about!* Presently, you could smell it—scents of citrus and vegetation and burning wood, the first variation to greet my nostrils in twenty-six days!

"Congratulations, sir, a perfect landfall!" O'Malley said. I looked back to see Trent nodding acknowledgement of the compliment.

Eight bells were rung. O'Malley went below as Fox took over the helm.

Trent joined me a few minutes later. "I'm afraid your various lessons are all over for the moment, Mr. Dordrecht," he said. "We'll all be needed at our posts until we anchor, and then we've some months of work on Statia before we can resume."

My lessons were the last concern on my mind, but I worked up some feigned dismay and thanks for what I'd received. "When will we be anchoring, then, Captain Trent?"

"Oh, we've forty miles yet, to Statia. Mid-afternoon, I should think. Come down to dinner at noon. No reason we shouldn't finish off the burgoo!"

I barely acknowledged him—having spied a small fishing smack with three black men hard at work. I nearly hollered out "We've just come all the way from New York!" but fortunately restrained myself. I spent the entire morning gawking at the sights, smells, and sounds, so completely different from the flat, gray, snowy land I'd left behind.

The officers were in an expansive mood at dinner, this having counted as "an extraordinarily good passage." And Trent had allotted an extra grog. But landfalls were not new to them, and I squirmed with eagerness to go back on deck as their conversation turned mundane. "I was wondering," Fox said to the captain, "when you told Griggs the firm's name was the same as ever … do you suppose they'll change it?"

"What, change 'Castell, Leavering & Sproul'?"

"Just wondering."

"You mean because—"

"Yes."

Trent cleared his throat. "Well, I've really no idea. What would you think, Mr. Dordrecht?"

Preoccupied with the thrill of my arrival in the tropics, I couldn't even muster a response.

"Will they take on a new partner, do you suppose?" Fox persisted.

"Did Mr. Glasby mention anything of the sort?" Trent asked. "You're his *protégé*, are you not?"

I forced myself to concentrate. "Yes sir. No, the issue was never remotely raised that I heard. We were busy dealing with the simple facts of the matter and the immediate problem of assisting the Leaverings in their distress."

"Did you happen to be present when they first found out?"

"Well yes. In fact, I accompanied Mr. Leavering and the coroner to identify the body."

They were electrified. "I hadn't realized that!" Trent exclaimed.

Though we might have discussed it at length on dozens of occasions over the past weeks, they only *now*, while prodigious wonders of the Antilles were undoubtedly passing the purview of the deck, detained me for nearly an hour to recount every detail and every perplexing mystery surrounding the death of Daniel Sproul in New York City. When the subject finally ran down, they all shook their heads in dismay. Fox, I learned, had known Sproul for a decade, and Trent, for a quarter-century.

"It's not right, somehow," Fox complained. "It's just not *right* that such a fine gentleman should die in such a way!"

"He was always too trusting a soul," Trent added lugubriously.

Chapter 5

Finally they released me, and I rushed back to the deck, just remembering to mind my head. Facing aft, I was disoriented to see that we were retreating from a large island.

"You've made good time, I perceive," Fox said to O'Malley as he came up after me.

"In sight, now," O'Malley replied.

"That one?" I squawked, pointing slightly off to starboard. There were islands all around the horizon, faint in the haze, and it was impossible to tell whether they were large and far away or small and nearby.

"Dead *ahead*, Mr. Dordrecht," O'Malley said with excessive patience.

"The little one to the right is Saba," Fox said. "Also Dutch, but even smaller than Statia, too small to offer any protection to shipping."

"Statia has the sharp edge to its mountain?" It was still faint.

"That's the one. Who's on lookout?" he asked O'Malley.

"Parigo. I reminded him!"

"Reminded him what?" I asked Fox.

"This last can be one of the more dangerous legs of our trip, Mr. Dordrecht. Privateers, navies—"

"It's broad daylight, Mr. Fox!"

"Exactly. Many have been caught and condemned in these politically dangerous waters. Until we are inside Statia's periphery, the ship remains at risk." He must have noticed dismay on my face. "Another two hours, perhaps."

Whether his skittishness had any practical impetus, I couldn't tell, but less than two hours later, without incident, we rounded the northern cape into the lee—and the sovereign waters, guarded by a few cannon mounted on makeshift walls—of Saint Eustatius. There, as we approached the town and the tremendous mountain behind it, we discovered an open anchorage of dozens—I counted ninety-two—of merchantmen flying at least ten different national flags. Over the ensuing hour I was twice told to keep myself out of the way while the sailors lowered the anchor and attached us to *terra firma* for the first time since we'd left Sandy Hook. The process, which involved backwinding the sails to test the sureness of the anchor's hold on the bottom, struck me as interminable.

I occupied my impatient self by examining the landscape, which bore no resemblance to any other of my experience. The perimeter of the island is smaller than that of Manhattan—it's but five miles from north to south—yet half of it is as hilly as the country up-valley from New York City, and the other half … has the tallest mountain I've ever seen, jutting two thousand feet near straight up from the sea. It's this prodigy, I understand, that shelters the harbor from the prevailing easterlies, permitting the extensive commerce despite the lack of protective land barriers on the north and south. The openness of the anchorage, Trent had explained, also made it dead easy to get in and out, the latter of which might come in handy should one of the area's fearsome *hurricanoes* blow up. The sole town of Oranjestad, nearly as populous as New York City, was named for the chief aristocratic house of the Netherlands long before one of its scions became king of England. It is located on the southwestern quadrant, on two levels—the lower town is at sea level but is only one road in depth, backing into a vertical cliff-face that reminds me of the New Jersey Palisades, on top of which is the larger upper town. One steeply inclined road, hewn out of the rock, bridges the fifty vertical yards separating the two.

"What are those strange, tall trees over there, Parigo?" I blurted out, having been stumped by their bizarre appearance within the general greenery.

Parigo was preoccupied with seeing the sails properly furled. "With naked gray trunk and spray of leaves at top? Palm tree, Mr. Dordrecht. Where coconuts from!"

"Palm trees," I repeated, committing the name and image to memory. "Source of coconuts."

Mr. Fox was nearby, verifying that the anchor rode was correctly belayed through the hawse. "When will we be able to go ashore?" I queried him, standing on tiptoe to see over the bowsprit.

"Beg your pardon?"

"When can we go ashore?" I asked again, wetting my lips.

"Oh. Oh, not before Monday, I shouldn't imagine."

"Monday!" I fairly shrieked.

"Aye," Fox said complacently. "Unlikely they'll be out so late in the afternoon for our papers, and tomorrow's Sunday, you recall, so—"

"Do you really mean we can't go … just over *there*, before *Monday?*" I pointed to the stone mole not two hundred yards away.

"Oh, it's no matter, Mr. Dordrecht. We'll be having visitors from all and sundry within the hour. You can be about your business directly, never fear!"

I ground my teeth in frustration. Of course I *did* want to be about my business, but … Surely there are some moments in life when business can be postponed just for a little while—to *explore!*

And yet the parade of people and boats paying business and social calls that evening was truly fascinating. Almost before Parigo reported the spanker sail brailed up, there were primitive canoes tapping against our hull, offering oranges, plantains, breadfruit, fish, canvas, rum—and women. Petty exchanges between the sailors and the small craft commenced immediately, but none were suffered to gain the deck for a full hour, when Trent and Fox at last declared the *Dorothy C.* "squared away."

That declaration was hustled just a little bit when the captain perceived a handsome gig being rowed in our direction from another merchantman flying a Union Jack. "Enos!" bawled the heavyset man in the sternsheets. "Welcome to Statia!"

"Why, Timothy Pine, upon my word!" Trent roared back. "Come aboard, come aboard!"

Fox and O'Malley shrugged at each other as the man, taking one look at the slime-covered steps built into the side of the hull, demurred. "Thank ye, Captain, but I'm just stopping by to invite you to dinner tomorrow at two bells."

"Most kind, I thank ye! May I bring—" Pine held up one finger. "Oh that's wonderful. Certainly I accept!"

"Excellent!" His coxswain handed Pine a small parcel. "Ah, and here's the latest from London!"

News! Pine rather ineptly flung the parcel up toward us. My heart skipped a beat as Parigo, leaning on the rail, risked tumbling into the sea to catch it with two fingers. He had to be hauled back in by three of the sailors, as he was more over than aboard.

Parigo presented the packet to Trent after he'd waved the gig farewell. He opened it and made a face on extracting the February *Gentleman's Magazine*. "Oh! No need to have risked yourself for this, Parigo!" He barely scanned the front page and shrugged. "I'll get to it tomorrow. You want it, Fox?" Fox shook his head. "O'Malley?" A shrug. "Mr. Dordrecht?"

"*Yes!*" I was amused that I was so hungry for news of the rest of the world, having been perfectly content in my separation from it for near a month. And how peculiar it felt to be reconnected to that larger world when still afloat opposite this tiny speck of land hundreds of miles from any continent. Yet it was the same periodical that I'd often picked up at Fischl's store on Pearl Street and left for other readers at my family's inn in New Utrecht.

For once, I felt enervated by the surfeit of fascinations. I could barely concentrate on anything. There was that enormous mountain looming over the island, the people and horses struggling up the road to the main town, and the sway of the palm trees. Bumboats came and went, and the cook leaned over the rail and bargained vociferously for fruits, vegetables, and fish—with the aid of Sergei, speaking a tongue I'd never heard before that sounded vaguely French. Whistles from the crew drew me to the opposite rail, where four Negro women—not especially young or pretty, but definitely female—were selling the same sort of brightly colored and patterned cloths they themselves were wearing—all from a dugout canoe. When these distractions subsided for a moment, I turned to the magazine and found printed confirmation that Britain was, in fact, at war with Spain, and there was open speculation how this might develop further and how the outcome would affect the balance of power in the world. Portugal had allied itself with Britain against Spain ... which meant that, here in the western Atlantic, Brasil would be on our side against Cuba, Mexico, and Florida. It all made the mind spin.

At supper an hour later, I relayed another item of news the magazine had deemed beneficial: the Russian Empress Elisabeth had expired suddenly on the sixth of January, and her successor had instantly reversed her policies, taking Russia out of the war. Since she had been allied with Austria against our ally Prussia, this was wonderful—particularly since Frederick of Prussia's forces were near total collapse, and the Russians had briefly occupied Berlin, their capital.

The others looked at me blankly. "I could never remember which was Russia and which was Prussia," O'Malley said drily.

"Prussia's German-speaking and Russia's the big country to the east," Trent observed tolerantly.

"Uh huh." Conversation again halted.

"Can you imagine those Russian soldiers," Fox surprised me by speculating, "being told that, because one woman died, everything they had been fighting for all these years was suddenly ... not important? Imagine your brother had been killed fighting the Prussians, and now, since January sixth, they're not your enemy anymore? It was all a mistake?"

I was dumbfounded both by the thought and the fact that Fox had voiced it.

"The way of the world, ain't it, Mr. Fox?" O'Malley said.

"Wicked!" Trent pronounced.

Another minute of stymied conversation was helpfully interrupted by the eight bells heralding the commencement of the first watch—and of what was expected to be the last shipboard gam before our return trip. That, I had learned from O'Malley, was because the crewmen eagerly anticipated spending Saturday evenings carousing ashore. "Not that we can ever allow more than half ashore at any one time," he added.

As I retrieved my guitar to go on deck, Trent pulled me aside to say he expected me to join him as Captain Pine's guest on the morrow. The invitation was to be construed as a matter of business, he explained—which conveniently exempted him from having to choose between Fox and O'Malley. "Wearing your finest, if you please, Mr. Dordrecht!"

Despite the frustration of continued restriction to the ship, the crew's gam was as merry as ever. All were pleased with the successful passage, and the captain again tipped his men with extra grog. With the sun down, the two lines of lights on shore next to those flickering aboard the ships, mixed with the tropical scents and the gentle evening breeze, transported me like Aladdin's magic carpet to a heady sensation of earthly paradise. It was not so late in the year, I mused, that there might not still be snow on the ground in New Utrecht!

Heaven had something to do with Captain Trent's sermon in the morning, but I couldn't parse exactly what, perhaps because I was suddenly nervy about the forthcoming dinner. Sergei had barbered me, and no one had made a face at my suit, so I supposed I looked all right. I had read courtesy books explaining proper gentlemanly deportment, and had often experienced the hospitality of the Leaverings without committing any solecisms that I knew of … but still it was a social challenge. Among complete strangers, I was now to represent the interests of my firm and myself as a worldly man of business. I conjured my cousin Charles at his most peevish, sneering at my foibles one instant, encouraging me the next … *No matter!* We were presently in our gig being pulled up next to the quite substantial merchant vessel *Rachel Peabody* of New Bedford, Massachusetts. Parigo gave me an encouraging wink as I took a deep breath before following Captain Trent up the side ladder.

My captain and Timothy Pine, I now learned, were first cousins—natives of New Bedford, who'd not set eyes on each other for nearly a decade. After polite introductions, I was left in the care of the mate, a slight fellow of thirty or so, named Gerald Yarmouth. He tactfully offered me a tour of the ship while the two captains caught up on the fates of their mutual relatives. Remarking my surname, he observed that his mother was Dutch; he was, interestingly, a native of Saint Maarten, the younger son of a British planter who'd settled there. Though his English was perfect, he observed—in Dutch—that officialdom here on Statia would be gratified to be addressed in their native tongue, and we continued our conversation in that language. "Mind that they are all notorious for hard-bargaining here, Meneer Dordrecht!" he warned.

"Are they known for actual sharp practice, Meneer Yarmouth?"

"It does happen, sir," he said, grinning and pointing expansively around the harbor, "but, as you can see, it doesn't happen often enough to drive the world away!"

I inquired about the effect on Statia of the commencement of hostilities between Britain and Spain.

"For Statia, it's been only good, as all the trade that had migrated west toward the larger islands came right back here. What's had greater impact has been the British capture of Martinique, because—"

"I beg your pardon?"

"*Eh?* Oh, it's still news, to you, of course! The British under General Monckton took Martinique. Middle of February. And St. Lucia, and Grenada, and St. Vincent."

I was as much thrown by his locution of 'the British'—as if the British were not *us*—as by the facts. "My gosh!" I stammered.

"And, as I say, the impact is that all those French planters can now trade with you northerners openly and directly."

He seemed quite composed about this, for someone whom I imagined to have a stake in the locality. "I fear that might be devastating to your trade, sir!" I said.

Yarmouth grinned sardonically. "I have a British father, a Dutch grandfather, and a French father-in-law, Meneer Dordrecht, and all three counsel letting Father *Time* work his wonders!"

We were called to dinner, which was served for four under a canopy on Pine's quarterdeck with a fine show of silver that widened his cousin's eyes. Captain Pine had evidently done quite well for himself. He set to work over the turtle soup, reciting all the products the *Rachel Peabody* had left to sell, and demanding a verbal bill of lading for the *Dorothy C.* in return. He was full of good-humored, though bibulous, advice on where and to whom to market our goods. Though I did not feel constrained to follow Captain Trent's example of refusing a second glass of claret, I did assert that I felt bound by my employers' strict injunction not to buy or sell anything during my first week on Monte Cristi.

"Well you're in Saint Eustatius, lad!" Pine boomed cheerfully. "They can't gainsay you here!"

I smiled with what I hope was an inoffensive attempt at modesty, and allowed Yarmouth to commence a tale about the cask of pickled pork that had spontaneously exploded during an inspection by none other than Lieutenant Griggs of the *HMS Artemis*.

From the fact that Captain Trent conversed cheerfully with me on our brief trip back to *Dorothy C.*, I gathered that I had passed muster.

Though Captain Trent, Mr. O'Malley, and I were ready to go ashore at Monday's first light, it was an hour later before the customs official made his appearance. When introduced, I greeted him in Dutch, smoothing over the testiness with which our captain had noted the man's tardiness. As a reward, I was apprised—in Dutch—of one particular firm that was especially eager to sell off its stores of molasses. When he at last proclaimed us welcome to the Netherlands Antilles and left, I shared that advice with the captain … to smooth *his* ruffled feathers.

Our crew rowed us in—yours truly crazed with anticipation—and we climbed awkwardly off the heaving launch onto the stone mole. When I stood … I suddenly felt that the entire earth was veering madly up, down, and around. Trent deftly grabbed me under my armpit. "Sea legs!" he exclaimed, hauling me forward to the beach. "Sort of a reverse seasickness, Mr. Dordrecht. It'll soon pass. After so long aboard ship, you're unused to the steadiness of Mother Earth!"

I wanted it to pass instantly, but I was very grateful for a log that lay on the far side of the road. After two minutes, the world ceased swimming about quite as haphazardly. "You'll pardon me, Mr. Dordrecht," Trent announced, "but I'm going to leave you in O'Malley's care today. I must immediately attend to my own affairs. I'll meet you both here after the first dog watch."

Woozily, I stood up. "Yes sir, thank you sir," I said as enthusiastically as I could. We shook hands, and, with a third admonition to have a care for my purse, he moved into the vortex of the bustling commercial street, where he immediately disappeared. I sat back down, feeling myself recovering, but not yet vigorous.

"Ain't you ready yet?" O'Malley demanded. He'd been as dizzy as I, but was first to compensate.

"Give me a minute?" I asked.

He grunted and sat down.

"You been here before, O'Malley?"

"Twice. Like all the other towns down here, except madder. Busiest place I ever seen." We watched an African woman swathed in pink cotton as she passed us, the plate atop her head surmounted with a pyramid of melons. "You can get one of those for two shillings down this road a ways."

"Two shillings for a *melon?*"

"Two shillings for a *woman!*"

Oh. I took it that he was familiar with the going rate. Perhaps I could cite my employers' prohibition against premature commerce if he were to press me to join him. I stood again and was relieved the dizziness was much reduced. "That's the palm tree?" I asked pointing twenty feet down the road. "How amazing that it has no branches!" I walked over and pushed against the sixty-foot high trunk; the tree swayed, but it was surely not because of me.

"You don't want to be there when a cocoanut falls!" O'Malley warned, pointing to husks on the ground. I hefted one for weight … and agreed with him.

"Let's go!"

From the ship, one could see that the commercial street of the lower town followed the shoreline for over a mile, but from the southern entry, where we were, you could barely see four buildings ahead. The path between the houses and hostelries, built into the steep hillside on the right, and the warehouses and retail outlets, built into the sea on the left, was scarcely wide enough to accommodate a cart. Much of the loading and unloading was done on the water side, where the structures were built out so that small craft could directly reach their back doors. The street was tighter and more jammed with hucksters than any I'd ever seen—and New York City boasts its share! Through a heavy miasma of tobacco smoke, my eyes darted, fascinated, from the staggering array of wares to the staggering assortment of human beings selling them. O'Malley set off smartly, shouldering his way down the middle of the road … and appeared stunned and irritated that I had stopped dead at the first table, where attractive blue-and-white Dutch fireplace tiles were offered in an abundance I'd never seen at home. The proprietor and I struck up a quick acquaintance. The reason I'd never seen so many in New York, despite its thousands of Dutch-descended folk, was that the British requirement to ship all goods only on British vessels made the product prohibitively dear. "They're selling quite well here, though, sir," he asserted. "I fear I shall soon be sold out of all I have left!"

It took considerable will to thank him, remind myself to check back, and proceed onward. "Don't you want to go through the street to the end?" O'Malley asked impatiently. "There's an ordinary at the north end—sells a nice local beer, I recall!"

The next shop's display of steel farming tools caught my eye. "Well … you head on, then. I'm trying to—"

"Captain Trent told me to watch over you today," he said miserably.

"Oh. Is it any good if I release you? I don't need—" He shook his head. "Well, I'm sorry, O'Malley, but … Aren't you *interested?* Aren't you—"

"I could see all I want of this island in half an hour!"

It took me a few seconds to get my breath back. "Don't know what to say, man. By my lights, you can set your sails however you wish. Me, I've got work to do." I turned away to the hardware vendor, whose products and prices were all in British units, which was curious, because the seller spoke halting English with a heavy French accent. I asked after the auger, which was identical to one I'd seen on Ann Street; my brother had wanted one, but couldn't afford it. This one he could afford—even after my markup! The vendor told me it was because his goods had been purchased directly from the manufacturer. Again mindful of my resolution, I thanked him and passed on.

"Direct from the manufacturer!" O'Malley scoffed, startling me.

"That *is* dubious, isn't it?"

"In the middle of a war, Froggie walks into Sheffield and takes away a warehouse-full?"

"So what do you think?"

"Smuggled, of course. Huge business on the coasts of England and France. We nearly collided with a smuggler as we approached Plymouth one night. They're built to outrun the Revenue lads. He'd have sunk us if I hadn't altered course in time! In a tear of a hurry to avoid the king's excises!"

But his enthusiasm faded as I rushed to the next emporium—a draper's—featuring great rolls of elegant upholstery fabric. Though the cloths were Flemish, the seller was Irish—but O'Malley hung back from our exchange, having spotted a crucifix about his neck. For my part, I've now had enough commerce with Quakers, Baptists, Romanists, and Hebrews to have banished the assumption of my childhood that the Reformed Dutch were God's one and only chosen people. I haven't met a Mahometan yet, but …

"What on earth are you doing?" O'Malley demanded, seeing me holding the end of a roll of patterned burgundy damask to the light.

"I'm estimating the thread count," I explained. "Ninety! Excellent—although I should have thought to bring a tape measure."

"What …?"

Might as well try to make conversation with him! "The tighter the weave, generally, the finer the cloth. One of the things I learned when Mr. Leavering ordered me to go shopping with his wife and Mrs. Glasby, when the Glasbys were furnishing their new home."

O'Malley was horrified. "He asked you to wait upon the women like a house slave?"

"I protested too, at the time, but Mr. Leavering insisted on it. He said, 'Just you keep silent, Thomas, and observe their deliberation. You'll learn a great deal about merchandise!' I had never sought out such finery before, though I've spent much of my life in markets, so perhaps he was right."

O'Malley shook his head. "I just want to be a sailor."

"Sea captains regularly need to engage in commerce, my friend!" He'd absorbed Captain Trent's aversions, I feared; such indifference would hurt him should he ever be deemed capable of full command. "The more you know about—"

"I'll meet you back at the mole with the captain." And he fled. Perhaps I was getting preachy, but … *Oh well.*

Later that afternoon, I actually *did* meet a Mahometan! *Ha!* He was from Algiers, on the Barbary Coast. Selling fine carpets acquired all the way from Persia. Spoke perfect French. Extremely polite and attentive of manner.

Hours later, Trent and O'Malley breathlessly collared me in an apothecary shop. "Mr. Dordrecht, it's long past six!" the captain protested.

It is? "Gentlemen, I do beg your pardon!"

"From now on, you shall have to pay the dock boys to ferry you back to the ship, sir!"

"I quite understand."

"Did you get no further than this?" O'Malley demanded. "You're barely a quarter of the distance!"

"An excellent day, I assure you!"

My first day proved a true harbinger of the weeks to come. With difficulty, I did manage to restrain myself from either buying or selling for the first week—and a good thing too. Visiting every house and every ship—goods were also trafficked directly from ships' holds—I discovered bargains superior to many to which I at first had been impulsively inclined. I was three days into the second week before I finally bought eight dozen of the Dutch tiles. It was three weeks after that when I had the good fortune to locate an eager buyer of Vrouw Van Voort's barley. Curiously enough, the manager was a Dutch woman, who had been aboard the ship to inspect the barrels but who constantly retreated to an anteroom of her shop as we dickered over the price, "to consult with my ailing husband." The few words I overheard were French! But we struck an agreement—to be paid in gold *louis d'or*—that I calculated was nearly twice what the barley could have fetched at market in New York. Elated with this success, I floated out into the street … and chanced across Mr. Fox, who was rather despondently "enjoying" a day at liberty ashore. We dined companionably at the public house O'Malley had recommended. Perhaps to ensure conversation, Fox—an excessively modest man—asked me for my impressions of Saint Eustatius.

After some minutes of enthusiasm concerning the climate, topography, sights, sounds, smells, wares, and exotic populations of the island—all of which appeared to intrigue Fox as if he'd not been exposed to them independently—I more calmly said, "Do you know what I've not seen? I'd heard that Statia is famous as a market for Africans, yet I've seen no trace of that trade as yet, although—"

"The slave mart is well out of town—it's that fort on the shore to the north of the anchorage. The business is all kept separate. The slaves are brought in, sorted, sold, and shipped out directly from there, with no access to the rest of the island."

"Ah," I said, beginning to understand. "Yet the town surely does not lack for Africans."

"Oh no, but they're the ones chosen by the residents here."

"They are unusual in the degree of their apparent freedom of movement, it seems to—"

"Well, where would they move *to?*" Fox countered sensibly.

"They seem to be even less subject to oversight than slaves in New York City. I've found not a few left in full charge of their stores, taking in the coin of all nations!"

"A goodly proportion of them are actually freedmen, as I understand it, Mr. Dordrecht. Some are even trained in letters and numbers."

"Extraordinary. Is this how things stand on all the islands down here, Mr. Fox?"

He nearly choked on his ale. "Good lord, no! Statia is like none other. All the others keep their blacks under tight reins. In all the others, the blacks outnumber the whites ten to one. Here, the ratio is far more equal."

"In the town, at least."

"Oh yes, but the town is virtually the whole."

"Why is that, do you reckon?"

"I'm told it's because the way this island makes its money is so different. All the others grow sugar, sugar, sugar—but Statia doesn't get enough rain, and is too small besides, so it has become this enormous mercantile enterprise."

"Necessity, mother of invention!"

"So it would seem, Mr. Dordrecht." We finished our repasts. "Have you seen the horse mart?" he asked. "I was thinking of walking on to the horse mart."

"Do you have need of a horse?"

"Oh no, I'm just … seeking to occupy myself. Would you care to accompany me? It's barely a mile over the hill, I gather."

Though the idea seemed implausible at first, I quickly agreed. I was ready for an excursion out of the town and glad to see more of the island. And I reasoned further that all markets should be of interest to a man of affairs, whether he trades in horses or not. After climbing to the crest of the rise, we were even with the mast-tops in the harbor, and able to view both the lower and upper towns and the towering Quill mountain behind them. Curious that one almost forgot it—the sight being obscured from the lower town. We could also see both shores of the island, just as one can see the East and North Rivers from the steeple of a Manhattan church, and its smallness struck me anew. "Have you ever climbed the mountain, Mr. Fox?"

Fox looked at me, dumbfounded. "Climbed the … Whatever for, Mr. Dordrecht?"

"Oh. Just … for the experience of it, I suppose."

Fox evidently found my whimsy so bizarre, he was rendered mute. Through fields sown with grains and vegetables—and some sugar, I noted—we presently came across a fenced pasture with a dozen horses running freely about. A man greeted us, clearly hoping that we would join the bidders, but content with his half-dozen others when we explained our mere curiosity. It was but twenty minutes later that the auction began. Although no great judge of horses, I noted the bids made and was impressed by the large amounts surrendered for plain workhorses. "Have we ever transported livestock in earnest, Mr. Fox?"

"Not in *Dorothy C.*, sir. She's not equipped for it."

"Come to think of it, I don't recall finding livestock on any of the firm's manifests. Perhaps we should consider it!"

As we made our way back, one of the bidders overtook us on his new mount. "I say, gentlemen," he called to us, "you may wish to divert yourselves to the north fort, where we are selling off a boatload fresh from the Gambia delta." *Slaves.* "They are all in prime fettle, as the trip required but thirty-nine days!"

We waved acknowledgement to him as he galloped off. "I have no desire to attend that, Mr. Dordrecht," Fox announced, "but I surely will not impose if you wish to."

Again contrary to my expectation, I was torn. Though I'd once conducted a private transaction, I had never before observed the organized sale of Africans. I constantly passed by the market on New York's Wall Street, but I had somehow never found the occasion to investigate it. And though I would certainly abide by the policy of my firm's Quaker principals not to deal in slaves, there was no certainty that I'd spend my whole career in their service or that I might not someday start my own business—in which event I should at least be familiar with a commerce well-known to be profitable. Perhaps this was as good a time as any to extend my education to the market for slaves, as well as that for horses.

Fox was rather surprised—and I thought faintly disappointed—when I elected to part company with him. I followed the horseman's northwesterly path up a hillock past two rather handsome plantation houses, each with numerous outbuildings apparently devoted to warehousing and some manufacturing purpose—likely rum distilleries. Soon I reached the top and was looking down onto the shoreside fortress that I'd seen at a distance from our anchorage. As I approached the forbidding, solitary structure, built of the porous black stone found everywhere on the island, I heard a hubbub from inside it, but couldn't see an entrance. A dark-skinned man noticed me, waved me to the far corner, and pointed up an exterior staircase. "I'm afraid you've missed all the prime males, sir," he said with a disconcerting, lopsided grin, "but there are eight dozen females yet to be sold off!" I climbed up to an open balcony behind the fort's parapet. A score of buyers were looking down into the courtyard ... where a slight, bent, balding African clad in a loincloth was inspiring only desultory bidding, despite raucous encouragement from the auctioneer. With the sun in my eyes, it took a minute to make out the dais below and the cowering, chained group underneath the far gallery. Though the auctioneer's harangue was in English, I heard a great deal of French and Spanish discussion among the customers.

The fellow who'd passed us on the road approached. "Ah, welcome, young sir! Your friend could not join?" He didn't pause for an answer. "Do you expect to be bidding? We require payment in—"

"I shall only be observing."

"Ah!" he said, disappointed. "Perhaps another occasion, then? We expect a large parcel from the Congo any day. Please make yourself at ease."

By the time I sat down on the hot stone, off to the side, the old fellow was gone, and a hobbling sixteen-year-old lad was on the block. Instantly I wondered—I never had before—if Floris Van Klost's timorous, crippled slave Sander had ever been through the like. Against all appearances, the auctioneer was assuring us that his leg was merely sprained; none evidently believed him, and so the resultant sale was for only seven pounds. As he was dragged away, a woman on the opposite side began screaming. Slapped repeatedly, she wailed the louder until a tie was put in her mouth. It was not because she was to be bid, but because an eight-year-old boy was being pulled away from her to the center. Two slave overseers tied the woman's hands behind her, as she was attempting to crawl out and grasp the lad, who was himself contesting with his restraints to rejoin her. As he appeared sturdy and whole, he attracted slightly more interest, was sold at twenty-two pounds, and was taken off after the others amid the muffled wailing of the woman.

"That's the last of the males, gentlemen, but as you can see, we have some fine wenches for you ..." The auctioneer nodded at the two overseers. "Yes, let's see if we can't get her off-loaded before she starts the rest of them wailing." The woman I took to be the lad's mother was dragged forward, despite her unrelenting protest. She brought her knee up into the groin of one of the overseers, felling him to the ground to the huge amusement of the crowd. Two additional men rushed to replace him. One held her hair tightly to force her to face forward, as she only wished to look after the boy. As some spirited bidding commenced, I recalled that I'd just seen a mare separated from her colt at the horse auction. They had been physically proximate to the moment when each was led forward for bid. If the mare realized they were about to be parted—which I doubt—she made no overt protest, and the colt seemed only slightly skittish to have his bridle taken by someone unfamiliar to him.

When the woman, sold for eighty-six pounds, was bodily carted off to a different door than her son, her screams could be heard, despite the gag. A smiling French-speaker leaned over to the successful bidder and said, "You shall have quite the *handful,* there, Monsieur!"

Revolted, I forced myself to sit through three more sales before I could endure it no longer, and left.

Walking back along the beach path, I resolved that, whether he was employed by Quakers or not, whether he saw any sense in the rantings of John Woolman or not, Thomas Dordrecht would never deal in slaves.

Transferring the barley into the buyer's warehouse would have been difficult enough, given that Saint Eustatius lacked a true harbor and any deepwater mole to which we could securely attach the *Dorothy C.* for the purpose of off-loading. It was a tribute to Statia's mercantile attractiveness that shippers put up with the clumsy necessity of off-loading from the anchorage onto small work-boats, which then laboriously hauled the produce into shore or to other ships in the offing. The buyer of the barley desired it to be transferred directly onto another ship, a three-master named *La Fleur de Lys*, supposedly out of Rotterdam. The process, every step of which required my attendance, consumed the better part of a fortnight.

When that was finally completed, I took the opportunity of a showery morning to climb to the upper town to pursue a tip I'd garnered from a factor aboard the *Fleur*—that the governor's son-in-law, a fellow Harmanus's age, had several building projects afoot and probably needed nails. The upper town of Oranjestad—it was my first visit—was far less crowded and raucous than its seaside brother, with neat, sturdy, modest wooden houses surrounded by small gardens, all on a slope coming down from the mountain to the edge of the sheer drop. Inquiring at the fort, I was directed to a house "just beyond the synagogue." I was again astonished by Statia—the brick-built structure was one of the more impressive—but I pressed on and located the home of Meneer Johannes de Graaff. When a slave cordially requested me to state my business, I explained, in Dutch, that I had a shipment of nails on offer. De Graaff, who did remind me of my brother—at least in respect of being formidable in bearing and severe in demeanor—presently appeared and invited me inside.

He set directly to business, carefully examining the dozen sample nails I'd brought for consistency in length, straightness, and point. "Made in England?"

"No sir, made in New York."

His brows arched up, and I took it that he knew well that New Yorkers were not supposed to be manufacturing nails. "Much cheaper for us when they don't have to be shipped so far," he murmured.

And when you evade the duties, I forbore to add. We commenced a relaxed round of bargaining. He had undoubtedly noted as well as I the price of British nails in the hardware emporia of the lower town. We soon came to an agreement we found mutually pleasing.

He offered me tea and queried me regarding the state of business in the northern continental colonies for a few minutes. "Your name is Dordrecht?" he said after a lull. "Odd. Your family comes from that city?"

"I presume so, Meneer, but all I know for certain is that my paternal forebears are all American-born."

"I could vow I've heard the name before. We do have families that once lived in the New Netherlands. Have any of your relations trafficked here in the past?"

Rather startled, I could only reply that I was from farmer stock, and the first of my line to essay participation in commerce.

Meneer de Graaff was pleased to suggest that I might not be the last, and he continued by asking my impressions of Statia. After reiterating my positive enthusiasm at some length, I was inspired to take advantage of the man's frank and intelligent nature and ask a question that had intrigued me. "I've not been to many places, sir, but others have given me to understand that Statia is, *uh*—"

"Unique?"

"Yes, exactly, sir. And I can't help wondering how it is that all this"—I pointed to the crowded anchorage, visible outside his window—"should have come to be?" Meneer de Graaff was smiling wryly. "It's such a small place, you see. It's half the size of New York island, and there's no continent surrounding it, so how—"

"It was a deliberate choice, Meneer Dordrecht. Once the original founders had settled here—because the land here was free, there weren't even natives to be contended with—they realized that, unlike all its neighbors, it was unsuitable for large-scale farming. So trade was their only recourse. And for that, they had three great advantages—location at the corner of the island chain, easy entrance to the harbor, and the simple fact of being Dutch. The Netherlands has cleverly avoided most of the endless contentions of France, England, Spain, and the German states, and so have we, in the Netherlands Antilles."

"But you say it was a deliberate choice?"

"Indeed, and that was not so long ago. Our commerce expanded enormously after our petition to the States-General—to allow us to be a completely free port—was granted. There is nothing that calls business to you like the promise that the commerce of all nations is welcome without prejudice, and will face no hindrance or tax."

"But what sustains your government, then?"

De Graaff shrugged. "Harbor fees are really quite adequate for that. The point is that the residents become wealthy because the trade sustains them."

"How can you afford any defenses?"

He grinned. "Our true defense—I daresay you've noted our fortifications are almost laughable—is that all the other islands in this sea *need us*, Mr. Dordrecht, as do you on the continent. The great powers might ignore the moral barrier of our sovereignty, but they think twice before tampering with our success, much as it galls them to see us thumbing our noses at their vaunted mercantile protection systems."

"But ..." I halted to absorb his observations, but a contrary notion intrigued me. "What if others ... What if *the whole world* should attempt to free its commerce in so extraordinary a manner? Wouldn't that—"

De Graaff laughed. "It's an appealing thought, rather! Surely the *people* of all countries would be the richer."

"But wouldn't that hurt you, here on Saint Eustatius?"

"Oh ..." He shrugged again. "Well, we'd no longer be unique, I suppose. But I shall not lose sleep over the thought, Meneer Dordrecht. The interests of the powerful will not easily be overcome."

"Ah."

"And even if they were," he added with a cheerful grin—all the more unexpected on a usually sober face, "we have a reputation for quality already built that would support us, even in the absence of our unique financial virtues. The Danes, you know, have tried to imitate us on Saint Croix island."

"Indeed?"

"They're doing well enough, but it hasn't hurt us."

Another caller was admitted to his anteroom. We quickly made arrangements for transferring the nails, and he expressed a hope that I'd visit his island again. As we stepped outside, we faced the mountain, and ... "Is there any way to go to the top, Meneer de Graaff?"

"The top of the Quill?" He smiled, startled. "Haven't done that since I was a boy! There's a trail the lookouts use. You'd need mules. Ask at the fort."

A ship arriving from the north brought our first communication from home, a letter from Mr. Glasby dated May 26, jointly addressed to Captain Trent and myself. It was unusually to the point, even for him:

> Relieved to get your letters from St. Eustatius. Approve decision. Mr. Leavering returned a fortnight since, still unwell. Has only been twice to office. City business in uproar as General Amherst has decided his inability to provision is result of trading with the enemy. Has threatened to arrest captain of the *Dove* for treason! Six French merchants have been incarcerated & their papers seized. Gov. Colden has imposed a general limited embargo on all exportation of provisions from this port! Whether this will affect return of *Dorothy C.*, I don't know, but hope to write again in time.

Having first read it privately, Trent and I presently shared it with Fox and O'Malley. "That's it?" the latter demanded.

"I know Captain Carlisle of the *Dove*," Trent said, ignoring him. "Good man. A trader, just like ourselves. Can't imagine why he should suddenly be facing such charges after all these years."

"I conjure that Mr. Glasby is somewhat overwhelmed," I said to O'Malley.

"If the redcoats paid the going rate for provisions, they wouldn't have any problem!" Fox asserted.

As none of us argued with him—though I know many who would—conversation halted. "So what do we do?" O'Malley asked.

We all looked to Trent, but he was vacantly shaking his head, stunned. "Carlisle accused of treason!" he rasped.

Fox and O'Malley looked at me. "We proceed about our business as best we can, of course," I said.

However, my business was beginning to trouble me. I had not yet sold the consigned flour, which was, after all, the main reason for the entire journey and a wasting asset. I had had two firm offers for it, and had turned both down, believing that I might do better. Now I was doubting the wisdom of my refusals. At the time, my reasoning had concerned the proffered exchange of flour for molasses. Specie—hard coin—however desirable, was not to be hoped for as payment for a shipload of flour, even though specie was somewhat more prevalent here than at home. The problem was that I was hoping for sugarloaf, rather than molasses, and it appeared that European ships had made off with a year's supply of Antillean sugarloaf just before we arrived.

Suspecting that I might have neglected the establishments at the northern third of the road, I revisited them, openly asking for sugarloaf. At one, I was referred to "Koopvaarder's, two doors down." Proceeding there immediately, I found a relatively large emporium with a section of empty shelves that suggested recent wholesale business. A well-dressed man of apparently equal European and African parentage stood up behind the counter and greeted me with the traditional offer of assistance. Thinking to gain a stronger impression of the wares before asking for the master, I avowed that

I was merely browsing. "Please be our guest, sir," was the suave reply.

It was just past noon, and having the place to myself, browse I did. Like some of the other stores, it appeared to be organized more by the geography of provenance than product category. One aisle contained offerings of North America, one those of Europe, and another those of the tropics. Given the clientele, this was perhaps more practical than it might at first sound. I tended toward the European shelves, and found Flemish wools, Irish linens, and French satins; tools from England and Germany; tulip bulbs and tea from Holland; and books from all over. As always, the last detained me, as I compulsively scanned each of the scores of titles, searching for matter to enlighten, or at least entertain me, on our return voyage. I had selected two when my eye glanced upon a display of playing cards, notable only for the fact that they resembled—no, they were *identical* to the four I had found in Mr. Sproul's tract. Their backs showed the same cobalt and white floral motif his possessed, and the King of Clubs, visible despite the maroon ribbon holding each deck together, had a cape of the same figured pattern as the Varlet of Clubs. I carried the books and a deck to the counter. "I don't wish to purchase the cards, but I'm curious if you can tell me anything of them. Do you know, perchance, where they were made, for example?"

"Austria, I believe, sir, though they contain the French complement of seventy-eight cards. Why?"

"Are they very rare?"

"Not that I know of, sir. What we have on display are the last of two dozen we acquired a few years back."

"I've only seen the like in New York once before."

"Ah, that'd be because of your king's imposts, no doubt. You can buy this deck, here, with four face cards and all the tarot cards, for less than a plain English deck would run you." I stared stupidly at the cards for five seconds. "Would you like to buy them after all, sir?"

"Oh! No thank you, just the books."

"Very well. You are visiting us from New York, I take it? That's between Philadelphia and Boston, is it not?"

"Yes," I replied, rather astonished at his awareness of geography. "Still a great distance. Nearer Philadelphia."

"Ah. Mr. Koopvaarder came from there, some thirty years ago."

"Indeed! Did he come from the city, or upriver? I'm unfamiliar with the surname, and …" Something caught my eye. "Excuse me, are those sugarloafs offered for sale?"

Behind his chair, on the floor, were two cones, nearly three feet in height. He glanced at them and smiled. "Ha, that didn't take long! They are from the test batch, and were brought in just this morning."

"I've not seen any here since I arrived over a month ago."

"Very popular item. These were made at our own manufactory."

I struggled to restrain any show of excitement. "Is that so? Are there … any more?"

"We have a large run soon to be completed, sir, it's—"

"Perhaps I should speak to Mr. Koopvaarder in person. I am the supercargo of the *Dorothy C.*, and we have some four dozen hogsheads of fine New York flour that we—"

"Oh yes, the *Dorothy C.*, I've seen her. A noble ship! You are representing what firm, may I ask?"

"I am with Castell, Leavering & Sproul. Is Mr. Koop—"

"I thought that was a Pennsylvania company?"

At every step, this fellow—who had to be a bondsman, he lacked the shirt-front red ribbon that denoted a free black—was surprising me. "It has been expanded recently, and I proceed from the New York City office."

"Tell me, is your flour whole wheat or is it—"

"It is ground to the all-purpose level. Surely I should be discussing this directly with the master?"

He stood, rising to my own height, but evidently taking no offense. "Oh, I'm sorry, I am Absalom, sir, Mr. Koopvaarder's agent in full charge." He made bold to offer me his hand, which no other member of his race had ever done. After hesitating, more from surprise than disinclination, I shook it—but rather limply, I fear. "Mr. Koopvaarder is at the plantation today, overseeing the drying of the next batch. There are some fifteen hundred loaves that will be ready for sale in another week." He paused to look at me expectantly, and I again struggled to contain my excitement. "Perhaps you would care to visit the plantation and tour the works this afternoon, Mr. *uh*—"

"Thomas Dordrecht."

"Mr. Dordrecht. I'd be pleased to escort you directly!"

"I—"

"It's less than three miles away. I'll have the carriage brought round."

"I … Why, I'd like that very much!"

"Excellent! Thys!" he shouted at an open door toward the back. "It will be thirty-seven pence for the books, Mr. Dordrecht," he murmured while a commotion occurred in the rear room.

"*Ja, Meneer Absalom?*" said a tall, grinning African lad of probably sixteen years, coming toward us.

"Get the carriage, Thys," Absalom said, in Dutch. "I am going to show Mr. Dordrecht the plantation works. Then change your shirt. You will have to mind the store until I return." The boy, who also lacked a red ribbon, positively whooped, "Yes sir!" in English, as he ran out to the front.

I settled for the books and noticed Absalom making careful observation of the amount of coin in the drawer during the moment we had to wait for the carriage.

Two fine gray stallions were pulling one of the more elegant open carriages I have ever stepped into, with two upholstered seats. Absalom offered me the one facing forward, climbed in after me, and told the liveried driver to take us to the mill. As we proceeded out of town, we moved further up the mountain than I had been hitherto, and I found the view ever more breathtaking. Absalom, however, was articulately explaining the processes involved in the production of sugarloaf—chopping, shredding, and crushing the cane; repeatedly boiling the liquor using the bagasse—the vegetable detritus—as fuel; pouring the concentrated product into inverted conical molds when the sugar was thick enough to crystallize; and finally drying out the loaves for an extended period at low heat. In sum, a time-consuming, labor-intensive, and yet immensely profitable business.

"You've not explained how the raw cane is nurtured," I observed as we passed into Meneer Koopvaarder's fields. "I've always heard that, too, is a difficult process."

Absalom was happy to acknowledge an attentive listener. "Ah yes, well, you can see over there we are harvesting at the moment." He pointed to a field of what appeared to be an acre or two of extremely tall grass.

A slave with a bundle of ten-foot-long canes on his shoulder was struggling toward a waiting sledge. He lowered it and sucked his hand, which was bleeding, as he returned for another load. "How much sugar will eventually result from, say, that bundle of cane?" I asked. "A pound or two?"

"More like half a cup, Mr. Dordrecht."

We passed the cane warehouse, a structure larger than the barn on my family's twelve-acre plot. "Does Meneer Koopvaarder have other fields?" I asked, curious at the disparity.

"There are a few," Absalom replied. "They are sown with cotton and yams. There is also a lemon orchard and many animal pens. Ah, over there you see the cistern that sustains us through the dry months. And here is our factory."

It was a long, single-story, rough-hewn stone building with a shingle roof. Absalom proudly walked me through its production areas—cutting, pressing, three vats of progressive boiling, and finally the molding room and the drying room. Suffocatingly hot work, all through. At one point, Absalom left me for a minute to confer briefly with the sugar-cooker, who he said was the most valued slave on the plantation. As they indulged in a rather worried-looking chat, I silently multiplied the rows and columns of drying loaves and confirmed the self-proclaimed agent's estimate—more than enough, quite possibly, to exchange for Mr. Helden's flour. "When will these be ready for sale, *uh…*"—Should I address him as *Meneer?*—"Meneer Absalom?"

There was a brief smile on his face as he urged me out onto a shaded porch, where a girl was waiting for us with lemon water and cakes. "Another six to eight days, Mr. Dordrecht. None are spoken for, to my knowledge. Is the *Dorothy C.* soon planning to sail?"

"Captain Trent has given me to understand that we must be under way well before the storm season but, other than that—"

"Aha!" Absalom was no more able to suppress a quiet smile of satisfaction than I was. "I am certain Meneer Koopvaarder would be pleased to make your acquaintance, sir," he said somewhat evasively, "but I am informed that we have missed him. He has repaired to his house in town. We shall at least pass the big country house, Haven Plantation, on our way back." He nodded at the girl, and she amused me by walking out to the path and emitting a whistle for the driver that overrode the racket of the factory. As we began down a sharply declining path, Absalom reassured me that the carriage had sturdy brakes. He pointed out the plantation house—a solid but unpretentious two-story structure, not actually very big, also built of the soft black stone I had learned was volcanic rock. "I should be interested to inspect the flour barrels on board the *Dorothy C.*," he said with a casualness that I couldn't positively affirm was studied. As I again thought that this, *surely,* was a matter for the master, and not an agent of any description, he asked if the next morning would be acceptable.

"Well, yes, of course," I stammered.

"The change of the morning watch, perhaps?"

"Yes, but … Will Meneer Koopvaarder be joining us?"

"Ah, I daresay not," Absalom replied easily. "I'm afraid he is unable to tolerate even the slightest motion of the seas."

Every reason for Koopvaarder's absence was perfectly plausible, and yet … it all seemed so bloody odd. I wondered if another question I had might shatter Absalom's cultivated veneer. "Does all your sugar come from your own fields? From what I've seen of this island, your factory must consume more cane than is grown on all of Statia!"

He grinned, showing quite fine teeth. "Aha, you are most acute, Mr. Dordrecht! But I'm afraid I can't answer that, it is—"

"Can't, or won't?" I demanded, not finding it quite as amusing.

"It is a secret of our trade, if you will."

"It is the *voudou*, perhaps, Meneer Absalom?"

He laughed. "Yes, our so magical *voudou!*"

Meneer Yarmouth of the *Rachel Peabody* had already explained that secret to me: Statia's fishing boats made stops almost daily on the shores of St. Christopher's Island—ten miles away and ten times Statia's size—where they'd throw a tarpaulin over a load of raw cane and throw their daily haul of fish on top of that, thus avoiding the excises a British exporter would normally have to pay. I decided to rest content with the local fiction.

At the foot of the road from the upper town, I demurred on his offer to deliver me to the dock where I could secure a conveyance to the *Dorothy C.*, knowing I could walk the distance faster through the dense street. "I do thank you for the tour. I had no appreciation of the process at all."

"Ah, but there's so much more to it than we showed you just now! Until tomorrow, then!"

The solstice having just passed, it was still fully light, and I decided I was hungry enough to splurge on supping ashore. I was hailed by the Hollander merchant who'd sold me the fireplace tiles, and gladly joined him at his table. When our conversation rolled around to business gossip—which never takes long on Statia—I enquired his observations on the Koopvaarder firm. After protesting for ten seconds that he never credited scandal, he authoritatively informed me that Staats Koopvaarder was a notorious souse whose slave-dealing business preoccupied him to the exclusion of all his other affairs. Noticing that my face undoubtedly fell into despondency, he added, "It's that mulatto slave fellow, Absalom, who keeps the emporium from running into the ground. You should deal with him, if you can!"

Koopvaarder's agent punctually rapped on the hull of the *Dorothy C.* at eight the next morning, requesting permission to come aboard. As I'd forewarned the officers that a mulatto man was to be expected to do business with me, he was properly received. O'Malley had objected that he didn't want to take any orders from any African, and Trent, more used to Statia's ways, told him, "Very well, it's time we tarred the shrouds again. You can see to that!"

Fox, Parigo, and two other sailors accompanied Absalom and me down into the hold. Parigo and the sailors moved a few of the closest barrels to the side, much to the annoyance of Dorothy the cat, and Absalom minutely examined the condition of two that were underneath them. Following the same practice I had learned in New York, he then had us remove the bungs of these two and extract a cup of flour from each—"for Meneer Koopvaarder's inspection."

The process, conducted with cheerful efficiency, required but an hour. Absalom had kept his launch waiting. Stopping at the rail, he told me he was completely satisfied with the integrity of the barrels, and his impression of the flour was good—though more examination was required—and that he believed the grade of flour was much in demand. He promised to contact me again within the week.

I spent the rest of the morning alone in the stuffy cabin, calculating on paper various terms I might negotiate in order to exchange a great quantity of New York flour for a great quantity of Caribbean sugarloaf, mindful of Mr. Leavering's insistence that the price must ensure not merely a *quid pro quo*, but pay all the expenses of the trip plus a substantial portion of the overhead of the firm, and also ensure a profit in addition that would offset the great risks that the firm was running and would incur again in the future. I struggled to quantify such other imponderables as the quality and consistency of the sugar, variations in the size of the loaves, packaging, and the manner and timing of deliveries. At length, my head swimming, I decided I could not further improve my estimations of the minimal, feasible, and optimal ratios of flour to sugar. I set my notes aside and gratefully ascended to the deck.

"Mr. Dordrecht!" Captain Trent accosted me. "Would this afternoon be suitable for us to visit the firms you suggested?"

Trent was having more trouble selling his goods than I was with mine, and my apparent progress must have served as an opening for him to accept the offer I had made ten days before. His problem was that he habitually dealt only with familiar customers and was stubborn about exploring new relationships. Worse, he so disliked going into the town that he tended to market only directly with the other ships. In my explorations of Statia, I had noted several firms that might be interested in his marine supplies and quietly suggested them to him. But he'd neglected to pursue them, preoccupying himself with the endless repairs and improvements that were doubtless necessary to the seaworthiness of the *Dorothy C.* As June was drawing to a close, however, none of his regulars had taken his bait, and the situation was belatedly alarming him. Happily, going ashore would admirably serve my need to clear my head. "By all means, Captain!"

We called on three establishments that afternoon—none of which Trent had previously visited. He was astounded when I was greeted by name in each. But a curious incident occurred as we were examining cordage in the last.

"Captain … Trent, is it not?" exclaimed a well-dressed gentleman of middle years—apparently another customer. Trent looked as though he recognized the man, but couldn't place him. "Peter Wardener," he explained, offering his hand, "captain of *Four Daughters*. We met perhaps two years ago, in Philadelphia."

Recognition dawned. Trent shook the hand enthusiastically and introduced me. "What brings you to Statia, Captain?"

"Ah! Therein lies a tale, Captain Trent! But I say, I'm parched, and there's an ordinary next door with a porch that catches more breeze than any other in Oranjestad. Might I offer you gents a quaff?"

Wardener seemed perfectly guileless; eager for refreshment, I was glad when Trent announced that we'd done enough for one day.

We'd not sat and made ourselves comfortable when Wardener ordered a bowl of rum punch—made here rather tastily with tropical fruits—and promptly launched his yarn. "It was the middle of March when we left Philadelphia, heading as usual for Monte Cristi."

"Ah!" Trent and I both exclaimed, guessing what would come next.

"Well, we arrived early in April and found the harbor deserted, save for a few fishermen. We made bold to move toward them, not having seen any suggestion that plague was afoot, and be damned if the castle didn't fire a cannonball right at us! No warning at all! It bounced on the waves and touched us on the stem, but we were far enough away that we weren't damaged. We turned and fled into the offing, only to be waylaid two hours later by His Majesty's Navy! Now, I had by then already decided that I would make sail for Statia, though that would take us weeks against the wind, but my papers had been made out for Kingston, and our excellent tars declared that they would be only too happy to escort us on to Jamaica!

"There was no way to refuse this ever-so-kindly offer, so we put in to Jamaica the week after Easter and made the best sales we could of our cargo of tobacco."

"Must have cost you dearly!" Trent said sympathetically. "But what then brings you here after all?"

"I fooled them!" Wardener exulted. "My main cargo was planed maple lumber. I had it loaded first so that it appeared to be no more than the floor of the three lower decks, with the tobacco barrels atop it."

Trent snorted with amusement. "They didn't spot this ruse?" I asked dubiously.

"They did not, happily. Helps if you distribute a few dead fish below just before Customs arrives!"

"Indeed!"

"So we cleared back for home—and made a slight detour!"

Trent made the mistake of asking Wardener to describe his trip from Jamaica, prompting another ten-minute saga of a month of storms, breakage, illnesses, near-mutinies, and self-professed brilliant seamanship. Finally, Wardener recalled his manners, made some enquiry of us, and learned that we were representing Castell, Leavering & Sproul.

"Oh, of course, they have a New York office now. Mr. Castell explained that to me some time ago."

"Ah, you have met our Mr. Castell, then?" Trent asked.

"Yes, but it's Mr. Sproul with whom I am far better acquainted. Our wives, you see, are very … Is something wrong?"

Taken aback, Trent looked to me to explain the necessary facts. "Captain Wardener, I am very grieved to have to inform you that Daniel Sproul is dead."

Wardener froze in the act of lifting the punch bowl to his lips. "No!"

"I fear so, sir."

"But when did this happen? We had a most pleasant afternoon with the Sprouls early in March, and … and I paid a call at his office the very morning of my departure! I was rushing to beat a snowstorm and had a little room left, and I hoped he might have some goods that might easily be consigned. He was in perfect health. Was there some horrible accident?"

Once again I was forced to recite the bizarre circumstances in great detail.

"I still can't believe it!" Wardener said at length. "I'm very distressed! He was always so vigorous, so …"

"What?"

"Do you know, he *was* strangely agitated that morning when I last saw him. Said he'd not slept. I didn't much think about it because *I* was so agitated. The glass had dropped like a stone overnight, and I was afraid the river might freeze back and I wanted to make haste."

"Did he have any goods for you?" Trent asked.

"No. He even apologized that he had nothing in. I said it was no matter, because I'd just received eight barrels of mineral pitch from Goodman & Benchley, across the street. I had to sell them in Jamaica at statute prices, *alas*—the Navy was very happy! He then inquired what my base cargo was, and I explained my gambit with the lumber, and … He didn't laugh, he got very angry. Yes, I'd never seen him so angry—it was unlike him. Positively growled that General Amherst was causing such a fuss over trading with the enemy when there was wholesale corruption in his procurement procedures that cost the Crown ten times as much. I had no idea what to make of the outburst, so I said as a jest, 'Well, you tell him!' And he gave me the most peculiar stare … until I finally said I really had to depart, and he shook himself and said 'I do wish thee safe passage, Peter.' And that was that."

"Did you avoid the storm?" Trent asked, disrupting a thought I had.

"Oh, not entirely. We did make it down into the bay before it hit the next morning. But then we anchored and waited it out. Nasty, but brief."

"Can you recall exactly which day it was you left, Captain Wardener?" I asked.

"Oh surely, Mr. Dordrecht, it was Wednesday the seventeenth. First entry in my log of the voyage, you see."

"We left on Tuesday the thirtieth in another snowstorm," Trent exclaimed jocularly. "I never want to do that again!"

As he launched into *his* yarn, recounting our flight from the press gang, I found myself compulsively committing everything Wardener had said to memory.

Chapter 6

Four days passed before I had a word back from Absalom. The boy Thys rowed out in a dinghy and conveyed his message verbally without coming aboard. Absalom had been satisfied with the flour, he said, but there was a delay because the sugarloaf was taking longer to cure than expected.

"What about Meneer Koopvaarder? Was *Meneer Koopvaarder* satisfied with the flour?"

"Oh yes, sir, I do believe he was, sir!"

"I see. Well, tell Meneer Absalom I hope to hear further from him very soon!"

The following afternoon, having received no additional communication, I visited the Koopvaarder store … and found the boy in charge. Absalom, he explained, was at the refinery. Koopvaarder was at the plantation house. I have not yet so mastered the *finesse* of commercial relations that I can express impatience for a resolution without betraying excessive eagerness for a sale. It was now July. All I could manage was to turn on my heel and flounce out, as if I had felt personally insulted.

The boy rapped on the hull the next morning, bearing the message that Absalom would be pleased to show me the final product … if I would be so good as to attend him there for tea the *next* afternoon. Chagrined by my previous display of impatience, and determined not to repeat it, I disdainfully inquired if the carriage might be available, and the boy—a quick-witted fellow—said he was sure that if I were to have the launch deliver me to the Koopvaarder wharf in the rear of the warehouse at two o'clock, he could have the carriage waiting for me in the front.

Frustrated, I again worked over my calculations, belatedly admitting that my arrangement with Koopvaarder's was insubstantial. Then, delegating Sergei to watch for sharks, I had a quick swim by the boat, after which I went to town looking for alternative purveyors of sugar.

But Absalom was a reassuring model of commercial acuity at our meeting the following day. He immediately took me into the drying room, where the loaves were now freed from their molds and sitting upright, glistening white as they awaited the blue paper covers a slave woman was applying. We walked among the tables, examining the product. "How close are they in weight?"

"They average fourteen pounds, two ounces," Absalom replied, "and seldom vary by more than three ounces. They can be judged individually, if the customer wishes."

I decided to consider later whether that step might be required and preoccupied myself with multiplying fourteen pounds, two ounces by the number of loaves on display. "There are fewer loaves than I saw last week, no?"

"True. It's not uncommon for even ten percent to be judged inferior, and withdrawn to be boiled again."

"Aha. Did Meneer Koopvaarder make that judgment?"

He hesitated for just a second. "No. The sugar cooker and … I make those decisions. Can we interest you in sampling some, Meneer Dordrecht? Choose any loaf, and we'll have sugar with our tea."

Many years back, I had once spent an afternoon watching my Aunt Betje at work baking apple tarts. She had employed me nipping and grinding the sugar—during which she cheerfully explained a great deal about its variant grades. I chose a loaf that looked a trifle oddly-shaped. Absalom removed a substantial chunk and handed it to the serving girl, who propitiously appeared with a mortar and pestle. Having ground it down, she poured it easily into the Delft sugar bowl that Absalom had retrieved from a cabinet, and we repaired out to the porch. In the light—and in the tea that was ready and waiting—the sugar was consistent in color and granularity—all that might be desired.

Some sweet cakes were placed on the table. "These were made this morning with the sugar that was removed from the lot," Absalom announced, daring me to find anything wrong with them. I couldn't. I again wondered where the owner was while he had the girl explain the cookie's recipe.

"We would like to offer you nine hundred twenty loaves for your flour, Meneer Dordrecht," Absalom announced abruptly. "That's thirteen thousand pounds in weight and—"

"*We* would? Meneer Absalom," I said testily, "this is Meneer Koopvaarder's sugar, is it not? Surely the exchange of a boatload of flour for a boatload of sugar is a matter that would merit his personal attention?"

Again Absalom shrugged as if he conceded that my qualms were entirely understandable. "Indeed. But I fear he is detained out at the slave market today. However, you may rest assured that he will endorse any agreement you and I should come to." I looked him in the eye, and he rather fiercely stared back. "And I'm sure he'll be pleased to tell you as much tomorrow, when he insists you come out to Haven Plantation for Sunday dinner with him and Lady Vatusia!"

It took me a couple seconds to absorb this. Finally, I uneasily decided Koopvaarder's imprimatur, after the fact, would have to serve—and we still had much to negotiate by way of price and performance. "I shall be pleased to accept," I said—rather too sharply. "With, *um*, delight!"

Once it was settled that Absalom was to be my sole bargaining partner, we got back to business. I made an equally ludicrous counter-offer, of the entire run of sugarloaves for forty barrels of flour. We digressed on the subject of barrels and crates and delivery methods for nearly two hours, but at length arrived at an agreement that all the flour should be exchanged for eleven hundred loaves of sugar which, he asserted confidently, could be packed in my presence into four dozen crates that could easily fit in the space vacated by the equal number of hogsheads of flour on the *Dorothy C.* According to the calculations I'd already done, such an exchange would enrich

Mr. Helden, more than satisfy Mr. Leavering, and add luster to the reputation of Thomas Dordrecht.

As he related the particulars of the morrow's engagement, I habitually outstretched my hand to conclude our bargain. Absalom seemed equally as pleased as I as he took it.

The weather was especially fine as I was again conveyed up the side of the Quill, this time directly to Haven Plantation. I had no particular worries about the meeting with the mysteriously reclusive Meneer Koopvaarder and his "Lady Vatusia"—other than securing a firm personal commitment to the agreement that his agent had made. As I climbed the wooden steps to its porch, the front door was thrown open, revealing an interior of surprising opulence. A tall, black factotum in full livery of pink sateen, white lace, and powdered wig welcomed me.

It took at least five seconds for it to register on me that I recognized the spectacular *major domo.* It was Absalom!

I was about to splutter my confusion when a side door was opened, and Absalom boomed, "Meneer Staats Koopvaarder, may I present Meneer Thomas—"

"Yes, yes," Koopvaarder boomed heartily back, coming between us to embrace my shoulders, "our colleague from New York. Welcome, sir, to Haven Plantation!"

Koopvaarder was an extremely imposing man, whose fading blond hair marked him in his late forties. He was taller and broader than me and tending to stoutness. His florid face, which had probably been comely in youth, was unmarked by pox, but deeply lined by some habitual response to the world—I couldn't yet imagine what. He was be-wigged and dressed in full fashion—a burgundy velvet suit with an embroidered cream waistcoat, with *gold* buckles on his shoes! I had seen portraits of the King's Privy Council members that looked less ostentatious.

"Thank you, sir, it's a pleasure to meet you at—"

"Do come into the salon, lad, and we'll have some punch!" He took my elbow and started toward the other room. I uneasily realized he was already intoxicated. "Fetch the punch!" he snapped at Absalom, who, to my dismay, nodded and tamely departed in the opposite direction. A rustle was heard at the top of the elegant staircase. We turned, and I beheld the hem of an extremely elaborate white satin apparition descending. "Ah!" Koopvaarder exclaimed effusively. "And here is the Lady Vatusia!"

It wasn't only that the gown would have done Madame Pompadour proud—or that she was wearing more gold than I'd ever seen on one person before—that completely stopped my breath. It was the plain fact that "Lady Vatusia" was African, as black as coal. Dumbfounded to the point of speechlessness, I simply gawked—and sensed that Meneer Koopvaarder was quite enjoying my discomfiture.

But the woman did not lack for aplomb. She approached me and—only once seeking Koopvaarder's reassurance—curtsied, as neatly as anything I'd seen at my dancing class. "Welcome, sir, to our humble abode," she said, her mellifluous voice slurred by the fact that she, too, was somewhat inebriated.

Still befuddled, I collected just enough wit to nod and say, "Ma'am!"

As she preceded me into the salon, I observed that she possessed quite beautiful features, and yet she was long past the age at which casual mistresses of the powerful are reportedly sent out to pasture. Koopvaarder gestured elaborately—there was a hint of condescension—that I should follow. The large, rectangular, cantaloupe-colored room was pleasingly light and airy, and almost as elegant as those in New York City. Handsome furniture pieces, obviously imported from Europe, were placed about, including a polished mahogany table set with china and silver for three.

Vatusia settled herself on one side of a divan, Koopvaarder took the heavily carved oak armchair, and I sat on a straight chair upholstered in purple damask. Absalom followed us, bearing a salver with a porcelain punch bowl that would have done great credit to my family's tavern. He had put it on a sideboard when the lady imperiously commanded him to set it next to her. He removed a vase of yellow hibiscus flowers from the end table, placed the punch where required, and served us each in individual goblets. "That's all," she told him. Absalom promptly retreated out of the room. "Your good health, sir!" she toasted me. I noted that a red ribbon was sewn into her bodice.

"And yours!" I responded, lifting my potion for a sip. The punch was even stronger than that I'd drunk with the two captains.

"You don't like it?" Koopvaarder demanded, having taken a goodly swallow. "Statia's finest rum!"

"It's excellent, sir. I just like to take my time to savor it."

"Ah, tip it down, lad!" he said after another gulp that would've left me gasping. "We've got plenty!"

"Thank you kindly, sir," I said, taking another sip and attempting to gauge whether half could be surreptitiously poured back into the bowl.

"So you're from New York!"

"Aye—and I understand you are as well?"

"A long time ago, my lad. How is business in New York these days?"

It was a relief to change the subject. "Our recent letter suggests it's in quite a lather, Meneer Koopvaarder. The city was doing very well until the army decamped last year, but matters have been slowing since, and recently the general—Amherst, in charge of all His Majesty's North American forces—has decided to take some of his problems out on the mercantile community."

"Oh, isn't that always the way!" Koopvaarder fretted, cynically shaking his head. "What is it this time?"

"He complains that the merchants are trading with the enemy."

"Well, they *are*, of course!" Koopvaarder roared, laughing. "The best account we have in New York is with Trans-Hudson Produce. They send me three ships a year full of salted pork that they know perfectly well I trade for molasses from Guadeloupe!"

"With Aaron Colegrove?"

"Aye, that's the name. With his agents, of course." My distasteful memories must have shown on my face. "You know him, I take it?"

"A former employer, sir ... It's not that I'm horrified by what he's doing, it's that he's one of the loudest patriots insisting everyone should back Amherst to the hilt!"

"Is that not so!" Koopvaarder exclaimed. "And we've been tattling on him!" He and Vatusia found this uproarious. "I take it your firm has no scruple about preserving the French in the Caribbean from starvation?"

"The principals of my firm believe that wars should be fought between armies and not between peoples."

"Good heavens, Vatusia! *Rousseau! Voltaire! Wilkes!* In our own drawing room!" Again they shrieked with mirth. "But seriously, lad," he said after another swallow, "I can only concur that the whole business of the war is most disgraceful. Disgraceful! A passel of spoilt children, these kings and ministers." While I briefly wondered if perhaps a meeting of minds was conceivable, Koopvaarder and his lady began a parody of head-shaking disapproval. "Not that *I* have any objection to their wars, good sir! Oh no, I love their wars! Their wars are very profitable *for me!*"

"For all of us here on Statia," Vatusia added generously.

"Not perhaps as lucrative as my trade in Africans, but valuable nonetheless. I say, I've not seen you down by our slave auctions. We've a particularly fine lot from Angola to be sold on Tuesday. You must be sure to—"

"Thank you, sir, but I … my firm does not elect to deal in slaves. They—"

"What! Why ever not? Preposterous!"

"Many of the officers are Quakers, from Pennsylvania."

"Quakers!" Koopvaarder sniffed. "*Agh*, such hypocrites! As if they didn't run half the ships that bring our stock to us!"

I knew this overstatement to be untrue of our own firm, and was smarting from the insult to my employers. But he blared ahead before I could rejoin. "Surely *you* don't fall for any of this radical nonsense that the trade should be suppressed? A few weak-kneed preachers in London would bring down all this!" He gestured about his salon. I couldn't tell whether Lady Vatusia was meant to be included in the survey or not. "Why, slavery has been the basis of all our civilization since time immemorial."

"The basis of *every* civilization!" Vatusia stiffly concurred—staring at the corner cupboard.

"Surely they must allow you, as supercargo, to trade on your own account? Why don't you pick up just three or four? You could sell them handsomely as soon as you returned!"

I had a purpose to attend this afternoon; this was not the time to indulge in argument. "I shall be quite content with the profits of trading flour for sugar, thank you, Meneer Koopvaarder."

"Ah, well now, if it's profits you're interested in, my lad, you need to forego both slaves and sugar!"

Are we changing the subject, please? *And will he desist from calling me his lad?* "How so, sir?"

"The biggest *coup* that passed through Statia this year—which I am furious did not include me!—was between the quartermaster of royal George's army in America and some firm in Philadelphia, *um*—"

"Atlantic something," Vatusia offered.

"Aye. Tens of thousands of pounds' worth of military stores—artillery, muskets, ammunition, uniforms, tents. All supposed to go directly from Britain to the colonies, of course ... having paid the requisite duties, of course."

"Yes?"

"Ah, but who actually knows what their route was, across the broad ocean? Who truly can say what excises were or weren't paid? Certainly not your high and mighty generals!"

"Oh no, no, no!" Vatusia exclaimed, smiling coyly.

"Ship after ship from England—over two dozen in the last year—arrived here with cargo they hadn't declared on their manifests, and it was all trans-shipped by that firm and sent on to New York, where the army paid full price for it!"

Although my cousin Charles often insinuated that such treacherous commerce existed, I was appalled to hear it asserted as a plain fact.

"If you're ambitious for profit, my friend, *that's* how you go about it! And if you can manage an arrangement on that order, Staats Koopvaarder will be only too glad to service it here on Saint Eustatius, by God!" He gestured for a refill to Absalom, who'd been standing in the threshold. "Isn't it ready yet?" he demanded as his goblet was refilled to the brim. The enslaved agent nodded.

"Our guest's too!" Vatusia commanded.

"I've a sufficiency, thank you!" I protested.

"But we insist!" There was no help for it. Absalom topped my glass and then hers.

Koopvaarder downed another healthy swallow, and I realized he'd likely reach incoherence before I could accomplish my chief purpose. "Meneer Koopvaarder, I beg your indulgence for raising the business at hand, but—"

"Oh heavens, my lad!"

"But I do want to know for certain that you approve the arrangements that … your agent"—I nodded at him—"and I have made, regarding the exchange of our flour for your sugarloaf. Is that entirely to your satisfaction?"

"Seems fine," Koopvaarder said unenthusiastically.

"Are the details precisely in order, by your lights, sir?"

"I'm sure you and he have managed perfectly well, *um,* sir," he said impatiently.

How I yearned for the guidance of Mr. Leavering or Mr. Glasby! What a completely exasperating way to conduct business! I gritted my teeth with the realization that this, my first major international transaction, critical to my career and reputation, has been negotiated with a slave who doubles as a butler, on behalf of a drunkard who can't remember my name!

While I struggled to think of anything to say, the girl who'd waited on us at the factory appeared by the door and nodded to Absalom, who presently brought in a steaming soup tureen and set it on the table. "I do hope you'll enjoy our conch stew, sir," Vatusia said, moving to take the center chair Absalom held out for her, "it's a local specialty."

"I'm sure I will, ma'am." Koopvaarder and I rose and took our seats on either side of her.

"Let's drink to confusion among the generals," Koopvaarder bawled jovially, raising a crystal glass of claret. "May they never discover what's transpiring behind their backs!"

Vatusia joined him in laughing at this witticism. I drank, now hoping only to put the meal past me as deftly as possible. However, the wine was delicious, and the stew, precisely served by my stiffly controlled colleague, was a toothsome novelty to me. My hosts were paying far more attention to the wine, but I saw no reason not to tuck into both.

Trying to keep discussion remotely about business, I inquired how basic services were provided in the lower town and how dear the warehouses were. "I noticed that yours was unusually commodious and very well-organized."

"Oh we thank you, good sir!"

"Perhaps it is a tribute to the care of your steward," I said, nodding at Absalom in the clumsy hope of easing him into the conversation.

Koopvaarder caught my intention. "Maybe you'd like to buy *him*, eh?" Absalom froze with the stew bowl in his hands. "I'll sell him to you!" Koopvaarder held my horrified gaze for seconds before bursting into hilarity. Vatusia joined in, but Absalom's fists were tightened as he set the bowl down. "Absalom! The New Yorker wants to buy you! Your price is being bid up! It'll take you another year to buy yourself out—"

"We have an *agreement*," Absalom said through clenched teeth.

"*Ha!* Jesting! Only jesting! Bring the meat out!"

By now my mood was thoroughly disgruntled, though my appetite was not. Conversation devolved to the safe topic of the provenance of the comestibles and the room's appointments. Fortunately, Vatusia enjoyed hearing herself talk, so the pretense of civility was precariously maintained as I ate heartily.

But that mood was suddenly disrupted again, in the oddest manner. Seeing me with a clean plate, Absalom said, "Would you care for another slice of the mutton, Meneer Dordrecht?"

Koopvaarder suddenly gasped, turned pale, grabbed his wrist and demanded, "What did you say?"

"Are you unwell, sir?"

"What did you just say?"

"I asked if Meneer Dordrecht would like another—"

Koopvaarder rose, bolted from the room, and dashed up the stairs.

"Well, look after him, you fool!" Vatusia ordered, after a few seconds of bafflement. Absalom ran out, and the woman collected herself and asserted, "Do be seated, sir, I'm sure it's nothing. May I offer you another slice?"

For a few moments, she stumbled about, trying to chat while I shamelessly ate and drank my fill, rather relieved by the absence of my host. Presently Absalom returned. He was taking my plate and making apologies for Koopvaarder when the latter abruptly reappeared, considerably disheveled and distracted of mien. He moved purposely toward me, shoved Absalom aside, and pulled over the straight chair. "*Where* are you from?" he demanded fiercely.

"Sir? From New York City, as we—"

"Where were you *born?*"

Resolving to handle myself sensibly in the face of a drunk, I said, "Oh I doubt you've heard of it, sir, it's just a tiny farming hamlet in Kings County, called New Utrecht."

Breathing heavily, he stared intently at me for a quarter minute. "Are you Frederik's son, or Rykert's?"

Both Vatusia and Absalom froze in numb mystification. My unease grew. "You have the advantage of me, sir!"

"Your parents?" he demanded, nearly shouting.

"I am the son of Rykert and Chastity Dordrecht, Meneer Koopvaarder."

"*She* still lives?" Disconcerted even more, I made no reply. He continued to stare at me, unmoving—and I was impelled to examine him in turn. "My name isn't Koopvaarder," he rasped at length, occasioning a visible shudder from the other two. In the instant he said it aloud, I guessed, and recoiled: "It's Gerrit Dordrecht."

In the full minute we regarded each other in silence, I realized it had to be the truth, but a cold perturbation suffused my entire corpus, and I vowed I would never address the man by the name of *Uncle*, to which our consanguinity would entitle him. "Your family has believed you to be dead since before I was born, sir!" I stated coldly. His lips trembled, but he made no response. How many ills, I wondered—from Grootmoeder's senility to Frederik's lassitude to my father's intemperance—might conceivably be laid at the door of this man's cruelty?

"I always meant to …" His voice drifted away.

I stood uneasily, suddenly aware that I had overindulged. "Thank you for dinner," I said to the wall.

"I'll call the carriage," Absalom said as I made my way past Vatusia and came face to face with him.

What was to become of our agreement? For ten seconds I debated renouncing it before caution restrained me. "I think I'll prefer to walk, thank you."

"Meneer Dordrecht, I—"

I turned blindly toward the exit ... and collided with the serving girl, causing her to drop a tray of postprandial cheeses. "Not now, you clumsy slut!" Vatusia bellowed.

Feeling myself the cause of it, from ancient habit in my family's tavern, I squatted to assist the girl as Vatusia rose in a fury. "Can't you see—"

"But your son said—" the girl wailed in protest.

"*Silence!*"

Yet it was out. Stunned, I forewent any assistance to the girl and looked back at the three. I caught both Koopvaarder and Absalom in a simultaneous gesture of turning the head and raising an eyebrow that I characteristically associated with just one other man: Cornelis Dordrecht, my grandfather, fourteen years in his grave.

Naught else could explain it. Absalom was the issue of the union of Koopvaarder and Vatusia—the son of my uncle Gerrit Dordrecht who had made a joke out of the idea of selling to me ... *my first cousin.*

I pulled myself up by the doorframe, turned, and, with great care, walked out and descended the steep steps. But then I began to move quickly and finally to run to the road and onward, down toward the town. After fifty yards, I grabbed onto the trunk of a palm tree, leaned to the side, and retched everything in my stomach.

"Why, good heavens, it's Meneer Dordrecht! Are you taken ill?"

Unsteadily, I got myself upright from the glade where I'd collapsed. "Meneer De Graaff!"

Johannes De Graaff and an attractive woman I presumed to be his wife were sitting in a halted carriage. De Graaff jumped out to take me by the arm. "It's not advisable to nap in full sunlight, young sir!" The sun was at the same angle I last recalled; I couldn't have been long on the ground. But I was still feeling the liquor and was suffused with mortification at the picture I had to be presenting. "You *are* ill! You must let us take you down to town!"

"Oh no, sir, thank you, I can manage!"

"Nonsense, I insist!" With his driver's help, he practically forced me up into the carriage. "This is the young New Yorker who sent us that lovely keg of cider, my dear," he explained.

The lady fretted and patted my forehead considerately with a perfumed handkerchief. "You do need a hat, sir!" she exclaimed. "And why dress so formally to take your exercise?"

The punch and the wine having loosened my tongue, I soon blurted out the entirety of what had just transpired.

"And so Koopvaarder is your uncle?"

"I don't care to claim him, sir. He has disowned his family by allowing us to believe him dead for thirty years!"

A thought suddenly struck De Graaff. "That's where I've seen the name before! When I first took up my position, there was an open case, years old, involving a man who'd evaded his indenture to a shipper ..."

"After three decades, he surely couldn't still be concerned to conceal his name because of that!" Vrouw De Graaff observed.

Suddenly, I was impelled to voice my anxieties regarding my pending business arrangement with Absalom. De Graaff thought it over. "I doubt Koopvaarder would dare to interfere, sir," he said. "The merchants here watch each other more carefully than they let on. With care, you should be able to complete the transaction."

"Even though my contract's been made with a slave?"

"Ah, no matter," he said dismissively, "many here have the like. And he'll soon buy himself out." I must have looked incredulous. "We do things differently here, Meneer Dordrecht!" he added. He and his wife shared a knowing smile.

We reached the intersection of the road from the lower town, and I refused their repeated kind offers to convey me further.

"Do you know," I heard Vrouw De Graaff saying as they pulled away, "we should have realized that 'Staats Koopvaarder' rings false as a name!" I halted, looking out over the harbor, pondering the remark. She was clearly correct, and I smote myself for a simpleton. If you render it into English equivalents, the name would be something like *Eustace Merchantman.*

A note addressed to me was dropped across the rail and retrieved by Parigo. When Trent put it in my hand, I was still in my bunk. I had delayed returning to the ship until late in the evening and had shammed a tipsiness that had long since passed, to avoid having to discuss the day's events. In the morning, still nursing my miserable thoughts, my pretense had been a hangover.

> Meneer Dordrecht,
>
> It would indeed be understandable that you, as agent of Castell, Leavering & Sproul, might hold me, as agent for Koopvaarder's, culpable for the offenses you suffered yesterday, for which I can only express the deepest regret. I beg that you will not do so, however, and will permit our commercial agreement to proceed as scheduled. I promise you that the proprietor was in truth ignorant of your surname (of which he had never deigned to make any inquiry), and that both I and Lady Vatusia were unaware that he himself had any name other than that one by which he has always been known on Saint Eustatius. Please trust that I remain, sir,
>
> Your most humble & obedient servant,
> Absalom Koopvaarder

Still in the bunk, I read this missive over at least ten times, doubt and mistrust contending with its frank and eloquent appeal. What quite took my breath away was not the wish that the business should go through, but the writer's temerity—his impudence, some would no doubt say—in claiming Koopvaarder's spurious patronymic for himself. A New York slave would face a whipping for such effrontery, yet I … could not help being impressed. But how do I deal with him, knowing that we have a blood relation? Do I tell him he has a grandmother in New Utrecht? Uncles, aunts, and a host of cousins?

After half an hour of this, I thrust myself out of bed, shamed. Whatever my personal hesitations and inclinations might be, I had a clear duty to my employers to secure the best available sale of the flour.

"Well, you've perked up!" O'Malley exclaimed.

"*Eh?*" I hadn't noticed he was in the cabin.

"Wish I could recover so easily from a hangover!"

"*Uhh* ... yes. Well, indeed!"

When I presented myself at Koopvaarder's warehouse an hour later, Absalom greeted me with strict formality and made no further reference to what had taken place at Haven Plantation. When I agreed that our compact should proceed, he relaxed slightly and said, "Then we have a great deal of work to do, sir, if your captain hopes to depart 'ere the month is out!"

That work commenced immediately, and much of it was organized by Absalom. He set me in charge of a section of the plantation to oversee the crating. I sensed he was bending over backward to ensure my confidence in the exchange—and in him. He ordered an elaborate iron *CL&S* brand to be fabricated and given to me, to be impressed upon the crates as they were sealed in my sight. Meanwhile, he and Thys began rearranging the warehouse to accommodate the flour. As the transaction progressed, the officers and crew of the *Dorothy C.* became involved as the hogsheads of flour were finally disgorged from her holds, and boxes of sugarloaf replaced them. Happily, Captain Trent had also concluded arrangements with a merchant to whom I'd introduced him, exchanging his goods for barrels of rum. Our section of the anchorage became the locus of frenetic activity from sunup to sundown.

On the many occasions when I was driven past the plantation house on the way to the manufactory, I scanned about in search of Koopvaarder or Vatusia, but I never saw either again. I felt more regret in the formality that continued to strain my interactions with Absalom, but I understood it to be a necessity for both our sakes—and honored the fortitude implicit in his discipline.

After his service on the last Sunday in July, Captain Trent called Fox, O'Malley, and me down to the cabin. "This is for no one's ears but ours, gentlemen," he said quietly. "We shall be leaving on Thursday night. Mr. Dordrecht's last crates are expected tomorrow, and the last of the rum should be stowed by Wednesday. I'd like you two"—O'Malley and myself—"to start topping the water and acquiring our fresh provisions, while Mr. Fox and I quietly clear the decks aboard here."

The conspiratorial air was somewhat mystifying. "May I ask, Captain—I can certainly comply, but why is this secrecy necessary?"

Fox smiled grimly as O'Malley smirked and rolled his eyes. "Have you not noticed that none of the other captains who have left the port have stopped to say farewell beforehand?"

"There are spies ashore, Mr. Dordrecht," Trent said patiently, "and we don't want anyone to alert the privateers or the navy of our departure."

"They'll guess easily enough that it's imminent," Fox added, "but we mustn't give them any help."

"Did you have any other business unfinished, Mr. Dordrecht?" Trent asked.

I hesitated to express a desire I knew would bewilder them. "I … I had hoped to find a day for an excursion to the mountaintop!"

The three of them collapsed in laughter. When it finally subsided, Fox said, "Well … but if he starts off on Thursday morning, no one in the town will ever guess we're thinking of leaving on Thursday night!"

That was good enough for Trent. "He shouldn't go alone!" O'Malley warned. When it was instantly ascertained, to my tacit relief, that O'Malley did not care to accompany me, Parigo was nominated—whether he liked it or not.

But he did like it, though he was clearly mystified why he'd been spared from the ongoing heavy labors shipboard. We progressed through ever-wilder greenery on ever-more-precarious paths until we reached the lookout at noon, alarming a pair of slave signalmen who'd never before seen recreational visitors. They enthusiastically named the five inhabited islands that could be seen from their promontory and showed us the system by which they could alert the fort below if any threats were perceived on the horizon. They recommended we leave the mules with them if we really wanted to pull ourselves up to the summit, still half an hour's climb away, via the ropes strung between tree-trunks.

We did and … I confess to being thrilled as we achieved the top, where we could see the world three hundred sixty degrees around from a vantage far higher than any masthead. Not only could we see the tiny ships coming and going, we could see down into the crater of the volcano—a concave hole that I'd forgotten must exist! I wanted to go all the way down into it, but Parigo reminded me the lookouts had warned us against snakes, so we retreated after half an hour. We shared our comestibles with the signalmen and arrived back at the fort at dusk, sore from riding on the mules. Thinking we still had ample time, I treated Parigo to the convivial tavern I'd discovered on Sunday, where there was music in addition to good food, and they were only too happy to ply you with their rum punch. It was late when we reached the mole, arms about each other's shoulders, bawling at the top of our lungs:

The women all tell me I'm false to my lass,
That I quit my poor Chloe and stick to my glass!
But tell me, ye lovers of liquor divine,
Did you e'er see a frown in a bumper of wine?

Two of the regular launch boys rushed toward us. "Meneer Dordrecht! Hurry! You must hurry!"

"Hurry? Why? What's wrong?"

"Just get in boat!"

They rowed out with a prodigious show of splashing oars. "Anchor cable hove short!" Parigo observed blearily.

"Oh thank God, here they are at last!" O'Malley said. "Get aboard, quickly!"

I just remembered to pass the farewell notes I'd written—with a coin—to the launch boys.

"Up anchor!" Fox called as Parigo reached the rail. "Parigo, get to the bow! Where the devil have you been?" he demanded.

"Sorry? It's … still Thursday night, unless I'm mistaken!"

Bells on other ships could be heard ringing the change of the first watch … but not ours. "Anchor's aweigh!" Parigo called.

"Loose sails and trim to starboard!" Trent commanded from the helm.

Only now was our bell rung eight times. "Close, too close!" Fox wheezed as the *Dorothy C.* gained way. "Mr. Dordrecht, it's now

Friday. You can*not* commence a voyage on a *Friday!* It's … not done!"

"It's bad luck!" O'Malley scowled. "Don't you know *anything?*"

Chapter 7

"*Quiet!*"

I had been regaling Sergei with the splendid day Parigo and I had enjoyed when Trent crossly rebuked me.

"We're trying to leave without drawing unnecessary attention, Mr. Dordrecht!" Fox whispered, recalling me to our circumstances.

It appeared to me that the crew remained in a state of considerable tension.

"Night departure's very tricky, Mr. Dordrecht," Fox said when I pressed him to explain it. "To avoid navigational hazards and the privateers and the navy, we must maintain a perfect course and precise dead reckoning for two days at least. Once we get out of the tropics, I trust our nerves will be calmed."

We were *leaving* Saint Eustatius! The first pangs of homesickness for New York had touched me this week ... but the day's jaunt had been so much fun, I was still reluctant to leave. When might I ever return to this blue-and-green paradise? I watched the lights of the town and the anchorage fade. And I'd never set foot on even one of the other islands!

The moon rose, now in its last quarter. I stood at the rail until I could no longer distinguish the island's silhouette from the sky and the sea.

"Time for your seamanship studies to recommence, Dord– *er,* Mr. Dordrecht!" O'Malley called, with vicious jauntiness, at two bells in the forenoon watch.

I stretched—as much as that was possible—in my bunk, thinking that if O'Malley hoped to bait me with such foolishness, he was picking on the wrong man. "I shall join you directly, *Mister* O'Malley," I said. "I'm sure that will be a worthwhile discipline, and that all the commercial notations and calculations I have to attend to can wait a few more hours!"

The routine of the long journey home was thus initiated: lessons in seamanship, meals with the officers, hours alone to attend to my business notes or reading, the Saturday night gam, and the Sunday morning service. Parigo took me aloft and, with extreme trepidation, allowed me to go out on the yard with the others to unbend the mizzen topgallant sail, which needed a repair. I confess it took all my courage to step out on that rope, seventy feet in the air, but I insisted on making the attempt. O'Malley lectured me on steering, but refused to let me take the wheel until Fox intervened; and then he derisively pointed at the ship's unsteady wake. Fox more kindly explained the points of sail and the optimal trim for each angle of the wind relative to one's direction. And Captain Trent agreed to explain the intricate details of the calculation of lunar distances that reckon our longitude—a training he'd not yet provided to O'Malley. Noting my mathematical predilections, he eventually had me double-checking his own estimations.

Everything proceeded swimmingly for seventeen days. *Dorothy C.* made good progress in her everlasting north-northwesterly course, mercifully escaping both criminal and official notice on the high seas. A fish was occasionally caught, I completed my notes and letters and finished reading several books, and Fox proclaimed that if I really wanted to be rated an Ordinary Seaman, I could be. It was grand.

And then we ran out of wind. On the passage south, we'd had light winds for a day here or there—and they permitted one to walk easily about. But to have the wind and, of course, the boat *stop dead* for four days in broiling August, northwest of Bermuda, was sheer torture. It was surprising how stoically the sailors endured it. I felt myself on the brink of going mad, gibbering nonsense to the cat to induce any feeling of change.

And then, finally, the long-predicted blessed deliverance, whose reality you'd begun to doubt, arrived. For a day, the universal relief was palpable in every cranny of the ship. It then blew more strongly, and I began to think of my priorities ashore.

And then it blew *more* strongly, and more, and still more. One by one, the sails were furled tight. The topmen would return to the deck, exhausted, only to be sent immediately back for another. "Not too anxious to climb those ratlines now, eh?" O'Malley teased. Given that he was struggling to hold the wheel, I contented myself with thinking that he wouldn't be too anxious to go aloft either. Fox called Parigo and me and three others to go below to double-lash the cargo. The thought of the cargo's weight suddenly shifting to one side was horrifying.

It was dark when we returned to the deck. We were reduced to two small fore-and-aft sails and heading west of our rhumb line to keep control of the ship. The new hat I'd bought in Statia instantly blew overboard. When Parigo reported eighteen inches of water in the bilge, my first concern was for the sugar. Captain Trent ordered me to join three others at the capstan pump. When twenty-two inches were reported an hour later, I realized the ship itself could be in danger.

And then the rain came, and the winds blew it horizontally, punching into one's face. It hailed, and one of the strongest seamen broke his arm slipping on the ice. He was nonetheless ordered to help work the pump with his good arm so that one of our foursome could replace him on the deck. Hour after hour, we marched in a circle, struggling to hold ourselves upright against the unprecedented pitching and rolling of the ship. A slimy gray dawn arrived, and the rain abated, but the wind continued. Anxiety showed on all the men's faces as Trent ordered us to heave to, to turn directly into the wind as we had for the navy's inspections. The danger under such circumstances, Fox had said, was being unable to complete the turn, and thus to be caught broadside at the waves' mercy. But we succeeded, and I was sent below with the understanding that I'd be summoned again in four hours.

When I was shoved awake, I could hardly believe any time had passed. For yet another watch, I pushed around in a circle, a human ox. The bilge level stayed dangerously high, but did not rise. It was the legendary medieval drowning cell of Amsterdam made manifest! The winds did not drop, but the motion was easier, and the officers remained certain that we'd not been pushed so far westward as to lack sea room relative to the coast. I was permitted another watch asleep, and endured a further turn at the pump. When Fox next shoved me, he said the wind had dropped somewhat, we were back on course, and I'd been allowed two watches asleep, but was needed one more time at the pump. "It's over, then?"

"The worst is over, Mr. Dordrecht."

"*Whoof!* I guess that's about the worst the ocean can do, *eh*, Mr. Fox?"

The look he gave me instantly made me glad I hadn't voiced such a stupid remark to O'Malley, who was snoring nearby. "Mr. Dordrecht," Fox said simply, "those who suffer the *worst* the ocean can do generally don't come home to tell the tale."

When it was finally possible again to take sights, the captain determined that we were roughly three hundred miles from Cape Hatteras, in North Carolina, far to the west and about a hundred miles farther overall from where we had been before the storm. Fox and I inspected the holds, and I was relieved to find that, thanks to the relentless pumping from which all my muscles still ached, the bilge had never risen over the floor. We set a northerly course, unbent the sails, tended wounds, repaired damage, and began to anticipate our landfall within the week.

Land was sighted dead ahead at dusk on Saturday, the twenty-eighth. Our reckoning of longitude was clearly off, as we had expected to find New Jersey on our port side, rather than Long Island in front. Unable to discern exactly where we stood along that featureless coast, we headed back out to sea and hove to, awaiting the sun. But when dawn arrived, it was sheathed in fog so thick, it was impossible to take sights, and was accompanied by only the lightest southerly breeze. Captain Trent conducted a surprisingly perfunctory Sabbath service, sent two men aloft, and ordered an extremely cautious northwesterly course.

The captain was not too proud to ask our location of a black fisherman an hour later. We were south of Freeport, fifteen miles east of the lower bay. We found a coin with which to buy half a dozen of his cod and headed west with raised confidence. Before noon—with fog still impeding visibility—we were surprised to find a fisherman pursuing *us*. "It *is* her!" a man shouted, waving his arms. "*Dorothy C.! Dorothy C.!*" Trent allowed the sails to flap, and we slowed even more as the fisherman approached. "Message for you, Captain!" the man at the tiller bellowed. The two hulls knocked together with a great thump. Parigo lowered a bucket to him. He took the coin out and placed a small envelope inside, saying, "Glad I didn't toss this over! We was afeared you'd gone down with that storm!" He found that very funny.

"Not at all," Trent returned tolerantly. "Many thanks!"

The envelope was jointly addressed to Trent and myself. We took it aft. It was in Mapes's scribbled pen, with Glasby's signature. How many times had they copied it out?

> Situation much changed. Urgent avoid HMN. Do not venture NY bay. Amboy, Marcus Hook below Phila., Newport if must. J. Glasby

"My God!" Trent breathed—from him, a vehement statement!

I sank onto the rail in great disappointment as Trent passed the note to Fox and O'Malley. Here we were, practically—no, actually, as the weather had cleared slightly—in sight of the Narrows, yet ordered to sail elsewhere. We had had but one further missive from Glasby before we left Statia, which had suggested that relations had worsened between the army and the city merchants, but this was quite a shock.

O'Malley was scanning the horizon with the telescope. "I doubt you want to head for Perth Amboy, gentlemen," he said. "There's a full-rigged representative of His Majesty's Navy at anchor inside Sandy Hook!"

Groaning, Trent took the spyglass for a minute. "He's right," he sighed, lowering it. "Let me pray on it a moment." He nodded to Fox, and they descended to the cabin—to examine their charts, I presumed.

"May I?" I asked O'Malley, who was holding the telescope. An alternative notion had occurred to me. It was still hazy, but I now had my bearings. I turned my gaze to the northeast … and found what I'd hoped to see. "Mr. O'Malley!"

"What now?"

"Look here. How big would you guess that ship is?" I pointed to an anchored three-master visible behind a sandy spit. "As big as *Dorothy C.*?"

"Likely."

"With as great a draft?"

"Possible. Where is that?"

"Sheepshead Bay. South coast of Kings County."

"So?"

"It's just three miles from my hometown, eight miles from Brooklyn. And I happen to know everybody and every barn in between."

He lowered the telescope, a wry smile on his face. "Maybe there's a point to having a landsman on board after all, Mr. Dordrecht! Worth a look!"

I hurried below to confront Trent and Fox.

"Ah, Mr. Dordrecht," Trent said, immediately including me in the ongoing conversation, "it's likely we could reach Newport a dozen hours sooner than we might reach Marcus Hook, but you would probably have more difficulty getting your goods to market in New York City from—"

I blurted out my suggestion.

"*Sheepshead* Bay? But that's … just three miles away."

"If we can get in at all, we can get in before dark."

"But Mr. Dordrecht," Fox objected unhappily, "if we have seen the warship, the warship has seen us, and—"

"But *they'll* never get into that bay," Trent countered.

"They could send the army!"

"By the time the army gets there," I asserted—with perhaps an excess of bravado, "I'll have everything off the boat and stored in three dozen barns all over the county! They'll all be empty now in anticipation of the harvest, and before the harvest arrives, we'll have moved it all overland and via small boats into the city."

"But what if—"

"I've got that fisherman back alongside," O'Malley bellowed down from the deck. "Says he can pilot us in!"

"What's the depth, for heaven's sake, O'Malley?"

"Ten feet around the bar at low water—but we just passed the low, he says."

Captain Trent inhaled and exhaled deeply. "I'll leave the decision to you, then, Mr. Dordrecht! Both Philadelphia and Newport are perfectly viable options, as far as the ship is concerned. But I've never even seen this harbor before."

"I think we should try it, Captain Trent. Even at the worst, if we somehow lose a quarter of the cargo, the firm will be better off than if it has to be moved so far overland."

"Fox?"

"What happens to *Dorothy C.*, once she's off-loaded?"

"We'll see if we can't contact Mr. Glasby for an answer by then," I said.

"I've no objection, Captain."

"Then let's be on with it!"

Trent and Fox hurried up the companionway, and, in my enthusiasm, I once more struck my head on the lintel. No blood was drawn, but I was again chastened in caution's favor. And of course, once on deck, I realized that I faced two hours of inactivity yet before I could be put ashore. Parigo was already sounding the depth with the lead line. Following our amateur pilot, we kept on well to the west of Breezy Point before Trent ordered a jibe to turn us toward the harbor entrance. Excited as I was to watch, I'd have no better moment to dash off some notes of my own, so I repaired to the cabin.

"That's the stupidest-looking hat I ever saw!"

My cousin Bertie Hampers was the first person I saw as I rode into New Utrecht. After surviving another bout of sea legs, borrowing a horse, and riding it as fast as I dared to my hometown, I'd completely forgotten that Parigo's makeshift bonnet was back atop my head. I ripped it off; then, not knowing what else to do with it, I replaced it.

"But welcome home anyway, Thomas!"

"Well thanks, Bertie. Where is everyone?"

"Still in kerk," he groaned, nodding across the road. "The dominie is developing a thesis on the *conferentie*, and this is the third week he has inflicted it on the entire congregation."

"How'd you escape?"

"Feigned being deathly ill this morning!"

I laughed. "You can still get away with that—as a twenty-four-year-old father of three?"

"Father of four, Thomas! Jenneken gave me another son in April!"

"Oh yes, Mother wrote me. Congratulations! But—"

"Your family is also set to increase!"

"Ah! All are well?"

"Aye. Except Uncle Rykert was in a brawl a few weeks ago, up in Brooklyn."

"What!"

"A bad one! Lucky to escape with a couple bruises and cracked ribs—but they made him resign as schout." I groaned over this blow. My father's sinecure as the town's sheriff was his last hold on any public respect. "When did you get back?" Bertie asked.

"An hour ago!"

"An *hour* ago!"

His startled reaction finally gave me the opportunity to assert my pressing quest.

"Well, why not—*Ha, a hymn! At last!* You could address the whole town at once, Tom. You'd better go in there, because the lot of them are going to *run*, right after the benediction!"

He was right, so we walked over and put our ears next to the kerk's blue doors. "Aha!" Bertie said. "He's about to close. It's now or never, lad!" He pulled the door open for me. "*The hat!*"

I whipped it off again and strode into the church—and had the distinct sensation that everyone was shaking themselves awake from a deep sleep. Certainly my arrival occasioned a good deal of comment! I proceeded down the aisle and indicated to the dominie that I would like to speak.

I had feared that Van Voort would be outraged, but I underestimated him. "Thomas Dordrecht! We have prayed, weekly, for your safe return, and here are our prayers answered!"

Amid the cries of *hallelujah* that followed, I managed to blow a kiss to my mother, sitting with the family in the Dordrecht pew. I drew myself up to address the assembly, apologized for my abrupt appearance and for disrupting the service, and then stated my mission as succinctly as I could, begging that every available man, woman, child, slave, horse, cart, and barn might be commandeered to the temporary service of Castell, Leavering & Sproul within the hour. No one appeared to have any difficulty when it became obvious that the necessity derived from an imperative to avoid the royal authorities, nor even when I urged them not to boast of it about the county. However, when I suggested that, of course, some form of reward would be found for their effort—

"Thomas, this is the Lord's Day! You cannot ask us to *labor* on the Sabbath!"

For a second he stumped me—and then some blessed inspiration evoked, "I'm only begging a neighborly favor, Dominie!" His congregation was clearly eager to garner a little unexpected coin—not to mention desperate for exercise—and so Van Voort conceded that, *in that case ...*

We Dutch are nothing if not a practical people!

Even he himself was pressed into service—to hand-deliver my urgent letters to Glasby and Leavering, with a stop at my sister's in Flatbush.

As all fled out to fresh air, there was a moment to embrace my family. The excitement was so high, nobody even remarked the extraordinary recovery of Engelbertus Hampers from the dire malady that had prevented his dutiful attendance four hours before. My niece was begging Harmanus to take her along. "Certainly not!" he decreed.

"But you're taking Hendrick!"

"That's different!"

"Wait a second, Harmanus," I said. "Berendina, how is your penmanship coming?"

"Vrouw Nijenhuis gave me high marks!"

"Is that so!" She nodded with eager enthusiasm. "She could be of use to me, Harmanus," I whispered.

"Oh very well. Run and change … and get all your writing gear!" Berendina and Hendrick ran back to the house. "Mind you watch out for her, Thomas, she's but eleven. I don't like it that there will be sailors about!"

"The sailors will treat her like a princess, brother!" He sniffed, unimpressed. "I must hurry back to the ship and make ready," I announced. "I hope to see everyone by Sheepshead Bay as soon as possible!"

Dozens of barrels and crates were already piled on the shore when I returned, as I'd requested. "People are coming?" Trent demanded nervously. "I don't forecast rain, but these goods should not stay here overnight!"

"An army of stevedores will be here shortly, Captain!" I assured him, simultaneously thinking that Hendrick could be made useful directing traffic counter-clockwise through the settlement. And presently they began to appear, led by Bertie Hampers and Eben Stanley, Marijke Van Voort's foreman. He had thought to bring three of Loytinck's burly slaves, whom I asked to assist with loading the carts. Harmanus arrived, and I set his daughter to taking detailed notes on the cargo and destination of every wagon as it headed out. I pulled Vrijdag aside to brighten his day with news of his nails.

Starting in mid-afternoon, with many making two or even three trips, the job was completed before dusk, much to Captain Trent's amazement. "It took five days to load that boat, and you've off-loaded her in five hours!"

"Ah, well, having a dock and dry land surely helps!"

A note had been returned from John Glasby, advising Trent, if empty of goods, to proceed into the harbor after all. An official document indicating that *Dorothy C.* had discharged all her goods in Charleston, South Carolina, signed by well-paid officials, was enclosed. "I fear another occasion for perjury may be required, Captain," I said. He grimaced. "All in a good cause!" I added, attempting levity.

"As you will, Mr. Dordrecht!" he said, shaking his head.

Harmanus and Bertie brought the last wagons. My brother collected his excited, but tired and cranky children, while Bertie waited for me to retrieve my dunnage and say thanks and farewell to the crew. Even though I expected to see them all again in the city within the week, after five exciting months aboard, the abrupt parting much affected me. Even with O'Malley!

Wonders never cease!

Having enjoyed a dandy nap while the rest of the town had been struggling to stay awake, Bertie was now far livelier than I, who was ready to admit to exhaustion. He begged a complete description of my entire journey as we trundled back to New Utrecht in declining light. I had barely recounted our escape from Sandy Hook when we saw the first houses of the town. "Oh! And I saw a ghost!"

"Sure you did! Your pious Quaker friend ranting against slavery, perhaps?"

If I'd forgotten poor Mr. Sproul, others hadn't. "Not funny, Bertie!"

"Sorry. You saw a ghost?"

"Gerrit Dordrecht is alive and flourishing on Saint Eustatius!"

His jaw—and the reins—dropped. I grabbed the latter and brought us to a halt in the middle of the road. "Uncle Gerrit is *alive?*"

"He's been there for thirty years. Uses a different name ..."

"What!"

Suddenly the revulsion I'd felt for my uncle made me sorry I'd opened my mouth. "Maybe it'd be better if we didn't talk about him."

"Why?"

I groaned, stuck. "Promise to keep it just between us?"

"*Huh?* Oh, all right. If you say so."

Chapter 8

My rumbling stomach—and the awareness that I'd need to get myself into the city in the morning—finally prompted me to halt my own tale and demand we drive on to the inn. There, I devoured the midday meal that my mother had warmed over—my first fresh grub in a month!—and begged to be excused to sleep.

"So, Gerrit is still alive?" my mother asked as she served me breakfast late the next morning.

For a second, I was too dumbfounded to reply. "Aye. Bertie wasn't supposed—"

"It's all over town, Thomas. Katryne told me."

"Do they know … everything?"

"The African wife? The enslaved mulatto son? Yes. The children have already been teased about it."

"I'm … sorry."

"It's the truth, though? He is Gerrit?"

"Aye. Nothing else could explain his knowledge of our family."

My mother looked away pensively. "I've always felt … guilty about him."

"What! *You?*"

She sighed. "When your father first brought me out here from the city, Gerrit was fifteen, and I'm afraid he became infatuated with his older brother's intended. Nobody else was even talking to me—I knew no Dutch then—and so I … allowed him to carry on … But he was a foolish, impetuous boy, and he got out of hand and attempted to force himself—"

"Oh my God."

"Fortunately, I held him off until Rykert caught him. But then he and Cornelis beat Gerrit absolutely bloody, and he disappeared the same day. It was only weeks later that we learned he had indentured himself to a sea captain out of Boston—"

"From whom he ran away on Saint Eustatius."

She sighed again. "He was such a pious, earnest lad. Wrote poems for me."

Poems? Koopvaarder? I shook my head in disbelief. "He's a brute, Mother."

"I suppose he must be," she said with uncharacteristic gentleness and reluctance.

"Has anyone attempted to tell Grootmoeder?"

She shook herself. "No. And I strongly recommend against it. For thirty years, she's believed the only reason her son hasn't made contact was because he was dead and couldn't. She's beyond gossip. Why disabuse her now?"

I finished my breakfast.

"Brevoort has gone into the army again," she announced uneasily.

"Oh no. Whatever possessed him to …? You'd think after the Niagara campaign laid him flat for six months—"

"Needs the money. His wife wrote me—otherwise, I'd never have known."

"Where is he now?"

"I don't even know that. There was a great flotilla that sailed out of here two months ago"—this was news to me—"and the speculation is they headed south to attack the Spanish."

Would it never end? I took my mother's hand and squeezed it. "I have to rush into the city, Mother. I have to face my employers! I think they'll be satisfied with my commercial decisions, but I've stuck my neck out by landing it all in Sheepshead Bay."

"I'm sure you've done splendidly, Thomas!"

My bosom swelled at this declaration. We stood, and I embraced her. "There's much to tell of my trip that was wonderful, Mother.

I expect to be back very soon, perhaps even tonight." I gathered my possessions—and the notes my niece had left for me. I scanned them quickly. "Tell Berendina she did very well!"

I had contemplated trying to take a first cartload into town, but the imperative was to get myself there, so I made off straightaway on foot. It was not quite noon when I was stepped onto New York island, feeling a great flutter of excitement, though it was every bit as wiltingly hot as Saint Eustatius. I'd barely gotten off the reeking wharf when I inadvertently walked in front of a drayman, causing him to rein his horse to the side. He kept right on going, but shouted, "Arsehole!" back at me.

So good to be home! First, I went over to my boarding house on Chambers Street, where I retrieved my stored effects, negotiated a room, changed, and washed my face. I proceeded then directly back to the office, where Cyrus Mapes, the last to see me out, was the first to welcome my return. "Behold, the prodigal son!" he teased—loudly. I was startled to notice some gray hairs at the temples of his annoyingly cherubic face.

"Grand to see you too, Mapes!" I returned, nodding at the grinning others. "Are Mr. Glasby and the boss in?"

He shook his head. "Mr. Leavering is expected in an hour, and Mr. Glasby went up to Kip's Bay this morning, to scout for barges to haul your stuff across the river. They'll be hoping for a full report!"

"Of course. But … why did Mr. Glasby go so far north? Can't we just bring goods across here on the ferry, or on our own barges directly to the slip?"

Mapes lowered his voice. "Ah, things have gotten *very* tight in the last months, Dordrecht! There are inspectors, there are *spies,* all over the waterfront! We have to go around them."

"I gathered there were problems from your note, but—*spies?* How many times did you have to write that note out?"

Mapes groaned. "Thirty-five times! Then we had to get them distributed all around the lower bay. But the fishermen are getting used to the drill. We aren't the only firm trying to scare off its returning ships!"

"Huh."

"And yes, spies! There's a sharply dressed fellow loitering about the wharves, says he's hoping for work as a stevedore. No one's been foolish enough to hire him, yet he's returned daily for over a month now."

"Not a very competent spy, in that case."

"That may be. But someone is rewarding him for the attempt. Along those lines, incidentally, are you certain none of the hometown people you pressed into service yesterday will betray us?"

"Oh, for heaven's sake, man!" I spluttered, outraged.

Mapes shrugged. "As I said, things have … Did you know that they've declared a general embargo against all provisions leaving the port? No, you couldn't have received that letter, I suppose. But have you seen the harbor? Full of idle ships!"

"I thought something looked wrong as I crossed on the ferry."

"Aye. What really poured sand in the works, though, was when they brought criminal charges against eighteen merchants at once!"

"Eighteen! *Criminal*, not civil?"

"That's right. Mr. Glasby even speculated that Mr. Leavering might well have been included … if he hadn't been fortuitously out of the city!"

"Oh no!"

Mapes was getting riled just retailing this history. "Aye. He got back just in time to add his name to the four dozen merchants who publicly protested."

I shook my head. "All of this is Amherst's doing?"

"Amherst? No, General Monckton is our governor now—yet another military governor! Monckton came north as Amherst went south with the fleet."

"I did hear about that. Where … ?"

"The betting's on Cuba, I understand. Havana being the richest city in America, they hope to plunder it before a general peace is finally declared! Finally doing something sensible!" Mapes laughed.

"You're jesting, right?" He shrugged. "When will Mr. Glasby be back?"

"Soon, I should imagine, so we can all confer."

"Ah. I'd better reorganize my notes, then. My niece wrote down my calls of the contents of each wagon and its destination, but what we'll need now is to ponder what goods are in each barn."

"Aha, yes, I'd say that's a priority!"

We separated, and I moved to sit again at my desk. For just an instant, I mused that, while it was good to travel, it was also very wonderful to return—but perhaps I was just relieved to sit down after hours in motion. I then went to work. I reread Berendina's lists, decided how I would proceed, opened the desk to retrieve quill, ink, and paper ... and found a faintly familiar envelope. I pulled it out with the materials. *Oh, the one from Mrs. Leavering ... with the cards.* I opened it again. Dully, I noted that the design of the cards *was* exactly identical to the deck Absalom Koopvaarder had shown me. But why had she sent them back to me? Oh, because she was in great distress at that time, I recalled, and perhaps not thinking clearly. How on earth could I possibly return them to the rightful owner? I contemplated dropping the entire envelope into the waste bin—but Mr. Leavering returned just then, and I stuffed everything back in the desk.

When he first came into the room, I had to turn my head away for a second to master my reaction. In the five months since I'd last seen him, Benjamin Leavering had aged notably. He had lost a great deal of weight, which one might think would work toward a contrary impression, yet he was sallow, halt, and short of breath. I walked over to present myself and, to my great relief, something of the man I'd known and admired for years reasserted itself. "Mr. Dordrecht!" he boomed, taking my hand firmly. "How good to see you safely back among us!"

He, Mapes, and I retired into his private office, and Mr. Leavering postponed personal details and got right to business. "First of all, Mr. Dordrecht, can you summarize what you've brought back from the islands?"

"For the firm's account, sir, there are four dozen crates of sugarloaf, totaling approximately fifteen thousand, six hundred pounds, and—"

"Sugar*loaf*? Oh excellent!"

"And thirty-two casks of Saint Eustatius rum, totaling about a thousand gallons, that Captain Trent exchanged for the naval stores."

"Aha, well, this is a very good haul. I—"

"Plus, we have eight rolls of raw Irish linen—about five hundred yards; a bill of exchange for fifty pounds sterling ..." I extracted the bill from my notebook and handed it over.

"This was all in exchange for the flour?" Mapes said incredulously, looking up from the notes he was making.

"No, it was part of Captain Trent's arrangement for the naval stores. The flour was matched evenly by the sugar. Oh, plus three barrels of lemons, which I dispatched to my sister's care in Flatbush. We should market those as soon as possible."

Mr. Leavering looked impressed and pleased. "And what did you acquire on your own account, out of curiosity?"

"Three crates of Dutch fireplace tiles, sir, and some two dozen iron and steel farming tools."

"Indeed! Well, you should—"

"And a spinet and two violins."

"My goodness! You should be able to dispose of all those fairly profitably. Now, the ship is entirely off-loaded, I understand? Do we have any word of her, incidentally?"

"She was spotted in the Upper Bay this morning, Mr. Leavering," Mapes asserted, "anchored by the Kill Van Kull awaiting the incoming tide."

"*Hmm*. Might be as good a place as any for her to sit tight!" At my baffled reaction, he explained, "We have nothing to put back into her, Mr. Dordrecht, that we are currently permitted to export from this city!" He thought for a few more seconds. "Yes! Mapes, let's send word immediately to Captain Trent, that though we'll be glad to see him at his earliest convenience, the *Dorothy C.* should be secured inside the upper bay, but not brought to the wharf." Mapes nodded and left to attend to this errand. "How did you fare as a sea-traveler, Mr. Dordrecht? I'm told that was a hurricane, last week!"

"Mr. Fox says it was only a gale, sir—though I will frankly tell you it was terrifying enough. But I can boast that I never once forfeited my dinner to the slop bucket!"

"Excellent. Perhaps you'll be commissioned for travel again sometime."

"I should like that, sir—though perhaps not right away! And may I inquire how you and Mrs. Leavering fare?"

Instantly I realized the question was wrongly timed. "*Ah* …" he replied evasively.

To my rescue, Mapes reappeared, with John Glasby following. "Thomas!" the latter exclaimed, beaming, clasping a shoulder as he shook my hand. "I rejoice to see you back with us … Mr. Dordrecht," he added, recalling our more formal commercial proprieties, to Mapes's relief.

"Mr. Dordrecht has just summarized the accumulated goods returned on the *Dorothy C.*," Mr. Leavering said. Mapes handed him his listing.

Glasby whistled. "We may make some money on this voyage after all!" he exclaimed—to my dismay, as I'd assumed the firm would profit handsomely.

"Was it not a good idea to debark in Kings County, then, sir?" I asked somewhat meekly.

"No, no, it's not that. It will be far less costly to retrieve goods from Long Island than from Newport or even Perth Amboy, but … our entire market is drastically down from its level six or twelve months ago, so we expect to net substantially less than we might have hoped for when you left.

"But to return to the matter at hand," Glasby continued—with Mr. Leavering standing aside, nodding complacently—"where are all the goods now? First of all, how many cartloads were there?"

Thus commenced the detailed planning of the retrieval of the ship's abruptly off-loaded goods, which took over an hour. Mr. Leavering excused himself in the middle, asking Mr. Glasby to manage it.

"He seems a little better today, don't you think?" Glasby inquired of Mapes as he returned from seeing the boss to the door.

"That's the longest he's stayed here in weeks," Mapes agreed. "Perhaps the success of the voyage has encouraged him." Mapes, I had learned in passing, had been promoted, in recognition of his assistance to Glasby during Leavering's and my absence, so that he and I were now equal in rank. And that, I was glad to discover, seemed to relieve his combativeness toward myself.

It was decided that Mapes and I would travel to Flatbush directly and retrieve the two cartloads in my brother-in-law's barn. Mapes would see them back to New York while I would continue on to New

Utrecht. From there, I would oversee the loading of carts to be sent to various waypoints—Red Hook, Brooklyn, and Maspeth in Queens—where Mapes would attempt to manage inconspicuous transport across to Manhattan. The roads being decently dry and hard, we estimated the whole could be accomplished within the week. Fortunately, the firm had amassed several hundred bit pieces of Spanish dollars, with which silver I could recompense everyone for their help to date. Glasby pulled me aside as we prepared to leave, to express the hope that he and his wife would soon be able to entertain me to supper.

In Flatbush, Mapes had to endure ten minutes of familial gushing before we got him on his way with the lemons and the four kegs of rum that had been stored in Berend's brewery. Geertruid presented me with baby Frans Kloppen, my latest nephew, who had actually been born in January, before I left. She pressed me to linger, but I declined, wanting to reach home before dark. For next four days, I stayed at the inn—as a paying commercial customer!—and was continuously occupied with the logistics of organizing, borrowing, renting, loading, and moving, with not a little buying and selling and keeping notes in between. Each of our deliveries had to go to a different place; Mapes informed me each afternoon where he'd arranged for the following day's load.

Having had time to plan, Mother organized a family reunion for Friday evening. Even my sister Lisa Willett and her husband came all the way from Jamaica, in the next county. Though very tired, I rallied to tell everyone about the blueness of the ocean, the trip to the volcano top, and the gale. Once the children were tucked away, I also related the flight from Sandy Hook, the slave auction, and, of course, all about our long-lost uncle.

I walked Lisa and Roderick out to their buggy, tethered in front of the house. "Was I the only one who noticed that Pa was not present tonight?"

"No, Thomas," Lisa said. "But the others have grown used to it."

"It's almost as if they consider him already dead," Roderick observed grimly. "Sorry!" he added.

"Can't be faulted for telling truth," Lisa asserted.

"I've only seen him twice since I got back. Barely had time to wave."

"Mother told me he took it very hard when they forced him to resign. He's apparently trying to stay sober." Roderick made a dubious face and Lisa shrugged.

"Why did they suddenly decide they couldn't let him finish his term as schout?"

"The tavern brawl in Brooklyn was the last straw, I believe, Thomas. The whole county heard about it."

"A man was killed, you know!" Roderick added.

"Oh no! All Bertie told me was that Pa got banged up."

"I think the selectmen considered it a great embarrassment to the town," Lisa said.

"What does he do with himself, if he's trying temperance for a change?"

"Walks by the shore on dry days, plays patience on rainy days."

"Ye gods!"

We all sighed with regret … and exasperation. "We have to get moving, my dear," Lisa said. "If the moon doesn't cloud over, we shouldn't have any trouble, but still, it's a long way. Welcome home!"

"Oh! Marinus asked me to send his regards, Thomas!" her husband called as they started up the Kings Highway.

My friendship with his brother, a chum from our tumultuous months in the provincial army, had brought the couple together. "And mine to him, Roderick! Good night now!"

The only chore remaining was to move the goods I'd acquired on my private account into the city, where the firm would rent me warehouse space until I could dispose of them. I had already sold several tools and a third of the tiles for a smart profit right there in New Utrecht, but I presently realized it would require two trips to move the rest. After breakfast, I walked over to our family's field to the northwest of the town, where Harmanus had settled those goods in a barn. The sky was heavily overcast, and I realized rain would inevitably make this morning's trip a mess—but I should be thankful to have had six days without.

Inside the barn, my father was sitting on one of the chests of tiles, his back to me. "Joachim?" he called.

"It's me, Pa." He grunted—my enthusiastic welcome. Stung by his indifference, I proceeded to look about for the harness gear. "Joachim will be over in a few minutes, Pa, to help me with the cart, once he and Harmanus finish repairing the coop."

Pa completed his hand of patience, which he'd been playing atop another chest, and collected his cards.

"How are you faring, Pa?"

"Tolerably," he said without conviction.

"I hear you're—"

"I hear *you* found my sniveling little brother Gerrit alive and well after all these years, down there in the Caribbean! Topping it the swell, no less. If he were back here, I'd beat him up again!"

He was risible, pathetic.

I told him, "You're in no shape to challenge—"

"*And* he's consorting in sin with a—"

"Well now, aren't you a fine one to complain of the sins of others!" He folded his arms and pouted. I sat on the other chest, facing him. "Pa, I'm glad to hear you've sworn off the—"

"It's only temporary!" He refused to look me in the eye. "Until I feel better!"

"It must have been a shock to have them demanding your resignation?"

"That damned pompous fat-ass Van Klost! For God's sake, that brawl wasn't my fault! They—"

"What happened, Pa? When was this, anyway?"

"What's it now, September? Back in June, end of June. We was playing Piquet, like usual. Two toughs come in, no one's ever seen before, but they're friendly-like. They sit with us, and—"

"Who is that, Pa?"

"Joe. You remember Joe! Used to be the constable up there before he got so fat."

"Joe … Wicklow?" Pa nodded, and I recalled his unfortunate friendship with a thoroughly disreputable lout with whom I'd had briefly to deal, three years back. "You were playing cards?"

"Aye. They joins us for a few hands, everything's fine. And then, out of nowhere, the shorter one says to Joe, he hears his woman is the best whore the town's got!"

"Criminy!" Of course, one of my dim recollections of Wicklow was of him mooning after the most outrageous harlot I'd *ever* encountered. "So, he took offense, I gather?"

"Yeah, he popped the guy one. Foolish. The guy was twenty years younger than him. He jumps on Joe, and the whole place is in a roil. I throw a punch at the other guy, he grabs a chair and shoves it into my ribs, and I'm down right away."

"Are they healing up at all?"

He shrugged and rubbed his chest. "Suppose so. Still hurt like hell. Anyway, some of the other folks are fighting with the taller bloke, who's fending them off while the stocky little one is beating on Joe, and I'm trying to get back up."

"Where was the proprietor?"

"Trying to get his musket loaded. But before he did, the two of them lit off. Ran out and ran away, fast."

"*Huh!* But I heard a man was killed?"

"Well … yeah. Joe."

"Joe Wicklow was the man killed?"

"Aye. Everybody picked himself up, after, excepting him. He was gone."

I tried, but I couldn't marshal even the most perfunctory expression of regret. "Did anyone go after the men?"

"The ones who weren't limping, maybe. But they'd disappeared. There was no moon. Probably had their own dinghy, and just rowed away over to the New York side."

"My God!" No matter how little love I felt for Wicklow, this fracas was appalling. And the more I thought about it … it surely seemed *odd.* But Joachim arrived, and the two of us commenced loading the cart and hitching the horse.

A quarter-hour later, the cart full, it was time to say good-bye. I found Pa in the back, standing by the workbench next to the window, intent on another game of patience. "Pa, I'm off, and—"

The cards. My father's cards were the same as the deck Absalom had shown me! I impulsively grabbed one to make sure. "Hey! What the hell—"

"Pa, where'd you get these?"

"Don't you take that tone with—"

"No no, Pa, I'm just curious. This isn't one of the decks I bought for the inn two years ago, and I happen to know these are very rare."

"I didn't *steal* them, for—"

"I know that, I'm only curious, I say! Do you have the entire deck?"

"I have all fifty-two. Couldn't play without!"

"But not the tarot set? Or the fourth face cards?"

"*Huh?* No, just the … What's this all about, Thomas?"

I could hardly answer that question in my own mind. "Where'd you get them, Pa?" I persisted.

"Well, they were Joe's, if you must know!"

"Joe's?" Somehow my memory went blank.

"Joe Wicklow's, you ninny. Just talking about him! We'd been playing with them when it all happened. I picked them up after it was over."

"They were his, not the tavern's?"

"There you go again!"

"I just want to know!"

Pa snorted with irritation. "Yeah, they were his. He'd taken to bringing his own, because the tavern only had one deck."

"Huh. Had he always done that?"

He rolled his eyes. "I don't know … No. He only started bringing them a few months before. We sometimes just had to wait before that."

Joachim was gaping at the two of us, but I stood immobilized, unable to imagine even the remotest possibility of a connection between the odious Joe Wicklow of Brooklyn and the pious Quaker partner of Castell, Leavering & Sproul. "Which tavern was it, Pa?"

"Zank Gott fur da rain!" Joachim exclaimed joyfully—as I vainly turned up my shirt collar to hide more of myself beneath Parigo's hat, my only cover. "Vee needs it zo batt!"

It had begun to rain soon after we rolled out of New Utrecht, a light but steady drizzle that promised to continue for hours. It was warm enough and windless enough that neither of us would get chilled, but it was still uncomfortable, and the modest break in the terrible drought my brother was bemoaning occasioned no celebration on my part.

We were soaked through by the time we arrived in Brooklyn, and I was dismayed when told that the next ferry—unless a breeze came up—would be at the slack in four hours. So much for any thought of making a second trip today! However, the ferryman permitted us to load my goods into the boat, promised to keep an eye on them, and pointed me to a row of taverns where I might pass the time in some comfort. Had the ferry been running, I would have visited it at a later date, but there was no sense in wasting the time. I sent Joachim home and trudged along the shore toward the public houses. The scene of Pa's brawl, called *The Jug*, was the last and most rickety of the row, the only one specifically disparaged by the ferryman, and could only be entered this afternoon by stepping directly into a mud puddle.

Nonetheless, in I went. There were only two men and a dog inside the small, dark room, and all three were asleep. The barman, head on his folded arms on the bar, stirred himself at my entrance. The white-bearded customer, who looked like he might fall from his chair at any moment, kept right on snoring. The hound lifted its head briefly, and then settled back down onto the dirt floor. The barman, however, seemed to be shaking his scrawny adolescent self into some sort of alertness, so I ordered two beers, and asked him to join me at one of the four small tables. "Not much custom on a rainy afternoon?" I began.

"It should pick up," he replied, lifting his mug in a toast. "Saturday nights are our best." He regarded me warily, clearly finding my presence a puzzle.

I decided to get straight to the point. "My father was involved in a brawl here. I'd like to find out what happened."

He sighed. "We have a lot of brawls. Can barely keep two sticks of furniture intact."

"A man was killed at this brawl."

"Oh. *That* brawl."

"Aye. My Pa says he was playing cards with the victim, Joe Wicklow, when it happened."

"Your Pa's fifty-ish, gray-haired, a little bigger than most?"

"That's him. When did this happen? Back in June?"

"Yeah. It was a Saturday—last Saturday night in June. Big night, we must've had a dozen folks in here. Then those two goddamn sailors came in and busted it all up!"

"Sailors?"

"Well, they rolled as they walked, and they had long pigtails. I guessed they were sailors."

"You didn't recognize them?"

"Never seen 'em before or since. Mean-looking curs, one tall, one short."

"Did they start fighting right away?"

"No! Fact, they made theirselves real popular at first. Bought a round for everyone. I figured they'd just been paid out."

"Huh!"

"Then they sat down with Wicklow—and your Pa, I guess—and played a round of Black Lady."

"Did either Wicklow or Pa particularly invite them to join? Did they seem to know them?"

"No. I thought they might sit down here with the two girls playing cards, but they passed them by and went over there to the corner."

"And then invited themselves into the men's game?"

"Uh huh. After they'd bought the drinks, no one could back out just on account of they looked ugly, you know." He paused. "And after their first game, they bought the whole place a second round! I was thinking myself lucky at that point!"

"And the brawl started—"

"Still not right away." He closed his eyes, remembering. "About ten minutes later. And it was … all of a sudden, the shorter one and Joe were screaming at each other and throwing punches."

"Anyone try to break it up?"

"Yeah. Your Pa, among others. But the bigger one wasn't having it. He picked up a chair and started swinging it around, and nobody could get near them. I pulled my militia musket out from under the bar, but I spilled the powder, so …"

"New to militia drill?" The boy was probably just fifteen.

"Aye. Lots to remember! Anyway, the girls are screaming, the big tar is fighting off everybody else in the place, and I was just remembering that the axe was behind the keg, when the short one says, 'Done!' and the two of them drop everything and make right for the door."

"What was the dog doing?"

"*Eh?* Oh, I just got this mutt. In case something like ever happens again." The hound lethargically opened an eye. "Not sure he'll be much help!"

"You go after them?"

"I ran outside, and I seen 'em charging up away from town. There was a few loitering out of doors that ran after, but it was near midnight, and everybody was already drunk. Weren't no use."

"Dark that night?"

"Yup. Moon had set. In the morning I found tracks that looked like them in the mud near the shore, just two hundred yards up. I'm thinking they had a boat there."

"But they didn't steal anything?"

He looked startled. "No. Wrecked three damn chairs and a table, but …"

"So, what did you do then?"

"Well, everybody was leaving—some without paying up. I caught one and then had trouble making change. Then I tried to do what I could for your Pa, who was bleeding some … and really hurting bad. We thought Joe was just knocked out. It was ten minutes or so before old Titus there"—the white-beard was still snoring—"said he weren't breathing."

"Had he been stabbed?"

"No. Neck was broke!"

"Sweet lord!" I exhaled sharply. "Did I hear you right, the one fighting with Joe said 'Done!' just before they took off?"

"That's what I thought."

We took long pulls on the beer. "This is too odd. None of this makes sense, unless … unless they had it in for Wicklow in the first place."

He grinned. "Well, I'm damn glad somebody else sees that! Mister, I know when guys are spoiling for a fight. Those two *weren't.* They were after Joe, I say, plain and simple. I tried to tell the new constable, but he wasn't interested. Seems Joe had ticked him off plenty. Joe could do that, of course! Ticked *me* off plenty, but still ..."

"This would be the man who replaced Wicklow as constable? Wicklow was fired?" Sad he couldn't offer Pa some commiseration!

"Yeah, long while back. The new one just says it was another barroom brawl that went a little too far, and he hasn't a prayer of catching the sailors anyway."

"Well that could be true. They might have shipped out across the ocean before the sun came up."

"He could at least have tried! Lazy slug!"

"But still ... *why?* Why Wicklow, if they were complete strangers?"

"I talked about it next day with my neighbor, two doors down. She says she saw them skulking around outside here with a third man, just before eleven."

"Before they walked in?"

"That what she says. Says the third one was wearing a good heavy cloak with the collar up. In the middle of June!"

"So she can't describe him."

"More than middling height, not stout, is all she said. Couldn't see his face."

"Did Joe have any special enemies—that you knew about?"

"Used to have plenty, back when he was the constable. But now, no one much cared about him."

"Did he have any *friends?*"

"Well ... your Pa was the only one I saw regular. Oh, and Flora, of course, sort of."

"Flora? Sort of?"

"Flora who lives upstairs. She's friends with lads who ... are flush."

Oh. "Joe Wicklow was *flush?*"

"Had been while he was working. Then she dropped him. But they got back together this spring."

"*Hmm.* Where was she when the brawl was going on? Was she playing cards?"

"No, she was, *uh,* up in her room—with some other guy. Didn't come down until half an hour later."

"What was her reaction when you told her?"

"Ohh ..." He shrugged. "Yeah, she thought it were just another fight."

"But when she found out Joe was dead?"

"Oh, well, she seemed ... as sorry as anyone."

Not many to waste tears on the likes of Joe Wicklow! After debating with myself, I decided I wanted to talk with her. "Is this Flora around today?"

"Sure," he said, rising and walking to the narrow staircase. "Flora!" he bellowed, rousing the old guy and the dog. "Got a gentleman as wants to see you!"

"What!" a husky female voice yelled back. "Great, Billy! Send him up!" The young barkeep gestured with his thumb that I should proceed.

"*Um,* no, *uh,* Billy. Can you ask her to come down?"

"Flora! Wants you to come down first!"

"Oh Christ, he can see what he wants to see up here!"

Was it worth it at all? "Billy, I just want to talk with her. Tell her there's a sixpence in it."

Billy dashed up the stairs.

"Weren't no fight!" I turned, startled. The raspy voice belonged to the white-beard, Titus. "Man's neck don't get broke in a *fight.* Have to mean to do it!" He then had a coughing fit.

Billy and the woman were coming down the stairs, she protesting raucously until she clapped eyes on my disheveled self. "Oh!" she exclaimed, pasting a smile on her face—a face that might once have been comely were her eyes not completely inert. She was over thirty, and had hair dyed a hideous yellow, but somehow looked less brazen than many of the tarts I see walking the streets of New York at night. She had to be a professional, however, if yours truly, who'd just loaded a cart in a barn, unloaded it into a ferry in the rain, wore a makeshift hat, and stepped through mud to reach this shabby establishment ... could excite her.

At my nod, Billy poured a round for everyone. "Miss, *uh*—" I began.

Incomprehension. "You got a last name, Flora?" Billy prompted.

"Norts," she finally answered, still puzzled. "This about Joe?"

"Yes. Miss Norts, do you have—"

"You a friend of Joe's?" she demanded incredulously.

"My Pa was his friend," I admitted with completely unnecessary embarrassment. "Rykert Dordrecht."

"Yeah. Ryk. He was here a lot."

"Yes. He was here the night Joe was killed. Do you—"

"He got beat up too!" Titus supplied.

"Do you have any idea who those men were? Any idea who might have had it in for Joe?"

"Joe? Joe weren't worth nobody's fuss. I don't see them, myself."

"Was there anyone else who even seemed to know him?"

She shrugged. "Back when he was big man, maybe. No one paid him no mind since."

"Shacky?" Titus said.

"Oh yeah!" she said. "Forgot about him."

"Ain't seen him a long time," Billy observed. "Last winter?"

"Who is Shacky?"

"Shacky was some cousin of Joe's. Meshach. Only family I ever heared of. No good. Sponged off him. Didn't see him much, he lives over in the city."

"He sponged off Joe?"

"Well … not much. He was somebody Joe could look down on."

A service also provided by my father, I fumed. "Could he have had it in for Joe?"

She didn't seem to have an opinion.

"Could've used him *here* that night!" Titus cackled.

"Shacky was a brawler," Billy explained. "You know the type. Mean. He might have fought those sailors off but, honestly, I'm just as happy not to be seeing him around anymore. Kind of guy you don't turn your back on!"

"But would he ever try somehow to kill his cousin?"

"No," Flora asserted.

"Shacky couldn't think no further than his next drink," Billy said.

None of this was getting me very far. "He's from New York? He's Joe's cousin? His last name is Wicklow?"

"No," Billy replied. "What'd he say? Heyman? Hayter?"

"Hager," Flora said, yawning.

A church tower struck three o'clock. "My Pa has a fancy deck of cards with blue and white backing he says were Joe's. Any of you remember them? They weren't yours, were they, Billy?"

"Nah, I only got one set. Yeah, he shows up with them one night a few months back, says now he and Ryk won't have to wait for Titus and Wally to finish no more. Buys Ryk a drink to celebrate, like."

That sounded out of character. "Had he ever done that before?"

"Joe? Nah!" Titus thought the idea so risible he had another coughing fit. The dog barked at him.

"That was 'round when he decided to be nice to me again," Flora murmured. "Great while it lasted."

"Did he ever say where he'd got the cards?"

They each shook their heads in turn. Out of questions for them, I fell into small talk, which was halted, mercifully for me, a half-hour later, by the ferryman's warning bell. The rain was still coming down, but the breeze had picked up. I settled my bill, thanked *The Jug*'s denizens, and departed.

The ferry got halfway across the East River … and the wind died. The boat came to a halt, and its four passengers had to gird their souls with patience. The dismal rain continued, and I again became soaked through to the skin. I had idle minutes to wonder if my sudden preoccupation with the cards was ludicrous. After all, Wicklow's deck might have nothing to do with the cards found on Daniel Sproul's person. I had seen identical cards on Statia; there was no reason to think there was but one such deck on the American continent. And yet … what if there were a connection?

The only other lead to Joe Wicklow, it appeared, was this ruffian, Shacky, whose actual name was …

It suddenly struck me that I had heard the name Meshach Hager somewhere before. But I was damned if I could think where or when. The second officer aboard Wardener's ship in Saint Eustatius? The clerk in our customer's Hartford office? The divine being considered by the Reformed congregation in Flatbush?

The breeze picked up just enough to bring us in before the current began flooding in earnest, and I had work to do. I hailed a carter to back out onto the dock, and we manhandled my three crates and the tools out of the boat and into the cart in less than an hour. In another twenty minutes we arrived at the firm's new warehouse on Cherry Street, just north of the shipyards, to which Mapes had sent me the key. With another half-hour's heavy exertions, the two of us secured the goods in an empty corral at the back of the warehouse. Tired but relieved, I rode with the carter—a garrulous black fellow, apparently free—back down to Peck Slip. On the way, I listened with half an ear as he described the boxing bout he was looking forward to viewing later in the evening. It was a rematch between … somebody and somebody else, because the referee had been drunk and the challenger's partisans insisted "it weren't no fair fight." In his enthusiasm, by the time we arrived, he was urging me to attend the event too. Any disappointment he might have felt over my pass was quickly overwhelmed by the tip I gave him, which he'd more than earned by all the lifting.

For a moment, I stood immobile after waving him farewell. The rain had at long last ceased, but the weather remained overcast and humid. Dusk was approaching, but all I had left to do was return the key to the office and go home. Looking about, I noticed that, even though Saturday was usually a half-day, and it was already past six o'clock, the area was nonetheless unusually quiet. Because there were no ships at our wharf, I realized grimly, and fewer than normal all along the shore. With a sigh, I turned and walked toward the stairs leading up to the firm's office, a recalled phrase unaccountably forming in my mind …

"Meshach Hager weren't killed in no honest fight."

Yes! Someone had said those very words to me. Who? Who was it?

The stolid city constable, Officer Jennet.

And who was Meshach Hager? I sat heavily on the stairs, thinking back nearly six months.

Meshach Hager was the name of the coroner's *bravo.* Meshach Hager was the name of Mr. McCraney's snarling, rum-soused corpse—the man who'd been knifed the same morning Mr. Sproul's body had been found.

And Meshach Hager was a cousin of Joe Wicklow … who had also met a violent end … in another suspicious fight.

Chapter 9

It was getting dark. I stirred myself to enter the office in order to replace the warehouse key on its rack in the closet. I looked about the empty premises, feeling ever more queasy. Two men, blood relations, were dead—one who'd been killed the same day Daniel Sproul's body had been found, and another who'd possessed an unusual deck of playing cards that matched some found on Sproul's person. I was abruptly impelled to rush to my desk and retrieve Mrs. Leavering's letter. Yes. On yet another examination, they surely did appear to match up with those in Pa's possession, right down to a comparable degree of wear.

Daniel Sproul's demise had always been understood to be tragic, improbable, and inexplicable. But all my intuition was now telling me more—that it was *wrong*. The queasiness in my stomach settled into an angry demand that whatever was unnatural about it—and something clearly was—had to be investigated, explained. And that any human agency that had a part in it had to be exposed and punished.

Suddenly, I wanted desperately to trace all of Mr. Sproul's moves on his fatal trip from Philadelphia. But traveling to Philadelphia on such a mission was preposterous—far too expensive when I'd so little to go on. And, come to think of it, it wouldn't be necessary anyway, because we'd had a *letter* from him, from somewhere in New Jersey, when he'd been halfway. I'd not seen the missive, I'd only been apprised of its import.

But that letter would be right here in the office, in the correspondence file! I dashed into Mr. Glasby's room, where the files were kept, and nearly spilled the portfolio for March as I pulled it out … and there it was, right where Mapes had placed it! I took it out, returned the file, and walked to the south window to read.

> Sunday, March 21
> Carteret Hotel, New Brunswick, N.J.
>
> Mr. Benj. Leavering
>
> My Dear Sir,
>
> Thursday's heavy snowfall delayed my planned departure for New York until yesterday. As a consequence, I am detained here for the Sabbath. Though the snow is melting fast, our coach's progress has been tedious, and looks likely to be but slightly improved on the morrow. I have therefore little hope of reaching New York City in just one more day—a water passage from Perth Amboy being strongly discouraged by all I meet. Most probably, I shall reach Newark or Paulus Hook by Monday night, and be commending myself to thy hospitality as of Tuesday. I fear I may make thee a most tiresome guest, as I shall be occupied with business unrelated to either our family or our firm, which I shall duly explain on my arrival. Until then, trust that I remain
>
> Thy loving son-in-law, D. Sproul

Trying to read it a second time, I found the light inadequate. Taking both Mrs. Leavering's and Mr. Sproul's letters, I locked the office and got myself to my local tavern for a hearty meal. I sat at the end of the table and was fortunate that no one barged in on my fast-running thoughts.

On the occasion of my own trip to Philadelphia, in May of last year, I had taken the coach from Paulus Hook and broken the trip in New Brunswick. On the return, I had taken a boat from New Brunswick down the Raritan and up through the lower bay. This was the most common pattern of travel, recommended by Mr. Leavering, the only man who made the journey with any frequency. Thus, I had no specific idea where Mr. Sproul might have alighted in Newark or Paulus Hook—presuming he had, in fact, proceeded as he'd written. Yet there were not that many possibilities, and there was only the one coach company, so it might well pay to inquire. Mr. Sproul was distinctive enough in appearance and manner that he might well be remembered, even months after the fact.

Though I had a myriad of personal chores to attend to, my private commerce to sort out, and social calls that I really ought to make—and despite the fact that some might argue it was no business of mine in the first place—I resolved to take the morrow's first ferry across to New Jersey.

The red-bearded fellow at the helm of the ferry had to be, I recalled, the "otherwise useless nephew" of the ferryman with whom I had spoken back in March. He was quite useful to me, being more than willing to describe the Spartan amenities tiny Paulus Hook had to offer, which included two inns that had eluded my attention on my previous visit.

The terminus of the Convenient Coach Company's route was, I had forgotten, next to a solitary inn directly across from the dock, surrounded by its privy and a stable, but not a single tree. On the occasion of my trip, the coach had been awaiting the ferry, and so I had never set foot inside the building. This morning, in clear, blustery weather that made the preceding day's dreary rain a bad memory—for me, if not the farmers—the flimsy little dock at Paulus Hook was deserted within five minutes of the ferry's arrival and immediate return departure. The few who had arrived with me walked off directly, mostly up the road toward the interior, but some straight across the grassy mudflats toward, I presumed, remote farmhouses.

There was naught to do but to see if anyone could be raised at the inn. The paint on the inn's weather-beaten sign was so faded, I couldn't make out the name, and that was only the first indication of dilapidation. Inside, there was one large room with six round tables, a fireplace, and a bar; a hall appeared to lead back to a kitchen, and a stairway up to bedrooms. Its layout was not unlike a smaller, two-story version of my family's own tavern, except that it was perhaps the filthiest and smelliest excuse for a public hostelry I'd ever come across. Surely Daniel Sproul would have had to be desperate to have selected such an establishment. I was about to call for service when a lass my own age, clad in nothing but a chemise, came out of the hall, exclaimed, "Oh!" upon seeing me, and ran back in a fluster.

Presently, following a clatter of pots and pans, a slovenly, balding fellow in his mid-thirties appeared from the back. "Yes? What?" he said, more ignorantly than rudely.

"I'm trying to trace the steps of a colleague who might have stopped here back in March," I blurted out.

He stared blankly for seconds. "You're with the authorities?"

"No, no," I assured him. "I'm making a, *uh,* private investigation. Our colleague … went missing."

"Six *months* ago?"

"Yes." There seemed no point in attempting to explain. "His name was Daniel Sproul—a merchant from Philadelphia. We think he might have arrived—"

"I don't recollect no one by that name, and I don't keep no records. Can't help you."

Laziness, I thought, rather than deliberate evasion. "A trim, Quaker gentleman of middle height, aged in his late forties?"

"Nope. Don't think he stayed here."

"Might, *uh*, your wife remember him?"

He looked at me blankly for a second, then burst out laughing. "*Wife?*"

Time to change the subject! "This is where the coach line stops, isn't it?"

"Yeah. No coaches today. Sunday."

"Was there a coach yesterday?"

"Coach came in yesterday, leaves tomorrow."

"Aha. Where does the coachman stay?"

"Gunther? He stays in our stables. He's out there right now." He pointed in the direction of the other structure I'd noticed. "Feeding time."

"Oh yes? Perhaps I'll look him up, then. Thank you, Mr. …"

He was yawning. "That's all right." And so we parted.

The fresh air off the river revived me as I stepped back into the sunlight. As I walked around the corner of the building, I saw a tall, slight, middle-aged man carrying two pails of water suspended from a yoke on his shoulders and heading toward the other building. I caught up with him just as he set his burden down. "Gunther?"

"*Ja?* Who asks? Coach is dawn tomorrow. We go Newark, Elizabeth, Woodbridge, Piscataway—"

"No, no, thank you, Gunther. I was wondering if you might remember one of your passengers—a man who has, *um,* gone missing."

"Yes? I try. When was?"

"Well, this was back in March. Were you the coachman back then?"

"Yes. But I one of two. Sam also drive. Excuse, please?" He poured the pails of water into a trough for the horses and commenced brushing them. "March a long time ago, sir!"

"I realize. I'm trying to trace a Mr. Sproul. A trim, pleasant gentleman, about so tall, about your age? Would have traveled all the way from Philadelphia? A Quaker, in dress?"

"We have many those, sir," he protested, shaking his head. "I don't—"

"The exact date he ought to have arrived here was March twenty-second. His trip began on a Saturday, because there had been a snowfall on Thursday, and he wrote from the Carteret Hotel on the Sunday. Do you recall a postponed trip?"

He looked at me as if I was daft—and he was right to do so. "We postpone often, all winter long, sir. Last snow this spring was April twenty. Even in summer, we cancel in heavy rains. Not safe, you see. Mud!"

"Yes, of course." It was foolish to have thought a postponement would be as memorable to the coachman as it would have been to the passengers. "Tell me, are there proper hostelries in Newark? With all respect, I can't imagine Mr. Sproul willingly staying here." I nodded over at the other building.

"*Ach ja!* Well, there is place for the quality in Newark, but now we mostly leave them with Van Narden house, just there." He pointed westward toward what I realized must be the other inn, two hundred yards away on slightly higher ground. "Much more—" He made a gesture I interpreted to mean *decent*.

"I see. Well, thank you kindly, Gunther."

"Have a blessed day, sir!"

So I tramped across the marshy, unpromising turf—land over which the Dutch and the Indians had, a century ago, fought wars disastrous to both sides. Presently I came to a large, new, white farmhouse with two maple saplings and a tavern sign in front of it. Peering through the open door, I saw some three dozen people tightly crammed inside. Sunday worship was in progress. A man came around from the back, probably having attended to a personal emergency, and hailed me at the door. "What sort of service is this, sir?" I inquired.

"Why, Reformed, of course, lad. Do come in!" Given that I'd not be able to speak to anyone about mundane issues of real life and death until it would be concluded, I allowed him to tug me inside and squeeze me onto the end of a bench. Immediately, I realized something was radically wrong, but it took me half a minute to place it. The young dominie was preaching—barbarously to my ears—*in English!* It was wryly amusing that I—great arbiter of tradition and piety that I am—was scandalized. Presently, I recalled hearing that the quarrels of the New Lights and the Old Lights, which began twenty years back with the Great Awakening of all Protestants, have always been particularly divisive over here in New Jersey. But I'm afraid that this fellow was just as boring in English as New Utrecht's dominie is in Dutch, so my attention wandered. I shook myself, however, when he suddenly began denouncing various New York divines by name, including Wouter Van Voort! You may find me remiss in that I failed to rise in outraged protest to defend my family's pastor ... because I'd no real idea what the man was talking about. At length, the service concluded in the form with which I was familiar—other than the fact that it was in the official language of the province rather than that of the church.

As the congregation dispersed, I walked along the shore for a few minutes in order to avoid having to make small and insincere conversation. When the dominie and all the congregants were gone, I sought out the inn's gaunt, elderly proprietor, Van Narden. I debated in which language to address him and settled on English. This proved to be a mistake, as he spoke it with great difficulty and was relieved when I was able to switch. It still required several more minutes to convey my problem and gain his cooperation. The man was not a bright spark in any language. At length, he pulled out a guest ledger—which he apparently had trouble parsing. He was glad when I volunteered to take it from him and seek out the previous spring's entries.

I nearly jumped when I found "Daniel Sproul, Philadelphia," entered for the twenty-second of March.

"That's the man!" I exulted. "He was here!" Meneer Van Narden looked equally alarmed as pleased. "Can you tell me anything about this visit?" I asked.

"Saartje!" he called desperately toward the back of the building. Thirty seconds later, a prim, white-haired woman I presumed to be his wife appeared, hands clasped demurely in front of her. "Saartje," Van Narden said to her, "this young gentleman is asking after one of our patrons … this one," he said, pointing to the signature.

"Ah!" she exclaimed, evidently thinking there was some special significance to the name that her husband had missed. "But have you demanded to know who he is to be asking?"

Her husband reddened, unnecessarily embarrassed because he understood—as she obviously did not—that I'd comprehended every word. I hastened to respond, in Dutch, to her perfectly legitimate question. "My name is Thomas Dordrecht, Mevrouw, and I am an employee of the firm of which this gentleman, Daniel Sproul, was a partner."

It still took seconds for them to recover. "Is he no longer with the firm, then?" she asked.

"I'm afraid Mr. Sproul is deceased, Mevrouw." I hadn't meant to let it slip just yet, but there was no longer any point in withholding the truth. "In fact, he passed away at some point that night." They looked very startled and upset. "His body was discovered over in New York City at six o'clock the next morning."

Now they looked bewildered. "Ah! A heart attack?"

"It would seem so, though the medical examiner was unable to say."

"That's why he never came back," she murmured, shaking her head.

"'Came back,' Mevrouw?"

"I remember him perfectly well. He had asked if there was any way, beside the ferry, to get over to New York. This was even after he had paid for his bed! I thought perhaps he had come across one of the oystermen and persuaded him to row him across."

"Was it still light, then? Why was the ferry not running?"

"No, it was dark. The coach did not arrive until, oh, probably half an hour after sunset. We enjoy our best custom," she added apologetically, "when the roads are bad."

"*Uh huh.* Let me try to order this schedule. The coach arrived after dusk. Was Mr. Sproul the only passenger who stopped here?"

"Yes. Others had apparently stopped in Newark, but he had persevered."

"But he registered and paid for the night?"

"Yes. He left his luggage in the room, and—"

"His luggage!" I gasped. "It's not still here, by any chance?"

"Yes. We held onto it assuming he would collect it on his return … but then I think we just forgot about it."

"You didn't see his obituary in the *Gazette*?" I pointed to a copy of the Philadelphia newspaper on the table.

"We don't read it, sir. It's for our patrons." They couldn't read English, I realized, and might even be illiterate in Dutch.

"May I see the luggage, please?"

She blushed pink, confused. "Meneer Dordrecht, if the gentleman is dead, then we should turn the luggage over to his *kin*."

"Of course, yes, but …" It took me a second to realize the solution was in my jacket.

I extracted Mr. Sproul's letter—which they were unable to read. However, the signature, which compared exactly to the one in their ledger, convinced them. "Johan," she told her husband, "we put it in the back, near the chimney."

It was in the attic, and Van Narden needed my help struggling with his heavy ladder, to brace it against the wall, lift the ceiling cover, and then reset the ladder so he could climb inside. It took him several minutes to crawl about and retrieve the parcel, which he finally handed down to us. "There's this too," he said, forestalling my eagerness to inspect the cloth travel bag. He handed down a dirtied and damaged Quaker hat—to his wife's vexation.

"Where did this come from, Johan?" she demanded as he was toiling to replace the cover.

Van Narden waited until I'd helped him return the ladder and he'd caught his breath. "Wendell found it. He gave it to me the next day. He thought it must belong to him. I put it with the luggage."

The hat was more than dirty, it was unsalvageable: crushed completely flat, with muddy boot-prints on the top. The bag, however, was perfectly clean. "Who is ... No wait. Will you ... be so good as to observe and witness me as I open the bag? It ... may become important." They hesitated, disconcerted by the agitation I was unable to conceal. Before they could voice any objection, however, I proceeded to empty it out. They were quite relieved when nothing was found save a neatly folded set of good business clothes and a Bible. I was disappointed, however, and turned the bag inside out, felt carefully through the clothing, and riffled the pages of the Bible, in the vain hope of further discovery.

"There is nothing at all unusual, Meneer Dordrecht," Van Narden observed.

"Aye. That's so," I had to concur. "Let me try to understand what happened, in order, please. Mr. Sproul arrived, registered, paid, and went to his room. Yes?"

"Yes."

"Ah. Did you see ... My family are innkeepers, Mevrouw. I understand one is not supposed to show curiosity about this! Did you notice how much money he had in his purse?"

She blushed, as I would have, if someone had posed the query to me. Heaven knows it's nearly impossible *not* to notice! "Well, I did not mean to pry—but I had just seen the awful scars on the gentleman's hand, and ... There were several gold pieces in his purse, sir. We seldom see gold coins here, and of course silver is all that's necessary for us."

"A plain, brown leather pouch, with a leather thong tie?"

"Yes."

I was pensive for some seconds. When his body had been discovered twelve hours later, Mr. Sproul had had two pounds in silver in his purse, no more.

"Sir?"

"Sorry! Can you estimate how long he stayed in his room?"

"Minutes only, as I recall," Vrouw Van Narden said. "He came right back out, wearing the same clothes, and asked where he could get some supper, as he was hungry."

"We aren't able to feed our guests as yet," the man said. "We just took on this place a year ago."

"Ah. So what happened, then?"

"There's only the tavern by the dock, Meneer Dordrecht," she said.

"I see. So he left?"

"Yes." She shrugged.

"Was he wearing the hat?"

"I think so. I don't recall ever seeing him without the hat. We expected to welcome him back within an hour. But when the fire burned low, we left the door unlocked and retired … and we never saw him again. I doubt he was here more than twenty minutes."

"Was there anything to suggest he'd returned while you were asleep?"

"No. The bed was undisturbed in the morning."

"Did you ask the fellow at the tavern?"

She looked to her husband to answer. "We're not on speaking terms with Mr. Meed, sir," he explained.

Uh oh. Fortunate that I face no such restriction! "Who is Wendell, please?"

She smiled. "Wendell Brush is an oysterman. Lives alone not far south of here. He was just with us, for the service. The very thickset young man in blue?"

"Ah, with his hair not tied?"

"Yes, that's he."

Wendell's slipshod notion of Sunday dress marked him apart from the others. "He *found* the hat?"

"So he said," Van Narden asserted.

"Where? And when?"

"He didn't say, he just dropped it with me."

"How did he know it was Sproul's, or that Sproul was staying with you?"

"Well, he could see that it was a *gentleman's* hat."

And a gentleman wouldn't stay anywhere else. Right. "When was it that he gave it to you, Meneer?"

Van Narden had to think. "It was right at dawn. Wendell had been fishing all that night. In fact, it was before we realized the Philadelphian was not in his room."

"When *did* you realize that?"

"It was when the first ferry was about to leave," Vrouw Van Narden replied, "that we knocked again and found the room empty."

"I had put the hat under the counter," her husband added, "and then I just put it with the luggage when Saartje asked me to store it away."

I collected Mr. Sproul's effects, got directions to Wendell's abode, and thanked them for their helpfulness. "Pardon me if this seems rude, but why do you have your service in English, if you don't understand it?"

"Ah, but others do, Meneer Dordrecht!" she exclaimed.

"Our dominie believes we must speak the Word in the language of the land," he agreed.

"But—"

"Wendell is the newest member of our congregation, our great success!"

"Ah, I see." Frankly, I didn't see it at all—but my curiosity was more than sated, and time was wasting.

About half a mile to the south, following a path that had marsh on both sides for much of the way, there was a collection of huts, barely sturdier than slave hovels, about fifteen feet above the tide line. A woman hanging washing out to dry pointed me toward Wendell's.

Wendell's domicile was no better than the rest—unpainted clapboard with one window and a mud chimney. How on earth do they survive the winters? The door was open this afternoon, however, and the inhabitant had fallen asleep at his table, Bible in hand. The place was clean, but still reeked of fish. Wendell started as my shadow crossed his threshold, but he smiled broadly when he recognized me. "Oh! The new parishioner! How kind of you to pay me a social call, sir!" He gestured elaborately, awkwardly imitating people he had possibly seen arriving by the coach. "Pray, have a seat! Did you not find our dominie's sermon most exciting? He is famed for his eloquence all about the Bergen Neck! There's no finer preacher between the Hudson and the Hackensack, Mr. Van Narden says—and he should know, as he was on the committee—"

"Mr. Brush, is it not?"

"Oh yes sir, yes sir, yes sir. And who do I have the honor of addressing this blessed Sabbath afternoon?"

"My name is Thomas Dordrecht, Mr. Brush, and I'm not actually a member of your congregation—"

"Oh but you must be, sir! What a fine, godly body it is! What good souls, firm in the ways of—"

"I live on the far side of the river, Mr. Brush. I'm sorry, the Van Nardens directed me to you, because I'm endeavoring to trace the movements of a colleague who stopped at their inn and then disappeared, whose hat they say you found. This hat." I removed it from Mr. Sproul's bag.

"Oh yes!" Brush exclaimed excitedly, forgetting his passionate evangelism. "I was so happy to be able to save it for the gentleman, because I'm sure it must be a very valuable hat"—He couldn't tell by looking that that had ceased to be the case?—"and I'm sure he wouldn't want to have forgotten it, and—"

Wendell Brush evidently lacked for companionship, and needed to talk twice as much as necessary to make up for it. "I know it was some time back, Mr. Brush, but can you recall where and when you found this hat?"

"Oh now let me see. Oh yes, of course I can, even now, because it was so peculiar. I found it early that morning, on the cow."

"I beg your pardon?"

"Yes, I was rowing back to shore, I saw the hat lying on the cow."

Had his solitary choices of career and abode already driven the man mad? "I'm afraid I don't comprehend you, Mr. Brush. What cow?"

"Oh! The cow is the floating dock we use to set and haul moorings."

It took a few seconds. "The cow is a thing, not an animal?"

He slapped his thighs, laughing hard. "You thought there was a cow—a *cow*—in the middle of the water?"

Finally, the hilarity receded. "I still don't understand what this thing is, Mr. Brush. Can you describe it to me?"

It took over ten minutes—after which he casually mentioned, "It's right outside, we can just go have a look!" Sure enough, there it was, an odd floating work rig, moored fifty yards offshore, that I'd seen but not remarked upon as I walked over to find him.

The "cow" does need some explaining. Though the Upper New York Bay is a huge body of water, its shores become ice-bound for weeks every winter. The Hudson River has even been known to freeze over completely, notwithstanding its mile-wide breadth, and notwithstanding the fact that the tide still raises and lowers it six feet, twice a day. Ice being extremely destructive to boats, all boats are laboriously hauled out onto land for three or four months of every year. During the working months, the smallest and lightest boats—dinghies, skiffs—are beached after every use and dragged above the tide line. Larger and heavier boats, those with drafts greater than a foot, are generally moored for the season in shallow water and reached by rowboats. Their moorings are semipermanent anchors installed in the spring and removed every fall, as moorings, too, would succumb to the action of the ice and the tide; however, they provide a more secure connection to the ground and spare the sailor the daily effort of raising, lowering, and setting a temporary anchor.

Yet the semiannual chore of placing and removing the moorings, which are much heavier than temporary anchors, is itself an arduous undertaking. Remarkably, the impoverished community of oysterers, fishermen, haulers, and ferrymen occupying these squalid flats had organized a cooperative effort to expedite it, in order to maximize the number of days they'd be able to work every year, and had built the "cow" to save time and effort. Wendell's patience became exhausted trying to make clear to me things that were patently clear to him, and so he volunteered to row out to the bizarre platform to show me exactly where he'd found the hat. He jumped up and started for the shore; as I followed, I noticed he was barefoot and making deep impressions in the mud. I begged him to wait while I removed my shoes and hose. Had it been decent to do so, I'd have gladly spared my breeches by removing them as well!

The weight of the rowboat was a challenge, given that I am used to my Indian canoe, which I can drag single-handed. The tide was out, so we needed to haul it thirty feet across the sucking mud before it floated, which left me panting, much to Wendell's amusement. I shook my feet in the water to clear the mud before I climbed in … and wondered if Wendell owned boots to spare his feet in frigid December.

Five minutes later, we pulled alongside the "cow." It was a rectangular floating dock, about eight by fourteen feet, built atop six tarred barrels, and itself retained in place by a mooring. Although yesterday's rain had washed it, it was permanently stained the dull gray color of river mud. In the center of it, improbably, was a square hole, three feet on a side which, Wendell explained, permitted the hoist apparatus to raise and lower the heavy moorings. The hoist was hung from the four timbers that formed a pyramid directly over the hole, with a block-and-tackle arrangement that was cleated on one of the timbers. "Do they call it a cow because its business hangs below its four legs?" I mused aloud. Wendell found that riotously funny.

"This thing has no sails or oars, Wendell. How do they get it to the dock to collect or return the moorings, and then take it all to the right spot for placement?"

"How d'ye think? We tow it with a dinghy, then we toss over a day anchor while we work."

"What if you have wind like today, or the current is against you?"

He shrugged. "Takes longer."

"Very labor demanding!"

"Maybe. Maybe. But we get the whole job done a week earlier than before."

In December? I shuddered to think of it. "May I step onto it? Will it hold my weight?"

Again, Wendell found me a source of mirth. "Of course it'll hold your weight! It'll hold four men and a couple moorings, that's what it's for!"

Somewhat tentatively—the breeze was kicking up waves that were rocking the dinghy—I clutched one leg of the superstructure to pull myself onto the cow, which was steadier than I expected—and yet a very small space for a group of men to be working together in less than ideal weather conditions. I ducked to walk under the pyramid and nearly hit my head on the next leg of it, which might have tumbled me into the central hole. It felt safer to be on either of the ends, where one could stand upright—but without any railing. "Where exactly did you find the hat?"

"The hat? Right where you're standing now. How come—"

"It's a wonder the hat didn't blow off!"

"Weren't any wind that night. Not a breath."

The incongruousness of Wendell's find being discovered on this workaday contrivance out in the bay was overwhelming my poor intellect. Surely Daniel Sproul would never have had reason to be here. If he'd found someone to row him across to New York, there would have been no occasion to stop at the cow. Could he have lost the hat overboard, after which it floated long enough for someone else to retrieve it and set it on the cow? "It was crushed and muddy when you found it, Mr. Brush, but was it wet? I mean, soaked through?"

He shook his head. "There was a little dew on it."

"How on earth did that hat end up out *here?*" I grumbled to myself. And how did it get the bootprints all over it? "Oh, let's go back," I said despairingly. Brush obligingly agreed, and rowed quickly into the shore, where we dragged the rowboat back to safety. Rather absently, I walked back to the man's hut—he following along. "Mr. Brush, you found this hat at dawn, I take it, and you took it to Mr. Van Narden's. Why did you assume Mr. Sproul was staying at Van Narden's?"

"Who is Mr. Sproul, sir?"

"Oh. The owner of the hat."

"The Quaker gentleman?"

"Yes. You recognized it as a Quaker's hat?"

"Well, yes, because I'd seen him wearing it, and Mr. Van Narden said that's what it was—a Quaker hat."

"You'd *seen* Mr. Sproul, then?" I said, my excitement overwhelming my impatience that he'd not mentioned it previously.

"Oh yes, the evening before. At Meed's."

"About when was that, please?" I asked, rebuckling my shoes.

"What time? Oh dear. At least an hour after dark. The gentleman was having his supper when I came in for a tipple. I always have a tipple before I go out at night. I only go out at night two times a week, because there's a taverner up in Hoboken who wants fish on Tuesdays and Fridays, you see, and I bring them right to his dock, which makes him very—"

"But you are sure it was the same gentleman?"

"Oh yes, there weren't two like that. And we spoke, of course."

"You *spoke* to him? How did that come about?"

"Well, John Meed told me to speak to him. Said he'd asked to speak to anyone who owned a rowboat."

My mouth went dry. "And … ?"

"And so I went over to his table. He was just finishing his plate, and he invited me to sit down, and he bought me my whiskey! Nobody ever bought me a whiskey before, nobody! And he wasn't even having one himself!"

"What did he want?"

"Well, he was hoping that someone would row him across to New York. Said, 'I could make it worth thy while,' if it could be done right away. Funny way to talk!"

"And what did you say?"

Brush had to think. "Well, first of all, I couldn't—because I had to catch fish for my regular buyer. I didn't want to risk losing his business, you see! But then, it only made sense to discourage the gentleman, because there was no breeze, and the current was running strong—and would stay strong for at least another three hours. I told him he'd do better to get a good night's rest and take the ferry in the morning. I asked where he was staying, and he said up at Van Narden's, and I said they'd be sure to wake him in good time for the first boat."

"That all sounds logical. What did he say to that?"

"Well, he sighed like he wasn't too happy, but he allowed that I was probably right."

"He didn't offer any reason why he was so anxious to get across, by any chance?"

"Said he wanted to spare his in-laws any worry."

"Did you observe him as he left the tavern?"

"*Uh,* no. I nursed my drink for a spell, and then I left."

"Oh. About how long would you say you were in the tavern?"

Telling time was not Mr. Brush's long suit. "Oh … near an hour, I guess."

"Near an hour! Then it must have been after eight o'clock before you left?"

"I … guess so, if you say so."

"Did you have any other conversation with Mr. Sproul?"

"Oh … not directly."

"How do you mean, 'not directly?'"

"He was talking to someone else, mostly."

Someone else! "Aha! Who was that?"

"Another stranger. Also a gentleman with nice clothes—except he had a funny-looking wig. Staying there at the inn, I guess."

"Oh yes? You were still at the table? Did you overhear anything of their conversation?"

"Oh yeah, but it didn't sound like anything special. They talked about the weather, how fast the snow was melting, that sort of thing."

I'm sure my dismay showed.

"They were playing cards, you see."

Chapter 10

I stared at him, amazed that the very factor that had prompted my venture across the river had slipped my mind. "Cards?" I asked hoarsely.

"Aye, this other gentleman came down the stairs, asked Mr. Meed if he had a deck of cards and if he thought anyone might like to play."

"Yes? Please go on."

Curiosity finally struck Wendell Brush. "Why are you asking all this, Mr. Dordrecht? Why didn't the Quaker gentleman come back for his own hat?"

Our conversation was diverted while I informed him of Mr. Sproul's mysterious demise and my reason for interest in it. He appeared much affected, and eager to offer further assistance, but did not seem to comprehend that the event might be deemed questionable. "You were saying that this other gentleman asked the bartender for cards. What happened then?"

"Well, Mr. Sproul overheard them talking, and he immediately pipes up to say he'd like to play, and the gent with the wig comes over. Mr. Sproul asks me if I'd care to play, but I don't know how, and I had to leave sometime soon anyway, so—"

"Did Mr. Meed provide a deck of cards?"

Brush looked confused. "I don't know. Must have, I wager. The man had a deck when he came over."

"Do you remember what the cards looked like?"

"What the cards *looked like?* Mr. Dordrecht!" He laughed again.

"Did they look at all like these?" I produced the four varlets, showing him both sides.

He did seem to recognize them, but he shook his head. "I can't be sure, sir. John Meed would know!"

Indeed, so he would! And it struck me that, however unsavory Mr. Meed's establishment might be, it had to be more comfortable than Wendell Brush's pungent abode. "Would you care to accompany me over there, Mr. Brush? It's Sunday, so I doubt I can treat you to a whiskey, but perhaps—"

"Oh he serves on the Sabbath, Mr. Dordrecht," he said cheerfully. "Mr. Van Narden and our dominie disapprove of it, but I have to admit it is a refreshment … from time to time."

"He doesn't get in trouble with the law?" I asked while struggling back into my hose and shoes.

"It's against the law too?"

We stood and stretched, and I gathered up Mr. Sproul's luggage. "Let's find whatever's on offer, shall we?" He was completely amenable. I surmised this was the most entertainment he had known for weeks. Outside, I took a grateful deep breath—and Brush's elbow, to more purposefully direct him on to the inn. "So the two gentlemen began a card game—and you stayed to watch?"

"Yes. Plus the other gent offered me a tot of rum. Right kindly, I thought. Right kindly!"

"Rum? You were drinking whiskey!"

Brush shrugged. "Well, he'd bought a whole jug, you see."

A whole *quart?* "Did he offer a drink to Mr. Sproul?"

"Oh yes, and I think he was sorry he'd bought the jug when the Quaker turned him down!"

"I happen to know that Mr. Sproul was an abstainer."

"Yeah? Mr. Van Narden is one too. Wants *me* to become one! I … don't see how a man can live without, I really, really don't!"

"Do you recollect what this other gentleman looked like?"

"Oh that's hard, Mr. Dordrecht, that's hard. He had his back to me most of the time."

"Why was that? I thought you said you stayed for a spell?"

"Yes, but there were two others as joined in the game."

"Oh?"

"Didn't like the looks of *them* at all! I don't think the gents did, either, but they wanted to play Whist, and it takes four hands."

"Was it Mr. Sproul who proposed Whist?"

"No, it was the other one."

We walked in silence for a few paces. "Please tell me whatever you can about all three of these men."

Brush looked perturbed. "Never saw any of them before or since, Mr. Dordrecht! And I've spent more time with *you*, now, than I ever did with any of them! I'd surely like to help, but—"

"I understand that, sir, and that it was months ago." Was he flattered or annoyed that I'd called him *sir*? Can't stop to worry it! "But I'd appreciate whatever you can remember."

After one more look such as he might have cast on a gibbering madman, Brush bent to the task. "Well, this other gent was much younger than your Quaker fellow. Fairly tall. He was carrying a fancy greatcoat. The other two ... *Agh*, the slaves around here keep themselves cleaner!" *Brush* was complaining of their hygiene? "Big brutes too—big. Older one—forty-five, maybe—was really heavy. Younger one had funny teeth and a scar on his forehead."

"You've a better recollection than you credit yourself for, Mr. Brush!" His descriptions were compatible with my own memory of the *bravo* and of Joe Wicklow, who had made quite an impression on me three years ago. I cleared the mud off my shoes on the inn's unexpected amenity, a boot scraper, and we walked inside.

"*Eh?*" Meed, the tavernkeeper, said as I reentered his dismal domain, still bereft of patrons. "Oh hey, Wendell!"

"Afternoon, Mr. Meed."

"An ale for me, please, Mr. Meed, plus whatever Mr. Brush would like—and could you bring them to the table there along with a drink for yourself? I've something I believe may interest you." As Meed lethargically poured libations—looking as if nothing anyone might ever say could interest him—I had a second to muse that, in this splendid weather, he could have easily set up a pleasant table outside.

Meed set the drinks down, sat, and took a swallow without ceremonially waiting for Brush or me. "What is it then?"

Brush lifted his whiskey in acknowledgement as I extracted the playing cards and set them on the table. "Do you recognize these?"

Meed started, finally shaken into attentiveness as he turned them over. "Where'd you get these? Where the hell are the rest of them?"

"They belong to you, then? They were in the possession of the Quaker gentleman I asked you about this morning. I've learned he was—"

"Damned useless without the main pack!"

"He had registered to stay with the Van Nardens." Meed rolled his eyes. "This was on the evening of March twenty-second, as I said before, and this is evidence that he stopped in here."

"Well, I don't remember him if he did. Lots of strangers pass through here."

Only once, I felt certain. "Mr. Brush recollects him!"

"Do you know where the rest of the cards are? They'd be right handy to get back!"

"Matter of fact, I do, Mr. Meed, and I'll get them to you if you'll try to help me out. Do you recall *when* they went missing?"

"*Um*, months ago. They ain't called for every day. Here, I—" Meed got up, rummaged behind his bar, and returned with a score of cards that he dropped on the table as he sat back down. They were the matching tarot set.

Mr. Brush's face turned crimson as the girl I'd seen earlier came downstairs, wearing only slightly more by way of clothing. She dropped herself into a chair behind me, languidly put her feet up, and commenced mending the hem of a petticoat. He cleared his throat and prompted, "The man he's interested in came in after dark for supper, and asked for anyone with a rowboat. He bought me a drink—right neighborly!—even though he wouldn't have one for himself."

Meed shook his head a few times, then stopped. "A Quaker? With one of those dumb flat hats?"

"Yeah."

"Uhh …"

"Then there was another gent," Brush continued, "who asked you for the cards and played with the Quaker. Younger fellow, fairly tall?"

"His wig was too big and was always about to fall off?"

"That's the one. Then there were two others, castaway lads—I'd never seen them before, either—who joined in the card game."

Something jogged in Meed's memory. "Ohh … Yeah, because it was strange seeing those two rowdies playing with the two gents! The gent with the wig bought a whole jug of rum!"

"That's right. That's right. Now you have them!"

"I remember the younger one with the scar and the wild hair," he said, pointing to his temple. "He made me check for my musket! But … nothing went wrong."

"I only stayed a short spell," Brush continued, "but I remember they got upset with the Quaker because he would only ante up a penny. But then they clammed up after he took the first hand!"

Meed actually laughed. "Yeah. And he won the other hands too. They could've lost plenty!"

"Do either of you recall any of their names? Surely they introduced themselves?"

"Not that I heard," Meed instantly asserted.

Brush massaged his eyes, thinking. "The wild one said his name was something like *Jackie*, I thought. Something like."

Meed had no reaction. It sounded close enough to *Shacky* to me—but I presumed it wouldn't do to prompt him by suggesting it aloud. "Was anybody else present in the tavern that night?"

"What time did you say this was? This all began after dark in March? That's late!"

Right, right: you get west of the Greenwich road, and an hour after sunset, *everything's* "late"! "Uh huh. But can you recall anyone being around other than Mr. Brush and the four at the table?"

"Now how the hell would I remember that after six months?"

"Well, it's not *likely* there were others, is it?"

"No, it's not likely."

"Do you recall it, Mr. Brush?"

"I don't think so, Mr. Dordrecht. I stayed much later than I'd planned, because of the drinks and the game. I don't think there was anybody else … oh, except maybe, uh …" He nodded in the girl's direction.

"She don't count," Meed asserted, brutally loud. The lass reddened as I looked around, but pretended to ignore us.

That judgment, I noted tacitly, would have to be revisited. "So then, Mr. Brush left after an hour. The four men continued playing cards? How late did they stay?"

Meed looked at me impatiently. "The only thing I really notice is if I don't get paid or if there's a fight. Otherwise—"

"Well, they played at least once again, right?"

Meed managed to look thoughtful. "Several times. The Quaker fellow kept winning. If they had been playing with his cards, I'd have wondered!"

"Would you guess an hour?"

"I was sure ready to close up! But you can't push customers out—even if they've already bought all they're going to buy. And besides, I didn't want to rile the two bullies."

"Had you seen any of these men before?"

"No."

"Is it unusual to have four men you've never seen before keeping you open late at night?"

"Well … yeah, it is. Sometimes our locals bring in some visitors or day laborers, but—"

"This was abnormal?" He nodded. "So, if I calculate right, it must have been nearing ten o'clock before it broke up?"

"Must be. We don't hear any church bells unless the wind's still, and—"

"It *was* still, that night," Brush asserted. "No wind at all."

Meed looked at him vacantly. "Right … It was. Yes! They were intent on the game, and I heard the Trinity bells, and I counted them to ten! That's when I knew I could edge them all out and finally close up and go to bed."

"You did that?"

"After they finished that round, yes."

"Did they all leave together?"

"Pretty much, I think. I was right glad to see the back of the two louts. They went first … Oh! The gent with the wig found out that the Quaker man was staying up the road, and said if he could ride behind him, he'd carry him there, because his horse was out by the stable, and he had to go on toward Newark."

"Newark! Good lord, that's five miles! In the dark!"

"Beautiful gray mare. I saw it when I went to the privy. Road's not that bad!"

"Where do you suppose the other two went?"

He exhaled derisively. "Not my business to worry about it, mate! I reckon they had somewhere they could hole up for the night. Just as glad it wasn't here."

I sighed, perfectly confounded. "So Mr. Sproul—the Quaker gentleman—left here after ten o'clock, in good health and state of mind?" And completely sober, I added to myself.

"Of course he did." Meed—not much livelier than Brush—was suddenly intrigued. "Why?"

"Because his corpse, dead of no apparent cause, was discovered over on the New York side, at six the next morning!"

Meed stared. Brush stared, even though I'd told him before. The girl fidgeted. "You must be jesting, surely?" Meed said.

"I'm afraid not."

"Well, that don't make any sense!"

Do tell!

"Say now ... How is it that you found these cards and brought them here?"

How much, I wondered, should I explain? "As I said, I'm trying to retrace Mr. Sproul's movements ... and the cards were on his person. He must have forgotten that he'd separated them out."

"Well, I wish you'd brought all of them!"

A customer appeared in the door—the ferry having docked shortly before. "Be with you in a minute!" Meed told the sad, impoverished-looking fellow.

"Sorry. I'll get them to you presently. Could I be introduced to the young lady?"

"The who? You want her?"

Wendell Brush flushed crimson, declared it was urgent that he get on, and ran out after hastily mumbling thanks for the whiskey. Meed stood and stretched.

"I want to *speak* with her, Mr. Meed. Does she have a name?"

"Just go ahead, for Christ's sake!" His customer wanted a bed for the night as well as something to eat. I walked across the room.

She was perhaps a little older than I'd first thought, but not as defeated-looking as Flora Norts. The red hair was her own. Her plain blue muslin skirt was absurdly trimmed with a dozen flounces. I smiled inwardly to imagine my mother and sisters finding out that I seemed to be making a habit of consorting with harlots! She was at least pretending to concentrate on her sewing. "May I speak with you for a minute, miss?"

"My throat is parched, mister!"

"Mr. Dordrecht," I announced, signaling to Meed to bring her something. "And you are?"

She smirked ruefully. "They call me Miss Paulette."

"Ah." Meed delivered a hard cider. She took it without acknowledgement, and he returned to the customer, who was protesting the rate for a bed. "Did you overhear most of the conversation we just had?"

For a second, I feared she was going to play coy. "Yes," she said, forthrightly looking me in the eye.

"Aha. Well, Miss Paulette, can you tell me if you recall that evening back in March?"

"Maybe."

Have I misjudged again? "It would be a great help if you could!" I said earnestly.

"Yeah? To whom?"

Try once more! "To me. And to the cause of justice for a dead man."

"Few of them worth any breath!"

"Daniel Sproul was one."

Finally, she melted a little. "The Quaker?"

"Aye."

She took a long pull on her cider. "Yeah, well, the 'other gent,' as you call him, had spent some time in my room."

I had speculated as much. "When did you first see him?"

"Late that afternoon. John was out, I don't think he even knew he was up there with me."

"Had you ever seen this man before?"

"No. I was down here alone. I saw him through the window on his fancy tall gray mare, looking the place over, careful-like. He went around behind, and I thought that was it—but he came in. Said he lived over in Newark."

"Did he give his name?"

She smiled sarcastically. "You really think he *would?* He said to call him 'Steve.'"

"What did he look like? How was he dressed?"

"Not bad. Better than most of my, *uh*, friends." I disdained to pursue that. "Tall as you. A little older, late twenties? Trim, dark, clean-shaven, brown hair."

"They said he was wearing a wig!"

"The wig came off while we were … That wig was plain wrong for him. Stupid looking! I think he just bought it cheap, in case anyone might see him consorting with the likes of me!" She shook her head. "Had a blue cutaway suit with velvet trim, heavy green wool cloak—nice enough."

"Have you ever seen him since?"

"I thought I saw him once from upstairs, a couple months ago, stabling a flash dappled brown stallion. Probably—"

"You said the horse was gray."

She seemed confused by not having realized the discrepancy, but simply shrugged. "I was hoping he'd come back for me, but I suppose he was only taking the ferry. Wouldn't mind him again, he paid up front for his privileges. He talked about staying the night, that one time, but he never came back up after going down for a tipple. I was surprised he was still here when I went down."

"Did he talk about himself at all?"

"Don't they all? Trouble is, you never know if any of it's true … Said he'd been in the army, both at Québec and Montréal, but now he had some job with the province."

In Newark? Not a big place! "Do you have any idea what brought him to Paulus Hook?"

"No, course not. You're asking a lot about him. You got it in for him?"

"I just want to ask him what he knows of Mr. Sproul."

She smiled mechanically. "Why don't we talk about *you?*"

Uh oh. I straightened up in my chair. "I'm here with a purpose, ma'am."

"Oh. Then I need another drink."

I signaled to Meed to refill both our glasses. "Can you recall anything more about him? He was with you for a couple hours, right? Did he do or say anything out of the ordinary?"

She sighed. "Oh … Yes. He took his time—unlike most. But he was always jumping up to look out through the window. Any time there was a racket, he'd break off and go peek through the curtains. He'd stay a couple minutes." I must have raised my eyebrows. "Yeah—without a stitch on!"

"Did you guess what he was looking for?"

"Not at first. But … after we had, you know, the first time, he said he wanted to take a walk, but I shouldn't take up with anybody else. I said that would require another payment—and he *paid!* And then he went out for, oh, half an hour. I lay down for a nap until I overheard him talking out by the stables. He was with those two sharks—the ones he and the Quaker were playing cards when I came downstairs."

I gulped. "You're sure it was the same men?"

"You couldn't miss the one of them, with his buck teeth and that scar on his forehead, and the other—big, fat oaf. I was amazed anyone in Steve's class would give them directions to the privy, but he was out there a while with them."

"Ten minutes? Twenty minutes?"

"I guess. I heard him ask if they'd brought everything."

My jaw dropped. "So … he definitely knew them!"

"Must have. The fat one was carrying a lantern and a coil of rope, and the other had a torn quilt under his arm. Then Steve had something he wanted them to see. He went behind the stable—I suppose to get it off his horse—and then he came back to the side where there was still good light."

"It was getting dark by then?"

"Just starting to. Anyway, it was— You know what a bosun's chair is?"

"Yes?" A bosun's chair is a lightweight plank for a seat, with a canvas back, but rather than having legs, it has straps that come together above the chair, so that the entire apparatus—with the boatswain belted into it, of course—can be safely hoisted to otherwise unreachable spots in a ship's high rigging. Parigo was up in one almost every day. "But how is it that *you* know what a bosun's chair is?"

"I grew up next to a shipyard in Perth Amboy," she said grimly.

"Oh."

"Wasn't all bad," she said. "Workmen used to let me swing in one when the overseer wasn't looking." She was waxing nostalgic. "When I was but six or seven."

"Aha. And ... what happened next?"

"*Eh?* Oh. I remember wondering what on earth they were doing with a bosun's chair, of all things. There's no yard anywhere near here, you know!"

An excellent question, Miss Paulette! "Quite so. But what did they do then?"

"They ... They all went behind the stable, and Steve came walking back alone toward the tavern, so I got back in bed."

"You didn't see the other two again?"

"Not until I found them all playing cards together, along with the Quaker gent."

"Uh huh." And we don't have to ask whether "Steve" got his money's worth in between. "About what time would you say you went down to get your supper?"

"*Oof!*" She shook her luxuriant—and actually fairly clean—russet tresses, apparently hoping I'd withdraw the tiresome question. I waited. "Well, it had been dark for a while before Mr. *Steve* left for his tipple. Then I waited for, oh, half an hour—I usually give them their time—before I got hungry and came down for my supper. Besides, it's warmer downstairs, that time of year, with the fire."

"I see. Now, who was in the tavern when you got there? Were there any of the locals?"

"Besides John and Wendell? Was Pedro there? No, it would have been way too late for Pedro, he's always gone before dark. No, it was just John and Wendell … and there was Steve, playing cards with his slimy chums and the Quaker gentleman."

"You know Wendell, I take it?"

She smirked. "Oh yes, I know Wendell!"

However pruriently entertaining a tale might lurk behind *that* response, I decided my own quest took precedence. "Did you join the table while you had supper?"

"Oh no, no. Girls like me are not welcome when you gentlemen are gaming with other gentlemen, I know that full well! *Steve* pretended like he'd never seen me before."

"Aha. And how did the—"

"No surprise to me, of course!"

"Did the others acknowledge you?"

"Acknowledge? Wendell blushed like he was twelve—he *is* twelve—and the Quaker man seemed affronted and turned his head away. But the other two …" She shuddered. "The one with the scar looked ready to pull my dress up right there and then!"

No wonder he lost the game! "So what did—"

"John and I ate our supper over here, while they continued playing where you were sitting before." She pointed up at the candleholder by way of explanation—a rusty iron ring suspended from the ceiling, supporting six candles.

"Did anything happen while you were eating? Did they talk?"

"Oh yes. Not much, though. I thought the two gents were put out because the other two were playing so badly. They obviously didn't know the game at all. Wendell picked up and left, soon after I walked in. He always does."

All right. "Did any of them ever address each other by name?"

"Ooh. No, it was always *sir* this and *sir* that." She quaffed a long swallow. "Wait, the one with the evil scar called the fat one something once. What? 'Joe,' it was! And 'Joe' right away kicked him in the shins! I saw it, the gents didn't."

"You're sure? Joe, not Jim? Or Bo?"

"No, it was Joe. That important?"

I wasn't prepared to say. "Important for me to know what you heard. Nobody ever quarreled or snapped at each other, that you saw?"

"Nope. I could tell John felt real nervous with those two toughs in the room, but they seemed to be on Sunday behavior to me." Obviously, *she* hadn't been to church for a while! "Besides, I knew that Steve probably wouldn't deal with them if they were, well, violent."

I was beginning to think she might have been mistaken, there. "How long did you stay?"

"Oh, I watched for a couple hands. What else do I have to do? But I was still hoping Steve would come back up, so I left, thinking he wouldn't want the others to see him going with me."

"But he didn't, anyway?"

"No. Last I saw of any of them."

"Aha." I thought for a minute and then stood up. "Well, you've been very helpful, ma'am. Would you care for another drink?"

She looked startled. Perhaps no one had ever called her *helpful* before. "I would, actually."

I nudged Meed, who was nodding off at the bar, asked him to get her another, and settled my bill. He—who clearly tolerated or even encouraged her prostitution—looked vaguely jealous of the time I'd spent with her in plain sight. "A wench like that ain't made for *talking*, mister!"

I ignored him and walked toward the door. "So what do you think really happened to the Quaker?" she called.

"I honestly … still don't know," was all I could answer.

My eyes smarted from the bright sunshine, and I regretted having had to spend so much of this gorgeous afternoon in that dank and dreary tavern. There was nobody about on the ferry dock. A young black couple were walking along the shore, holding hands, each using the other hand to secure a straw hat against the breeze. Asked when the next ferry might be expected, they said it had only left a few moments before—but should make good speed with all this wind. Straining my eyes, I could see it approaching the Manhattan shore. It would still be near an hour's wait.

Was there any point in staying here in New Jersey? Even having learned so much, I felt no closer to understanding what had happened to Daniel Sproul. But I couldn't imagine who else might make matters clearer—other than "Steve," if I could ever locate him. But it was far too late to attempt a trip to Newark to chase after a wild goose.

Frustrated, I set Mr. Sproul's luggage down on the rough bench by the dock and started ambling up the desolate, treeless shore toward Hoboken, the next hamlet. But once I passed a sandy stretch where four crude dinghies were beached, the land became so marshy, I turned back, fearing the complete ruin of my shoes. On the way, I walked behind the stables. There were two doors in the rear and two in front, so traffic could move through as needed. The hitching post in the back was five yards behind the structure, to avoid interference, which made it—I checked—out of sight of the house. The coachman's bunk was at the front. I saw it as I waved to Gunther, who was blacking his harnesses with the door wide open.

Meed's privy was closer to the tavern on the landward side. It was serviceable, but one of the less salubrious I've ever used. The back of the house, I noticed as I came out, had not been repainted the last time the front was whitewashed—a tawdry economy. It was half as large as my family's tavern. There was one protrusion from the rear, which I assumed was a kitchen, and there were but two windows on the second story, one in back—Miss Paulette's *seraglio*—and one in front. Yes, she would have been able to view activity on the western side of the stable, but not the north side, where the hitching post was. Would there be any cellar so close to the tide line? Doubtful.

I scanned the panorama and was briefly entertained only by a flock of sandpipers on the shore. I walked back to sit on the bench. The ferry was still tied up on the far side. After a few seconds of self-irritation, I recalled I'd brought paper and pencil, and that, if I didn't start writing down some of the bewildering details I'd heard, I'd never remember them. So I fell to. It improved my disposition, no matter how useless it all seemed.

"Mr. Dordrecht! Mr. Dordrecht!" a man called. But looking up, I could see no one. Surely it couldn't be from the ferry, still a quarter-mile away. "Mr. Dordrecht!"

"Mr. Brush!" No wonder I couldn't see him: he was sitting in his rowboat, holding onto one of the ferry dock's pilings, the top of his head below the level of the dock. I stowed my notes and walked over to him. There were three pails full of oysters on the floor of the rowboat—plus a great deal of reeking mud. "Looks like you've had a profitable afternoon!"

"Oh aye, but I thought of something else I wanted to tell you."

"Oh yes? What's that?" The ferry would arrive in five minutes.

"I remembered *why* I went in by the cow, you see. That morning."

It took a second to understand what he was talking about. "Well, it's moored near your house. Don't you usually go past the cow?"

"No. I was coming back from Hoboken, along the shore, so it was out of my way. And by that time I was fighting the current."

"Uh huh. So …"

"When I was fishing, earlier that night, I was … Oh, you see where the ferry is now? About three cables further south."

"Yes?"

"And I seen a light. On the cow."

"On the *cow?* A lantern?" *He's just now remembering this?*

"Aye, and there were men there too, at least three of them."

"On the *cow?* In the middle of the— What time was this? Can you guess?"

"It was just after eleven. I could hear the church bells that night, like we said."

"What on earth were they doing? There was no moon for working, yes?"

"Right. I dunno. Could be crabbing, I suppose."

"They could do that right here at the dock! Did anybody else see this?"

"Anybody else? I'm the only body ever up, that hour."

"Could you hear anything?"

"Couldn't make nothing out. They'd talk loud, and then they'd shush each other." He smiled. "One of them called somebody a 'Jackass!'"

"Aye?"

"Sounded just like the gent who bought all the rum!"

Like *Steve!*

"I thought maybe I should go in and see if they needed any help …"

"Yes?"

"But I got a bite just then—finally, nice big shad!—and when I looked over again later, it was all quiet."

"You think they were gone?"

"Not sure, but the light was out."

Though grateful he'd come forward, I was completely exasperated with his dullness. "Had you *ever* seen anybody working on the cow at night before, Mr. Brush?"

"*Uhh* ... well, can't say I have, no. That's why I thought I'd go by it, in the morning. Just curious, you see."

"And you found the hat."

"Aye. And I gave it to—"

"To Mr. Van Narden, right." The ferry thumped against the other side of the dock, nearly pitching me over on top of the oysterman. "Listen, good sir," I said while running back for the luggage, "thanks for telling me this! And, *um*, if it should happen that you would be needed as a witness in a court of law—"

"A court of *law!*"

"Just in case! You'd be willing to do your duty and go across to testify in court, wouldn't you?"

"What, across the river?"

"Aye."

"I've never been to New York City!" he said, grinning.

Uncontrollably, I *looked* at New York City to make certain it was still there, just one mile away. Some depths are beyond the fathoming! "Well then, it'd be a real exciting novelty for you!"

"Huzzah!"

The ferryman rang his bell. "Huzzah!" I called back to him as I scrambled aboard.

There had been a light on the cow that night.

"If you'll all please sit on the port side," the ferryman said.

"He means the left side, mother," a smug seven-year-old asserted.

In something of a daze, I found myself amid a gaggle of children who'd apparently come across with their mother for a picnic.

At least three men had been aboard the cow that night.

"That's it, you can brace your feet against the far thwart. It will be a bumpier ride than usual, this afternoon."

"Sit *down*, Jeremy, oh please!" the mother moaned.

The ferryman cast us off, the sails caught the wind, the boat immediately heeled sharply to starboard, and the children screamed in unison.

But I remained lost in my own thoughts. *A man who sounded just like the gent who'd bought the rum had called another a jackass.*

Two of the older lads, probably eight or nine, recovered themselves and began to skylark about. "Sit ye down, boys," the ferryman warned—to no avail.

He'd bought a jug of rum, not gin or whiskey—the same spirit that had permeated—

The mother shrieked with all her might as one of the little wretches tumbled overboard. "Damn!" roared the ferryman. "Sit down, all of you!" he commanded, struggling to bring the boat around.

"I can swim for him!" I shouted, tearing off my jacket.

"No!" the ferryman roared, shoving me back down. "Need you to pull him out! All of you, sit! He'll last until we get there!" the boat rounded onto the other tack. "Haul that line about for me, mister," he said to me calmly. One further tack brought us to a halt abreast of the terrified youngster within two minutes of his immersion. Not knowing even how to paddle, the child was frantically slapping the water. A few minutes more, and exhaustion would overwhelm him. "You hold onto the man's legs!" the ferryman instructed the other boy, as I leaned far over the gunwale to catch the flailing arms. Several muscles were strained as it took all my might to haul the sopping lad, and then myself, back inboard.

The family crumpled together in a heap of tears as I collapsed, panting, back on the port side, and the ferryman stoically regained the way of the boat. "You all right?" he asked. It was the same man I'd interviewed in March.

"Aye. I'll feel it tomorrow. You?"

"*Ugh.* Hate it when that happens! Second time this year! Never lost one, though—*Thank you*, Jesus!" He strained to hold his tiller against a sudden puff. "I've lost chickens, lost purses, lost hats by the dozen, but never lost man, woman, or child—*Praise* God!" He scanned ahead for other boats. "Ten more minutes, folks!"

One had to admire his composure. Mine was tested by the aches I felt in my struggle to get my jacket back on, plus the discovery that I'd torn my shirt and scratched my belly on the gunwale. Still wheezing, I leaned back, enjoying the warmth of the sun.

My eyes lit on the distant shore of Staten Island, about where we'd been that first snowy morning when my hat had blown over the side of the *Dorothy C.*, and Parigo had impudently told me the only reason anyone would have tried to save *me* was because they assumed I was Leavering's grandson. In my lessons with Fox and O'Malley, I'd learned much that would justify his assertion that the ship, ten times the size and burden of this ferry, would have taken far longer to maneuver its way back to any specific location where a man had been lost overboard. Yet still, had I … Had anyone explained simple doggy-paddling to this child, today, he'd have survived without trouble for an hour in the river, rather than being endangered in minutes by his own panic! But I'd told Parigo I could swim, and yet he'd still doubted my survival, because of the …

Because of the cold.

And suddenly I had in my mind's eye a complete and hideous picture of the foul manner in which the worthy Daniel Sproul had been brought to his untimely end.

Chapter 11

"Well, Thomas Dordrecht! It's about time you paid me a social call! You've been back a week, and yet … My dear, what's wrong? You look all done in!"

Adelie Glasby pulled me inside the threshold of the home she and her husband had leased a year ago on the smart block of Maiden Lane, just off Broadway. Within a minute, she had me seated comfortably in the small, handsomely appointed sitting room, called Mr. Glasby from his study, and furnished me with a glass of ale.

"So, did you manage to get your goods safely into the warehouse, despite all that rain?" John Glasby boomed, entering the parlor. Seeing his wife's worried face and my attire—hardly appropriate for Sunday visiting—he stopped short. "Where on earth have you been just now?"

I took another long draw on the ale, having difficulty mustering my thoughts.

"Are you concerned about the business, Thomas? Perhaps I should withdraw, and let—"

"No, no, Adelie, it's not that! Please stay. It's …"

As I'd staggered off the ferry, numbly acknowledging the mother's effusive blessings, I'd grown more and more apprehensive of relating my intuitions of the lethal plot I'd just envisioned. For twenty minutes, I had walked aimlessly about, debating whether I'd do more harm than good if I told Mr. Leavering how I suspected his son-in-law had been killed—without any absolute proof—though I now felt utterly positive about it. And I could still not point to any conceivable motive for the plot. How would it affect an already weakened and grieving man—a man who is my employer, mentor, and, I dare to say, my friend? In the most dire case, might it fatally distress him?

"John, he's trembling! Perhaps some brandy, instead?"

"No! Thank you, I—"

"Are you in some sort of trouble, Thomas?" John asked.

"No, it's not that, either, it's—" There was no avoiding it now. Perhaps that was why I had come to them. "It's about Mr. Sproul."

Adelie and John Glasby looked at each other, and me, stunned and bewildered. "Mr. Sproul?" both said.

And finally, having gotten the sentence out, I began to regain control of myself. "Aye. Mr. Sproul's death, which has always seemed so unnatural to us, because of his good health and sanguine disposition?"

"Yes?"

"It's because it *was* unnatural. Mr. Sproul, I fear ... I feel positive ... was murdered."

It was their turn to gasp and tremble. "Murdered!" Adelie breathed, raising a handkerchief to her face.

"Thomas, that's a ... very serious ... thing to say!" John Glasby protested softly, taking her hand. "How ...?"

It took nearly an hour. I daresay it was not the most coherent recitation, either, but they prompted me for enough clarification that the narrative emerged. It commenced with the accidental discovery of the cards and proceeded back to the lamentable friendship that began years ago between my father, the former schout of New Utrecht, and Joe Wicklow, the former constable of Brooklyn. And from there, I detailed all my activities and thoughts of the last thirty-six hours.

"You pulled the boy out of the Hudson! You're a hero, Thomas!"

What? "Oh. No, the ferryman was the hero, Adelie. I nearly jumped in and caused him twice the trouble."

"Explain this ghastly machine to us again, Thomas," John demanded. "I can't picture it."

"It's not a ghastly machine, John, that's just it. It's a perfectly sensible, utilitarian tool—perverted beyond speaking."

"It's a floating platform, with a hole in the middle?"

"Right. With a pyramidal framework that suspends a hoist directly over the hole."

"All right. So … your surmise is that the two ruffians, Wicklow and—"

"Meshach Hager, known as 'Shacky.'"

"—were waiting behind the stables when Mr. Sproul came out, following this Steve person?"

"Aye. And rather than coming to his defense, *Steve* joined them in subduing Mr. Sproul. Mr. Sproul may have been in fine fettle, but when three men, each larger than himself, combine—"

"Oh, how vile!" Adelie exclaimed, voicing the emotion sickening the three of us.

"They must instantly have put a hand over his mouth," I ventured, "and somehow constrained him from crying out—which might have been disastrous to them on a quiet night, with the coachman asleep just on the other side of the building. Then they stripped him down and—this is a guess—rolled him tightly into quilts or blankets, which they then secured so that no marks would be left on the body. Then—again, I'm guessing—they tied him into the bosun's chair right there on the shore. It would've been far easier to do ashore than on the water."

"I see," John murmured. "Or I think I see."

"Once they'd gagged and immobilized him, they loaded him into a rowboat and rowed out to the cow, where they had to light the lantern briefly, in order to see where anything was." I gulped. "They attached the bosun's chair, with Mr. Sproul in it, to the hoist … and lowered it until he was neck deep in the water … which at that time of the year was cold enough to cause the strongest man alive to perish within half an hour."

"Dear heaven!" Adelie moaned.

"They must simply have stood there," I theorized, "*waiting*, until they were sure he was dead!" Now her husband looked ill. "Then they hoisted him out, extricated his body from the bosun's chair, redressed it in the dry garments, got it and themselves back into the rowboat, crossed the river, and quietly deposited him in the yard of Roberson's hotel on the Greenwich road." A thought occurred to me.

"Perhaps they deliberately splashed the clothes with rum, to make people think … Or perhaps it was an accident …"

We sat in silent contemplation for a moment. "It was the fisherman who showed you this 'cow,' because he'd seen a light there in the night," Adelie asserted. "But how was it that you came to speak with him, in the first place?"

"Oh! Because it was he who had discovered the hat!"

"What hat?"

"Ah, Mr. Sproul's hat." I'd not shown them. The luggage was by their entryway, where I'd deposited it as I came in. Producing it caused yet another sensation. "We had wondered where his hat and his luggage were. He'd left the valise at Van Narden's, but he wore the hat when he walked down to Meed's tavern for supper. My guess is that they had planned to put the hat back on him, but they simply forgot about it—a flat, black hat in pitch dark—and they'd stepped on it, flattening it even more."

"It's ruined," Adelie observed, morosely setting it back with the clothes.

"Yes. If they recalled it later, they probably assumed it would most likely blow off the cow and sink before anyone discovered it."

"And … after they left the body?" John asked.

"They rowed away as quickly as possible, I reckon, but they only went a mile or so to the north, and beached again near the foundry. And there—I can only guess there was a quarrel—Hager was done in, knifed, with none of the *finesse* that was expended to divert us with regard to Mr. Sproul."

"But Wicklow was related to Hager!"

"Aye, a cousin of some sort. But … if he was still present with the other two, it doesn't appear that he came to his cousin's defense. More likely the contrary, as Hager bore no marks of having attempted to defend himself—probably because someone was restraining him."

"And Wicklow himself has since met a bad end," John stated.

"An extremely suspicious end, John, though it passed for a common tavern brawl at the time."

"So both of the accomplices of Miss Paulette's gent from Newark … are dead!" Adelie observed.

We all nodded at the significance of this fact. "I think we should tell Mr. Leavering!" Glasby announced with sudden conviction.

"And *Mrs.* Leavering!" his wife added tartly.

"And Mrs. *Sproul*, for that matter," he rejoined. "In fact, whatever the consequences, they have a right to know. Whether we regard the supposition of murder as incontrovertible or not, we are certain that we now know his whereabouts until late that evening. We *must* tell them!"

"Ah, but it's too late, tonight, John, they'll have retired. They've been retiring very early ever since this happened, Thomas."

That was sad, as they used to enjoy the evening life of the city. "When can we all visit them, then?" I asked.

My host sighed. "I absolutely have to be in the office tomorrow. We have people coming to buy all that sugar you've brought us! And *you* have to be there too, Thomas—Mapes is completely swamped!"

"*I* shall tell them, tomorrow morning!" Adelie announced firmly.

John looked as if he would protest for a second, but thought better of it. "Well, if anyone can break it to them gently, it is my wife," he conceded.

"Have you had any supper, Thomas?" Adelie asked. Upon consultation with my innards, I confessed I was absolutely famished. "Then you must stay!"

By tacit agreement, we did not discuss the matter of Mr. Sproul at table. Rather, I had occasion at last to describe some of the wonders of my trip. Saint Eustatius was already beginning to seem as remote as a dream. But I could tell my hosts were too agitated to concentrate on it. When I at length finished my second helping, they hastened to suggest we return to the parlor for a glass of port.

"So this 'gent,' this 'Steve,' hails from Newark?" John resumed.

"If we grant that he was telling Miss Paulette the truth," I said. "All we really have is his physical description, which is confirmed by Meed and by Wendell Brush. She herself cast doubt upon the name."

"And for that matter," Adelie added, "we may well wonder what *her* real name is! Did she show any hesitation or deviousness when you spoke with her, Thomas?"

"Well … I wouldn't doubt that she'd be capable of it, Adelie. But I don't think so, in this instance. She seemed indifferent to her recollection of him—save for her, *um,* emolument."

"You're rather delicate with these ladies, Thomas!" she teased. "Perhaps you're not quite as insensible to their charms as we supposed?"

"Adelie, please!" I protested. "If my sister Geertruid hears—"

John Glasby came to my rescue. "Didn't you say 'Steve' claimed to work for the province in Newark?" I nodded. "Well, then he would likely be one of the port officials. Any other province officials would reside in the capital, in Elizabethtown."

"A tax collector!" Adelie exclaimed with clear distaste.

"Just so. Maybe … someone could go and search him out!"

"Do you think we can take this to the authorities, John?" she asked.

"The authorities!" he huffed, with unexpected vehemence. "The *authorities* have got yet another war on their hands, and the only thing they care about at the moment is that it should be fully supplied. And to do that, they're ready and willing to turn every consideration of law and equity on its head! The Crown's attorneys will be too busy prosecuting shippers and tradesmen to bother themselves with a mere case of murder!"

"John—" Adelie cautioned.

"Do you know that Mr. Leavering was prevailed upon to pledge eight hundred pounds toward the surety of two of his friends who have been *jailed* on charges of trading with the enemy! Trading *wheat,* mind you, not saltpeter! The firm will be unable to invest in any new ship or warehouse or factory until that fortune is released. And at the rate these lawyers and politicians stumble along, it could be years before the matter is resolved. Years!"

I'd listened to businessmen's complaints on this score since I'd joined the firm, but this was a new level of outrage from the usually modest and conservative John Glasby. I had thought Mapes was surely exaggerating. Obviously, I'm out of touch with the news of the world!

"My dear, you're ranting!"

He caught himself. "Ah! Of course you're right, my love, I beg pardon!" He finished his glass. "We must consult with Benjamin for our next move. Even at his weakest, his common sense has never failed us!"

It was clear, however, that they both remained upset—the unprecedented public upheavals only exacerbating the private turmoil we felt. It seemed a good moment to thank them and take my leave. Both my body and my brain needed a good night's sleep, so the sensible thing to do was to go home and get it. And for once I did the sensible thing!

Refreshed in the morning, I strode through Monday traffic with renewed determination to tackle all problems at work and elsewhere. As I drew within sight of Peck Slip, however, I noted an unusual grouping of men huddled intently on the far corner. Curious, I crossed over and discovered them observing a young black fellow who was swiftly creating a pencil sketch of a sailor. The entertainment apparently lay in the dexterity and precision with which he was capturing the mariner's unremarkable features. After two minutes, he halted and said, "There! That's done it!"

Though the seaman was pleased with the likeness and avowed he'd send it to his lass back in old England, he quarreled with the sixpence charge … until an onlooker jested he should cough up a shilling for the improvements that had been made upon nature. He paid and the crowd dispersed. "Would you like your own portrait sketched, sir?" the artist asked me as he picked up his easel.

"Oh! No, at least not today, thank you." I turned back, but halted at the curb to let a drayman pass.

"If you ever should, sir, you can ask for Jones at the Negro tavern on Bridge Street!"

"Aha, very good!" I was within five paces of the office stairs when something jogged my memory. I turned back, but the fellow had disappeared. Where had I heard of a sketch artist named Jones before? From the coroner's driver!

Without an instant's hesitation, I turned on my heel and stepped off smartly in the direction of the morgue. As I moved, I rationalized this quixotic decision on the ground that I was a *little* early to work now, and would therefore only be a *little* late after I had made my inquiries. As I turned the corner approaching the structure, I saw a slave adding oats to a horse's feed bag directly in front of it. He and I recognized each other—but I couldn't recall a name. "Aston I is, mister!" he announced, pointing to himself with a grin.

"Yes! Thomas Dordrecht," I stated. "It was you who said that Jones made a sketch of the cadavers who were to be interred in the potter's field!"

"Aye?" he agreed warily.

"Would they still have one that would have been made back in March?"

"*Hoo!* Don't know, boss. We can ask!" He tethered the horse and led me inside and up to the first floor. He reiterated my request to the functionary in charge—who pointed him to a room further back without seeming to need any justification of my purpose—and I followed him through a heavy door into a large closet with only one window. Our storeroom at the office looks pristine in comparison. A constable was interrogating a smooth-cheeked lad who was sitting on a stool with his wrists tied behind him, about the knavery of a gang of petty thieves. The boy had red welts on his face, and the constable looked very annoyed at the interruption. "Morgue pictures?" Aston demanded.

The constable grunted and pointed at one box among many in the corner. "Overdue for winnowing," he muttered.

Aston overturned the box onto a table. "Last December!" he grunted, pointing to a date notation. "Only supposed to keep them three months!" He turned more pictures over, having the sense to maintain what little order they had, and presently came to March of this year. "What we looking for?"

"March twenty-second. Meshach Hager."

"Oh yeah, the slimy Shacky. Here is!" He passed the paper to me.

It was smudged and torn, but the drawing was as true as the sailor's, instantly bringing my actual viewing to mind—particularly in that Jones had captured the repellent sneer and bloodied wildness of the corpse. "May I borrow this?"

"It's yours. Should've been thrown out weeks ago."

"What are these numbers?"

"Grave location, just in case. But he still there—poisoning the worms!" He laughed at his own joke.

"Aston, get out of here, will you!" the constable ordered.

Making an impudent gesture as soon as the speaker's back was turned, Aston unhurriedly reset the pile in its box and pulled me into the other room. Through the door, I heard the bound lad screaming. "I collect you now," Aston said, ignoring it. "You and Jennet and me went over to the Greenwich road ... Wait! You the fellow McCraney want to see! I drives him down to your office when he looking for you, but there weren't nobody knew anything."

"McCraney, the coroner?"

"The assist, yeah. He probably downstairs. We only find one stiff for him this morning!" Aston held out his palm expectantly. The smallest coin I had, unfortunately, was a sixpence, so that's what he got. But at least he appreciated it!

I proceeded down below, ignoring the church bells tolling eight o'clock, and knocked on the door of the morgue.

"Yes? What is it?" Immediately the door slid open, and McCraney, in a bloodied apron and bloodied hands, looked at me blankly.

"Thomas Dordrecht, Mr. McCraney. I understand you wished to see me." I took a glance over his shoulder at the body on the table—and resolved not to repeat the error.

"Oh yes," McCraney said at length. "Give me a moment, please?" I gladly nodded. He shut the door, and I paced the outer room for three minutes until he reappeared, cleaned up. "Sorry to hold you, sir. You were involved in the curious case of Mr. Sproul, isn't that it? Last winter?"

"That's right. I made the official identification of his body for you, because it was so distressing to my employer, Mr. Leavering."

"Mr. *Leavering*, yes. Now I remember. After you left, I was so dissatisfied, I went over the corpse again, until the undertaker came for it."

"Indeed?" I said breathlessly.

"Well, I didn't find much, that I recall, but I wanted you to know ... Let me locate my notes." He sat at the desk and began to rummage about, finally putting his hand on a journal. "Ah! It didn't seem that important, so I didn't get around to visiting your office for a week, and I was informed that the principal was in Philadelphia, Mr. Glasby was spending a day in the firm's warehouse, and you were gone abroad!"

"I see, yes. But what else did you discover?"

McCraney spent a minute locating and rereading his notations, and then he cleared his throat. "There were very slight contusions around the ankles and just under the rib cage." He scanned further, nodding to himself. "But even more curiously, there was a small piece of torn cloth, about an inch square, caught in his back teeth."

"Cloth? Could you tell what kind?"

"Wool. Red. About the thickness of a winter scarf."

"Uh huh! Anything else?"

"Well, I had been embarrassed when someone—Oh, it was you, wasn't it?—pointed out that his clothes were saturated with rum, so I examined them, also. And I found that the rum was not only on the front of the waistcoat and jacket, where you might expect to find spillage, but all over the clothes—on the breeches and on the back of the waistcoat! How he managed to get rum on the back of his waistcoat, I can't begin to imagine!" He read further. "Also, there were a few spatters of very pungent mud on the jacket. Not regular farm soil, a much sharper odor." I nodded. "That's about it. I thought you should …" He noticed the sketch I was holding. "Isn't that one of our morgue drawings? What on earth do you want with it?"

"This is the one of Meshach Hager." McCraney looked at me blankly. "You called him a '*bravo*.'" I put the sketch in his hands, but it still brought no recognition. "His corpse was brought in just an hour after Mr. Sproul's. In fact, we used it to compare the temperatures of the two torsos."

"Oh yes. A petty thief and rapparee. But … why do you—"

I decided to rehearse my suppositions as a test of their plausibility. "Through an unusual and fortunate happenstance, Mr. McCraney, I have only yesterday discovered that Mr. Sproul and Meshach Hager had encountered each other before their bodies were simultaneously brought into your office for examination."

His jaw dropped. "The Quaker gentleman … and this *ruffian?*"

"Aye, sir. I have taken the sketch in the hope of more positive identification, but circumstances and the verbal descriptions of witnesses make it most likely that they were among a foursome playing cards over in Paulus Hook the evening before Mr. Sproul and Hager appeared here."

"But this Hager was obviously a noisome and repellent figure! Why would—"

"I think Mr. Sproul was possessed of a democratical and tolerant disposition—and he was very eager to relax with a game of cards."

"I would be most reluctant to remain in the same room with the like!"

"And you would be wise in that, Mr. McCraney, because it is my theory that Mr. Sproul's fellow card-players—there were three of them, one to all appearances a gentleman—accosted him late that evening outside the tavern where they met … and overpowered him and … murdered him."

McCraney now looked as though it was crossing his mind that I might be a lunatic. "How could this be?"

Without retelling the process by which I'd deduced the events, I explained the mechanics of how I believed Mr. Sproul to have been killed. The details he'd just added, I observed, were completely consistent with my theory. He was still shaking his head in disbelief—which reminded me that I had evidence to show him—Mr. Sproul's luggage and hat, which I was carrying to the office for safekeeping.

It was the hat that intrigued him. He pointed to the largest splash of gray mud. "Do you mind if I scrape this off?"

Although mystified, I had no objection. "The hat's ruined."

He scraped the dried mud into a small ceramic bowl, and sniffed it. "No great odor," he observed. Then he added a tiny bit of water and mixed it with his index finger. Again, he subjected his nose to it—and recoiled. "Smell!" he commanded, handing me the bowl.

"*Oof!*"

"Awful, isn't it! But it's the same as the mud that was on his coat. I can't imagine where such repellent soil is to be found."

I could. "It's from the river bottom, Mr. McCraney. It was all over the cow device. I smelled it just yesterday."

"I … see."

I carefully formulated a question. "Do you perceive any objection to the proposition that it is *possible* that this is how Mr. Sproul died?"

"You mean, from the evidence of his corpus?" He thought. "No. The only implausibility is external to that, it's … disbelief that any murderers would go to so much trouble when they could have as easily garroted or stabbed him without producing a commotion."

"They were concerned to avoid any uproar over the fact of murder, it seems, Mr. McCraney. They wanted no public clamor or investigation."

"Still … it is very convoluted!"

Church bells rang the half-hour. "I must run, sir. I am terribly late for work."

We stood. He handed me the hat and I packed it again into the bag. "Oh! If you were away, you must have missed seeing your Mrs. Glasby in *The Recruiting Officer*!"

Remorse struck me, because I hadn't even thought to inquire of it since I returned.

"She was most amazingly humorous! Please tell her how greatly I enjoyed her performance!"

He was yet another of her conquests, I thought—with an absurd twinge of jealousy. "I will do so, sir!"

Mr. Glasby and Mapes both scowled at me as I arrived at quarter to nine. But I could tell, as he demanded an explanation, that he was equally alarmed as irritated. He'd not slept well, he admitted, the scenario of Mr. Sproul's murder having haunted him. When I explained my delay, he only seemed more upset. He asked me to work with Mapes to ensure that the Saint Eustatius goods were completely located, organized, categorized, and readied for sale. I should then sit with the bookkeeper and clarify the dozens of expenses I had incurred getting the shipments from Sheepshead Bay to their present locations. I then needed urgently to attend to the bookkeeping issues related to all the transactions of my five-month travels. "Even if you've kept good notes, Thomas, it's easy for this to get away from you!"

Although I had believed my notes to be meticulous, I hadn't spent half an hour with Mapes on the first problem before I realized that much of my own handwriting was nearly illegible to me, not to mention everyone else in the world. It didn't help that Mapes, so far from gloating, could barely concentrate, as Glasby had just informed him of my suppositions regarding the death of Mr. Sproul.

All of this was disrupted before ten o'clock by the unanticipated appearance of Mr. Leavering, followed by Mrs. Leavering and Mrs. Glasby, who seldom visited the office. Still panting from the stairs, he said, "John, I'd like to see you directly, please! Thomas, Cyrus!"

I think all three of us—and everyone else in the office—were surprised to be addressed by our given names at work, but it was clearly an order. He marched directly into his office and installed his wife in the most comfortable chair.

"We have completely misjudged them both!" I heard Adelie Glasby whisper, smiling to her husband as we followed.

"Close the door, please, Thomas!" I did so, noting the restoration of a self-possessed tone not heard since that ghastly instant when McCraney had pulled back the blanket. "Cyrus, have you been brought to date with our speculations concerning Mr. Sproul's demise?"

"I have, Mr. Leavering. Mr. Glasby just—"

"Excellent. Mrs. Glasby has just done the same for Hermione and me." He paused a second. "I think it is imperative that we pursue this matter without delay! What Thomas has revealed is evidence of a …" He shook his head.

"A most heinous, unspeakable crime!" Mrs. Leavering emphatically finished for him.

"Exactly so. And I am resolved that everything possible must be done to reveal the villain and bring him to justice!"

"Hear, hear!" she exclaimed.

"And I am prepared to devote my personal funds to this effort, as the affront to my family has been severe. If the firm should incur costs in the effort, I shall make it up out of my pocket. I am hoping we can ask you, Thomas, to dedicate your full energies to this matter, until it is resolved, as we believe—"

"We are greatly in your debt for the initiative you have voluntarily shown thus far, Thomas!" Mrs. Leavering asserted warmly.

Overwhelmed, before I could muster the appropriately modest reply that I'd done only what I felt *I* owed to Mr. Sproul's memory … the moment passed.

"Despite having been away these many months, Thomas has a clearer grasp of the sequence of events that took place during Daniel's last hours, and he has spoken directly with many of the individuals who saw him then, thus giving him a leg up on any further investigation. John?"

"Well, that's undeniable, Mr. Leavering, it's just—"

"What?"

"We need all the help we can get *here*. A good sale of the *Dorothy C.*'s cargo is probably our last chance for profit in this fiscal year, and—"

"Nonsense! I shall be in the office to assist with that!" Glasby and Mapes exchanged a startled look, and exhaled with relief. "I fear I have been remiss in allowing a personal tragedy to undermine my duty to the firm," Leavering admitted, coloring slightly, "but I hope I can now make amends for that. Thomas, may we count on you to undertake this matter?"

This time, I was prepared! "Sir, it would be no more or less than what I feel *I* owe to Mr. Sproul's memory!"

"*Ooh*, well done!" Mrs. Glasby mouthed, beaming at me.

"Excellent. Now, how shall we proceed?"

After a second's pause, Glasby spoke up. "I was thinking we might inquire of our competitors down on Rodman's Slip, who lade some of their ships in Newark, if they know of the officialdom there. Perhaps they—"

"I'm thinking we should send Thomas directly to Philadelphia," Mr. Leavering asserted, overruling him. "Whatever precipitated this plot must surely have originated there. Somebody knew, better than we did, that Daniel would be in Paulus Hook that night. Thomas?"

"I think you're right, sir. This scheme was unquestionably premeditated, and from Philadelphia."

"I shall write to my daughter and Mr. Castell immediately. How soon do you think you could go?"

"High water today?" I asked Mapes.

"One thirty."

"Well ... I could get there fastest by taking a boat to Perth Amboy this afternoon, but I'd prefer to take the coach, to retrace Mr. Sproul's route, as it were, even though the next one won't leave until

Wednesday morning. Waiting might also give me an opportunity to show some of the people I've talked to the morgue picture of Meshach Hager that I just acquired."

That had to be passed around the room; no one recognized him. Mrs. Leavering, hearing revulsion from the likes of Mapes and Glasby, balked at looking at it. "An evil face," Mr. Leavering observed.

"If ever there was one," Mrs. Glasby concurred.

"Very well then! But if you have any extra time before departing, you might spend it here, Mr. Dordrecht, helping Mr. Mapes get a firmer overview of the cargo." He'd reverted to formal address, we all noted. "That is the firm's priority. The accounting is important, but—"

"I have a concern, Benjamin," Mrs. Leavering interrupted, "before we disband here."

"Of course, my love."

"And that is, that a certain amount of reticence, of discretion, is called for, by all of us. If Thomas is correct in his inferences, this fiend who dresses as a gentleman has done in not only my son-in-law, but his own two accomplices. He is clearly a most desperate character, of horrific ruthlessness! I would recommend that we all—what's the phrase?—*keep mum!*"

"Well advised, madam!" Mr. Leavering agreed. "Can we all submit to this discipline?" He sought out nods from all present and must have noticed doubt on my visage. "Well, Mr. Dordrecht, we realize you may need leave to relate some aspects of—"

"We are concerned that you should not become yet another victim of this villain, Thomas!"

"Thank you, ma'am, I stand warned! But we do have in our favor the fact that he cannot be unaware that there has been no outcry about any of these crimes in the six months that have elapsed, and therefore may well have become somewhat complacent."

"Don't press your luck, young man!"

"Point taken again, ma'am! But beside that, Mr. Leavering … I may wish to engage with my cousin Charles on this matter."

"Oh, I see," he said. "*Umm* …" They all looked uncomfortable. Mapes had a very sour face, having once met Charles and taken an instant dislike to him.

"With all due respect to your cousin, Thomas," Glasby said, "Mr. Cooper is a notorious gossip, and—"

"On the other hand, John," Mrs. Glasby broke in, "Charles is probably already aware that something's afoot, and you know he'll worm it out of us despite our best efforts."

"He will, that!" Mrs. Leavering agreed, smiling.

"And while he gives the impression of being a flagrant tattletale, he's actually very careful and deliberate in his gossiping."

Her husband shrugged, and Mr. Leavering concurred that Cooper might be included in our cabal. After announcing that he was very happy to be getting back to work … he enjoined us all to do the same and closed the meeting.

I took the opportunity to escort the ladies down to the street, and then attempted to clear my head by walking alone around the block. Before heading off to Philadelphia, I needed to settle my personal affairs, at least by collecting the remainder of my supercargo goods from my brother's barns—not just because time was wasting until I should dispose of them, but because he'd become frantic over the approaching harvest. Also, I wanted to stop by *The Jug* again to show the sketch of Hager. The weather, I observed, looked likely to hold dry for another two days, at least, which would allow me to accomplish a Long Island trip on the morrow. Therefore, I had no reason not to return to the office and see if I could get some work done.

So I did.

My cousin Charles tracked me down before I even began to look for him. He was sitting on a barrel on Peck Slip, reading a newspaper, when I left the office at six thirty. "Suppertime!" he announced, taking my elbow and steering me up the waterfront to yet another of his haunts, a "low tavern with a high kitchen manned by two slaves captured on Martinique."

"How long were you sitting there waiting, Charles?"

"Not long, lad, but if the sun had gone down, I'd have barged into the office to drag you away."

Oh sure, I thought.

"I enquired for you yesterday at your residence, hoping to hear of your trip. But not finding you, I applied to Mrs. Glasby for the latest, this afternoon, and—"

Aha! "And so, as usual, you already *know everything!*"

"Of course. Save for everything else, which you're about to tell me!" Impatiently, I frowned at him. "Given that, supper is my treat, of course!"

Once again I speculated whence his ready cash emanated—and dismissed the issue. "Tell you what, cousin—thou who knowest all—I, too, want some information, some news, given that I've been almost completely out of touch for half a year, and—"

"Have you heard the latest from Russia?"

"*Russia?* I was thinking of—"

"It's *too* delicious! The tsar of Russia, who gained the throne only in January, has been deposed!"

"Deposed! Peter, right?"

"By his wife!"

"His *wife!* But how—"

"The nobles and the army like her better than him, don't you know! So all the palaver of the law of primogeniture and the sacred blood inheritance—*hist!* out the window!"

"But—"

"He asked only to retire in peace, stupid sod. Lasted a week before he suffered a most *unfortunate* accident!"

I had to laugh too, though I wondered how funny the populace found it.

"And to top it, Catherine—her name, a spunky lass by all accounts—reversed the imperial war policy yet again, and has withdrawn her forces from any support of our own beloved ally, Frederick of Prussia, throwing Whitehall into yet another tizzy!"

I drifted off for a minute, recalling Mr. Fox's musings on the previous royal accession. Would the enemies of the past six months now be friends again? Would the allies of half a year be deemed enemies anew?

We reached the establishment he'd selected, the appearance of which was quite dubious: peeling paint on sagging wood. I had to duck to get inside the door. Suspiciously unpopulated. "We're early," Charles offered lamely.

But the beer came promptly and was good enough to dispel my qualms. "What I actually was wondering—"

"*Eh?*"

"Was what has been going on here in this city? Mr. Glasby waxes nearly apoplectic over—"

"And for once, I agree with him!" Charles and John Glasby maintain civility out of their mutual love of Adelie and the Leaverings, but are frequently impatient with each other's political views. "Notwithstanding the departure of the unlamented Earl of Chatham from His Majesty's government"—unlamented by Charles Cooper, that is—"the dolts have successfully embroiled us in war with Spain, as well as France and half of Europe! This, when the kingdom will need a full generation to pay off the public debt already incurred, no matter that we have all the wealth that can be plundered out of *Canada* to assist! Such a shame that no one realized beaver hats have gone out of fashion!"

The onslaught of his sarcasm, as usual, was nearly overwhelming. However, as I was coming to agree with many of his contentions, I nodded mildly and quaffed my beer.

"And the governor and council of our very own province have dutifully made contributions to these follies, in our name, that will ensure that *we* shall spend our lives paying off the debts *locally* incurred for this war. Meanwhile, eighteen honest commercial men await their trials for trading with the French sugar plantations, the embargo on all trade has idled dozens of ships in the roads, business is declining anyway, the drought has the farmers in a panic, and the *HMS Enterprise* can find nothing better to do than accost one ship after another in the hope of a condemnation that will bring a two-eighths share to its patriotic captain!"

"The *Enterprise* is still on our shores?"

"Aye, curse the bastard! It was she who brought the news of war with Spain, she who dragged the *Dove* into court—"

"It was the *Enterprise* that drove the *Dorothy C.* out of Sandy Hook into a blizzard!"

"What!" Charles was thrilled to hear of yet another malefaction with which to berate the hated vessel.

"She hadn't been anchored more than an hour before she dispatched her boats to press men off ships waiting out the storm. We got wind of it, and Captain Trent elected to brave the shoals without a pilot rather than risk losing his crew."

"My God! Extraordinarily dangerous! You could have been killed!"

"The men made no complaint. And, as one of them pointed out, *I* could have been pressed!"

"I dare say. And you've already done your share for the war effort."

"My sentiments as well."

"I don't *believe* in the war effort, Thomas."

"Understood, Charles."

"I think we—"

"Would you gentlemens care to order?"

A young black lass was apparently to be our improbable servitor. And immediately, my cousin's passion veered from politics to venery. With amazement and alarm—her race constituting no barrier—I saw his hand reach around behind, and—

I heard it before I realized what I'd seen. She'd smacked him, hard across the chops! The manager rushed over to push the girl back to the kitchen as I fell to pieces laughing at the reprobate's pout. The manager rushed back, blithering apologies, and avowing the girl would be thoroughly chastised. Charles was hilariously trying to recover his dignity.

"Nah, bring her back—and have her do it again!" I roared, unable to control myself. Charles looked ready to bolt the place, which only provoked me the more. Finally, he seemed to regain his shame-faced self-possession. "You asked for it, cousin. You know you did!" I told him. The manager took our glasses to refill them. I leaned across the table and whispered, "I wonder if *Sejanus* will be reporting this moment to a gossip-hungry public?"

"You wouldn't!"

"I'll have to think about it," I teased.

The manager placed our refilled glasses in front of us, declaring he would whip the girl himself. Charles took a deep breath and caught his wrist. "Don't whip the bitch!" he wheezed.

"But—"

"Not necessary. Don't whip her."

Now the manager looked irritated that Charles was interfering with his disciplinary methods. He swallowed it, however. "*I'll* be happy to take your orders, gentlemen."

Though I was still chuckling, and Charles was panting from the effort of the closest approximation to a true apology I'd ever heard pass his lips, we managed to put in an order for food.

"Mother says Brevoort went back into the army. She thinks—"

"Your brother's a fool, Thomas."

There was no point in taking offense. It was near my own opinion, and Charles would have been even more scathing about *his* brother. "She thinks he may have been on a flotilla that left here over the summer?"

"Likely. It was huge." I waited for further elucidation. His morale finally repaired, Charles said, "Cuba."

"It *was* for Cuba?"

"Havana. Where the dons stage the flotillas of gold and silver from Peru and Mexico."

"Well defended?"

"Of course … No, I haven't heard anything yet."

Food was placed before us. The manager offered more apologies until Charles waved him away. But my cousin's choice was vindicated: notwithstanding the drab surroundings, my ham steak was excellent. Presently, our spirits revived. "All right, your turn! What prompted your dash to New Jersey yesterday, Thomas?"

Even though he'd heard it all from Adelie just hours before, he demanded every detail again, from me. It served to clarify his understanding, he claimed. I dare say the repetition served the same purpose for my own thinking.

"What you must look for in Philadelphia, Thomas," he dictated as we were served apple pie, "is not primarily who did this, but *why* it was done! Someone knew that Sproul was traveling to New York, and they even knew how he was traveling to New York. Why did they need to kill him? Why did they go to such lengths? Why did they need to make it seem accidental? Why was his gold stolen, but not his silver?"

"All good questions, cousin. Yes, I shall certainly pursue the answers. Tell me, do you know anything of the port of Newark?"

"Ha! Not really—other than all port officers are notoriously corrupt, and the New Jersey ports garner less oversight than New York and Philadelphia, so …"

"An officer of the province stationed in Newark—"

"Is more than likely to be bent!"

True to his promise, Charles paid for the meal. He accompanied me all the way out to my boarding house, still culling particulars. "You haven't belabored me for an accounting of our disreputable Uncle Gerrit, Charles!"

"Oh that. Old news, Thomas! Mother heard it all from Aunt Betje last week. I must say I enjoyed retailing it to my brother, the Reverend Henry Cooper, however." He smacked his lips. "He was *so* mortified, poor fellow!" He drew a theatrical sigh. "And how was I ever to know that three of his congregation were eavesdropping upon our shameful family dirt?"

Chapter 12

"Pa, I'm going to show you a sketch from the city morgue. It ain't pretty, but I want to see if you recognize the face."

"What?"

The sobriety resolution having evidently held for another three days, Pa's orneriness was intensified, but his mind, I sensed, was clearer. "Pa, it's important, but, as I say, it's ugly. This is a picture of a dead man."

"Oh for—" He snatched the paper from my hand but sucked in his breath after turning it over. "It's Shacky!" he said incredulously. "He's dead?"

"You knew him?"

The belligerence relaxed. "Met him a couple times last winter. Some cousin of Joe Wicklow's. Joe didn't really like him much. Always whining about money."

"When was the last time you saw him?"

"When? Can't recall. Snow still on the ground."

"Why did Wicklow abide him at all? I don't conjure Wicklow as a tolerant type."

"Nah. Maybe Joe liked the fact that Shacky scared people. Last time I saw him, I had the notion they were up to something together. I even asked what it was—thinking maybe they could use a hand, you know—but Joe wouldn't tell me."

Thank you, lord God in heaven! "You got no gist at all?"

"Wily type fellow, Joe. Liked to tease big and then leave you guessing. He was in funds, suddenly, the last few months, but wouldn't say how it happened. And he was hinting that more was coming where it had come from—but he wouldn't *say* where it had come from. Oily bastard! Makes you tired!"

"Joe never happened to mention what had happened to Shacky?"

"No. Where'd you get this, Thomas? Why—"

"Shacky's body was in the morgue the same morning that I went there and identified Mr. Sproul's corpse, Pa. Back in March, a week before I left. Joe never told you he'd been killed?"

"No! Flora asked about him once. Joe said he'd lost touch."

"You never asked after him?"

"Hell no. Shacky wasn't one you'd *miss!* How'd you ever—"

"That's the other thing, Pa. I bought you a new set of cards." I set them in front of him. "Got them at Fischl's yesterday. I need the others as evidence. They're the connection, you see, between Wicklow and Shacky and Sproul."

"*Sproul?*"

"Mr. Sproul had four cards that matched—the varlets—buried in a pamphlet in his coat. That's why I got so excited on Saturday."

"Your Mr. Sproul had something to do with Joe and *Shacky?*"

It took some minutes to describe my reasons for conjecturing that Joe and his cousin had abetted Steve in murdering Mr. Sproul, and that Steve and Joe had later turned on Hager and eliminated him.

"But Joe wouldn't …" My father turned his head away uncomfortably. "He wouldn't …"

"Not even for money, Pa? You said—and Flora said too—that Wicklow was spending freely this spring."

"But—"

"And both Billy and old Titus say that the fracas there in *The Jug* wasn't any spontaneous brawl, but deliberate murder. Maybe Steve found out that Joe was talking about getting more money where the first money had come from!"

My father looked abashed and nauseated—as I daresay I would if I thought I might've been keeping company with homicides.

"Could I have the cards, please, Pa? I have to get right back to the city." He stacked them and handed them over. "Mr. Leavering's sending me to Philadelphia tomorrow, you see."

"Philadelphia!"

"Aye, to work with Mr. Castell to see if we can't determine Mr. Sproul's motives for traveling to New York."

"They must trust you."

It was such an unexpected and oddly gratifying statement, I was briefly speechless. It didn't matter that Pa hadn't noticed that the firm had once before sent me to Pennsylvania, or that it had recently entrusted me with a shipload of goods to the far Caribbean, this was the first time in years that my father had ever expressed anything approaching real pride in my accomplishments. "Yes, thank you, Pa, I believe they do." I was greatly tempted to capitalize on the moment of our harmony to plead that he should continue in the path of temperance ... but I stopped myself in time. The man has enough people preaching at him. My joining the chorus would only alienate him. "Can you tell Harmanus that everything is cleared out now?"

He nodded.

"I'll say farewell to Mother, then."

It was Vrijdag and his six-year-old, Kaspar, who accompanied me to Brooklyn that afternoon—Joachim having protested that only he knew how to harvest the beets properly. I had enough time to be impressed with the lad's liveliness—and to hope against hope that his father's recently-enhanced savings might eventually redeem him, too, from the prospect of becoming the inheritance of Jenneken Hampers and my cousin Bertie. He might suffer worse fates, but still ...

The ferry had just departed when we reached the dock. Vrijdag and I off-loaded the cart where the ferryman's wife could watch over my goods. I sent the slaves homeward and walked over to *The Jug*. The young bartender was standing precariously on a chair atop a table, changing the candles in the chandelier. "Be with you in a second, mister!" he said.

"Don't rush," I admonished. The chore was once mine, at home, because my elder brothers were both violently averse to heights.

He collected the excess wax for reuse and got himself down. “What can I— Oh hey, mister, *uh* …”

“Thomas Dordrecht. A beer, please, Billy.”

He smiled and hastened to pour it. “Didn’t expect to see you again. You live here in the county?”

“I live in the city, but I come from New Utrecht and have family all over.” I quaffed a gratifying swallow of the ale as he nodded, and decided I had to cut the small talk short. “You recall my interest in that brawl? I’ve learned a lot since Saturday, and … here, have a look at these.” I produced the deck of cards. “You recognize these?”

He did, right away. “Yeah. Wicklow left them here once when he was drunk. I saved them for him. How’d you get them?”

“My Pa took them, the night Wicklow was killed.”

“Oh. Haven’t seen much of him since then.”

“He’s been shocked into abstinence—at least for the time being.” With the same forewarning I’d given Pa, I produced the morgue sketch, which Billy, too, identified as Wicklow’s cousin. I then had to tell him all I’d adduced about the incident that had done Wicklow in.

“You want to see Flora too? She’s, *um*, busy at the moment.”

He’d given all the confirmation I really needed, and I didn’t want to miss the next ferry. “No, *uh* … Billy, you said there was a neighbor who had noticed the sailors talking to a third man that night, before they came inside here?”

“Aye. Widow Steenburgh. She watches out for us. She’s two doors down.”

“Yes? Might she be available?”

He shrugged. “I’ll go with you! You can bring your glass.” With no more concern than I’d have felt in New Utrecht, Billy simply walked out the door, turned left, and strode into his neighbor’s establishment, calling out “Lenoor!”

“Well, hello, lad, how—”

The woman, though presumably in fact a widow, could not have been more than a decade older than myself. She reminded me of the formidable Marijke Katelaar Van Voort—a large, solid woman who brooked no nonsense. Unlike Vrouw Van Voort, however, she was unprosperous, direct, and not at all bashful. Billy looked to her with something approaching adulation. It sharply occurred to me that he'd never once mentioned his parents. "Lenoor, this is Mister—Oh, I forgot again!"

"Thomas Dordrecht, mevrouw, your servant."

"And he's interested in the brawl that happened in June, when constable Wicklow was killed."

"A terrible thing, Meneer Dordrecht, though I had little love for that Joe Wicklow. I don't like such things happening in our neighborhood! It has cost us all a great deal of custom since the event. What is your interest in—"

"My father, ma'am, was injured in that affray, and—"

"You remember Ryk, who was always wobbling around after Joe?" Billy suggested—to my great mortification.

"Oh yes," she said disdainfully.

I resolved to expedite the interview. "And there are other reasons, ma'am, which perhaps Billy can relate to you … but I'm in haste to beg a few questions before the ferry returns, if I may?"

"Of course, Mr. Dordrecht."

"You do remember the incident?"

"Oh yes. As I say, it was a small catastrophe for our area's reputation. I was at pains the next day to get the new constable—who is just as obstinate a fool as Wicklow ever was—to pursue the two sailors over in New York, but he—"

"Begging your pardon, ma'am, Billy said that you saw the sailors with another stranger, out in the street, before they went into *The Jug*?"

"Aye, I did."

"It's the third man that I'm most interested in. Can you describe him?"

"Ah. Well, this was long after dark, sir. We each keep a lantern in front, of course, but … Come outside." She led us out to the street. "It was very hot that night, and some of my patrons were sitting outside here"—she pointed to a pair of tables—"and I had brought them a last round when I noticed the three over by the sycamore." The tree was thirty feet away, closer to Billy's establishment. "I noticed the two sailors right away—the short one was in front of the taller, but both were facing this way—and I immediately felt alarmed. It's not as though we never see sailors here, and pretty rough ones at that, but … those two! It's also not usual for patrons to appear so late, here in Brooklyn. It's not like over in the city, where taverns are open at all hours!"

"Of course. But the—"

"But I was somewhat reassured by the dress of the tall man they were speaking with. He had his back to me, but I could tell he was wearing good boots and a fine officer's cloak—dark green, I think, with some fine stitchery—and a proper gent's wig. It was only after the tumult was over that it struck me how odd it was that he'd been wearing the heavy cloak, with the collar turned up, on such a stifling night."

"You never saw his face?"

"No, and I had a customer inside who wanted to pay his bill, so I didn't stay long."

"Did you notice the peruke, by any chance?"

"The wig? Nothing special. No curls, not one of those silly *macaronis* everybody hates." She hesitated, recalling something. "He kept adjusting it—a nervous gesture, perhaps?"

Or perhaps it didn't fit him properly, I thought. "You couldn't overhear anything being said, I suppose?"

"Oh no. If there hadn't been any fighting, I'd have doubted that they even knew each other. I'd have assumed the sailors and the gent just somehow met in the same tavern. But … We see sailors here, we see gentlemen here. But we don't see unknown sailors here, talking earnestly with unknown gentlemen late in the evening!"

"Did you see the gent again after you heard the brawl begin?"

"No. Never saw him again. I was inside when I heard shouts in the building between us—oh, near an hour later. I rushed out, assuming there was a fight, and saw the two sailors lighting out for the beach around the bend. I hollered to the men to go after them, but my customers were all too old and too sozzled, and the ones from this place"—the establishment in the middle—"got winded straightaway. Billy was out here, also trying to encourage someone to chase them, and I went to see if he needed help, once I realized there was no hope of catching them."

"A mess, weren't it, Lenoor?"

"It was that, Billy!"

"Did anyone see the two sailors again?"

"No. And I looked! I have marketing to do over in New York, and if our fool constable wasn't going to shift himself to go looking, I saw no reason I shouldn't! But I never saw any of them again. I'd recognize the sailors—but they could be anywhere from Barbados to Belfast, couldn't they!"

"You'd not be able to identify the gentleman in the cloak?"

"No sir. He was perhaps as tall as you—about six foot, yes?—and not heavy and not old. But beyond that ..."

I spotted the ferry tying onto its dock, and handed Billy the empty beer glass and two Spanish silver bits. "You've been very helpful, Vrouw Steenburgh. I thank you both!"

"What was that all about, lad?" I heard her ask Billy as I hurried away.

The first New Jersey ferry, the next morning, dropped me back in front of Meed's tavern in Paulus Hook. I imposed on the coachman and his two other passengers, who'd been waiting for the ferry, to dash into the tavern and speak to the proprietor. Meed was looking more disheveled than ever and had to struggle to recall me from three days before. He brightened when I produced the deck of cards, however. "Well, I'll be damned! I was afraid I'd have to—"

"I'd like you to do me a favor, Mr. Meed, since I've restored your property."

"*Eh?*"

"First, I'd appreciate your lending me back the four varlet cards that I gave you the other day. Surely they're very seldom needed!" He pouted. "And more importantly, I'd like you to promise that if you're ever called upon to testify about them in a court of law, you'll still have them."

"What! *Aww* ..."

"It could be a highly important matter, Mr. Meed. It could bring a certain honor to your establishment!" I cooed. I'm sure he had no idea how ridiculous I sounded to myself. "Ah! And I have to put an unpleasant sketch of a deceased individual in front of you, to see if you can identify him. Ready?"

"Huh?"

I unrolled the parchment before his bleary eyes. I wondered if he'd ever seen any sketch of an actual person before. "*Ugh!* That's the one who got me so worried."

"You're sure?" He nodded. "Thanks, then." I took the four varlets, which he'd at least produced. "Sorry—they're holding the coach for me outside. Good-bye!"

I didn't see either Miss Paulette or Wendell Brush in Paulus Hook, but I did tip my hat to Vrouw Van Narden as we passed her establishment.

As we trundled through Newark about two hours later—a longer trip than I'd recalled, because of the delays for ferries across the Hackensack and Passaic Rivers—I kept a half-hopeful watch for anyone who might remotely be "Steve." I didn't spot a candidate, and so I naturally began to fret over the possibility that everything about him was a fabrication, invented for Miss Paulette. But the contrary thought was, why would he bother inventing such a fable to impress a harlot?

Later that afternoon, as we rumbled along the long stretch leading to Piscataway, it happened that I was the sole passenger. I set aside my reading—Oliver Goldsmith's *The Citizen of the World*, a fantasy of a Chinese traveler in England—and took the occasion to seat myself next to the driver. Sam, Gunther's partner, though more fluent, being a native of the province, lacked Gunther's forthright helpfulness. Every statement he made seemed premised on an expectation of emolument, which made for very slow, unpleasant conversation. I asked if he could remember his passenger of early spring, Mr. Sproul.

"Yeah? I saw Gunther the other night, and he told me a guy was asking after some Quaker passenger. I might recollect more if I were promised a drink at the next inn!"

"That you shall certainly have," I said, concealing some irritation. "*Do* you recall Mr. Sproul?"

"Nah! We have lots of Quakers traveling." I described Mr. Sproul—who had spent two days in Sam's proximity.

"Can't place him."

Sam's inability to recall him might stem from his irritating habit of never looking anyone in the eye. "Do many of the Quakers travel all the way to the New York ferry?"

"Enough."

"You don't happen to recall ever hearing an altercation behind the stable at Meed's, back then, while you were in your bunk in the front?"

"I'm a sound sleeper, lad. It ain't easy driving a coach!"

I was beginning to regret that I'd be buying him a tipple for nothing when I recalled something Miss Paulette had mentioned. "Sometimes other customers stable their horses there. Do you ever remember ever seeing a horse that was described to me as a very tall, handsome gray mare?"

He looked off into space for several seconds—until his horses wandered onto the verge and he reined them back. "Well, yes. I know that horse. Belongs to Mr. Lewes, down here in New Brunswick. I did see her once at Meed's. I had to look twice. Lewes never lets her out of his sight—'less he's *very* well paid, don't you know!"

Although a little hesitant—How many handsome gray mares might there be in New Jersey, after all?—I asked if he recalled when he'd seen the beast at Paulus Hook.

"Last winter sometime, I reckon, because I was upset to find the horse outside in the morning, without a blanket, even."

"Really?"

"Yeah. I'd seen her waiting outside in the evening, and figured whoever had leased her would ride her off after supper—but then she was still waiting, poor beast, when I got up at first light!"

"You don't say!"

"Well, I figured she needed food, and old Lewes would be right grateful if she got some. So, once my own nags were fed, I brought out some oats for her—and it was just then this fancy man in a military cloak shows up, wants to know what I'm doing, as if it weren't obvious. Some gall! I let him have a piece of my mind!"

"This would have been right at dawn?" *On what day?*

"Still before sunup. He startled me, came from out of nowhere—not the house, maybe from the next town north."

"Why had he let the horse stay out, if it was cold?"

"Didn't say. Wouldn't say much of anything. Looked a little strange, like he'd been up all night. Kept holding his cloak closed in front of him, as if he'd freeze if he let it spread open for a second. Then he recalls he's not wearing his wig. He pulls it out—he's carrying it—and he puts it on right away, but *backwards*. Backwards—he looked such a fool!" Sam roared with laughter. "He straightens it out, all the while trying to keep his cloak closed. But he don't take kindly to my laughing at him, of course, and he mounts up, all huffy, even though the mare is still eating. 'Hey,' I says, taking the bag away from her, 'You owe me for this!' And he just starts moving away, I couldn't believe it. So I ran after, and he spurred her into a trot and all I could do was curse!"

"Sam, this is important, can you try to—"

"I got Lewes to pay me for the oats, of course!"

Of course you did! "Can you describe the fellow, what he looked like?"

"I was looking at the poor horse, more than him!"

"What age, would you guess?"

"Thirty?"

"Lean, or stout?"

"Not stout."

"Height?"

"Taller than me."

"As tall as me?"

"About that, I guess."

"Anything particular you can … I suppose his hair was close-cropped, without the wig?"

"No. That's funny, ain't it? He had his own hair, tied back like most, and he put the wig on top of it!"

"What color hair?"

"Dark. Brown, I guess."

"What color was the cloak?"

"Dark. Blue? Green?"

"Which?" He gave me a very exasperated look. "Well, you must have looked right at it while he trotted away!"

"Green. It was green."

"Sam, can you say when exactly this was?"

"Now you're really jesting! Months ago!"

"No. I'm serious. This could be a capital matter."

"A what?" He snorted. "You need me to try that hard, boy, I'll need a stout meal along with my drink!"

Sam and I were clearly not fated to be bosom friends. "Very well, then! Was it in the beginning or the end of the winter?"

Sam shook his head and negotiated a bend in the road. "Toward the end of it, I think."

"Wait! What day of the week would it have been?"

"What *day?*"

"You have a regular schedule, you and Gunther. Which mornings do you leave Paulus Hook?"

"Oh. Mondays, Wednesdays, Fridays—normal-like."

"So it was one of those three mornings in the late winter that you saw the horse?"

"Yeah. Would be—'less the schedule was fouled up, because of a snowstorm."

"Aha! There had been a snowstorm. Now can you remember—"

"We have snowstorms that throw the schedule all winter long, mister! Anyway, Lewes will be able to tell you, he keeps the stables down here in New Brunswick."

Of course. *He's* the one I should be treating to supper! But we were at last at the Piscataway stop, and I didn't want to pursue the matter when other passengers boarded the coach.

Once finally arrived in New Brunswick, I booked a bed where Mr. Sproul had stayed, in the Carteret Hotel—my expenses having been guaranteed by Mr. Leavering. Then I walked down George Street to Lewes's stables, where Sam was chatting with the owner while currying his horses. "There's the young gent I told you of, Mr. Lewes," Sam announced. "Show him Clarissa!"

Lewes was a scrawny old fellow whose mannerisms had seemed a tad foggy until his horse was mentioned. "Well, she's *not* for sale, young sir," he immediately stated, leading us a few stalls in, "but I don't mind showing her off to you. There, you see! There's not a prettier beast in New Jersey, I assure you!"

Clarissa had a sleek silvery hide and did indeed strike me as a notably fine specimen. But I'm not one who pays much attention to horses. Had I not perhaps seen the like on the better streets of the city? "Is she truly that uncommon, Mr. Lewes? Or are you just using a well-turned phrase?"

"Oh no, sir! Well, I mean, *I* don't see her match passing through here—and I see a lot of horses, you'll warrant!"

"Uh huh. Actually, it's not the horse that interests me so much, Mr. Lewes, as the man who rented her from you last winter—when Sam here saw her up in Paulus Hook."

"Oh, that one! Never saw a man in such a hurry! He tore in from Philadelphia, his horse was ready to drop. A fine chestnut roan stallion, ridden almost to death! But even though it was past noon and terrible weather, he just *had* to keep going. Wouldn't take no for an answer!"

"Really!"

"Arrogant swine too. Just kept saying, 'How much?' like she weren't my pride and joy!"

"Terrible!"

"So finally I said I'd need *fifty pounds* collateral. That's way more than even Clarissa is worth, but be damned if the man didn't open his purse and starting counting it out! I was still so untrusting of him, I told him I'd charge five pounds for the rental. And he agreed to that too! I keep the horses for the post-riders, you know, for ten guineas a *year!*"

"Nice deal, Mr. Lewes!" Sam crowed.

"How long did he want to keep the horse?"

"A week, he said—but he brought her back after four days."

"She was undamaged?"

"Aye, but I doubt it was any thanks to him! She was exhausted and ravenous when he got here, so I believe it when Sam says the fool left her out overnight!"

"He must—"

"I did deduct a shilling, 'cause he'd somehow lost her blanket."

Curious. "He must have given you his name, Mr. Lewes?"

"Oh yes—William Smith, of Philadelphia."

"Any business address?"

"No. But I was trusting he'd want his gold and his own horse back."

"Did you see … I presume, when he left, he headed back toward Philadelphia?"

"No! He looked as bad as Clarissa when he got here. He *orders* me to saddle his horse while he gets himself a drink in the tavern—as if that ain't a courtesy I wouldn't always do! He comes back, we settle up, and he's off without a word. No matter I'm five quid richer, he's got me so riled, I watch to make sure I'm seeing the back of him! I expect him to turn down the Princeton road, but he goes the other way, north, and crosses the Raritan!"

"Five pounds' worth of aggravation!" Sam exclaimed.

"Did he give any indication what his business was?"

"Said he was in trade—which surprised me, because his cloak looked like it was military."

"How was that?"

"Fancy embroidery, you know. Dark green, heavy wool cloak. Royal monogram."

"George Second, I presume, not the new king?"

"Aye."

"Did he, perchance, wear a wig?"

"He did, yes. But I think maybe he wore it to keep his ears warm. He had his own hair underneath, you see."

If the man had intended the wig to disguise himself, it was certainly a miscalculation! Even with the variant name, which was suspiciously common, I felt certain Mr. Lewes's *William Smith* was Miss Paulette's *Steve*. "Mr. Lewes, I know this sounds odd, but can you put an exact date on this event? It's very important to me."

Lewes's interest was fading. "Oh, I don't know, lad. Around one of the last snowstorms of the past winter."

"What date do you *want* him to say?" Sam interposed, unhelpfully.

"I want to know the *actual* date, of course, Sam!"

"I've no idea, really, sir. It was right around when … Oh yes! One reason I didn't want to rent Clarissa was that I'd been planning to ride her to Cousin Tillie's funeral. She'd died the day before, and I had to go to the service the next morning."

"Aha! What day was that, then?"

"Oh heaven, who knows? I ended up riding *his* horse to the funeral."

"You remember what day everyone in your family died?" Sam challenged.

"Might your wife recall the date, Mr. Lewes?"

"She would ... if she hadn't beaten Tillie to the grave by five years!"

"Ah, I'm sorry!" Could we never manage to determine one straightforward datum?

"It'd be on her tombstone."

"Ah. Where's that, Mr. Lewes?"

"Princeton. You'll go right past it tomorrow. Sam knows the church. Northwest corner of the yard."

Well! That would serve. Relieved, I invited Lewes to supper—thinking his company would leaven that of Sam's—and I learned a great deal about horses that I trust will one day prove useful in commerce. Later I spoke with the hotel's manager, who was unable to add anything to my catalog of Mr. Sproul's movements or behavior.

On the pretext that Tillie was *my* relative, I imposed on the other coach passengers for a three-minute stop in a Princeton churchyard the next morning. There I found a recently erected red sandstone marker embellished with a winged angel-head, inscribed, "Here lies Matilda, widow of John Quarles, died ye 18th March, 1762, aged 85 years, 1 month, 7 days." Bless you for securing a plain fact, Cousin Tillie!

"Beg pardon, would thee be Thomas Dordrecht?" My interlocutor was a sallow, slack fellow whose long, florid nose stood out on his round face. He was of early middle age, dressed in the plain style favored by Quakers, and he seemed cordial enough.

"Aye! Good afternoon!"

"Welcome to Philadelphia, Thomas Dordrecht. My name is Christopher Enniston. I am a clerk for our mutual employer. Mr. Castell asked me to await thee and conduct thee to his home, where he and his wife are holding supper for thee."

"Oh. Very kind!" It was a relief not to have to find my own way. On the previous trip, I had stayed in a boarding house and had not been invited to anybody's home. I collected my luggage from Sam—I was carrying Mr. Sproul's bag as well as my own—and Enniston led me to a waiting carriage. There I was recognized and warmly greeted by the black driver, Francis Goode—not *Francis*, not *Goode*, always *Francis Goode*—whom I knew to be a salaried retainer, as Castell, too, abhorred slavery. Enniston held the door and we climbed in. After two days in the Spartan coach, sitting on an upholstered bench was very gratifying!

"This is not thy first visit, I collect?" Enniston said as we pulled away.

"No sir. I spent a week here a year ago in May, to become more familiar with the firm's facilities and procedures."

"Ah yes, just shortly before I was taken on." Enniston, I recalled, was roughly of my own and Mapes's ranking. "How do thee find our city?"

"Ah, quite splendid indeed, sir! The regularity of the streets is most impressive. And we are only now beginning to imitate your fine illumination system in New York!"

"Have thee ever visited our hospital, friend? Its welfare has become a major preoccupation of Reuben Castell."

"It would give me great pleasure, Mr. Enniston, though I fear the tour may need to be postponed until a future occasion." Rather than explain why—I recalled Mrs. Leavering's injunction to reticence—I changed the subject. "Have the authorities imposed a general embargo on Pennsylvania's commerce, Mr. Enniston?"

"No, but the continuing regulations are severe … though often honored in the breach."

"Aha. You are not blessed, as we are, with having the army and navy underfoot, perhaps?"

This produced a brief smile. "That may have an impact, I am sure. But the increasing restrictions on trade are indeed a cause for worry in Reuben Castell's planning."

Francis Goode halted the carriage briefly as we came to a noisy intersection. "I notice relatively few men dressing as you and Mr. Castell do, sir. Have the Quakers changed their style, or …?"

"Nay, friend. The town is flooded with Germans and Scots and all the riffraff of Europe. And many have been invited here by the proprietors themselves!" He shook his head with annoyance. The descendants of William Penn, I knew, were not much loved by anyone, not even by the Quakers—the heirs having disdained the creed of their famed progenitor. "The members of the Religious Society of Friends are become a minority in Philadelphia, though they founded this city but four score years ago!"

"Aha! Very like the experience of the Dutch in New York, Mr. Enniston! Well … times do change!"

Enniston did not appear to find the parallel amusing. We proceeded in awkward silence for a minute, until he was moved to inquire after my recent excursion to Statia. Since joining the firm, he'd become acquainted with both Captain Trent and Mr. Fox. Only too happy to recall my adventures, I enlarged on the subject until we arrived at the Castell home, a modest brick structure in what was apparently the older residential section on the northern edge of town. Francis Goode jumped to hand me to the curb as Mr. and Mrs. Castell, an elderly couple of somewhat austere demeanor, appeared at the door. Amid a very cordial welcome full of confusing *thees* and *thous*, I didn't notice before I was inside that Enniston had oddly disappeared without a farewell.

Severe though she might look, Mrs. Castell, whom I'd not met before, proved most genial in person. After offering me several bland potables, she shyly added that spirituous liquors were also available, though the couple themselves did not partake.

"I should not like to offend, ma'am," I said piously—though after the bone-rattling trip from New Brunswick, I was fairly desperate.

"Nonsense, young man. We do have ale and even whiskey!"

Now I adored Dorothy Castell—as was only proper, she being the namesake of "my" ship. "Ale would be perfectly wonderful, Mrs. Castell!"

As Mr. Castell and I made small talk while settling in the parlor and awaiting the refreshments, I looked about in curiosity. I had never before entered the home of a Quaker. At first, I was snidely tempted to discern *an ostentatious lack of ostentation* … but I quickly came to feel comfortable with the unadorned but finely made furniture and surroundings, particularly when being so warmly welcomed.

"There, Thomas Dordrecht!" Mrs. Castell said, presenting me with a large glass. "Now I must attend to our supper, if thee will excuse me?"

"Of course, ma'am," I said, "and thank you so much!" When she retired, I sat back down, took a deep and grateful swallow, and said, "Before we begin, Mr. Castell, lest I should speak out of turn ... have you confided the purpose of my visit to Mrs. Castell?"

My host looked somewhat perturbed. "Thou art most astute, Thomas Dordrecht. Normally I have no secrets from my wife. Surely neither Benjamin nor John Glasby would lead thee to think otherwise?"

"Indeed not, sir, but they themselves are unusual among my acquaintances in that regard."

"Ah, I see. But in this particular circumstance, following the caution that Hermione Leavering voiced, I thought discretion might be called for until after thy departure. Thee surmise correctly that I have not confided in any others, however. Evelyn Sproul is of course aware of thy purpose, but I believe we are the only ones in Philadelphia."

"That is eminently sensible, sir."

He took a sip of his lemon squash, and held up some papers that were lying on a pewter tray. "I have had two letters from Benjamin this week, and ... I must say, it is at least a fair thing to sense his sudden reinvigoration. He is all afire, not only with the news of your investigation, but once again with plain business matters! There was a time earlier this summer when I feared I might lose him on top of Daniel Sproul"—he cleared his throat as his voice went hoarse—"to the perfect ruin of all my life's work in commerce!"

"Ah!" I exclaimed, momentarily overcome. I'd not considered the perspective of a man eight years senior to Leavering, who naturally hoped to see his firm survive him.

"But ... to business, lad. Is there aught that's new since Tuesday? And how can I help thee?"

By the time I had summarized all that, my glass had been emptied. Francis Goode looked in, and Mr. Castell asked him to fetch me another—to my relief, as I really wanted it, but would never have dared to speak up.

"I know two men of this city named William Smith," Mr. Castell said in a rather puzzled tone, "but I can't imagine either riding to New Brunswick on the day after a snowstorm! Both are near my own age, and—"

"Begging your pardon, sir, I believe the name is false and was given as a ruse. The man is of course not honest. He gave another name to the, *uh*, hussy in Paulus Hook—which may equally be a ruse, though some investigation could be made of each."

"It grieves one to think of such evil in the world engrossing so fine a man as Daniel Sproul. The method you describe could bring on the most awful phantasms!"

"Aye sir, that is so." *But we cannot allow ourselves to dwell on it!* "Let us attempt to summarize what we have learned thus far."

"Yes!" Castell agreed eagerly.

"On Tuesday, before I left, I stopped in the New York Society Library to consult the newspapers of last March. The snowstorm, about ten inches' worth, not the worst of the entire winter, occurred on Thursday the eighteenth, the day Mr. Lewes's cousin died. Normally, the coach would depart for New York on Friday, but the storm delayed it until Saturday. Yet on the Friday, a horseman of some thirty years appeared in New Brunswick in tearing haste to proceed further north. The horseman has the same description as the man who consorted with the hussy in Paulus Hook on the following Monday afternoon, was observed playing cards with Mr. Sproul Monday evening, and was seen there again early Tuesday morning with Mr. Lewes's horse. Meanwhile, Mr. Sproul, we know, took the coach on Saturday the twentieth, the weather having turned much milder. He was delayed in New Brunswick over the Sabbath, arrived in Paulus Hook after dark—after the last ferry—on Monday evening, the twenty-second … and his corpse was discovered in New York City at dawn on Tuesday the twenty-third."

"I see. Very good."

"The coach always tries to reach Paulus Hook before the last ferry, but with melting snow turning the roads to mud, it was predictable on that occasion that it would not succeed."

"People hope to complete their journey in two days, of course."

"Yes. Oh, and the moon was in the last quarter on the twenty-second—the rise was at one a.m."

"Aha. Thus it was dark throughout the evening hours."

"Aye. But the essential deduction is that this crime was deeply premeditated. It cannot have originated in Paulus Hook. It involved considerable planning and expense. And a most critical inference is that the criminal perfectly comprehended not only what Mr. Sproul's travel goals were, but what he might practically *achieve* in those wintry circumstances." Mr. Castell looked thoughtful as I stopped for a swallow. "Further, though the action was premeditated, it cannot antedate Mr. Sproul's decision to travel, which by all reports was very sudden. And lastly, a great effort was for some reason made to disguise the fact of murder: the shadowy villain might have employed grosser methods with impunity on several occasions, had he not been so concerned to confuse us all. But he did not."

"Why would he avoid that, Thomas Dordrecht?" Mr. Castell asked.

"I can only postulate that the reason for the murder may be more damaging than the murder itself, sir. The criminal fears exposure of his motive more than he fears exposure of his crime." My host appeared troubled and very pensive. "In addition to the bizarre method of the murder," I continued, "consider the calculation involved in restricting the robbery to the gold coins, leaving a considerable sum in silver untouched. It was Mrs. Leavering who caught that discrepancy, not the coroner and not me!"

"A most percipient lady, it is well known!"

"It follows that the motive for this crime was not petty or trivial. Nor was it committed in a frenzy of emotion. Mr. Sproul's movements were carefully and correctly anticipated, and his generous, trusting spirit was *depended upon* to preclude any foreknowledge of his own mortal danger."

Mr. Castell visibly shuddered.

"I believe it's inescapable that the motive for the crime must originate here in Philadelphia, Mr. Castell, and that we must determine what on earth prompted Mr. Sproul to travel so abruptly to New York. Was he pursuing someone? Was he afraid of something?"

"Well, I believe thee must be right … but I'm at a loss!"

"I have to ask this, sir. Was there anything happening in the firm's affairs that might conceivably have occasioned such unprecedented behavior?"

Mr. Castell was far too sensible to take offense. "We shall have to reexamine our files for the period. But in all candor, I cannot imagine … Thee has been in trade long enough now to know that nothing ever seems 'normal,' that there is always something that seems new and out of the ordinary. Yet there was nothing so special about, for example, the arrangements I was making for iron delivery … I spent that entire week away in Lancaster, where, as you know, we are partial owners of a mine and a foundry."

"Indeed, I once bought some iron rod from them on my personal account, sir."

"Oh yes, so I recall. But I'd been there before. There was no change in our arrangements … No surge or downfall in city business was anticipated, or I'd not have ventured away. That snowstorm also kept me from returning home, by several days!"

"When did you return, do you recall?"

"I got home—when?—on Monday evening. I went into the office on Tuesday and was profoundly startled to find Daniel Sproul absent. Christopher Enniston agitated me all the more by saying he'd taken it into his head to travel to New York City. I feared perhaps Benjamin or Hermione was laid low but, as I later discovered, Daniel's wife Evelyn was ill, and yet he had left town in all haste! But I had much to attend to that day, and so I let it all pass, anticipating an explanation on the morrow. But the letter I received from John Glasby on Wednesday … was hardly anything I expected and was … devastating!"

"Was the firm involved in any controversy with its competitors?"

Mr. Castell shook his head. "No. We have made a practice of eschewing all such. We consider that our goods' quality should speak for itself." He sighed. "Of course, Daniel Sproul was no stranger to *public* controversy. He was a man of profound and occasionally vehement opinions … but these were of a general public nature, as a rule, not such as might incite any particular individual to violence against his person. His wife will tell thee of them. I've made an appointment for thee to visit her and her aunt tomorrow morning."

"Her … aunt?"

He seemed surprised that I was unfamiliar with the family arrangement. "Miss Rhoda Leavering, Benjamin's sister, has lived with the Sprouls since Benjamin and Hermione left us for New York." Dimly, I recollected occasional disconsolate mentions of Mr.

Leavering's maiden elder sibling. "They are still in mourning, and the sad fact is that Evelyn Sproul and the two surviving children are having difficulty struggling with their loss. Daniel has been sorely missed."

"Will you be accompanying me then, sir?"

"I think not. Possibly thee might learn more in private conversations with each? I don't know. At any rate, I mean to reexamine the firm's records for March. I don't expect—"

Francis Goode came in to announce that supper was ready, and we immediately broke off our conversation and repaired to their dining room, where I struggled to recall more genteel manners from the crude habits built up on shipboard and in the boarding house. Both my hosts professed interest in my recent travel, neither having ever been further south than Baltimore. They welcomed even more details than my family had a week ago. Trusting that they—unlike some—would not hold my uncle's failings against me, I candidly related the full background of my profitable dealing with Absalom Koopvaarder. Mr. Castell astounded me by suggesting that, if Absalom were to be manumitted and allowed to continue in business in Statia, it would be to the firm's profit to cultivate a relationship with him. I had more or less planned to deal with him as long as I could, but I hadn't thought of formally recognizing him as a factor of the partnership.

"Our guest is drooping, Reuben!" Mrs. Castell observed. "Thee has had a hard trip, Thomas Dordrecht, and need thy rest!"

And she was right.

Chapter 13

The next morning, Francis Goode drove me about a mile, out to the Sproul home. Though it was completely surrounded by greenery and dozens of yards from any other building, he assured me the red-brick structure was precisely oriented according to the town fathers' surveyed grid and boasted an address on "Eleventh Street." The door was answered by a tall, prim, black-garbed lady too elderly to be Mr. Sproul's widow. "You would be Mr. Dordrecht then?" she said rather frostily. Preempting any effort to display such charm as I possess, she ordered me inside. "I am Benjamin Leavering's sister, and you are one of his junior employees, I believe?" Again, I only had time to nod. "I can't imagine why Benjamin is bringing all this up again *now!* My poor niece was almost fully restored in health—and you can easily imagine, it was profoundly shattered this year—but her father's latest conceit has destroyed her equilibrium and brought on a relapse. Is this—'investigation,' he calls it—truly necessary?"

The reception was rude enough that I resolved to be direct. "Ma'am," I protested, "you do understand that we have very strong evidence that suggests that Mr. Sproul's demise was not natural, but an act of premeditated murder?" I held my voice down in case the children were in the house; Francis Goode had told me all three would most likely be at school. "Surely the matter must be examined, lest those responsible get away and become tempted to repeat the crime!"

"Oh!" she scoffed. "Why can we not have the simple humility to accept that the good lord sometimes taketh away what he giveth? For reasons that are not given to us to know! I am distressed that Benjamin has seen fit to overturn this household yet again with—"

"Is that Thomas Dordrecht, Aunt Rhoda?" It was a soft-spoken woman's voice coming from the top of the stairs.

Miss Leavering's demeanor instantly mellowed. "Oh. Yes, it is, my dear. But you needn't trouble yourself to come down. I'm sure I can answer all of the gentleman's questions, and—"

"Father wrote that I must speak with him personally, Aunt! Please offer him refreshment and ask him to come up!"

Seeing her aunt's look of consternation, I again vigorously shook my head to indicate that no refreshments were needed. "I *should* like to speak with you, however, ma'am. Perhaps after my interview with Mrs. Sproul?"

Her impatience now conflicted with her self-importance. "If we must, young man. If poor Evelyn does not need any assistance, that is!" I dutifully indicated that I awaited her permission to proceed upstairs. "Oh, go ahead!"

Mrs. Evelyn Sproul lay propped up on a day bed in the upstairs sitting room. She was a pallid woman who somehow seemed frail, despite a physique that took after her portly parents. Her attitude of welcome, however, bespoke their characteristic hearty generosity. "I must apologize for my aunt, Thomas Dordrecht; she is far too protective!"

"None is necessary, ma'am!"

"In truth, I would prefer to speak with thee privately. Father writes that thee has uncovered evidence that indicates that Daniel was …" She looked askance, unable to pronounce the word.

"Yes, ma'am. I fear it is so."

"Do thou believe in ghosts, Thomas Dordrecht?"

She quite startled me. It was the last thing I'd have expected from the daughter of Hermione and Benjamin Leavering. "No, ma'am, I don't."

"I never did, either, before … this. And yet … I feel my husband's presence so strongly, Thomas Dordrecht! Six months have passed, and yet I sense his proximity constantly! Not a moment goes by that …" I looked into my lap as she gasped and reached for her handkerchief. After a few seconds, however, she controlled her breathing. "I must be strong, however, for his sake! For his memory's sake, that is!" She took a sip of water from a glass on the nearby table and mastered herself. "Besides, if I am overcome by tears, my aunt will be rushing up to beat thee with the fire poker!"

"You are very brave, ma'am—and I appreciate your concern for my back!"

"But … one thing more. My husband's … shade, if thee will, has always seemed to me *uneasy*."

"Uneasy, Mrs. Sproul?"

"Aye. Not vengeful, not rancorous, yet still … unsatisfied. Oh, Daniel did not believe in any regime of perfect justice, Thomas Dordrecht. He thought any human attempt to mete punishments that pretended to exact perfect retribution for crimes to be impious. Such apportionment is the domain of heaven, he would say." I inclined my head, wondering where this thought was leading. "But he did believe that worldly justice had its place, that those guilty of violence should be apprehended and prevented from further incursions upon the innocent!"

"In all this, I personally would concur, ma'am."

She took another sip, formulating a new thought. "I could never say why, but *I* have been unsatisfied with the narrative of Daniel's death from the very first. He was too …"

"I understand, ma'am: too strong, too vital. You are supported in this by everyone who knew him."

"Exactly. So—in contrast to the fretting of my aunt, who has truly concerned herself for my welfare and my children's—I feel somewhat encouraged—even liberated, perhaps—by the horrible suggestion that my husband did not die a natural death. Is that reprehensible in me?"

"Assuredly not, ma'am!"

She sighed deeply, having gotten that burden off her chest.

"I sensed something of the same reaction in your parents, on Monday, ma'am. And Mr. Castell reports a renewed vigor in your father's correspondence!"

"It may be so. It may be so." Again she sighed, refreshed herself, and pushed herself more upright on the couch. "Now then, thee must tell me, pray, all thee know of this matter, and then tell me what I may do to further our knowledge."

If anyone was entitled to a comprehensive recital, it was certainly the victim's widow. Even though I'd now repeated the tale many times—its organization, I hope, having improved with each effort—we spent over an hour examining all the facts. She managed not to flinch but once, when I explained my theory of murder by forced immersion in the barely thawed river.

In answer to the query she then conscientiously posed, I said, "Given that Mr. Sproul's decision to go to New York was apparently very abrupt, ma'am, I need to know all you can tell me of the last week or so he was here in Pennsylvania."

"Ah! If only … It is most unfortunate, but I saw very little of my husband during that week, because I was so ill. I contracted a terrible colic early in March, and I stayed abed here, fearful that he and the children might succumb as well. I have often since revisited that week and … fretted that I failed him, in my weakness, because he was unable to confide whatever was worrying him—as something undoubtedly was!"

"Can you—"

"I think he was endeavoring to spare *me* worry!"

"Ah. You mustn't reproach yourself for having suffered a malady, ma'am!"

She smiled. "Exactly the sort of thing *he* would say, Thomas Dordrecht!"

"Can you specifically recount the progress of the malady, Mrs. Sproul?"

"Ah me! It took forever to conquer it! Terrible wracking cough! But … I came down with it on the day of the first meeting in March—"

"A Sunday?"

"Yes." She smiled. "We go to 'meetings,' not to 'services.'"

"I see."

"And it progressed through the week. Daniel called in a doctor—we have several in Philadelphia—and I was bled, and

I ingested the vile medicine, but … the worst of it was the following Sunday. Daniel took the children to meeting by himself, and Auntie stayed here with me. I think they feared for my life as the afternoon progressed, but the fever broke that evening, and I slowly began to mend."

"Do you recall, despite all this, anything that struck you as abnormal in your husband's behavior?"

"Ah, yes, that's the issue, isn't it! But no, at least not before the worst was already over. He was very busy, trying to keep the children from mischief. And of course he was busy at work, because Reuben Castell was away in Lancaster, and many on the staff were new …"

"But something did seem odd to you?"

"Only the next night. Daniel looked in and was pleased that I was improving. He said he was debating whether he should go to a card party the following evening. It was not a scheduled engagement with his regular playing partners; he was being asked to stand in for a man who was indisposed, as a favor to the host. It wasn't just that he was concerned for my health, he seemed unsure whether he truly wanted to go. But he thought it might be conducive to good business relations. I begged him not to hesitate for my sake, and he promised to excuse himself at the first opportunity. But … contrary to his pledge, he came home *very late* that night—after ten o'clock—and he seemed terribly upset by something. I never learned what, or even whether it was something at the office, or at the party, or here at home … I still don't know."

"This was the Tuesday evening, then, before he left?"

"Yes. Yes, that's right."

"But you must have spoken with him many times again before Saturday?"

"Oh yes. But … The next day, I suffered a mild reverse. And the day after that was the day it snowed. Daniel came home shortly after noon, having dismissed the staff. I was asleep, and he went into his study. That evening after supper, I was alert, and he told me, to my astonishment, that he had to go to New York City on the morrow, despite all the snow! He said he was glad I was recuperating, because he wouldn't dare go if he believed me endangered, but he wouldn't explain the purpose of the trip, because he didn't want to add to my troubles. And then … Oh, then there was some commotion with the children, which halted the discussion before I could protest."

"But he didn't leave on Friday?"

"No. He meant to. Francis Goode took him down to the coach terminus, only to learn nothing would move until the next day. It took them three hours to get to the center of town and back! Again, I was sleeping that afternoon, and … I never learned what was on his mind, much to my subsequent frustration. He promised he'd write as soon as he could."

"And he did leave on Saturday?"

"Yes. The weather was much improved, though I imagine the roads were still horrendous." She stopped, not wanting to add that that was the last she'd ever seen or heard of him.

"Oh, I should tell you, ma'am, that I brought the valise with Mr. Sproul's town suit, which I found at Van Narden's. It's downstairs. Plus what remains of the hat."

"Ah." She sighed. "Well, I thank thee for that. I suppose I … ought to give the suit away."

"It's in perfectly good repair, ma'am."

"Daniel was … The Friends insist on simplicity in dress, but this can be combined with considerable fastidiousness in quality."

This observation recalled a curiosity that I'd forgotten. "The woman who found your husband's corpse in her alleyway, ma'am"—she winced, and I cursed myself—"said that his waistcoat was buttoned incorrectly." She looked baffled. "But a waistcoat has so many buttons, I know I can go for hours before I even notice that I've—"

"Not Daniel! Daniel would never allow that! Every morning as he left, he'd ask me to check for just that sort of lapse."

She was again near to tears. "Do you know anyone named William Smith, ma'am?" She shook her head. "Does the description of the fellow elsewhere called Steve have any familiarity at all?" Again, a negative. "Well, there's but one thing more I can think to ask, which I fear may be painful to consider. Can you imagine any reason why anyone would wish to kill your husband?" She seemed to be debating whether to speak. "Because … somebody did."

"Do thee know, I have been considering that ever since I received Father's letter this week, but the only notion I can conceive … stretches credulity, and—"

"Would you tell me, nonetheless, ma'am?"

"Thee remember the pamphlet that was on Daniel's person?"

"It was I who returned it to Mrs. Leavering."

"Oh, yes. Well, Daniel was more than an admirer of the author, John Woolman, he was an ardent advocate and defender."

"An anti-slavery zealot, ma'am?"

"Perhaps thee can put it that way, Thomas Dordrecht. Daniel considered John Woolman our personal friend and even urged him to take his ministry beyond the Society of Friends, to the general public! I hope I do not upset thee?"

"Nay, ma'am—although I do find it most … quixotic."

"Many found it more than quixotic, Thomas Dordrecht. Many were profoundly offended and antagonistic!"

I sighed. "When one attacks what people consider to be their property, ma'am, many will—"

"Daniel had no quarrel with the right of property, but he argued it could not apply to owning human beings, all of whom were created in God's image, and all of whom are God's children."

"Even … Negroes?"

"A horse cannot read the gospel, Thomas Dordrecht. A dog cannot remonstrate, and a cow cannot pray!"

Perhaps to cover my own confusion, I hastened back to the matter at hand. "Do you conceive that this stance may have caused some to hate him so intently as to plot his mortal harm?"

She shrugged and shook her head. "Honestly, I cannot. Most people blithely dismiss the idea in cavalier fashion. John Woolman has occasionally faced down threats to his person, even from some among the Friends, but has never—*praise heaven!*—been attacked. And Daniel's opinions on slave-holding, however strong, were seldom voiced in public, and never, to my knowledge, outside the Friends." She paused. "He did have the ambition—for well in our future, after our children were grown—to take the word through the country, to follow John Woolman's lead … but this was at present an aspiration only."

We had a few more minutes of conversation, mostly wistful reminiscences of her husband, and then, vowing that I would send her reports of all developments, I excused myself—only to be collared by her aunt at the foot of the stairs. "Well?" she demanded belligerently.

Damned if I was going to be intimidated! "I should now be glad of whatever refreshment you might be able to provide me, Miss Leavering!"

"*Hmpf!* Follow me, then!" She led back through the house to the kitchen. "Coffee?"

"Do you have any beer?" It was only ten o'clock, but that never stopped any proper New Yorker.

"We do keep some on hand ... *for the workmen.*"

"Grand!" Uninvited, I sat down at the table, which was comfortable enough. "Many thanks!"

"What did—"

"Rather than repeat all the details I've learned of Mr. Sproul's last hours, Miss Leavering—which I'm sure Mrs. Sproul will be glad to share with you at her leisure—I'd like you to tell me your recollections of the last days he spent here in this house. Mrs. Sproul was ill and unable to move about; you must have had some difficulty managing the children?"

She heaved an almighty sigh of reluctance and sat down—while I marveled that this disagreeable person could possibly be Benjamin Leavering's sister. "Not that much more than usual, really. Mr. Sproul normally spent a great deal of time at his office. To give him credit, he would endeavor to spend a few minutes daily with his offspring."

"When did you first learn of Mr. Sproul's intention to travel to New York?"

"When he came home, the afternoon of the big snow. I was quite furious! Evelyn was not fully recovered, and the children were underfoot. Castell was away on business, and he suddenly elected to leave the city!"

"He'd never done the like before?"

"Certainly not! Outrageous! I mean, *de mortuis nil nisi bonum* is all very well, but that was ..." Her thespian shudder would have read clearly on the far side of a racetrack.

"Did he offer any explanation?"

"He did not! He insisted he could not say, and that he would write to Evelyn at the earliest opportunity. He said he'd be less than a fortnight, and—"

"He *did?*" She nodded, irked at being interrupted. "When did he say that? Why wasn't this generally known?"

She looked blank. "I thought everyone … No one ever asked me!" She shrugged. "He had just told me he had taken most of the gold from the household coffer, because Mr. Castell had depleted the office petty cash for his own excursion."

"Aha! That's important too! Did he say exactly how much in gold he had taken?"

"He did, but I doubt that's any of your business, sir!"

"I understand your misgivings, Miss Leavering, but by now they're surely neither here nor there! I am curious because I know that Mr. Sproul casually searched his purse to pay for the hostelry in Paulus Hook, and gold coins were observed by the proprietor, yet when his corpse was discovered the following morning, there were only two pounds and change in silver and copper discovered. At first that was enough to trick us into thinking there had been no theft, no foul play. Now I simply wish to estimate how much must have been stolen."

"Well, in that case … He told me he had taken out eight pounds, and left us three in gold and a quantity of silver that should certainly hold for the duration of his absence."

Eight pounds! That might explain Joe Wicklow's sudden ability to buy drinks and be *nice* to Flora Norts … but it could hardly constitute a motive for a man who'd unhesitatingly poured out fifty-five pounds to lease a horse. "Did he even remotely express any apprehension about his trip, Miss Leavering?"

"Apprehension? Nerves? Fear? *Daniel?* No. The man was, if anything, headstrong to the point of …" She simply shook her head.

Fearlessness was evidently no admirable quality in her estimation! "Did you have any further conversation? On the Friday, when he was unable to leave?"

"I was so incensed, I … No. When he returned on Friday, he and Francis Goode did take the children out for a sleigh ride, but then he dropped them back in my lap and retired to his study. I never even saw him on Saturday morning."

"I rather encouraged Mrs. Sproul to imagine why anyone might wish Mr. Sproul dead, Miss Leavering—quite against her will, I'm afraid. The only thing she could think of was that his anti-slavery positions might have—"

"*Bah!* Stuff! He talked Benjamin into dismissing the three that were the only good thing his wife brought into their marriage"—I was briefly dazed to realize she was speaking of the intelligent and charming Hermione—"but nobody other than a few of his fellow pietists knew about it."

"His position was not public knowledge?"

"Not really, thank heaven! But I can tell you what *was*, and what surely infuriated the good citizens of this province!"

Oh yes? "If you would, please, ma'am, I conceive it's necessary to—"

"With your Dutch name, Mr. Dordrecht, you must be of the Reformed persuasion?"

What now? "Well, I ..."

"A sensible religion, as these things go, even if not the king's! Not one of your ranting, shaking, quaking, New Light hystericals, at any rate!"

"*Uh*, no."

"Well! You should understand that the sectarians to whom our good King Charles was deluded into handing over this fine province have done their utmost, ever since, to wreck it—to surrender it to the savage aborigines and the papist French!"

"How is that, ma'am? There were Pennsylvanians aplenty when I fought at Ticonderoga a few years—"

She interrupted me just as I was realizing how futile it would be to venture an argument. "The *Quakers*—" Her voice took on a certain tremulousness. I couldn't decide whether it was satirical or evidence of overpowering emotion. "I shall never forgive Benjamin for sitting still while my darling niece was suborned into such impiety!" The tremulousness, I decided, had to be genuine. "You know, of course, of our most notable citizen, Dr. Franklin?"

"I esteem Dr. Franklin very highly, ma'am!"

"As you should, young man! Well! When the current conflict began, Dr. Franklin made the modest proposal that a militia should be formed—as in all the other provinces—to prevent heathen massacres on the frontier. And the *Quakers*, with Daniel Sproul in the van, I regret to say, opposed him!"

"Indeed?"

"And they succeeded in keeping this wholesome initiative off the table for two years! Again, one of the most outspoken opponents was your firm's Mr. Daniel Sproul! He—"

No matter that I found the alleged position incomprehensible, the substance was not germane to my inquiry. "Yet the Quaker opposition failed, ma'am. And this would have to have been at least three years ago?"

"That's so, but there are many who have never forgiven it, and—"

Presently, after ascertaining that she had no additional specifics to offer, I concluded our interview. Wishing heartily for yet another beer to still the ringing in my head, I passed outside and into the carriage that Francis Goode was faithfully holding for me.

"We must head in to the office, Francis Goode. Mr. Castell and I are to dine together."

"Very well, sir."

"Would it be a difficulty if I were to sit outside with you? I need to ask some questions of you."

"Me, sir?" I nodded from the curb. "No, it's no … It's not usual, but …" He started to get down to help me up, but I precluded that by bounding up next to him.

"Besides, I can see more of the city from this vantage!" Francis Goode shrugged, flicked the reins, and started us on our return. "I doubt you've been told, Francis Goode, but my visit to Philadelphia does not concern regular company business."

"Sir?"

"I'm investigating the last days of Mr. Sproul here. I've come across evidence that shows he didn't die of any natural cause, but was foully murdered." Francis Goode turned to stare at me. "Whoa, watch the horse!"

Francis Goode yanked the reins and the carriage lurched to a halt, alarming some of the townsfolk but causing no calamity. He got hold of himself, looked about, and started on again. "I ... sorry, sir. Mr. Sproul ... good man. I ... *I* regret him!"

"And I'm sorry to have mentioned it so brusquely, Francis Goode. Do you think you can answer some of my questions?" He solemnly inclined his head as he again flicked the reins. "Well, then, it's the second week of this past March that I'm concerned with. Mr. Castell was away in Lancaster, Mrs. Sproul was ill, there was a heavy snowfall on the Thursday, and Mr. Sproul took a coach for New York on Saturday morning. You remember all of that?" I could sense that he, like the others, recalled the week in detail—as we all tend to do about periods that culminate in dramatic reversals of our fortunes. "You must have seen a good deal of Mr. Sproul during that week?"

"Yes, I do."

"Uh huh. Well, I'd like you to tell me all you can remember."

"Week start with Reuben Castell—takes Lancaster coach, Monday morning. I look in on Missus, do errands. Do errands both missus on Tuesday, but take Daniel Sproul to Prentice house Tuesday night. Him play cards, he say, but not regular friends and he don't like. After, he upset, he go back to office, not home. Already three hours after dark, and he go back to office! He in there half hour, I ... hear him argue with Christopher Enniston."

"With Mr. Enniston? Arguing? What was Mr. Enniston even doing in the office so late?"

"I never know, sir. He don't say." He negotiated an intersection. "Wednesday? Wednesday nothing ... I fetch firewood for Dorothy Castell."

"Thursday it snowed."

"Aye. I hitch sleigh again. Early afternoon, Daniel Sproul ask me to attend him at home Friday morning, to go take New York coach."

"He didn't tell you *why* he wanted to go to New York?"

"No. He say very, very important. I try to say, with snow, no New York coach Friday. He don't hear. So, Friday morning, dawn—snow stop only then—I fetch. We try go downtown. Streets bad, very bad. Drifts so high in one, I shovel road. I tire, Daniel Sproul shovel! One block take half hour! We get to coach, coach not gone, coach not *going*. Daniel Sproul talk me whether we can go New York in sleigh! I willing, though never been New Jersey before. He finally say no, go home, not fair to women folk for him and me both go away. Say don't tell them he even consider."

"Really? So he was asking you to keep a secret? Had he ever done that before, Francis Goode?"

"No! He not usual, he … wrestling devil!"

"Yet you took the children out when you got home?"

"Yes. Happy time!"

"He wasn't 'wrestling with a devil' at that point?"

"All different, all back regular. But he say we try again next day."

"And on Saturday?"

"Roads clear enough, we make coach. He tell me watch family and Dorothy Castell. Last I ever see."

He pulled over to the curb in front of the office. "Francis Goode, can you think why anybody—*anybody*—would want to kill Mr. Sproul?"

He looked horrified to the point of tears. "No! Nobody! Daniel Sproul, he good man! He tell Marse Leavering free me, free wife, free son!"

"It was *you* whom Mr. Leavering set free?" I hadn't realized Francis Goode had ever had a wife and child.

"He! He! All peoples love Daniel Sproul!"

The home office of Castell, Leavering & Sproul on the Delaware riverfront is naturally somewhat more impressive than our outpost in New York, but few shipping firms will ever inspire architectural comment, much less commendation. The entry is on the ground floor, with the warehouse's main portal in the adjacent structure. I walked in, waved and shook hands with those I'd met the previous year, and knocked on the door of Mr. Castell's room. "Ah, Thomas Dordrecht!" he said, looking up from his papers-covered desk. "I've been reviewing our activities of last winter, and I'm afraid nothing suggests anything out of ordinary. We had three ships going to or from Britain, one in harbor, and, of course, the *Dorothy C.* was being loaded for Monte Cristi in New York. Perhaps thee can review these after luncheon?"

"Have you examined the correspondence files, sir?"

"I went over mine and I examined Daniel's very carefully. Again, perhaps thee can find something I see not."

"Are there any others?"

"Correspondence? *Um*, I think the clerks …" He rose and reopened the door. "Christopher Enniston is … ?"

"Down by the wharf, sir," a lad responded.

"Ah! Fetch me his letters file, if thee please!"

The boy had it on the desk by the time Castell sat back down. Mr. Castell looked through it, finding the period at issue, turned several leaves over, and stopped. "Ah!" he said, looking puzzled. "I'd forgotten this! I wonder why he put it here, rather than in my file."

> Thursday
>
> Reuben,
>
> For imperative reasons, I travel tomorrow for New York. As soon as I can, I shall write thee. Meanwhile, Christopher Enniston can give some explanation. I hope to return before the month is out.
>
> Daniel
>
> PS: Evelyn is on the mend, but I'd appreciate it if thee could look in on her.

"You must have asked Mr. Enniston about this?"

"Yes—but he said he'd no idea. He said that Thursday was the day it snowed, and speculated that Daniel had been planning to speak with him but perhaps forgot in the haste of closing the office."

"I see …" I made a mental note that a frank discussion with Enniston was in order.

"And, of course, it was the first thing I saw on my return after eight days' absence, and it was before we knew anything had gone wrong, and there was business to attend to, so I never …"

"Perhaps we can inquire again this afternoon." He shrugged and placed the missive in the battered notebook he invariably carried about with him. "But before we repair to luncheon, sir, if I may, there's one question I feel I must ask in the privacy of your chamber."

"Oh? Well, go on."

"This would ordinarily be an effrontery, and I promise to keep it in as strict a confidence as I can, sir, but in the circumstances—"

No matter his equable appearance, Mr. Castell *was* a seasoned business executive. "Get on with it, lad!"

"Do you know what personal financial dispositions Mr. Sproul may have made, by way of anticipating his eventual demise?"

"Had he made a will, thee mean?"

"Aye, and were its provisions known in advance by those concerned?"

"He had, and they were—a very responsible man, and properly aware of the mortality that waits us all. I am his executor as"—he grimaced—"as he was mine." He sighed. "I was hardly anticipating that *I'd* be the one burdened with the task!" I waited. "Evelyn Sproul inherited everything, of course, given the children's ages. Everything, as is only proper."

"The partnership?"

"Of course. She now owns—this *is* confidential—the one-quarter of the equity that he had contributed. Given the continuing frailty of her condition, I've not yet pressed her regarding the disposition of it."

"It must be a considerable sum, sir?"

"Kindly reaffirm thy pledge of confidentiality, Thomas Dordrecht. Not even John Glasby knows these details!"

"I promise, sir."

He sighed. "It's of course a goodly sum in the eyes of a young fellow such as thyself, but … it is hardly a great fortune. Most of our warehouses are leased. Two of our boats are partnered with other firms. Thy *Dorothy C.*—Captain Trent owns an eighth share of her!"

"I see. Can you—"

"Two unprofitable years in a row, and we'd be out of business, Thomas Dordrecht!"

Though trying to maintain my focus on the matter at hand, I confess I found it daunting to realize that my employer saw his business prospects as far more fragile than I'd imagined! "Can you think of anyone inside or outside the firm who might have—or even think they had—a pecuniary interest in Mr. Sproul's death?"

"None at all. None at all! Daniel Sproul was needed *alive!*"

Ignoring the curiosity of his staff—who were doubtless wondering why I was to dine with the chief rather than with *them*—Mr. Castell led me to a handsome tavern that had a pretty back garden with small tables, where we could have a repast without fear of being overheard. At his instance, I retailed what I'd learned of Mr. Sproul's last week in Philadelphia from his wife, her aunt, and Francis Goode.

"How I wish I'd postponed that trip to Lancaster!" he mused. "I could easily have gone the following week. It was only on the Saturday previous that I made up my mind to attend to it."

"Did many of the staff know you would be travelling, sir?"

He had to think back. "Well, they knew I'd be going ... sometime, but not exactly when. I discussed it with Daniel late on the Saturday afternoon, after they'd all gone home. So they'd have learned of it Monday, from Daniel."

"Did he express any apprehension about your trip?"

Mr. Castell shook his head. "None at all."

"Given Mrs. Sproul's illness, would he have urged you to postpone your trip if he'd had any thought of traveling out of town himself?"

"Most certainly he would! Our families are very close, and ..."

"Then his decision to go to New York must certainly have postdated your decision to go to Lancaster."

He nodded after pondering it for a second. "It would have to be so. Certainly he never even hinted the possibility to me."

"From what I learned in his household, it appears that nothing seemed at all out of ordinary before the Tuesday—aside from his questioning whether to accept the invitation to the card party. Francis Goode said he took him to 'the Prentice house.' Do you know a Mr. Prentice?"

"Not personally. Daniel had met James Prentice through their mutual participation as volunteers in the Union Fire Company—a most worthy endeavor. He is a factor for some of the largest mercantile firms here, and I know Daniel considered it possibly worthwhile to solicit business from him, but …"

"But what?" I asked at length.

"But he has a reputation as a habitual inebriate. I discouraged even approaching the man, even though no overt complaints have ever been raised against him, but I know that Daniel was unconvinced. Perhaps also his regrettable weakness for cards led him finally to accept an invitation." I tried to keep my face blank at this stricture against gaming, which I found excessive and tiresome. "But I can't imagine what might have happened at a *card party* that might have prompted what followed!"

"Mrs. Leavering said Mr. Sproul would never wager more than pennies, so unusual monetary losses cannot have been a factor."

"Assuredly not. In all our years as partners, I never once had reason to doubt his probity."

I was about to raise my questions regarding Mr. Enniston when Mr. Castell proposed we exercise ourselves by taking a circuitous route back to the office. I fear I slowed the elderly man down with my demands for descriptions of the many handsome and imposing brick structures we came across. But our conversation inevitably returned to Mr. Sproul. I solicited his opinion of Mrs. Sproul's and Miss Leavering's theories of the dead man's potential adversaries.

"Ah, they are both clutching for straws, Thomas Dordrecht! Neither notion makes any practical sense."

"Miss Leavering is the first person I've met who does not positively revere the memory of Daniel Sproul!"

He shook his head. "Rhoda Leavering, I am sorry to tell thee, is an Anglican zealot, unreconciled to her niece's change of heart. Were she not my partner's sister, I should be glad to avoid all commerce with her!"

"I confess, it perplexes me … Though I concur that it is unlikely to have had anything to do with his murder, I cannot fathom his position against the formation of a provincial militia!"

Mr. Castell halted, faced me, and earnestly took hold of both my forearms. "Can thee not? This whole sinful war has been waged for reasons not seen, Thomas Dordrecht—as Daniel Sproul well knew! It is said we endeavor solely to protect the innocent scalps of our frontiersmen, yet those same frontiersmen have been wickedly encouraged to place their scalps in jeopardy! All for the sake of those in power here on the seaboard, or in London or Paris!"

"But—"

"'Tis an attempt to steal the lands of North America by both kings and their royal lackeys and their wealthy servitors, lad. They all covet what is not theirs!"

"The French—"

"The French Crown is as reprehensible as our own, to be sure. There is blame on all heads. Yet—"

I inadvertently guffawed, forgetting who this suddenly ardent, elderly, radical speaker was. "I suppose you would then allow the Indians to keep us forever bottled up against the ocean, never to exploit the riches of the interior?"

"Nay, lad, nay. The point is that there is no call for *war* on this issue. It is a matter that reasonable men can adjust, piece by piece, year by year. There is no justification for the assumption that either the British or the French—or the Iroquois, for that matter—should forever dominate the continent!"

"But—"

"And that is why Daniel Sproul spoke out against Benjamin Franklin's proposal. Creating a militia would only further a war that should never have come to exist!"

"And the frontiersmen?"

"They should be encouraged back, just as they were wrongfully encouraged forward!"

"How were they encouraged forward, save by their own desire to be fruitful and multiply?"

"Aha! *That* is a good question, Thomas Dordrecht! That is the *right* question! They were encouraged with promises of land from officials who'd never laid eyes on the land and were careless of existing claims. They were encouraged by the army's having built roads to make it easy for them to venture beyond the civilized pale. They were most of all encouraged by open hints that their king and country would come to their aid if they got in difficulty—all at the expense of those prudent subjects who refrained from putting themselves in harm's way! All to secure quitrents and profits and glory for those who've done naught to merit them!"

An acquaintance of Mr. Castell's passed by and interrupted this oration with cheerful greetings, introductions, and inquiries after spousal health. When we resumed our walk toward the office, I said, "I shall surely consider your thoughts, sir. I know Mr. Leavering objects to the war, but I have never heard the case put so strongly!"

"God be with thee, Thomas Dordrecht!" Mr. Castell said, smiling. "There is much more. If gentlemen but knew the—*Ah!*"

A very strong gust of wind had blown his hat clear off his head and carried it to the far side of Lombard Street, where it landed in the gutter. Just then, two carriages, moving in contrary directions, passed with a great clatter, and the hat was swept even further away. Mr. Castell grabbed my sleeve just as I was about to leap in front of one of them. After they passed—and a check for other traffic—I ran across the road and retrieved it. "I fear it has gotten dusty, sir, but otherwise it's undamaged."

"I thank thee, lad. I am lucky it was not trampled."

We resumed our walk. "Are the hats matters of any religious import, Mr. Castell?"

He laughed. "Oh no, no, lad! They are not even prescribed, much less required. They are merely a common form in which some Friends observe our Testament of Simplicity."

"Is there one authorized manufacturer, or—"

"No no. Many. Why?"

"I notice your hat is considerably lighter than Mr. Sproul's, and—"

"Ah, well, you see, I carry my papers in a notebook, thus"—he raised his notebook to show me—"whereas Daniel would—"

We both stopped dead. "What?"

"Daniel would always stuff his papers *into his hat!* Thee say his hat, the one that was ruined, was heavier?"

"Enough to notice, sir."

"It was not just the mud?"

"No. Mr. McCraney scraped most of that off when he—"

Mr. Castell had grabbed my forearm and was tearing toward the office at a breathless pace. "Francis Goode! Francis Goode!" he bawled when we were still thirty yards away. The driver stood up expectantly. Mr. Castell opened the carriage door and practically shoved me inside. "To Evelyn Sproul's house, as fast as thee can, Francis Goode!"

"What is the meaning of this intrusion, Mr. Castell?" Miss Leavering demanded even as she was opening the door. "Evelyn is trying to have her afternoon nap, and—"

"The hat, Rhoda Leavering! Daniel Sproul's hat! Do thee still have it?"

She looked at the three of us in stupefaction. "The one that was crushed?"

"Aye!"

"The one that was in his bag of clothing that I gave you this morning, ma'am," I added.

"I … It's on the grate, awaiting the next chilly evening."

"Ah!" Castell exclaimed, pushing past her.

"It's very important, ma'am," I explained as I followed him. Francis Goode took it upon himself to close the door as she pursued us.

Castell was in the parlor, the hat in his hand. "Heaven be praised, it's not yet burnt!" He pushed the crown of it back into a semblance of shape—I'd seen no reason to bother with it—and looked underneath. "See!" he exclaimed, pointing at a loose area of the lining that had been crushed into the riser. He inserted his fingers into the cavity and extracted … "Aha!"

There was a sealed envelope and two loose pieces of paper, sharply folded. The envelope was addressed to Evelyn Sproul. He set it down on the table. "Aha!" he again exclaimed, checking the others. "This one appears to be the beginning of a letter to me, and this … is just … notes." He passed them to me after reading them. I read them and passed them to Miss Leavering, who read them and set them down. To my surprise—I'd assumed him to be illiterate—Francis Goode picked them up and followed suit.

The unfinished letter ran thus:

> Sunday, March 21
>
> Carteret Hotel, New Brunswick, N.J.
>
> My worthy Reuben,
>
> I am embarked on a mission I believe to be of great moment to our provinces. This past Tuesday I inadvertently discovered a fraud of staggering consequence to the King, the army, and the beleaguered rate-payers of our enormous empire. It was at a card party at the home of James Prentice. In attendance were only his neighbor, the importer Samuel Aldridge, and the latter's solicitor, whose name I never caught. After two rounds of play, Prentice excused himself to deal with a great row that had broken out among his wife and children that could be heard from the upstairs of the house. I excused myself to visit the necessary outside. When I returned—the family altercation still continuing—I stopped by bookshelves just outside the parlor, and overheard snatches of conversation. The substance was so horrendous, I restrained my first impulse to disclose my presence.
>
> The man was boasting of chicanery he'd engineered, to the foul amusement of his lawyer! Unsuspecting anyone near, he said quite clearly that he

"It appears that his hand became cramped," I observed, noting with dismay the irregularity of the penmanship that increased with every line.

"Daniel had great difficulty with writing. He would normally dictate to one of the clerks," Castell said.

The notes were barely decipherable scribbles:

> £267,000 imports
> Not a farthing tax

Inform J.A.
Transfer Statia
Tents, uniforms, powder, shot, salted beef
Atlantic Mercantile Co.—sham
C.E. asserts affiliated S.L.A.
Sent N.Y.—DeLancey? Colegrove?
Army "frantic" for supplies
Quartermaster—no scruples
Gov. too busy chasing traders
Artillery & muskets
Two doz. ships involved

Miss Leavering had turned quite pale. She was not even taking cognizance of the fact that a black retainer had seated himself in the family parlor. "But what … what could this all mean?"

Mr. Castell sighed. "What I fear it means is that Daniel uncovered a conspiracy to defraud the army—the Crown—of stupendous proportions. A quarter of a million pounds—"

Evelyn Sproul entered the room. All of us jumped up, embarrassed that we'd not called her before. "We have discovered some papers thy husband wrote while *en route* to New York, Evelyn," Castell said awkwardly. "They were in his hat." He handed her the two sheets. She sat and quickly scanned them. He then remembered the sealed envelope and passed it to her. Overcome, she clasped it to her heart and fled to the kitchen without having uttered a sound. Miss Leavering, Mr. Castell, and I sat back down.

"What would the excises on a quarter million of goods normally be, sir?" I asked.

"Close to thirty thousand," he replied after a second. "I assume he means sterling, not provincial currency. A royal ransom."

"Even if distributed among many … a huge sum."

"What is he suggesting actually happened?" Miss Leavering persisted anxiously.

"There have always been rumors," Castell mused aloud, "but … The bruited pattern is that all these goods, wanted desperately by the army here in North America, are smuggled out of Britain in small boats. Then they are transferred to oceanic shippers in Flanders or Holland or even France. The larger ships then take them to Saint

Eustatius Island in the Caribbean, where they are again transferred to American-registered shippers who bring them into New York, where the military is so eager to receive them … they make short shrift of the paperwork."

"And this man, Mr. Prentice's neighbor," I added, "apparently was in fact directing major aspects of such transactions, and doubtless pocketing the lion's share of the illicit profits!"

"This is infamous!" Miss Leavering declared. "Monstrous! How could—"

Mrs. Sproul's weeping could be heard from the back. Miss Leavering looked as if she thought she should go to her, then changed her mind.

"Who would 'J.A.' be, sir?" I asked quietly.

"I can't … think of anyone here with those initials. Can thee, madam? Can thee, lad?"

Miss Leavering was unable to name one. I observed that Mr. Glasby's middle name was Anthony, but I hadn't heard it used before or since his wedding ceremony. "'C.E.' would be Mr. Enniston, I surmise?"

"Well," Castell said, "he was mentioned in the note left at the office. I can't think of any other 'C.E.,' but I also can't—"

"Ah!" I said, catching Francis Goode's eye. "I didn't tell you, sir. Francis Goode took Mr. Sproul back to the office after the card party—this would be about nine o'clock—and found Christopher Enniston still there."

"Burning up our candles? For what possible reason? You saw him?" Castell addressed the driver.

"I hear him, sir. I know voice."

"And Mr. Sproul appeared even more upset when he left the office half an hour later."

"That's so?"

"So," Francis Goode replied.

"Well, we shall have to— How I wish he'd spelled out these initials! Now, 'S.L.A.' must be Samuel Low Aldridge, I suppose, but—"

"Mercy!" Miss Leavering exclaimed. "Surely *he* couldn't—"

"One of the very most substantial merchants of the city," Castell explained to me, looking dismayed.

I was rereading the abbreviated note. "Were there five or four at the party? It reads, 'his neighbor, Samuel Aldridge, and the latter's solicitor.' One would assume only four, if he'd been invited as a matter of necessity."

Francis Goode cleared his throat. "Beg pardon, sir. Samuel Low Aldridge live 'round corner from Mr. Prentice, on Second Street."

"Oh? Thee are sure?"

"Mr. Prentice man say so, sir."

"*Hmph!* Who is Colegrove? I know DeLancey, of course."

"Aaron Colegrove is a merchant in New York," I said, trying to restrain my distasteful memories. "He's related to the DeLancey family. Both Mr. Glasby and I worked for him at one point."

"Can thee imagine him participating in such a scheme?"

I squirmed for a few seconds, aware that it's impolitic to speak ill of former employers. "Candidly, yes, sir, I can. Mr. Glasby might be able to tell you more."

"Aha. So—"

Mrs. Sproul returned and sat again, having recovered some of her composure. She gestured for the two sheets, reread them, and passed them back. "The letter is … very personal, Reuben," she stated, "but I … I have heard some of thy discussion … Perhaps if I read some excerpts?"

"If thee would, my dear. We are learning a great deal."

"He says, first, that he can't write everything out twice, so he urges me to consult thy letter to learn his reasons for the trip, as he is 'hesitant even to engage a scribe.'"

"Ah!" Castell exclaimed, his jaw tight. "And he was unable to finish or post it. That means we shall learn little more!" All of us nodded, regretting that the ancient injury to Mr. Sproul's hand had inhibited his communication to the last.

"He says, toward the close, 'I deeply regret having so abruptly to abandon thee and the children, but it is for a worthy purpose, and I trust it will be brief.'" We all had difficulty restraining our feelings. "'It is imperative that I take my protest to the highest in the land, so that we honest merchants are not persecuted for the innocent trading of flour for sugar while others commit treason and highway robbery!'"

We all took this in as it became apparent she had no more to add.

A sudden insight nearly prompted a gaffe. "Oh my—" Mercifully, I clamped down on *Oh my God!*—which would have offended them all. "Oh my! 'J.A.!' It's *Jeffery Amherst!* He intended to put this information before General Amherst!"

"Who he?" Francis Goode could not help asking.

"In March," Mr. Castell replied, "General Amherst was the commander in chief of all His Majesty's forces in North America—and effectively the military governor of us all!"

"So … my husband's intent was to expose wrongdoing to the commander in chief?"

"Thus it appears, Evelyn—a massive fraud that has adversely affected every subject of the empire."

"But—"

"But someone must have discovered his intent … and forestalled him."

Mr. Castell and I shared a significant glance at each other. "Perhaps it's time we returned to the office, sir?" I said.

"Perhaps so, Thomas Dordrecht." We stood.

"It's this fellow Enniston that you suspect!" Miss Leavering cried.

"Nay, ma'am," I said, "it's known he was here in Philadelphia when Mr. Sproul was attacked."

"But he—"

"I would caution against all speculation, as yet," Mr. Castell said. "Particularly in public, ladies, Francis Goode! I recollect Hermione Leavering's warning that those who have once set upon their fellows to prevent their exposure may not hesitate to do so again!"

"Why that's appalling!"

"Yes—and must be taken seriously!" he lectured her. "Thee might consider not confiding in the children, just yet," he added gently to Mrs. Sproul.

She nodded. "Call on us again, as soon as thee can, Reuben?"

"I will. Let's be off, lad, Francis Goode."

I bowed as formally as I could while rushing to follow my employer's determined exit.

The carriage had progressed two blocks when I knocked my palm against my forehead. "When I was in Saint Eustatius two months ago, Mr. Castell—"

"Yes?"

"I was at dinner in the home of Meneer Staats Koopvaarder, the father of Absalom, who sold us all the sugarloaf. And he made reference to a recent local scandal, in which an enormous amount of goods smuggled out of England had been transshipped there to the army in New York!"

"Indeed?"

"And his, *um*, his woman said that it had been arranged by 'Atlantic something' of Philadelphia."

"'Atlantic something!' I see. Did thee learn anything more?"

"I … fear we had an altercation, sir."

"An *altercation?* With a supplier! I am distressed to think thee would ever stoop to—"

"The point of my host's story was his regret at not having been actively involved in the swindle, sir!"

"Oh. And … this is the man who'd enslaved his own son?"

"That's right. I was at pains to verify the contents of every crate I accepted from him!" He raised his eyebrows. "Mr. Mapes and Mr. Glasby have not reported any problems with the shipment, sir!"

"Oh. I see. So … thee are suggesting this scandal may bear relation to the scheme that Daniel Sproul discovered here?"

"I think it must be so, sir," I said—with private relief that my lamentable uncle was no longer the topic. "How many conspiracies of this magnitude could there be?"

"Not that many, one would hope!"

We progressed a few more blocks. "When did Mr. Enniston join the firm, sir?"

"Last August. He was previously … Oh my!"

I waited.

"He had worked for the Aldridge firm, for years!" He pensively toyed with his lips. "Daniel took him under his wing. They attended the same meeting."

"A different, *uh*, parish from your own?"

"Yes, so to speak. I've never been able to find much regard for the man … although his bookkeeping is faultless." He seemed to be debating further statement. "Dorothy has some regard for his wife. She is only recently with child, though they've been married for years."

"Ah."

"That will not make this interview any easier!"

The carriage arrived in front of the office.

"Christopher Enniston," Castell called, the instant we were indoors, "we would speak with thee!"

Startled—like everyone else present—by his grim visage and the tone of his voice, Enniston nervously rose and followed us into Mr. Castell's room, where I closed the door. "Sir?"

"Christopher Enniston, Thomas Dordrecht is not here to conduct any regular business of the firm—"

"Indeed! We were speculating as—"

"He has uncovered substantial evidence that shows that Daniel Sproul was murdered!"

Enniston emitted a yelp of dismay and began moaning, "No! Oh no!" After half a minute, he collected himself and begged leave to sit. For an instant, I thought Castell might refuse; but he acceded, and Enniston collapsed in the chair that I had placed behind him. "I … am most afflicted to hear thee say this, Reuben Castell. I …"

Castell indicated that he wanted me to sit next to his desk and question the man. "In your correspondence file, Mr. Enniston, we found a note written by Mr. Sproul to Mr. Castell that should have been filed with his correspondence. Why was it in *your* correspondence file?"

"It must have been … It was an oversight!"

"The note was written on the Thursday preceding Mr. Sproul's death, to convey the fact of his intention to travel to New York—"

"Yes."

"… and to mention that Mr. Castell might consult you, for some explanation of his trip."

Enniston's face was working nervously. "Yes. Well, as I explained to Reuben Castell at the time, Daniel Sproul must have forgotten his plan to discuss it with me … because we were … closing the office in view of the inclemency of the weather …"

Mr. Castell was staring at him coldly. Suddenly his face grew scarlet, he rose and slammed his fist on the desk. "Thou art *lying*, Christopher Enniston!" he bellowed, so loudly passersby on the street might have heard it.

Looking as wintry as the storm that had blanketed the day in question, Enniston quivered, terrified, in his chair.

If I'd had any doubt before that he *had* been lying, it was now gone. After a minute, I attempted to resume. "Let's go back to the Tuesday before he left. He attended a card party in the early evening, at the home of James Prentice, and then returned here and found—"

"I thought … I believed … They said he had expired of natural causes! Of heart failure!"

Had he truly believed it? Or just wanted to? "He was murdered in a very peculiar manner that left no marks, and thereby deliberately created the impression there had been no foul play. The subterfuge was so artfully accomplished, the coroner and all who saw the body were convinced—myself included."

"I … But then …" Enniston abruptly put his face in his hands and wept unrestrainedly. I think I'd know it if he were acting.

"Stop," Castell quietly ordered after a minute had passed. Enniston obediently used his handkerchief and pushed himself upright, still trembling.

"So then," I resumed, "do we understand that you *did* have some understanding of Mr. Sproul's plans?" Enniston merely gaped, his head lolling about drunkenly—whether from evasiveness or nausea was anyone's guess. "Francis Goode was waiting outside for Mr. Sproul that evening, Enniston! He heard raised voices—and recognized yours!"

Enniston moaned. "I meant no harm!"

"What were thee doing here that night, at such an hour?" Castell demanded.

"I … I don't like to go home. It's safer here."

"Safer? Ridiculous! And most improper!"

"I …"

"On that matter, Mr. Castell," I said, instantly regretting the fact that I had interrupted him, "can we imagine any reason why *Mr. Sproul* would have returned here, rather than going directly home after the party?"

Castell exhaled and shrugged. "I don't know. Daniel did not do things in orthodox ways, he was often impulsive, and—"

"He came here to fetch writing materials, he said. He had run out of his supplies at the house."

Both of us looked at Enniston, startled. The explanation was too absurd to be anything but genuine. "I presume he was not expecting to find you present when he arrived?"

Enniston shuddered. "Yes."

"And perhaps annoyed?"

"Yes."

"Why *were* you here, Mr. Enniston?"

Enniston reddened and squirmed.

"Tippling?" Castell proposed.

Enniston moaned and hung his head. "My wife … won't let me, at home, and.… Daniel Sproul remonstrated with me, made me empty the jug out the window, and led me in prayer. He warned me that … others might consider my behavior cause for dismissal."

"Others might indeed!" Castell growled.

"He sent you home?"

"He seemed about to—but then he asked me about my employment at Aldridge Brothers. He had been playing cards at James Prentice's house and inadvertently overheard Samuel Low Aldridge, who was one of the players, telling a friend about his profitable arrangements with Atlantic Mercantile Company. I told him my work was with Aldridge Brothers, but I had stumbled across evidence that Atlantic Mercantile existed as an unrecognized subsidiary of Aldridge's. I was concerned, as this seemed improper, and a month later I worked up the courage to speak to Ichabod Dabney, one of the officers, about it. He told me, succinctly, that it was none of my business!"

"You were keeping the accounts, and yet he deemed this none of your business?"

"Aye. That was last June. And in July, Ichabod Dabney found cause to dismiss me." Castell and I both stared at him. "He had examined the petty cash records in detail and … discovered discrepancies of his own, and I had to confess that I had borrowed monies from time to time … Daniel Sproul knew of this when he hired me, I told him all!"

"And he hired you anyway?"

"Daniel would do that," Castell said, shaking his head. "He may have believed that the repentance was sincere, and—"

"I had kept exact records of the funds I had borrowed, and—"

"*Pilfered!*"

Enniston reddened and swallowed and addressed me, avoiding Castell. "And over the next several months, following Daniel Sproul's suggestion, I worked out a schedule and repaid everything I owed to Aldridge Brothers, to the penny!"

"Good," I said without much enthusiasm.

"Daniel Sproul said he was pleased. And I thought that would be the end of it."

"It was not?"

"In January, Ichabod Dabney accosted me in the street and told me that unless I continued the payments, he would expose my defalcations to … He would post a letter to the newspapers! My parents, my wife … thee!" He was addressing our employer. "All would know!"

"Did you bring this threat to Mr. Sproul's attention?"

"Oh heavens, no! He'd done so much for me, I couldn't …"

"You did pay the man, then?"

"Aye, and it was most hard to bear. I had endured the difficulty cheerfully when restoring the debt, but …"

Castell looked askance, appalled at Enniston's foolishness.

"How long had you been employed by Aldridge Brothers?"

"Since I came to Philadelphia, over six years."

"And for how long had you been 'borrowing' from the till?"

"About fifteen months."

"And no one had ever … Do you think there may have been a connection between your asking Mr. Dabney about Atlantic Mercantile and his subsequent discovery of your embezzlements?"

"It was not *much* money! That much money gets simply misplaced, every month!"

"Oh, come now!"

"He had to expend a great deal of the firm's time to find me out!"

Castell raised his eyebrows thoughtfully, but said nothing.

"We're getting away from our chief interest. On the night Mr. Sproul found you here, what did he tell you of what he'd learned at Prentice's?"

Enniston sighed heavily. "He told me only that he'd been alarmed to overhear Samuel Low Aldridge boasting of a fraud he had perpetrated on the army. He asked if I knew aught of the business of Atlantic Mercantile Company …" We waited. "I was very startled to hear the name, as I'd never once heard mention of the company since the time I had asked Ichabod Dabney about it, but … in truth, I did *not* know anything of its enterprises."

"Nothing at all?"

"No. Daniel Sproul seemed very agitated by what he had overheard and, naturally, I expressed some curiosity—"

"Doubtless, thee would be gratified to divert discussion from thyself!"

Enniston reddened. "It … may be so. Nonetheless, Daniel Sproul said he was most tired, and thought he had better get some rest. He said we should continue on the morrow, but I had been scheduled to inventory the south warehouse, so I didn't see him again until Thursday."

A memory jogged. "You weren't present, then, when Captain Wardener stopped by to see if the firm had any last-minute goods for Monte Cristi?"

"Wardener? Of *Four Daughters*? He was here?"

"Captain Trent and I met the man in Saint Eustatius," I explained to Castell. "He was completely shocked to learn that Mr. Sproul was dead, particularly because he'd stopped in on the morning of his departure … which he had brought forward, in order to avoid the impending storm." I strained to recollect the conversation. "He said Mr. Sproul was out of sorts and complained of lack of sleep ... and amazed him by ranting on about procurement corruption and how much more it cost the Crown than trade with the enemy ... He even—*yes*, he even mentioned General Amherst by name!"

Mr. Castell contemplated this in silence.

"General Amherst was definitely on his mind when we spoke on Thursday!" Enniston broke in. "He told me everything he'd overheard, and carried on about how he was determined to go to New York and reveal to the general all about the criminal activities of Atlantic Mercantile."

Though I sensed he was now telling the truth ... "Mr. Enniston, why did you find it necessary to withhold this from Mr. Castell?"

"I ... I didn't ... What had struck me, at the time, was not Daniel Sproul's noble resolution to put a stop to this fraud ... but ..."

"But what?"

Enniston flushed again. "I realized that I now had information I could use to counter Mr. Dabney's extortions from me!"

"You mean—"

"I possessed an allegation with which I could threaten him in return!"

"Enniston, you didn't ..."

"After we closed here, on Thursday, I trudged through the snow and found Dabney still in his office. I told him I wouldn't be paying him any more money, because I now knew something he'd be very sorry for me to reveal!"

"And?"

"Well, he was very sensible! He agreed straightaway that the payments should cease. He even said he was glad to have some company that afternoon, as all his staff had left for their homes."

"Yes?"

"And he ... Well, he offered me a whiskey to ward off the chill, before I left ... and he asked me what it was that I'd heard tell of—out of curiosity, he said. And I said I knew what Atlantic Mercantile was doing and it was very wrong!"

I could see that Castell was finding this recitation almost unbearable, but we had to finish it. "Can I guess that he offered you a second glass?" I said.

"Yes! It was very gratifying that he bore me no ill will!"

"Did Dabney appear upset or horrified at the revelations about Atlantic Mercantile?"

Enniston considered the question—which had clearly never before occurred to him. "No … No, he did not. He seemed most interested in what I had learned."

"And did he ask how you had learned it?"

"No. He inquired how my work here was coming along, what we were trading, who I was reporting to … He appeared to have lost interest in his own projects and given up business for the day. We shared yet another tot before he closed his office."

"Did he ever inquire as to Mr. Sproul's activities?"

"Oh no … Well, he asked whether we expected to reopen for business the next day or Saturday, and I explained that, in view of the storm and Reuben Castell's absence and Daniel Sproul's traveling, we were closed until the Monday."

Dabney had ferreted out all he needed without asking a single direct question. "Did he perhaps find it odd that Mr. Sproul would venture abroad in such difficult weather?"

"Well … anybody would, of course."

Mr. Castell was studiously looking out the window, his jaw tight.

I, too, was troubled to keep my patience. I showed Enniston Mr. Sproul's page of notes. "Did he mention any details beyond these in your conversations with him?"

"Two hundred sixty-seven *thousand!* Dear heaven! No … and I had no idea so much was involved!"

I handed over the foreshortened letter. "Does this prompt any further recollection?"

"Ah!" he exclaimed immediately. "Poor Daniel Sproul! Thee can see how his hand troubled him! Often I would transcribe his correspondence for him, as—"

"Is there anything *more*, Enniston?" Castell demanded impatiently.

Enniston concentrated on reading through the missive. "But … But he told me he'd overheard Samuel Low Aldridge speaking to a *friend*."

"Yes?"

"Here it says, his *solicitor*, his *lawyer*."

"Yes?"

"But that's … Ichabod Dabney. That's Ichabod Dabney's position within Aldridge Brothers."

Mr. Castell's fists were clenched as our eyes met. "That will be all … for now, Enniston," he said hoarsely. After a second's hesitation, Enniston fled, closing the door behind him. "I shall fire him," Castell sighed, "as soon as I can find a replacement. I'll never be able to trust him again. I had no idea he was such a perfect fool."

Though I surely concurred, I made bold to offer a caution. "He may be needed as a witness, Mr. Castell, in—"

"We have no guarantee the ass won't go begging another drink from Dabney this very evening!" He rested his head in his hands contemplatively for a moment. "I'm sending thee straight back to New York tomorrow morn, Thomas Dordrecht! Thee will be safer there, until Benjamin and I decide—"

"But sir, I … We still have no idea how—or whether—Aldridge and Dabney might be connected to the man with the wig!"

Castell considered that thoughtfully for a few seconds. "Thee said he had claimed to be employed by the province of New Jersey?"

"So he told the harlot, sir."

Castell rose, opened the door, and called in one of the older clerks, an affable fellow I'd met on my previous visit. "Joseph is our expert on New Jersey," he explained. "Who are the port commissioners in our neighboring province, Joseph? In the north? I know Rushton across in Camden and the old cuss up in Trenton. What about Perth Amboy and Newark?"

The clerk was used to providing arcane tidbits of information. "The Raritan position is vacant at present, sir. I believe it is being handled temporarily by the new commissioner in Newark."

"Aha. And who is that?"

"A young military fellow appointed last year, sir. Oh, what was his name?"

"Military? Odd."

"Quite. There was some public controversy over the appointment, as—"

"Not the first time their governor's appointments have occasioned controversy!" Castell observed.

"Some more experienced local people were passed over. One of the newspapers noised the idea that money might have changed hands."

"Was this proven?" I asked.

"Oh no. But … such matters seldom are. It was rumored that the officer was a protégé of one of our wealthiest merchants, Mr. Samuel Low Aldridge."

We both gaped for three seconds. "Indeed?"

"Yes … Ah! Lieutenant Hardifant. Lieutenant Stephen Hardifant."

Chapter 14

"The problem of the moment," I explained to Mr. Leavering and his reassembled cabal after relating my Philadelphia adventures, "is that we have to be certain whether Lieutenant Stephen Hardifant of Newark is in fact *Steve*, the man with the too-large wig—the man who I think masterminded the murder of Mr. Sproul and his own two henchmen."

Though it was now Monday noon, every muscle in my body still ached from Saturday. In order to move myself as far as New Brunswick, I'd spent every sweltering daylit hour of Saturday on the back of a horse. I endured more time on a horse in that one day than in all my life before—and I shall be at pains to avoid ever repeating the experience! It didn't help that a storm blew up north of Princeton, and a bolt of lightning so frightened the wretched nag that it took off into a marsh and twice nearly killed us both before it calmed down. On Sunday, starting at high water before dawn, Captain Ford of the firm's coastal sloop *Janie*, under stern orders from Mr. Castell that he was to transport me immediately, despite the Sabbath, got us smartly down the Raritan and up through the Narrows, only to have wind and current turn against us, forcing him to anchor off Long Island for six very hot hours. We'd finally reached our dock at Peck Slip in a downpour at ten p.m.

"And how do you propose to do that?" Mr. Leavering demanded.

"Well ..." He had put me on the spot, as I'd not really been able to devise a plan. "There are, what, six individuals who we know saw the 'man with the wig' at different times: Wendell Brush the oysterman, John Meed the taverner, Miss Paulette of the oldest profession, Sam the coachman, Lewes the stable master of New Brunswick, and Vrouw Steenburgh, the neighbor to young Billy's tavern in Brooklyn. I was ... thinking perhaps of taking one of them with me to Newark while I sought Hardifant out."

There was universal agreement that no more harebrained plan had ever been voiced in the entire history of the human race. The prime complaint—which I had to allow—was that it would draw excess attention, and thereby put the witness, not to mention myself, in jeopardy to the suspect. "Well," I stumbled along, "perhaps we could get a drawing of the man? I could take Jones and we could see if we couldn't persuade Hardifant to sit for a portrait."

"You're sounding more demented by the minute, cousin!" Charles protested.

"You'll have to *find* Hardifant in Newark first!" Glasby observed.

"It isn't that big a place, John," Leavering said, "but still ..."

"Having a black man sketching people would cause something of a sensation in a small town," Mapes noted.

"Thomas should not be involved in this at all," Mrs. Leavering asserted. "Too dangerous! The wretch Enniston could have relayed his description to Hardifant through Dabney and Aldridge, just as he did Daniel's!"

"But—"

"She's quite right!" Leavering concurred, settling that issue—whether I agreed or not.

"*I* can sketch the man," Adelie Glasby said confidently. "He needn't be made to sit still for it. If I can get one good look at him, I can sketch him later."

"But, my dear," Glasby objected, "I don't want you going there alone when—"

"I shall go with her!" both Hermione and Charles exclaimed at once. The three of them looked as if this deadly business could be considered a great frolic.

"But how are you going to find him? Now be serious!"

Leavering had an idea, and he told Mapes to send one of the boys running out to the wharf to see if the *Janie* were still with us; if so, he was to instruct Captain Ford not to depart before hearing from him. "You could go by boat," he explained to the threesome, pointing to our large-scale wall map, "and present the Newark Port Commissioner with a story that you didn't know whether you had to register with him when all you were doing was … oh, taking a barrel of flour to somebody's brother in Essex County."

"Well, then they'd have to travel on into the county!" Mapes quibbled, reentering the room.

"No, no," Charles said, "we tell him we're waiting for the brother to pick us up. Once he's dismissed us as lunatics who don't comprehend the difference between transporting and importing—and Adelie has had sufficient time to memorize his features—he'll go away, and then we'll simply turn around for home!"

"This plan will all take a good deal of time in the best of circumstances," Glasby said, "but we really need to proceed as fast as possible. If the wind were to drop, you'd all be becalmed for hours, perhaps a full day, and—"

"*We* have time enough, John," Hermione said.

"We can bring some books—" Adelie said.

"And some wine!" Charles added.

"The point is, we'll need the sketch. Thomas will need to set it in front of all those people in Paulus Hook."

"Yes," I seconded, "and it would be especially wonderful if we could have it by tomorrow evening, because that's the next time Sam should get back to Paulus Hook. Here's what we could do. While you're taking ship, I'll cross on the ferry to Paulus Hook, rent a horse from Meed, and get out to the ferry dock on the eastern shore of the Hackensack. After you've seen Hardifant in Newark, you can stop by there, pass me the sketch, and then return to New York at leisure."

"Well, but this is all dependent on—ah, Captain Ford!"

The captain, a robust, portly, bewhiskered man of my parents' age, entered the room looking slightly baffled. "I was just preparing to cast off, Mr. Leavering, when your boy—"

"Yes, yes. How fast could you get the *Janie* to Newark, Captain?"

The poor man, already perplexed by the mixed assembly and Castell's directive regarding me, helplessly mouthed the word *Newark?* before shaking himself to answer. "Not much wind today, sir, but the ebb has just begun, so if we were to leave anytime soon, we could reach the Kill Van Kull before the slack. When the flood begins, it would have us arriving well before midnight. I confess I would prefer not to sail after dark, however, sir, begging your pardon."

"You have put in to Newark before?"

"A few times, yes, but—"

Leavering pondered a thought. "When will the next ebb begin here, Captain?"

"About two fifteen in the morning, sir."

"And barring complete calm, how long should it take, on an ebb, to round the point at Bayonne?"

"Three hours at the worst, I should think, sir."

"There you have it, then!" Leavering announced, his customarily decisive phraseology heartening us all with a sense of his reinvigoration. "You three shall board the *Janie* at five tomorrow morning, and can reasonably expect to be in Newark before noon."

"Then you can meet me at the Hackensack ferry dock about … How long will it take you, Adelie?"

"If I work fast, the sketch should be mostly complete before we cross to the other side of the bay, Thomas. If we have more time, I can add more detail."

"Do you not have any *goods* for me, Mr. Leavering?" Ford inquired plaintively.

"Ah, I'm afraid not, sir, our business is much diminished of late. However"—he took his wife's hand—"this is a most important trip, and very precious cargo!"

The three of them looked unbearably smug the next afternoon, as Captain Ford—mystified as ever—superintended his sailors while they tied the *Janie* to the muddy Hackensack River ferry dock. "Can't stay but a minute!" he called to me nervously. "It's high water now!"

I nodded; he'd forgotten that was the plan. Charles and Adelie had unquestionably been tippling. "It worked exactly as Benjamin imagined!" Hermione Leavering exulted. "The man was so self-important, he accepted our silly little fable that we didn't know whether we needed his services or not!"

The tiny dock was built to accommodate the ferry, and was too low relative to the *Janie*, so the ladies remained aboard while Charles climbed off to convey the sketch to me on dry land. "He noticed nothing amiss at all?" I asked him.

"Not a thing. Don't tell your friend Glasby, but Adelie worked him like a trouper! The swine was practically drooling over her! It was minutes after she'd signaled that she'd seen enough before Hermione and I could bore him to the point of leaving!"

I looked over the sketch. There were actually two pencil drawings: a full-body rendering next to a horse and a hitching post, and a detail of a hard-looking face, with strong, regular features, but cold and calculating eyes. Despite having been executed on a moving boat, the work was as sure and true as anything she'd done in the city. "He was wearing his cloak?"

"Cooler today. But my guess is he believes it embellishes his stature."

"No wig. What color is his hair?"

"Brown, neither fair nor dark. The cloak was forest green. Silver trim."

"Other than the absence of a wig, it matches everything I've been told about *Steve*."

"Perhaps today he was presenting himself in his own right, Thomas."

"Height?"

"Six feet, thereabout."

"Is that his horse?"

"He rode it confidently, I'd presume so."

"You saw him with it?"

"When he came down to examine us in Newark, yes. Nice horse!"

“What color is it?”

“The horse? Chestnut brown. And it’s a roan, you see the patches?”

Ha! “That’s how Mr. Lewes described the horse that *Steve* rode in from Philadelphia half-dead.”

“Really? Then the people over at Paulus Hook might recognize the horse as well as the man?”

“Uh, no. Because he left the roan with Lewes and took Lewes’s mare, Clarissa, to Paulus Hook.”

“Ah, well, there should still be enough for recognition … if he’s the one.”

“Aye. I feel almost … No matter.” Charles walked carefully back out and enlisted a crewman’s aid to climb back into the boat. “When do you think you’ll get back to the city?” I asked Ford.

The captain shrugged. “If we get enough breeze for any steerage, by dusk. Otherwise, it will be late before the tide sweeps us in. After midnight, perhaps.”

“Do tell Benjamin not to worry!” Mrs. Leavering ordered, waving gaily as the sailors pushed the boat back out into Newark Bay.

“It’s a great piece of work, Adelie!” I called.

“I trust no one will mistake that face for anyone else’s, Thomas!” she boasted.

She was soon proved quite correct. I mounted my rented nag, trotted back to Paulus Hook, and before dark, the sketch of Lieutenant Stephen Hardifant had been positively identified by Miss Paulette as her erstwhile patron; by John Meed as the man who had played cards with Mr. Sproul and the two rowdies; by Wendell Brush as the man he’d seen at Meed’s and heard on the cow in the harbor; and by Sam, whom I interviewed upon the coach’s arrival. Sam immediately said, “The roan!” I was confused—but he explained that he’d seen the roan in Lewes’s stalls while he’d listened to the stable master’s complaints about the infuriating man who’d rented Clarissa for a small fortune. He professed not to recall Hardifant’s face, but said the build, the height, and the cloak were familiar. He pays more attention to horses than to humans!

I arrived back in New York just at sunset. Realizing it was too late for the last run of the Brooklyn ferry, I launched my canoe for the first time in a year and got myself over to Brooklyn in the waning light. Vrouw Steenburgh, the only person who'd seen the third man with the two thugs, also couldn't be positive about the face—but she felt very sure about the cloak. The embroidery—Adelie had captured the filigree and the royal monogram—was unmistakable, she asserted. And who am I to contradict?

Returning to New York in the dark, fighting the current, I could just make out the *Janie*, settled back in port, as I paddled by Peck Slip. It took me another hour to get back to Old Slip, where I keep the canoe in a shed. Hauling it back out and stowing it was a nervous process, not only because I was alone on the dark, slippery pier, but because this was a very rough section of the town, the wharves being full of footpads, carousing sailors, and larceny-minded whores.

"So what's the verdict?"

I nearly tumbled into the harbor. "Good God, Charles, you … Can't you deign to announce yourself?" It was only the voice that enabled me to guess that the silhouetted shape four feet away from me was my cousin.

"Sorry," he said blandly. "So?"

"Yes, it's Hardifant. Four of them recognized the face, one the cloak, and one the horse."

"Good work, Thomas!"

I replaced the paddle and closed the shed. "When did *you* get in? How'd you guess I'd be here?"

"About eight o'clock. I saw Adelie and Hermione home, checked at your boarding house and the ferry dock, and then came here."

Church bells chimed eleven. "You've been sitting out on this dock for two hours?"

"Of course not. I was quaffing beer in one of yonder public houses!"

I shook my head. "You're taking your life in your hands in such dives, cousin!"

"Oh be serious. You used to like them!"

When I was sixteen I had not infrequently patronized establishments I'd be horrified to have my corpse discovered in today. "I was young and foolish, Charles."

He snorted. "*Pah*. You're no fun anymore, Thomas!"

"I'm beginning to think it'd be *fun* to throw you into the river, Charles! Shall we go?"

"Why not! However, we are bound for Mr. Leavering's. He asked us to rouse him whatever the hour."

I confess my heart sank for an instant. But Charles revived me by promising that our host's larder might be raided for food and drink.

When we arrived at Hanover Square, rather than employing the brass knocker, Charles rapped his knuckles gently against the door. After a minute, Mr. Leavering himself, in slippers and dressing gown, carrying a single candle, opened the door. "Is Hardifant the one?" he asked without preliminaries.

"Yes sir, all the witnesses identified him—or at least his cloak and his horse."

"Ha! Now we know. Come in, then. We must plan our next moves."

"Thomas has had nought to eat or drink for hours, Benjamin," Charles volunteered. "He's very cross!" I scowled at my cousin, irritated that he seemed unable to recall that, while I presume to count Benjamin Leavering as a friend, he is also my employer. As usual, Charles ignored me.

"That's so?" Leavering said tolerantly. "Well, why don't we settle ourselves in the kitchen, then? And there we'll be less likely to disturb my wife, who found her expedition quite exhausting!"

"She is quite as good an actress as the famed Mrs. Glasby, Benjamin!" Charles said. "Her display of total befuddlement regarding the procedure of 'importing' goods from New York into New Jersey was worthy of Drury Lane!"

Caught while attempting to light additional candles, Mr. Leavering briefly looked uncertain whether Charles was jesting. "Let me fetch you a beer, Thomas," he said—rather astonishing yours truly, his humble junior clerk. Once I'd had my first swallow, he said, "I've heard all of Hermione's, Charles's, and Adelie's adventures, Thomas. Now first, pray relate yours."

By the time I'd explained how I'd corralled each witness alone, and asked only, "Do you recognize this individual?" Trinity's bells had chimed midnight.

"This is not a situation with which I have any familiarity, gentlemen," Leavering said at length. "I'm still unfamiliar with the ways of the province, among other things. Where do we go from here?"

This question had occurred to me … but I, too, had no relevant experience and no settled thoughts on the matter.

Both of us turned to Charles, who—though the source of his omniscient knowledge was a perpetual mystery—could invariably produce plausible answers to such questions. "You must take it—take your accusations and your evidence—to John Tabor Kempe, Benjamin."

Leavering heaved a sigh. "Is there no one more … appropriate than that insufferable young man, Charles?" The province's attorney general was one of many royal officials who were currently at loggerheads with the city's business community.

"I'm afraid—"

"John Glasby tells me that if I'd been so unfortunate as to have been in this city in May, that man would have dragged me off to jail with the eighteen others!"

"Yes, but—"

"And he knows I am a subscriber to the protest against these shameful policies!"

"That may be, but—"

"I fear he will so take against me, personally and as a representative of the business faction, that—"

"Benjamin, the man deals in controversy every working hour! He takes none of it personally. He's one of those inflexible individuals who honor their duties to a fault. He may show excessive zeal in prosecuting the absurd laws against trading with the enemy, but he will also show zeal in prosecuting necessary laws against murder!" Leavering looked as if he were searching for another objection. "For better or worse, in short, the man appears to be honest."

I grimaced, recalling Captain Trent's characterization of Lieutenant Griggs, who'd forced him to perjure himself on the high seas. "You don't suppose Kempe knows where we landed the *Dorothy C.*?"

"I think you'd have heard of it, Thomas," Charles replied, "if he knew."

Mr. Leavering groaned. "We must dissemble regarding our commerce, then, even as we press the truth of Hardifant's viciousness?"

Charles sighed heavily. "It would … be politic, Benjamin." Again our host frowned with reluctance. "He's the Attorney General, sir; it's his job to deal with the capital cases of the province. There's really no alternative."

"How should we approach him then, Charles?" I asked.

"Ah! Well, you must organize your summation of reasons why you conclude Mr. Sproul was murdered, how it was done, and the consequences—the subsequent murders of Hager and Wicklow. How you *discovered* this—however interesting it may be to us—is less germane to him than the straightforward facts of the case. Toward that end, I would at least assemble a fair-copied list of all possible witnesses, with their professions and addresses."

"That should be easy enough," Mr. Leavering conceded.

"Would a chronological, sequential list of events be—"

"That might be *very* helpful, Thomas—very convincing. Mr. Kempe has been reluctant to involve the Crown in dubious criminal cases. If he can be actuated to commence a prosecution, we can be very hopeful of success. Perhaps you and I might closet ourselves tomorrow to prepare these documents. And then, you should call on him at the earliest opportunity."

Both Mr. Leavering and I noted the pronoun with dismay—and a certain sense of betrayal. "Shall you not be accompanying us, Charles?" our host asked coldly.

A certain hesitation shook my cousin's customarily imperturbable demeanor. "For many reasons, sir, that would be *im*politic on my part."

"But …" Leavering stifled his impatience with difficulty.

"Does this have anything to do with—"

Charles swiftly kicked me on the shin.

"*Hey!*"

Oh, I then realized, catching his glare: it somehow had *everything* to do with *Sejanus*—whose identity with Charles Cooper I was sworn never to divulge. "When shall we meet tomorrow?" I asked quickly.

A flash of relief crossed Charles's face, even as one of confusion crossed Mr. Leavering's. "I do think we've done all we can this evening, gentlemen," Charles said. "And perhaps a good night's sleep would be recommended. I propose that Thomas and I should meet at ten o'clock—perhaps at your boarding house?"

"Nonsense!" Leavering asserted, reconciled. "You must come here, and work in the dining salon where it's peaceful. Hermione will gladly provide all you need."

"Thank you again, sir," I said.

"Call on me at the office when you're done," he added, "and we shall proceed to Government House."

Organizing my notes into coherent form took us the entirety of Wednesday, and it was therefore not until Thursday morning that Mr. Leavering and I entered the building at Wall and Nassau Streets to seek an interview with the attorney general. We were told we'd have to wait, and sat in uncomfortable chairs facing the enormous new full-length portrait of H. M. George III. "*Overbearing sod!*" crossed my disloyal mind more than once as two hours passed in enforced indolence. The annoying delay also allowed me to fret whether even the wary Charles Cooper might have been fooled by the man we were attending—whether, in short, John Tabor Kempe himself might be a party to the Atlantic Mercantile deal.

Mr. Leavering was on the verge of walking out when a lackey finally appeared to escort us up one flight to Kempe's office.

John Tabor Kempe is a tall, very slight, dour, balding fellow who can't even be as old as Harmanus. The walls of his small office were covered with bookshelves loaded to the gills. Mounds of paper covered his desk. As we entered, he said, "Please be seated," and then he read and signed two pieces of paper before finally looking up.

"My name is Benjamin Leavering," my superior began, "of Castell—"

"Yes sir, I know," Kempe said. "Please state your business."

I could tell it cost Mr. Leavering some considerable effort to restrain his irritation. "Some six months ago, sir, my partner, Daniel Sproul of Philadelphia, left that city on a mysterious and unexpected visit to New York. He was seen at ten p.m. on March twenty-second at

Meed's tavern in Paulus Hook, in apparent good health and spirits … and was found dead of no identifiable cause at dawn the next morning in the yard of Roberson's hotel on the Greenwich road."

Kempe did appear slightly stunned. "A heart failure, I surmise?"

"I shall ask my young colleague, Mr. Thomas Dordrecht, to alert you to our suspicions, sir." Kempe regarded me with what looked like extreme distaste. "It has been he who has recently discovered many reasons to think otherwise."

"Yes?" Kempe said, disconcertingly staring into my eye.

"We have come to believe that Mr. Sproul was murdered, Mr. Kempe, with malice aforethought, and with the specific intention of avoiding suspicion by creating the impression of an odd, but natural death."

Kempe looked as though he were intrigued in spite of himself. "Go on."

"I propose to recite a series of events, sir, in chronological order, for which we have independent witnesses. We prepared a list of the witnesses—here—for your perusal. We would contend these incidents point necessarily to our conclusion. With your permission?"

"Go on."

"Mr. Sproul was a resident of Philadelphia, in the province of Pennsylvania, and—"

"I *know* where Philadelphia is!"

He was not going to make it easy! "On the evening of Tuesday, March sixteenth, he attended a card party given by a friend. At the party were two persons not part of his regular acquaintanceship—Mr. Samuel Low Aldridge, the proprietor of Aldridge Brothers, merchants, and Mr. Ichabod Dabney, that firm's solicitor. During a hiatus in the game, Mr. Sproul overheard Mr. Aldridge boasting to Mr. Dabney of major feats of chicanery. Mr. Sproul was much alarmed. We have retrieved some notes, in his handwriting, that indicate why he was so perturbed." I handed the paper to him.

Kempe's eyes widened instantly as he saw the amount involved … but he presently scowled. "This is the hand of a drunkard, Mr. Dordrecht! Is it not plausible the man was simply fuddled?"

"Nay, sir," Leavering broke in. "My late partner suffered an injury to his hand in youth and was never able to write properly. He normally dictated to a clerk. He mentioned in a letter to his wife, however, that he was reluctant to entrust these thoughts to any stranger."

Kempe stared at Mr. Leavering for ten seconds before allowing, "I see."

"After the party concluded, Mr. Sproul—unusually—returned to his office around nine p.m., to retrieve paper and writing utensils. He was distressed to find an employee there, Mr. Christopher Enniston, in an inebriated state. He remonstrated with Enniston but he recalled the man had formerly been employed as an accountant with Aldridge Brothers, and asked if he recognized the name of Atlantic Mercantile Company. Enniston said he'd encountered it once, that it was apparently an unacknowledged subsidiary of Aldridge Brothers, and that he had once inquired of Mr. Dabney, Aldridge Brothers' solicitor, concerning this impropriety, and had been sharply told it was none of his business."

"*Hmm.*"

"Enniston was not in the office the following day—he'd been scheduled to work in one of our firm's warehouses—but a Captain Wardener, who was a personal friend as well as a business associate, stopped in. Though very preoccupied himself, Wardener observed that Mr. Sproul was unusually agitated, and complained vehemently that corruption in military procurement procedures was threatening the realm, and that it was far more serious than the government's preoccupation with trading with the enemy!"

Kempe snorted derisively. "Indeed!"

"Sproul saw Enniston again the next day, Thursday the eighteenth, which was the day of the last big snowstorm of the winter."

"Ah! I recall it. There was a great deal of snow, but it melted away fairly quickly."

"Yes. Mr. Sproul closed the office around noon as the snow mounted up. Enniston says Mr. Sproul was still profoundly upset, and declared his intention to travel to New York City in order to bring these allegations to the attention of none other than General Amherst."

Kempe pointed to Mr. Sproul's note. "You think that's the reference of 'Inform J.A.' here?"

"Yes sir. And you can of course see that such a communication might have dire consequences for anyone associated with such misdeeds!" He nodded. "Mr. Sproul told Enniston he planned to take the Friday coach to Paulus Hook, and they parted. Mr. Enniston, however, did not go immediately home. For reasons of his own, he sought out Mr. Dabney, who, he alleges, had been blackmailing him, having discovered that Enniston had committed some petty pilferage while employed by the Aldridge firm. Enniston says he'd repaid the amount pilfered and foolishly thought he could stop the extortion with a counter-extortion based on Sproul's contentions. However, he says Dabney offered him spiritous refreshments, and admits that the entirety of Mr. Sproul's plans were presently wormed out of him."

"I see."

"On Friday morning, the snow ceased, but traffic was at a standstill. Mr. Sproul was nevertheless so intent on getting to New York that he and the firm's man-of-all-work, Francis Goode, drove down to the wharf, only to learn what should have been obvious, that no coaches were traveling. Goode says that Mr. Sproul even talked aloud of attempting to travel in the open sleigh—"

"Good heavens!"

"—before rejecting the idea and returning to his home, where he closeted himself in his study most of the day."

"Did he never …? I find it most peculiar that you've mentioned no one other than this one clerk having been informed of the man's concerns and plans! What about—"

"With respect, Mr. Kempe, his wife—"

"My daughter," Leavering interjected.

"His wife was ill with a colic. She was recovering, but she thinks her husband was reluctant to trouble her. The firm's third partner, Reuben Castell, was away in Lancaster on business."

"A son?"

"My grandson is too young as yet."

"He did confide in Captain Wardener, but that was apparently before he made a final decision, and Wardener sailed immediately after their meeting."

"Well … how did you ever find this out, then?"

"I met Captain Wardener by chance two months later, sir—on Saint Eustatius island in the West Indies."

Kempe's lip curled. "Statia, *eh?*"

It was clear that, like all officialdom, he had no love for the place. I'd have been smarter not to volunteer that detail! "Wardener was shocked and horrified to learn of Mr. Sproul's death."

"*Hmm.* Proceed."

"There was one individual who apparently did travel on that Friday, despite near a foot of snow. This sketch"—I handed over Adelie's work—"was executed surreptitiously just two days ago. It is of a Lieutenant Stephen Hardifant, who is currently the port commissioner of Newark, New Jersey, and acting commissioner at Perth Amboy. He is reputed to be a protégé of Samuel Low Aldridge."

"Is that so? 'Reputed' is insufficient, Mr. Dordrecht. Hearsay!"

"I admit the statement requires further investigation, sir." Kempe cleared his throat, and I pressed on. "Lieutenant Hardifant arrived in Lewes's stable in New Brunswick around midday on Friday the nineteenth, having ridden the chestnut roan in the drawing to exhaustion. To rent a mare from him, he paid Mr. Lewes a fee of five pounds, and left the roan *and fifty pounds* as collateral. He then proceeded northward."

"Fifty *pounds* for a common stable horse?"

"Mr. Lewes prized the beast highly and asserts the man was most persistent and appeared desperate to get on, sir." Kempe vigorously shook his head; I don't think it indicated doubt of my words. "On Saturday morning, Mr. Sproul did take the coach northward into New Jersey. The coach stopped in New Brunswick, and he spent two nights at the Carteret Hotel, as the coachman refused to continue on the Sabbath."

"Naturally."

"Yes. Mr. Sproul did some writing while detained there. He wrote and posted this brief note to Mr. Leavering ..."

Kempe all but snatched it from me. "'Business unrelated to either our family or our firm,' he says?"

"Exactly. He also wrote a personal letter to his wife, which she was reluctant to share—"

"She may *have to*, if capital charges are to be pressed," Kempe stated coldly.

Mr. Leavering flushed with indignation. "She did excerpt it for us," I quickly added. "There was a statement that Mr. Sproul intended to explain his actions by letter to his partner Mr. Castell, and that he considered it imperative that he should take his protest 'to the highest in the land,' as I recall the wording."

"General Amherst, then?"

"Yes. And as I noted from her recitation, 'So that we honest merchants are not persecuted for the innocent trading of flour for sugar while others commit treason and highway robbery!'"

Kempe cleared his throat. "Where is the letter to this Mr. Castell?"

"Here is what we have, sir. It appears that having written at length to his wife, his hand unfortunately gave out, and he was unable to finish it. Most likely, he intended to resume it after resting. The notes, I presume, outlined what he planned to explain to his partners—"

"Ah."

"And also to General Amherst."

"That would seem logical. I note with some dismay, however, the presence of the names *DeLancey* and *Colegrove* on this paper. It would be most unfortunate, gentlemen, should the names of two of New York's most upstanding citizens be casually bandied about in this context. I caution you that our empire has severe laws against defamation!"

He threw me—and Mr. Leavering too, I think—into a brief panic, as I'd not anticipated this and knew, furthermore, that *Sejanus* would never be deterred from having a field day with those names. "I … fear that it may already have gotten about in, *uh*, Philadelphia, sir."

He pursed his lips. "Most unfortunate, Mr. Dordrecht, *most* regrettable!" He sighed. "Well, get on with your story!"

"Mr. Sproul's journey resumed on Monday morning, in warmer weather that of course resulted in very muddy roads. The coach reached Paulus Hook only around six thirty, after the last ferry run.

Of Mr. Hardifant's activities since Friday afternoon, we have no specifics, but we can surmise that—"

"I'm not interested in your *surmises*, Mr. Dordrecht! Kindly stay with witnessed observations!"

"Yes sir. Beg your pardon! Well, then, Mr. Hardifant was next witnessed in the late afternoon at Meed's tavern in Paulus Hook, by, *um* … she calls herself Miss Paulette."

"A hussy?"

"Yes. She declares that he availed himself of her services."

"Meed's is that crummy little place right by the ferry dock?"

"Yes sir, with a stable five or ten yards to the north. Miss Paulette noted that Hardifant appeared constantly to be watching out for newcomers from her second-story window. After their first tryst, he dressed and went downstairs, and she observed him by the stable conversing with two men she'd also never seen before, whom she saw again later in the tavern's main room. These men have since been identified as one Meshach Hager, who was known as a public nuisance to our constables here in the city, and Joe Wicklow, at one time a constable himself, over in Brooklyn. Hardifant—"

"Wicklow? Wicklow? I remember the name. There were complaints about him, and he was dismissed!"

"That's the man, sir. It happens that I personally met him at one juncture three years back, so I was able to place him partially from witness descriptions."

"Really? All right."

"Miss Paulette observed Hardifant displaying a bosun's chair to the two men, with whom it was obvious he was previously acquainted, because he asked if they'd 'brought everything.' Hardifant presently left them and returned to her room for another, *uh*—"

"Yes."

"As I said, the coach arrived in Paulus Hook after the last ferry. Mr. Sproul debarked at the new Van Narden inn, a quarter-mile back from the shore. He engaged a room there and left his luggage to go for supper at Meed's, the only place in the locality that serves food. When he arrived, Mr. Sproul asked the proprietor if he knew anyone who might row him immediately across the river. Meed responded in the negative, and Mr. Sproul, apparently resigned, ordered a meal.

As he was finishing it, Wendell Brush, a fisherman and oysterman, came in, and Meed introduced them, because Brush owned a dinghy. However, there was no wind, and Brush refused all inducements to row across in the dark. Meanwhile, Hager and Wicklow came in and ordered drinks, much to Meed's consternation, as they looked unsavory even to him. And presently Hardifant came downstairs from his assignation and asked if anyone would like to play cards. It was well known among Mr. Sproul's acquaintances in Philadelphia, sir, that he found card games hard to resist, even though he eschewed ever hazarding more than a penny a card."

"Very peculiar. Very fastidious form of gambling, I must say! Personally, I disapprove of all such behavior!"

Oho! I note we can venture into digressions when *you* feel so inclined! "Hardifant appeared surprised when not only Mr. Sproul, but Hager and Wicklow—with whom both Meed and Brush assumed Hardifant was *not* acquainted—all readily agreed to play. Several hands ensued, in which two apparent gentlemen played amicably and without incident with the two rowdies."

The attorney general rolled his eyes as if he were imagining the wages of sin being meted out in purgatory. "Miss Paulette came downstairs for supper, and Mr. Brush departed to go out fishing. Hardifant also disdained to publicly acknowledge any prior acquaintanceship with the woman. Mr. Sproul won every game—the two rowdies reportedly played as if they'd never played cards before—but his three companions were each down by less than a shilling at the end. Finally, Mr. Meed heard the Trinity bells toll ten o'clock—which is only possible on a windless night—and insisted they disperse. Hager and Wicklow left immediately. Hardifant settled his bill, which was large because he'd purchased an entire jug of rum, and treated the others—Mr. Sproul, an abstainer, excepted—to all they wished. He then offered to give Mr. Sproul a ride up to Van Narden's, saying he planned to ride back toward Newark. They walked out together … and we have no report of Daniel Sproul ever being seen alive again."

"Shortly after ten?"

"Aye. Next we have a report from Wendell Brush, who was offshore, fishing in the river at eleven o'clock—again by the chimes—that a light was displayed, and several figures were to be seen, on board an apparatus kept anchored in the harbor by the fishing community, called a *cow*."

"I am too pressed to be in the mood for jesting, Mr. Dordrecht!"

"Sir, I avow, that is what it's called. Though I'd never seen the like before, it strikes me as a practical tool for setting and removing seasonal moorings. It consists of a rectangular floating platform with a large hole in the middle, over which is suspended a tackle that can lower and raise anchors weighing as much as five hundred pounds."

"A *cow?*"

"Yes."

He sighed. "Very well, proceed."

"In addition to having noted at least three figures and a light on the cow—an unprecedented occurrence at night—Mr. Brush maintains that he heard the voice of the gentleman who had bought the rum."

"Hardifant?"

"Yes. He heard Lieutenant Hardifant's voice coming from this platform at eleven p.m."

"Did this anomaly impel him to investigate?"

"Unfortunately not, Mr. Kempe. Partly because Mr. Brush is not very inquisitive, but mainly because he just then had a bite on his line. After he'd landed the fish, the light had been extinguished, and the voices were stilled on the cow, though he was not sure that all activity had ceased. He was impelled to row past the cow much later, at the end of his night's work, which is when he discovered Mr. Sproul's Quaker-styled hat. In order to save it from being blown off, he took it upon himself to give it to Mr. Van Narden, as he presumed Mr. Sproul was sleeping there. Neither Brush nor Van Narden took any cognizance of the fact that the hat was crushed, muddied, and improbably discovered on the cow."

Kempe shook his head. "It's unbelievable how dull some men can be!"

"Indeed!" I concurred. "Just at dawn, Sam Drucker, the coachman, who had spent the night on a cot in Mr. Meed's stables, discovered Mr. Lewes's mare—which he recognized from many visits to the New Brunswick facility—tethered outdoors, unblanketed, in the back of the stables. He grew indignant on Mr. Lewes's behalf and had commenced feeding the beast when Mr. Hardifant suddenly appeared and ordered him to desist."

"This would be six in the morning? The coachman positively identifies Mr. Hardifant?"

"Not precisely, Mr. Kempe. He is sure about the horses, and also about the cloak. However, he said that to be sure of the face, he'd have to see Mr. Hardifant wearing his wig, *uh,* backward."

"*What!*" Though trying to suggest exasperation, I sensed that Kempe, despite himself, was amused and possibly envisioning a moment of courtroom theatrics. "But the man in the sketch hasn't got a wig!"

"All six witnesses noted him wearing a wig that appeared to be improperly fitted, far too large for him, Mr. Kempe." He grunted. "I've been speculating it was a temporary and clumsy disguise."

"Let us eschew *speculation*, please, Mr. Dordrecht!"

"Oh, yes, certainly, sir!" But I complacently noted he'd caught the sense of it. "At any rate, Sam says Hardifant simply mounted the horse and rode off to the west without a word of thanks—in the direction of the Hackensack River crossing, that is."

"So we have observations of Hardifant at ten p.m., eleven p.m., and six a.m. Is that it?"

"Yes. Plus one more. Hardifant returned the mare to New Brunswick at one o'clock that afternoon. He must be an excellent horseman. He redeemed his own horse and the collateral from Mr. Lewes and departed back in a northerly direction."

"I see."

"At about the same time that Sam was confronted by Hardifant in Paulus Hook, Mrs. Roberson came across the body of Mr. Sproul in the yard of her hotel. She sent—"

"But how ..."

I waited for a second as Kempe caught himself. "We have no observations as to how it got there, sir." He grunted uncomfortably, and I continued. "Mrs. Roberson sent her slave lad to fetch the constable, and Officer Jennet took charge of the corpse about six fifteen. He and the morgue's slave, Aston, got it into a cart and delivered it to the morgue before seven. No sooner had Jennet returned to his rounds, however, than he was called to retrieve another corpse, a man who had apparently been set upon by more than one assailant and summarily done in by multiple knife thrusts to the chest. He was found on the shore near the foundry, about a mile north of Roberson's. This victim was known to Officer Jennet and Aston as a petty thief and hoodlum. It was Meshach Hager, whom we now know had played cards with Daniel Sproul just ten hours before." Kempe now seemed deeply intrigued. "Jennet and Aston then carted Hager's corpse to the morgue and deposited it in the same room with that of Mr. Sproul, where Mr. Liam McCraney was—"

"I know McCraney."

"He was about to pursue the sole clue he had to Mr. Sproul, a pamphlet with his name on the bookplate. He enquired at the Royal Exchange and was directed to our office, where he arrived shortly after nine in the morning. Mr. Leavering and I followed him immediately back to the morgue, where we had—*alas!*—no difficulty identifying the deceased."

Kempe, noting that Mr. Leavering was covering his face with his handkerchief, had the decency to offer him a glass of water. "I'm sorry, but we must soldier on, Mr. Dordrecht!"

"Mr. McCraney made several observations that morning. Mr. Sproul's corpse bore no gross evidence of foul play, but his detailed examination—conducted after Mr. Leavering and I left—found contusions about the ankles and a tiny piece of cloth in his back teeth, which he says would be consistent with strong but very carefully placed physical restraints. It was observed that Mr. Sproul's corpse was unusually cold. In fact, Hager's body was used to demonstrate that, by way of comparison."

Kempe was looking mystified. "You had no idea there might have been any connection, at the time?"

"It was the furthest thought from either of our minds, Mr. Kempe. But we compared the two in one other regard, as well. Hager was reeking of rum, and there was no question that he'd drunk a good deal. Mr. Sproul's clothes were impregnated front and back with rum, but Mr. McCraney could not detect that he had imbibed any."

"*Hmm!*"

"There was another curiosity with regard to the clothes. The woman who found the corpse, Mrs. Roberson, observed that his waistcoat was buttoned incorrectly."

"That's hardly—"

"But Mrs. Sproul insists that her husband was extremely meticulous in all matters of dress."

Kempe shook his head impatiently. "You're sure it was rum? No other liquor?"

"My family are tavern owners, sir. I'm very familiar with all spirits. One would have to assume Mr. Sproul's clothes had been deliberately splashed in order to—"

Kempe scowled at another clear lapse into *speculation*. "How did McCraney account for the discrepancy in body temperature?"

"He was unable to do so, sir. At least not until …"

"What?"

"Until I, very recently, proposed an explanation that he admitted was plausible."

"Oh yes?" he said, making a show of restraining annoyance. "And what was that, pray?"

"That Mr. Sproul had been overwhelmed by the three men, gagged, undressed, rolled in a quilt—and possibly a horse blanket too, it just now strikes me—to prevent bruising while being forced into silence and immobility. Then they tied him into the bosun's chair and rowed out to the cow, where he was suspended neck deep into the frigid water until he died of exposure."

"Dear God!" he breathed. "But he wasn't drowned, then?"

"No. A drowning victim is *visibly* a drowning victim, as I understand, sir. But somehow those who die of exposure to cold … expire in apparent peace."

Kempe had to shake himself of the horrors. "But this is only conjecture, on your part!"

"Aye sir, but Mr. McCraney allows that the conjecture is consistent with the observed facts."

"*Agh!* Anything else?"

"Yes. Mr. Sproul's purse was found with the body, and there were silver and copper coins totaling two pounds, eight shillings, and six pence in it—which led both Mr. McCraney and me to conclude that no robbery had taken place. However, he was known to have left Philadelphia with over eight pounds. Mrs. Van Narden spied gold coins in the purse as he arrived at Paulus Hook, and nothing he is known to have purchased that evening could conceivably have required more than a couple of silver pieces ..." I could see his eyes widening. "I'll leave any speculation on the cause of this discrepancy to *you*, Mr. Kempe!"

He disdained to find my insolence amusing. "Get on with it, please!"

"Mr. Leavering and I left the morgue and, as Mr. Sproul's partner and father-in-law, he arranged for an undertaker to prepare the body for return to Philadelphia for burial. Hager's body was interred that afternoon in the potter's field, but according to standard practice in the morgue, a sketch was made of him first. This sketch."

"*Ugh!*"

"This sketch has been identified by Mr. Meed, Mr. Brush, and Miss Paulette as one of the card players. It has also been specifically recognized as Wicklow's cousin by several people in Brooklyn."

"Brooklyn?"

"Yes."

Kempe thought for half a minute. "Where is this Joe Wicklow at present?"

"That's just it, Mr. Kempe. On the evening of Saturday, June twenty-sixth, Joe Wicklow met a violent—and improbable—death in what appeared to be a common tavern brawl in Brooklyn."

"I heard something about a man killed in a brawl over there at the end of June. No inquest was deemed necessary. A place called *The Jug*, if memory serves."

"That's it. On the waterfront, just north of the ferry dock."

"That was Wicklow, the former constable?"

"It was. More to the point, it was Wicklow, one of three men who played cards with Daniel Sproul on the evening of his death."

"How is this known? Was he positively identified by name on that occasion?"

"No. He is identified in retrospect by his possession of a set of Mr. Meed's playing cards."

"What! Oh dear, is that all?"

"When Hardifant asked whether anyone wished to play cards, Meed offered him a deck for the purpose. But it was an unusual deck, probably made in Austria—this is it—which has a comprehensive set of cards for all games—and therefore an excess of cards for many standard games such as Whist. Meed immediately separated out and retained the tarot cards. But in addition to the tarots and the four suits of thirteen, the deck possessed four varlets, excess face cards, which Mr. Sproul apparently removed and absently stuck into the pamphlet he carried in his jacket. And Wicklow, whether from forgetfulness or thievery, walked out with the main deck."

I had separated the three groups on Kempe's desk. "How can we be certain these were all from the same original deck, Mr. Dordrecht?"

"We can't," I admitted. "However, it's not a common design, and the circumstances suggest—"

Kempe hissed with exasperation. "You were speaking of Wicklow's demise in Brooklyn, I believe."

"Yes. But let me first mention that Wicklow's acquaintances, also regular patrons of *The Jug*, had remarked that he appeared suddenly and inexplicably to be in funds this spring. One even overheard him saying that he hoped more would soon be forthcoming from the same source."

"Which one was that?" he asked, pointing to the witness list.

"I'm afraid it was my own father, Mr. Kempe."

He glanced up sharply, and then immediately looked back at the list. "That would be Rykert Dordrecht?"

"Aye. My father was once the schout of New Utrecht, and unfortunately became a crony of Wicklow's when he was the constable in Brooklyn."

Some of our more pompous citizens, I knew and had considered with some trepidation, would jump on this connection as an excuse to dismiss the entirety of my contention. I met Kempe's eye and refused to cast my own downward. "How embarrassing for you," he said mildly. He sat back in his chair. "So what did happen on June twenty-sixth?"

"The proprietor—that's Billy, a lad who I believe to be an orphan—said that Wicklow and my father were playing with these very cards when two unfamiliar and very alarming men came in. Though they had the gait and pigtails of ordinary seamen, they bought two rounds of drinks for everyone, and joined the game. Billy was beginning to relax, when a quarrel suddenly erupted, and—"

"Such things happen all too commonly, Mr. Dordrecht!"

"It progressed unusually, however, sir. One of the sailors, who was shorter but very muscular, lit into Joe Wicklow. The taller one immediately made it his business to prevent any of the regular patrons from interfering. In the process he caused a couple of injuries and considerable property damage before the shorter abruptly said 'Done,' and the two of them immediately fled from the tavern, ran from the area, and were never seen again."

"I see. That's *not* a standard tavern brawl."

"No sir. Particularly when, as order was restored, the patrons discovered that Wicklow was dead, with his neck broken." Kempe looked up again. "I understand that necks are very seldom inadvertently broken as a consequence of fisticuffs."

"*Hmm.* Anything else?"

"One thing more. Billy's neighbor, Vrouw Steenburgh, the proprietress of a tavern two doors down from his, happened to observe the sailors before they entered *The Jug*. Though it was very dark, she saw them talking with a third man, a tall young man in a dark green military cloak, with a wig that was too large for his head. She couldn't see his face, but she immediately identified the silver embroidery pattern depicted as Lieutenant Hardifant's."

"An *embroidery* pattern?"

"She has done embroidery herself, sir, and is quite positive."

Kempe exhaled, looking somewhat overwhelmed. "Is that finally all?"

"Yes."

He looked out his window for a full minute, then turned back. "Well, what do you make of all this?"

"Mr. Kempe, you have charged us not to speculate! The question is, what do *you* make of it?" He looked out the window again. "But if I may be so bold, I cannot see any conclusion to be drawn from the incongruous facts of Hardifant's presence at Meed's that evening with Wicklow and Hager, the observation of figures on the cow at eleven p.m. with his voice specifically noted, the discovery of Mr. Sproul's hat on the cow late in the night, and Hardifant's presence by the shore at dawn ... other than that Lieutenant Stephen Hardifant ordered and directed the murder of Daniel Sproul."

"It's a bloody shame we didn't get to Wicklow before that stupid brawl!"

I caught my breath, alarmed that he might be seeking an excuse to dismiss all I'd produced. "That's so, no doubt. But if you admit for argument the conspiracy I've suggested, you'd have to see the great convenience that would accrue to the instigator if his two doltish and unreliable cronies were dead!"

"*Hmph!*"

"It is a most distressing business," Mr. Leavering announced after a long pause.

"And what would you have me do about it, sir?" Kempe demanded.

"We believe, sir, that a compelling case exists that Stephen Hardifant murdered my son-in-law! We believe the Crown should independently examine the witnesses, indict the man, and try him properly according to law."

Kempe looked out the window again.

"And we *also* urge," I added, perhaps too vehemently, "that Samuel Low Aldridge and Ichabod Dabney of Philadelphia should be investigated as conspirators in this case, and that the Atlantic Mercantile Company should be investigated for the egregious fraud that so exercised Mr. Sproul in the first instance!"

Kempe appeared somewhat unnerved. "We'll ... have to see what—if anything—comes from my investigation of Mr. Sproul's death."

Mr. Leavering and I looked at him hopefully.

"*If* I determine to pursue it, that is!"

Chapter 15

"But Thomas, what *do* you think happened?" Adelie Glasby pleaded.

"Mr. Kempe insists that my speculations are inadmissible!"

"*Oh phoo!* What does he know!" she said with a gay abandon I found very refreshing after an exhausting day. She, John, and I were in their parlor, having a tipple while waiting for Charles to appear for supper. Benjamin and Hermione were not expected. Mr. Leavering had found our meeting with the attorney general very draining, and his wife insisted she'd not yet recovered from the previous day, when she'd copied out every piece of paper we were to give him. Charles was, unusually, tardy. "Seriously, do you think Hardifant was prompted by Samuel Low Aldridge?"

I downed a third of the glass of ale. "What else would explain it, Adelie? Christopher Enniston let Dabney know that Sproul had overheard everything Aldridge had said at the card party ... and the very next afternoon, Hardifant is tearing north despite heavy snow! He realizes that he's got two days to prepare, because Sproul has no chance of reaching Paulus Hook before Monday night—and he'd not dare to travel by boat in that weather. He even realizes he'll not make it into the city before Tuesday morning, because the roads will be bad enough to delay the coach. And from either Aldridge or Dabney, he knows that Daniel Sproul can't resist a game of cards!"

"But how is it that Hardifant is so beholden to Aldridge that he'd be willing to commit murder to protect him?"

"Not sure. Certainly hope that question will be investigated! Quite possibly there's more to it than the obvious—the *rumor* that Aldridge contrived his appointment as port commissioner."

"Would that ever be such a consideration? Sounds pretty dull to me!"

"The office is a very powerful one, Adelie," John said. "Extremely lucrative. And the opportunities for corruption are legion." He and I shared a smile, which, of course, she noticed. "As importers, we are frankly very *grateful* for their corruption, in fact—because, if they *in*corruptibly defended the Navigation Acts and the war measures, we'd never get any goods in or out of North America!"

"But—"

"But there's corruption—and there's *murder*."

She turned back to me. "Hardifant must have gotten at least as far as Newark by the Friday night, then? What did he do until Mr. Sproul arrived?"

"Somehow he had become acquainted with Joe Wicklow, and he recognized him for a man without scruples, so he sought him out and engaged him. Wicklow, I imagine, brought in Shacky, his ne'er-do-well cousin, as the third. Hardifant's duties would have occasionally taken him to Paulus Hook, where he'd have noticed the cow and realized that, in March, it could serve as a means to do in Mr. Sproul without leaving a trace. So he acquired a bosun's chair and got Wicklow to bring a lantern, ropes, and a quilt—and had them both meet him at Meed's on Monday afternoon."

"Right," John said. "Now we've heard what went on inside Meed's. You believe the three of them set upon him as he was following Hardifant out behind the stables?"

"Undoubtedly. They had to be quiet about it, because Sam was sleeping in the front of the stables, and Meed and Miss Paulette were presumably still awake in the tavern. They stripped his clothes off, wrapped him in the quilt, and trussed him into the bosun's chair. Then they borrowed—stole—a rowboat, put everything in it, and got themselves out to the cow. There they had to light the lantern briefly, in order to attach the bosun's chair and …"

"I can't bear to think of it!" she exclaimed. "Literally as *cold-blooded* a crime as can be imagined!"

"So … afterward?" John prompted.

"Afterward, they hauled him back out, redressed him, put everything into the dinghy, rowed over to Manhattan, and fetched up near Roberson's."

"But they forgot the hat!"

"They forgot the hat, yes. Fortunate for us! It was dark out, the hat was black and flat, and they'd stepped on it and crushed it. If they thought of it later, they'd assume it would blow off and sink before anyone would notice."

"How long—"

"And they fumbled the waistcoat buttons."

"How long would it have taken to get across?"

"Nearly an hour, I'd venture. Current was slack just around midnight. I've done it faster in my canoe, but they had … a lot of weight. Hardifant probably jettisoned the chair, the quilt, and the rope in the middle of the river. At some point, they took the gold pieces out of his purse, but Hardifant was too canny to steal the silver as well. The point was to avoid suspicion." A thought came to me. "Maybe Shacky wanted the silver too! While they were on the cow, Wendell said he heard Hardifant call someone a jackass!"

"So they pulled up on the shore—"

"And they deposited the body the first place they could find where Mr. Sproul might plausibly have lain down, and hared away as fast as they could. They got back in the boat, rowed north out of town, and beached again, possibly so Hardifant could pay the others off. When it was that he decided it would be too risky to live with Shacky, when he got Wicklow to go along … I don't know. But one of them grabbed him and the other made short work of him."

"Positively reptilian!"

"Possibly there was an even number of gold pieces!" John suggested, his mouth in a wry smile.

"Then Wicklow and Hardifant parted company. Wicklow stayed in the city, and Hardifant rowed himself back to New Jersey. But he had a hard time of it, because the current was by then flooding in.

So it was dawn before he got back to Paulus Hook, where he'd left the horse."

"What happened to Wicklow, then?"

"Well, Wicklow—I met the man, you recall, Pa's terrible choice of a friend—wasn't much brighter than his cousin. My guess is, he ran right through all the money Hardifant had given him and decided he wanted some more. He was no match for Hardifant, of course, who again set his scene carefully, hired a pair of thugs to assist … and that was the end of Wicklow."

"Your pa was lucky to escape with a couple broken ribs!" John observed.

"Aye. I hope to—"

"He's going to do it!" Charles bellowed, having let himself inside the door. "Kempe's taking the case! He's going after Hardifant!"

"*Huzzah!*" John cheered.

"Congratulations, Thomas!" Adelie exclaimed.

"He had someone go over to Brooklyn this afternoon, to interview in *The Jug*, and just on the strength of their statements and Vrouw Steenburgh's, he's decided it's worth pursuing."

"Perhaps we can eat at last?" John hinted.

"Maybe Charles would like a drink first!"

Before I could also vote for supper, Charles said, "Oh thanks, Adelie, it's food I need. I've been drinking all afternoon!"

Buying tipples for every clerk in Government House, no doubt! But we repaired to the small dining room, and again none of us raised the curious question, *How is it that Charles Cooper knows all this before anyone else?* Adelie and I understood, and were sworn to conceal Charles's clandestine life; John, far from dull, had too much on his mind to worry it.

As the excellent repast progressed, I waxed enthusiastic in praise of John Tabor Kempe, whose mind—if not his manner—had much impressed me.

Charles injected some caution. "I'd be chary with your regard, Thomas! Indeed, I'd be very watchful of everyone who works in that building."

"Now why do you say that, Charles?" Adelie asked.

"Because the man is a very political animal. And as such, he's never to be trusted."

"Charles!" she protested. "How unjust! Here he's accepted our case—a very complex matter, one must admit—and you're already taking him to task!"

"I am merely suggesting that the man may have ulterior motives for his actions!"

"Oh, you think everybody has ulterior motives, Charles!"

"Everybody *does* have ulterior motives, dear lady!" She scowled with vexation, and I—and I think John too—felt a pang of anxiety that the squabble might disrupt the regard of old friends. "Naught to become distressed about, of course," Charles added in a more conciliatory tone. "Just a fact. If there's a transgression, it's in denying or falsifying ulterior motives, particularly when they contradict one's professed motives." She was still frowning. "It is *not* cynicism!" Charles is constantly accused of cynicism—and just as constantly denies it.

"Do you think Mr. Kempe's alleged ulterior motives contradict what he's just done?" she demanded.

Charles sighed. "I truly do not doubt that the attorney general would be pleased to send a man guilty of murder to the gallows. But I also think this case is something of a godsend to him at this moment in time."

Now he had all of us confused. "How is that, Charles?" John asked.

"Parliament and the Crown have put their colonial officials in a very awkward and uncomfortable position, you see, *vis à vis* the wealthiest of their local constituencies. Everything those officials do now to uphold imperial policy outrages those among whom they must live. They follow policy—and arrest eighteen merchants on criminal charges. They follow policy—and impound one trading ship after another. They follow policy—and impose an embargo."

"I will admit to being outraged," John observed drily, not raising his voice.

"Now then, what better way to defuse some of the personal rancor involved than to take on this matter—the case of a New Jersey tax collector accused of murdering a respectable Pennsylvania Quaker merchant and crudely leaving his corpse on the city's doorstep? By prosecuting Hardifant for murder, Kempe can forcefully suggest that he has the best interests of New York's business truly at heart—while doing nothing whatever to alleviate the continuing grievances that bedevil us daily!"

Each of his three friends was somewhat sobered. "Oh," Adelie said at length.

My cousin instantly changed the subject—to inquire whether Adelie had any plans to organize another theatrical production.

Which prompted me, finally, to inquire after the one I'd missed while I was away!

"It's out of our hands, now, Thomas," Benjamin Leavering told me privately the next day. "We must—both of us—get back to the life of the living!"

"Indeed, I look forward to it, sir! This has all been ... dizzying. I find it hard to believe my return from the Caribbean was less than three weeks ago!"

"Really? I'd lost track as well. Goodness! Well ... if you could apply yourself to finding buyers for the rest of that sugarloaf, I'd be obliged!"

Over the next weeks, we finally sold out the sugarloaf. Mapes had disposed of the rum in a matter of days. After straightening out my accounts, which seemed to take forever—I vow I'll be more careful in the future!—I marketed the farming tools at a good profit, just broke even on the fireplace tiles, and did passably on the musical instruments. Only when all was done did I attempt to reconcile my personal accounts and determine that I, too, had made a modest profit—disappointing, given my neophyte dreams—on the trip. I consigned the bulk of it to my savings, bought half a dozen books, two new shirts—and *another* new hat.

The consensus of our office and our associates was that, as Mr. Leavering had predicted, not just the city, but the entire empire was suffering a business contraction, and that that explained the reduced reward of our voyage.

I found an occasion to linger in a coffee house and read the news—the bewildering news from abroad. On July 21, forty thousand Prussians had battled thirty thousand Austrians in Poland, and our great ally King Frederick had won—because he'd asked his recent-allies-former-enemies-now-neutrals the Russians to stand pat long enough to addle the Austrians. On July 23, the French and the Saxons had defeated Prince Ferdinand—not King George's brother-in-law, the other one—at the Second Battle of Lutterberg. I inquired among the patrons, but no one could recall a thing about the *First* Battle of Lutterberg. On August 14, I read with much trepidation, the British, having brought a force of thirty thousand—including colonials—to bear, had captured the city of Havana, Cuba. On August 25, the Spaniards had invaded Portugal and defeated our ally at Almeida. But on the twenty-seventh, the British and Portuguese together had returned the favor at Valencia de Alcántara. On the thirtieth of the same blood-soaked month, the French had defeated the British and Hanoverians at Nauheim, in Germany. But, the report assured us, this was not critical.

And somehow, all of this—all of it!—had started in the wilderness in the far west of Pennsylvania.

"We've captured Havana!" I exclaimed when Charles sauntered in and joined me.

"Oh yes," he said indifferently. "But we'll just give it back when the war finally blows itself out."

"You're not serious!"

"I am serious. That's what happened to Louisbourg after the last war. Why shouldn't it happen to Havana?"

"They wouldn't give Québec back?" Fury suddenly gripped me. "They *better not* give Ticonderoga back!"

Charles looked at me quizzically. "A sore point, I collect?" He waited a few seconds for me to calm myself. "They'll think about it, Thomas," he said blandly. "They will! They have to restore something to the French—however that may annoy the heroic Earl of Chatham!"

Anything that might annoy William Pitt would obviously please my cousin inordinately. "But *why?* Isn't the argument that the French must be destroyed and humiliated, so they can never again disturb the peace of the world?"

"That's the argument, yes."

"But … ?"

"But it's silly, don't you see? What makes anyone think that defeat and humiliation in our time will be *permanent?* Short of the Carthaginian solution of selling the population into slavery and sowing the fields with salt, why should anyone assume the humiliation will not instead fester and burgeon into an implacable demand for revenge in ten, twenty, forty years' time?"

"Well … what would *you* suggest, then?"

"That's actually an unfair question, Thomas."

"How so?"

"You're effectively asking the sensible party—among whom I number myself, naturally—to extricate the foolish party from the untenable consequences of their absurd policies. The foolish parties made the bed, and they find neither side appealing—but they have to lie in it. At this point, those who might have suggested changing the mattress years ago … can't help them!"

"Are you talking of Whigs or Tories, here?"

"Both! Neither!"

"Come on!"

"I'm talking of anyone—there were many in both parties—so foolish as to argue that acts of *war* were the proper response when the French fortified a few insignificant trading posts on the Allegheny River."

I halted, suddenly lost in my recollection of Mr. Castell's defense of Daniel Sproul's argument against a Pennsylvania militia.

"But I have news, Thomas!" Charles announced, abruptly changing the subject. "Kempe sent the constable, Jennet, over to Paulus Hook for depositions last week!"

"Well, grand!"

"And the upshot is …" He took an elaborately prolonged sip of coffee, his pinkie raised in the air.

"Do I have to *beg* for it?"

"Stephen Hardifant has been arrested!"

The trial, Charles found out two days later, was scheduled for October 21, two weeks away. Further reports arrived that Kempe had an agent taking depositions in Philadelphia, but that Mr. Castell and Mrs. Sproul intended to brave the trip to New York in order to testify in person. Correspondence between the offices increased, and we learned that Castell had taken on a new clerk, purloined from the neighboring firm of Goodman & Benchley, and dismissed Enniston, whose drinking had only gotten worse.

Given the demands they surely faced at home, I was surprised when the Philadelphians arrived a full day ahead of the trial. Having caught the last ferry across the Hudson, they got in early in the evening. Mrs. Sproul, quite exhausted by the journey, was staying with her parents, but Mr. and Mrs. Castell were hosted by the Glasbys, and I was invited to an informal supper. "Thomas Dordrecht! I rejoice to see thee well!" Mr. Castell exclaimed, rising as I entered.

"And I you, sir!" I replied, taking his hand. I bowed to his lady in my best dancing-school fashion. "Your most obedient servant, ma'am!"

After pleasantries and refreshments had settled us all, Mr. Castell broke the mood by saying, "My friends, I bear one item of grievous news for you, which shall presently be general, so we may as well get it said."

The three of us braced ourselves.

"Our former employee, Christopher Enniston … took his own life, the afternoon before we left."

Adelie and John, neither of whom had met the man, murmured sympathetically. I was stunned.

"As I wrote to Benjamin, his behavior had become more erratic after his lying was exposed. I had fired him even before I was positive I had a replacement. When we heard of this, on Sunday, we went immediately to pay our condolences to his widow and were refused entry by her."

"Most unjust," Mrs. Castell huffed, "no matter what the—"

"She was distraught and ill, Dorothy, that's all. I shall try again in a month. However, we learned much from her neighbor, a washerwoman. She told us that Christopher Enniston had complained of being *haunted* by Daniel Sproul, that he had become mercurial and finally violent, and that he had struck his poor wife so terribly that she lost the child she was carrying. The neighbor rushed in to assist the woman, and found Enniston so overwhelmed with remorse as to be incapacitated. She upbraided him sharply … and he abruptly ran up to the garret and hanged himself."

Adelie and John shook their heads, horrified. It presently occurred to me that this tragedy might diminish the force of the clerk's evidence. "We heard that our attorney general dispatched an agent to take a deposition from Enniston, sir. Did that in fact happen?"

"Yes, it did. Last Wednesday, I believe. Both the wife and the neighbor were present, and they became furious at the agent for his insistence on detail when it was clear that Enniston was drunk and obstreperous. After the agent left, Enniston had an episode of tears, in which he constantly sobbed that *he* had killed Daniel Sproul."

"Oh no," I moaned. "But that's—"

"The neighbor knew enough about the case to assure him that was impossible, but he remained irreconcilable—and grew progressively more remote from his spouse until … the tragic end."

While the Glasbys elicited the fact that the wife had, thus far, survived the miscarriage, a gruesome notion came to my mind. Though it seemed implausible, I had to voice it. "Is there any … There's no suggestion that any agency but self-slaughter was involved, Mr. Castell?"

He sighed. "After what we believe happened to Daniel, Thomas Dordrecht, that had occurred to me as well. But no, I don't think so. No one beside the three was in the house at the time, and the neighbor was attending to Mrs. Enniston in the room that had the sole access to the garret … until the moment when they realized they'd heard no sound from above for too long and …"

"It was the neighbor who discovered him, poor, good woman." Mrs. Castell added.

The subject exhausted, John attempted to brighten spirits by inquiring after the couple's efforts to support the latest funding drive of the still new Pennsylvania Hospital and asking whether they thought an equivalent institution might be constructed in our city. It was a moment before I—briefly plagued with the grim worry that *I* might have contributed to Enniston's self-destruction—rallied to join in.

Mapes and I presided at the office the next morning, as neither Glasby nor either of the principals deigned to make an appearance. It was very odd, but such surplus intellectual capacity as I had was preoccupied with the trial impending on the following day. Mr. Leavering stopped in briefly at three o'clock—to invite everyone present to a supper reception for the Castells, for which he had extravagantly reserved Cranley's Assembly Room. Again I was too busy to consider more than once how strange it was to make a celebration of our anticipated victory in the trial prior to any such verdict. But a festive mood instantly reigned, and I was even more troubled to concentrate on getting my work done.

On arriving at Cranley's at six thirty, I was nonplussed to find the gathering larger than I'd expected. Many of our best customers were present, various dignitaries of the city ... and all the officers of the *Dorothy C.*, which had just returned from a run out to Nantucket! I'd spent five minutes with Trent, Fox, and O'Malley, explaining the case against Hardifant and receiving their good wishes for the morrow, when Charles tugged me away and said, "You have to tell me: *who* is the strange dark fellow with the *cat?*"

"What?" I looked about. "Parigo!"

He was sitting aside, tightly clutching the terrified animal to his shoulder, grinning hugely as he heard me call his name. "My cousin Charles Cooper—the boatswain of the *Dorothy C.*, Uzal Parigo," I quickly effected. "Why on earth did you bring the *cat?*"

"Well," he said sheepishly, "I hear namesake be here, so I think she should come too!"

"And have you been introduced?"

"No, not yet."

"Aha! Well ..." I spied Mrs. Castell on the far side of the room, sitting with Hermione Leavering and some other ladies. "She's a Quaker, Uzal, she'll call you 'thee' or 'thou.'"

"*Eh?* Oh. All right."

I led him across the room and made bold to whisper in Mrs. Castell's ear. Charles deftly pulled up a seat for Parigo to sit next to her. The three senior officers materialized, looking mortally anxious. But the happy result was that Dorothy Castell and Dorothy the cat of the *Dorothy C.* got along famously.

"A matter of high superstition on shipboard," I explained to my bemused cousin.

"I was afraid the beast might scratch her," he said. "It's certainly drawn blood out of *him!*"

Mr. Leavering tapped a wine glass with a fork for attention. "Ladies, gentlemen, dear colleagues and friends," he began portentously, "although the occasion that brings our guests to New York City is a grim one, we have some glad tidings for you tonight. And those will be announced to you by my beloved daughter, Evelyn, the widow of the late, deeply lamented Daniel Sproul."

Evelyn Sproul gamely stood up next to her father, who seated himself. She expressed her thanks for the condolences and assistance she'd had over the past months of her bereavement and added, "Many of you have doubtless wondered about the future of the company my husband worked so hard to promote. I am glad to tell you tonight that, as of final negotiations today, we now believe that future is assured. My husband's interest has been purchased by a new partner, to the great satisfaction of all concerned." I stared at her, slack-jawed, amazed that this had happened completely without my awareness. "And I can tell you truly that I believe my husband would agree that his name should not be forever associated with a firm over which he had no competence, and he would be extremely gratified to know his business legacy would persist in a firm henceforward to be known as Castell, Leavering … and Glasby!"

A storm of cheering broke out in which, however dazed, I joined. "You're *not* telling me this is news to you!" Charles asserted.

I shrugged. "I've had other things to think about!"

Charles rolled his eyes. "Thomas, it's been obvious for months!"

Again I shrugged, defeated. But then I mustered up, "What's *obvious* depends on where you're looking, Charles, and what you're looking for!"

"Oh, perhaps so," he allowed amicably … and wandered off to chat up the sailors.

Happy, despite my chagrin, I congratulated them all, ate my fill, shook hands around … and departed early. I could see why the party had had to take place that night, but I wanted on no account to be unready for the looming confrontation.

With John Tabor Kempe in charge—though a nominee of General Monckton was presiding—the trial of Stephen Hardifant got under way promptly at eight thirty the next morning, in the cramped courtroom of Government House, which soon became stuffy despite the refreshing autumn air outdoors. The attorney general had carefully organized his witnesses and depositions, and presented the recitation of events … almost exactly as I'd presented it to him!

I observed Stephen Hardifant for the first time with the detachment I imagine naturalists must feel on dissecting a beetle—a clinical perusal forcibly voided of revulsion. His military hauteur and frigid disdain for the proceedings almost convinced one of his unsullied and righteous innocence. But the façade blurred as witness after witness—deporting themselves impressively well, even Meed and Sam and Miss Paulette—irrevocably nailed him to times and locations that had no explanation other than association with the death of Daniel Sproul.

Some hilarity was in fact produced when Hardifant was required to put his wig—seized in evidence during his arrest—on backward.

At one point Kempe surprised Hardifant by abruptly asking if he knew of the Atlantic Mercantile Company. Watching him intently, I could see that Hardifant was not so good an actor that he could avoid a shudder. But he mastered his face and flatly denied it.

Over the objection of his lawyer, the odious Darius Gerrison, a creature of New York's most powerful elites, the deposition of the late Christopher Enniston was submitted in evidence, and the agent who'd taken it strove to explicate the connection of Hardifant to the cryptic notes of revelations Mr. Sproul was attempting to bring to New York. Though the agent appeared diligently to be trying, he was not an articulate or engaging individual, and I was irked to see some jurymen nodding off during his testimony.

Gerrison entered further objection to the submission of Mr. Sproul's written statements. He particularly protested the existence of "certain notable and unsullied surnames," and vigorously belittled the contention that the initials J.A. and S.L.A. referred to General Jeffery Amherst and Samuel Low Aldridge.

Yours truly was called and examined for nearly an hour. I thought Kempe's questions were precisely to the point and Mrs. Glasby affirmed that my responses came out well.

Liam McCraney was summoned after I stepped down and affirmed that my supposition of the manner of Mr. Sproul's death was more consistent with the observed facts than his original finding of *misadventure*.

A deposition from the port commissioner of Philadelphia occasioned a sardonic moment of revelation for me and for Hardifant, simultaneously. The deponent alleged that young Lieutenant Hardifant's prior experience as a regimental quartermaster had not remotely qualified him for his appointment. The man had been sufficiently incensed that he'd made independent inquiries, and discovered that Hardifant had been court-martialed in Québec for conduct unbecoming an officer—in respect of the maltreatment of prisoners, a suspicious number of whom had expired on his watch. He had in fact been convicted, but his sentence had been a mere fortnight's confinement within the camp. To Hardifant's growing agitation, Gerrison had sat still through all these assertions … but had leapt to take exception when the deposition proceeded to argue that the accused was "clearly preferred only at the insistence of Mr. Samuel Low Aldridge." Each of us had believed Darius Gerrison was present to defend Stephen Hardifant. *Now we knew better!*

I confess the chagrin I perceived on Hardifant's face brought me some wicked satisfaction.

However, the entire courtroom—me included—was electrified during the afternoon session, when Kempe unexpectedly called one Nacek Zamoyski to the stand. Zamoyski was an earnest, unassuming, recent Polish immigrant, a young fellow who required a translator. The jury became highly alert as the court required the translator to swear fidelity to the law and reciprocally administered the oath to the witness. Officer Jennet, having been ordered to conduct additional inquiries by the attorney general, had discovered that Zamoyski, who worked nights at the foundry on the Greenwich road, had been "attending to personal necessity" by the riverbank during the early hours of what was reliably identified to have been March the twenty-third, when he heard three men arguing some one hundred feet further down the shore. He had barely had time to compose his dress when, just as a load of fuel added to the blast furnace threw a lurid glow across the road, he saw a tall man with a wig and a military cloak repeatedly thrusting a knife into the chest of a man with wild hair, whose arms had been restrained by another. After the victim had crumpled to the ground, his assailants had calmly tugged something from his hands and parted company. The very fat fellow had walked back down the road toward town, and the man who'd wielded the knife had gotten into a rowboat and pulled away into the river. After several terrified minutes, Zamoyski had returned to the factory and tried frantically but vainly to explain the situation to his supervisor ... who entered a black mark against him for tardiness. Hours later, a worker arriving for the day shift had stumbled on the body and called the constabulary.

Gerrison mercilessly lampooned the accents of both the witness and the translator—but to no avail. Required to stand up wearing his wig and his cloak, Stephen Hardifant was authoritatively identified as the man who'd knifed a defenseless Meshach Hager.

Two hours after darkness had fallen, the jurors returned their verdicts on the several counts levied against the defendant. He was found not guilty of conspiracy to murder Joseph Wicklow. He was found guilty of murdering Meshach Hager. The foreman attempted to denominate his agency in the death of Daniel Sproul as *not proven*, but was required by the judge to change that finding to *not guilty*.

Though a capital sentence would inevitably ensue, I—and all who had followed my researches—felt robbed and bereft. I lowered my eyes in agony when I came to face Evelyn Sproul in the foyer. "I cannot see that justice was done to your husband, ma'am!" I moaned. "I'm so very sorry."

"Ah, Thomas Dordrecht!" she remonstrated gently. "Did I not tell thee Daniel himself did not believe in perfect justice in our temporal world? Let not thy heart be bitter, good my lad! Had thee not applied thyself so diligently, that vile man would never even have been accused—and would have roamed free to kill again!"

My ubiquitous cousin was waiting outside. He pulled me into a tavern to pump me for my reactions. "That wig is truly hideous," I thought dully, "but at least it fits his head!"

"You disappeared, last night!" he accused.

"I went home, Charles. You?"

"Showed Parigo and O'Malley the town!"

"What did Parigo do with the cat?"

"Gave the cat to Fox. Is there a joke there? No."

"Wait. O'Malley joined you *and Parigo?*"

"Until he got fuddled. Then we lost him. You should have joined us!"

Today was on my mind, far more than last night. Unnoticed by me, Charles had sat in the back row of the courtroom, so it was my perspective he wanted—*fancy that!*—not the plain facts. "It worries me that the judge so resisted any attempt to discern Hardifant's motives. Isn't it obvious that they need to be established in order to prosecute a case against Aldridge and Atlantic Mercantile?"

Charles halted with a fork halfway to his mouth. "Thomas … what makes you think there will ever *be* a case prosecuted against Aldridge and Atlantic Mercantile?"

The suggestion shook me even more unbearably than the verdict had. "But there … *has to be!*"

"Enniston was the prime accuser, Thomas, and now he's gone."

"But there *have* to be cases brought against Aldridge and Atlantic Mercantile; they're the root cause of the mayhem! They're the true source of the evil! Hardifant was just their lackey, he …"

"Aye. And?"

"You're not suggesting … ? You think they *won't?*"

He sighed. "Thomas, what do you imagine General Amherst's response would actually have been if Daniel Sproul had successfully gained an audience with him?"

"Why, he'd have been livid, naturally! He'd have had the quartermaster on the rack within the hour! He'd have demanded every account book for every one of his regiments! He'd … You don't think so?"

"He'd have been furious, yes. And he probably would have tapped an adjutant to investigate the worst abuses. But … he had a war on,

Thomas. Maybe he knew—though Mr. Sproul did not—that a new war with Spain was being arranged. But the military's concern is not with *how* they get their supplies; all they care is *that* they get their supplies. If the king and the rate-payer get defrauded in the process, they'd rather it were someone else's business to see it right."

"Charles, that would be nearly treasonous—to be indifferent to the Crown being defrauded. Surely—"

"They'd never *admit* to indifference, of course! But this is a perpetual pattern, Thomas. I fear Daniel Sproul was … somewhat *naïve* to assume that Amherst might put a stop to the corruption, and then to see the foolishness of persecuting every form of trade. Sproul was certainly naïve to trust Enniston!"

"You think he shouldn't have *tried?*"

"Of course not. I just wish he'd exercised more care—for his own safety—and learned that lesson without fatal consequences."

We ate in silence for a couple minutes. "I was hoping … that bringing Hardifant to justice and prosecuting Aldridge might at least make it seem that Mr. Sproul had not … died in vain."

"Oh," Charles sighed quietly, "not the first, not the last!" I swallowed my bile. "Maybe a better thought, though, Thomas, is that he did expose matters to some daylight. The names were all voiced aloud in court, the jurors passed his notes around, one villain will swing … Who knows what that unscrupulous hack *Sejanus* might reveal in the newspapers?" We both smiled. "And no one scores a perfect victory that instantly grinds an age-old pattern to a halt, so neither you nor he should be judged against that fantasy!"

We ordered a second round of beer. I mused that it was probably unprecedented that my cousin had actually made me feel better. "To the memory of Daniel Sproul!" I proposed as the glasses arrived.

"All honor!" he agreed, raising his glass to mine.

Four mornings later, I located Charles munching an apple amid a great horde of people standing on the Common. "What's the matter with you, lad?" he demanded. "You're late. I was afraid you'd miss it! You look awful! This should be a day of celebration for your superb forensic achievement!"

"I—"

Drums rolled, silencing the festive crowd. Stephen Hardifant, his wrists tied behind him, was led out from the jail by six dragoons and marched onto the scaffold. "Oh what fun—it's *Henry* presiding!" Charles whispered contemptuously. "Come on, Henry, you old fraud, this mob is salivating for a tearful plea to Jesus!"

Charles's detestation of his elder brother, the Reverend Henry Cooper, far surpassed any animosity I'd ever felt toward Harmanus Dordrecht. I will admit that Henry is one relative for whom I've never felt the slightest warmth.

And nothing he said could produce the prayed-for reaction from the condemned. Worse, as Henry bleated relentlessly on, Hardifant broke his icy disdain to roll his eyes, to the great amusement of us groundlings. Finally, with all pleas exhausted, the floor was released under him, and Stephen Hardifant was despatched, unshriven, to eternity.

"Is it over?" I said, once the *oohs* and *aahs* had quieted down.

"Yeah. You should've watched. He gave quite a show!"

I looked up at the repulsive remains. "I wanted to see him dead, Charles, but I had no interest in watching it happen."

"You're squeamish!" He poked me in the midriff.

"Stop it! I'm *not* squeamish!"

He stopped. "It still rankles that he wasn't condemned for Mr. Sproul's murder?"

"Aye, it does."

"Glad it's done, anyway?"

"I'm glad it's done."

"Time for a drink!"

Moving out of the Common, we passed and tipped our hats to Liam McCraney and then to John Tabor Kempe. "Someday I should be curious to hear how you discovered all the evidence you produced, Mr. Dordrecht!" Kempe averred.

"Why not join us now for a tipple?" Charles suggested—unaware that it would have been the last thing I wanted.

"Ah, I can't. I have matters pressing in regard to the case of the exporters accused of dealing with the enemy."

We both grunted—and managed to refrain from saying, *Some other time, then*.

Standing by his horse and cart at the curb on Broadway, was Aston, Officer Jennet's assistant. He saw me and grinned. "*Hoo*, didn't he *dance*, though!" Charles thought it very amusing.

"What *is* the matter with you today?" Charles asked, once we were seated and the waitress—who knew him—had taken our orders ... from a distance of six feet.

I found myself choking up. "There's been dreadful news, Charles, just this morning. My brother Brevoort—"

"Oh no!"

"Your cousin, Brevoort—"

"Oh no, oh no!"

"Dead, in Havana. August twenty-second." *There!* I'd gotten it out without disintegrating!

"After the capitulation? Battle wounds, then?"

"No. Yellow fever."

"Yellow fever! *Ugh!*" Watching me striving to maintain my self-control, he seemed to conclude I accepted this calamity with the fortitude he'd feel delivering similarly terminal news about Henry Cooper. "Well! At least he must have had the *great* comfort of knowing the town had surrendered!"

It was no good. I put a fist in my mouth, buried my face in the crook of my elbow on the table, and howled.

He rose and massaged my shoulders, both of us ignoring the spectacle I was undoubtedly creating. "Ah, Thomas, I'm so sorry, lad, truly." It took two minutes for the spasm to pass. I blew my nose and sipped the drink he pressed toward me. "I didn't realize you were that close to him."

"Wasn't, actually. He ... He'd grown so remote from the rest of us. Always wanted to know why ... and now ... Oh, it all seems so damned senseless, Charles! How are we to live in a world that's always so damned senseless?"

Charles looked me in the eye. "We *fight*, of course, Tom-*ass!* What's the alternative?"

Right. The man in the absurd wig was enjoining me *to keep fighting.* I shook my head—and then nodded in chastised agreement.

Comestibles arrived. Charles put a fork in my hand and pointed imperatively at my plate. "But I'm serious that you ought to get out and enjoy yourself more often!"

One has to hand it to my cousin! "Everyone *else* tells me it's beyond time for me to settle down, Charles. To get married, start a family!"

He snorted. "When you're good and ready—if that's your pleasure! But you *have* been working too hard, you know, and for years now!"

"I like my work!"

"Good! Excellent! But a little fun is not senseless, Thomas; it's one of the things we fight *for!*"

Fun was far from my thoughts at the moment, but … but …

"Well … perhaps you're right!"

About the Author

Photo by Margery Westin

Jonathan Carriel possesses a BA and MA in History from New York University. He lives in New York City and has spent decades supporting computer networks in each of its boroughs. As a recreational sailor, he has cruised the United States east coast and the Caribbean, sailed from North Carolina to St. Thomas, traversed the English Channel and the Aegean Sea, and crossed the Atlantic.

If Two Are Dead is his third novel, continuing the series of Thomas Dordrecht mystery and adventure stories that began with *Die Fasting* and *Great Mischief*. Each novel will take place in the context of a specific historical year in the turbulent second half of the eighteenth century—the decades of the industrial, American, French, and Haitian revolutions.

He invites his readers to visit www.JonathanCarriel.com, where they will find further material to pique their curiosity about the era, in addition to maps, photographs, genealogies, and text expanding upon these fictions.

Coming next in the series: ***Exquisite Folly***. In the autumn of 1765, Thomas Dordrecht returns to New York City after two exciting but fitfully profitable years in Europe, and finds the town in an upheaval. Delegates from nine of Britain's colonies have gathered to challenge the Stamp Act, and thousands of people are protesting—*rioting*—against it in the streets. When the wife of a wealthy and prominent merchant is found brutally murdered, tensions are heightened by clues that suggest a political aspect to the crime. With business at a standstill, Dordrecht volunteers, at no small personal risk, to search for the truth. As he investigates the private turmoil of the victim and both sides of the public controversy, he realizes that the convoluted machinations of the murderer, like the highly sophisticated reasoning of the British Cabinet, may be made of "wisdom spun too fine."